AngelFall
Books I, II, & III

A Novel of Hell

By S.E. Foulk

AngelFall – Books I, II & III

This is a work of fiction. All of the characters, organizations, and events portrayed in this novel are either products of the authors imagination or are used fictitiously.

AngelFall Books I, II, & III - A Novel of Hell. Copyright © 2011-2012 by S.E. Foulk. All rights reserved. No part of this book may be used or reproduced in any matter whatsoever without written permission except in the case of brief quotations embodied in critical articles or reviews.

For more information send an email to: mortuus.angelfall@gmail.com
  or visit http://TheAngelFallSeries.com

Cover Art:
Book I   - *Damned Cast into Hell*, by Luca Signorelli, Orvieto, Italy 1499.
Book II   - *The Last Judgment*, by Fra Angelica, Florence, Italy 1431.
Book III - *Lucifer, King of Hell*, by Paul Gustave Doré, circa 1861-1868.

ISBN-13: 978-1478215738
ISBN-10: 1478215739

Dedicated

to my wife

Mamo Kim, PhD.,

my Mom

Marjory Steiner,

Leighann Corey,

and last but not least,

my grandfather,

George Snow.

Book I

Table of Contents

Prelude	7
Chapter 1 - Aristotle Finds a Secret Place	13
Chapter 2 – Into the Undertomb	16
Chapter 3 - Aristotle's Plan	21
Chapter 4 – The Mystery of Socius	24
Chapter 5 – The Elders Poison	27
Chapter 6 - The Missing Elder Affair	30
Chapter 7 – An Earful from the Elder	33
Chapter 8 – Last Instructions and Exodus	38
Chapter 9 – Betrayal	40
Chapter 10 – Awakening	45
Chapter 11 – Emergence	47
Chapter 12 – Styx and Phlegyas	52
Chapter 13 – Phlegyas' Task	55
Chapter 14 – The Fugitives Trek	58
Chapter 15 – The Way Out	62
Chapter 16 – Paradise Found	65
Chapter 17 – The Stone Skull	70
Chapter 18 – The Mystery of the Skull	73
Chapter 19 – Across the Water	75
Chapter 20 – Caught!	79
Chapter 21 – Cry Wolf Demon	81
Chapter 22 – The Centaurs Unrest	84
Chapter 23 - The Search for Pholus	87
Chapter 24 – Battle of the Wood	92
Chapter 25 – Plutus Attacks	100
Chapter 26 – The Gates of Limbo	103

Book II
Table of Contents

Prelude	105
Chapter 27 - The Two Fugitives	112
Chapter 28 - Chiron's' Decision	116
Chapter 29 - Socius Rebukes the Elder	122
Chapter 30 - New Friends in Exile	126
Chapter 31 - Charon's Rage	131
Chapter 32 - Chiron's Promise	136
Chapter 33 - Rage and Pain in the Pitch	143
Chapter 34 - The New World	146
Chapter 35 - Limbo's Newest Elder	151
Chapter 36 - The Walk to Bremen	161
Chapter 37 - Meeting Benjamin	165
Chapter 38 - Panos On Fire	172
Chapter 39 - The Miners of the Pit	174
Chapter 40 - Clavius' Secret	184
Chapter 41 - Panos on the Rill	196
Chapter 42 - Pholus-At-Large	199
Chapter 43 - Old Friends	203
Chapter 44 - Meeting the Father	206
Chapter 45 - End of the Line	210

Book III
Table of Contents

Prelude	215
Chapter 46 - Fatherhood	218
Chapter 47 - The Missing Ferryman	226
Chapter 48 - Panos and the Centaurs	232
Chapter 49 - Identification	234
Chapter 50 - The Secret Society of Limbo	242
Chapter 51 - The Final Judgement	258
Chapter 52 - The Newcomer's Arrival	260
Chapter 53 - Demon Attack	263
Chapter 54 - Back to Circle Seven	279
Chapter 55 - Guests on the Blood River	289
Chapter 56 - New Tricks for Old Centaurs	292
Chapter 57 - Reunification	296
Chapter 58 - Secret Society No More	299
Chapter 59 - Nessus and the Centaur Rebellion	304
Chapter 60 - Inside the Cave	309
Chapter 61 - The Chronicler	316
Chapter 62 - The Flight of Militus	321
Chapter 63 - The Fall of Limbo	327
Chapter 64 - Limbo for Beginners	329
Chapter 65 - Emergence	335
Chapter 66 - The Encounter	339
Chapter 67 - Changing Priorities	344

Prelude

I was born, died, and went to Hell. Though at the time I did not know it, my journey began at age 13, when I found a small box in my parents' garage. I will relate the story of my journey as concisely as I can and with all the details I remember, but please bear with me for it was frightening, painful, violent and too horrific for words and to tell the truth, if I had known at the beginning what I would have to go through, I would've never left Limbo. After all, it was the best Hell had to offer.

Let me start from the very beginning. My family was typical; blue collar, divorced, living in an average neighborhood. I had just been sent to live at my father and stepmother's house, and I was unhappy most of the time. I was separated from my friends with whom I shared my juvenile delinquent activities while living at my mom's house. My mom finally had enough of me and my getting into trouble, and she called on my father to raise me. The fact that I was flunking seventh grade was Mom's strongest argument, not to mention the shoplifting and cigarette smoking.

It was a fun life, full of as much adventure as a 12 year old suburban child could get into, considering the time and place. If my mother actually knew half of what I was doing my father would have probably shipped me directly to juvenile detention. Burning down the soda machine at the local laundromat, attempting to break into the town thrift store after hours (Mom was the police dispatcher that night too), and stealing the change and valuables from unlocked cars were a few of my early-youth transgressions. Then there was the flunking seventh grade thing.

The clincher event which sealed my fate was when I stole a very nice hanging potted plant one evening from someone's backyard. I gave it to my Mom and told her my friend Eddie's mom wanted her to have it. Eddie's mother had 'tons of plants,' I explained. So why did Mom, generally a social twinkie, decide to be gracious and go say thank you that one particular time? It's beyond me. She must have intuited my deception, craftily reaching into my psyche and seeing the lie. Or maybe it was because of my general history of lying. Suffice it to say, my fate was sealed. I was packed up and off to live at my father's house by that weekend.

My father's household was restrictive, with unbreakable rules and many household tasks designed to keep me super busy, and thus, out of trouble. For my generally free-range, wandering lifestyle, it was like a prison. Eventually I learned how best to gain my freedom; get finished fast, get out the door and out of sight before new work could be found, because there was always some other goddamn chore to be done.

One day I was tasked with organizing the boxes in our garage for the annual church yard sale. My stepmother had magnaminously volunteered to run the yard sale, and thus I was enlisted, to my great unsurprise. Griping, I reluctantly set to work, separating the clothing from the household goods from the books from the crappy toys, and everything else, cursing and pissing and moaning all the while. Boxes full of things people could no longer use or did not want the guilt of throwing out, like canned pumpkin for the food drive, were everywhere. I worked hard, trying to find a quick way to pick and choose items that were useful and sellable. Luckily, it was a short time before I found the item which would change my afterlife forever.

The item: a book. It was *the* book. I could not put it down. It was a simple worn out paperback, a translation of Italian poetry into English. The cover was cartoonized medieval art; old looking, and rather uninteresting except the draw of people in misery and torment, but I did not open it until I read the back cover. I had moved a few hundred old books this day. Why this one stood out for me I cannot quite fathom, but it did, and I read. A journey through Hell written by some guy named Dante Aligheri from forever ago – and, it was poetry! So, this book was old, had an unknown foreign writer, and was a book of poetry – my personal 3 strikes for any book - the fact that it was poetry was usually enough for a quick dismissal. Yet curiously, I began reading, until I had no more time and had to return to my sorting.

This book didn't make it to the yard sale. It stayed with me, finally disappearing only when I moved out of my parent's house in my early twenties. I never forgot the story, as I had read it many many times as a thirteen year old, but the details faded over time. I grew older and with the loss of my youth, I turned my obsessions as a teenager to more adult interests. The fascination with an adventure through the inescapable landscape of doom became a slight memory, and my life moved on until the end.

I never expected to make this journey, I had no idea that it was an actual, real place. I still kick myself, because I had a chance to peruse Dante's work one last time before my death, as if the universe knew I would need some help. I saw the book again, an hour or so before the car crash. I wanted, for no real reason, to pick it up and read through it. It was instinctive, but I was far too practical now, short on time as always in my adult life. Suppressing my real desire to open it, I gathered myself and my good sensibilities, and dismissed the urge as childish impetuousness, walking out of the bookstore for the last time. Had I any inkling of my nearing demise, I would have read the book cover to cover right then and there. But I did not. So that's that.

The impact from the crash crushed my skull and upper torso instantaneously. I can only say I felt the violence of it, though not the pain. It was a moment, like a bad memory of discomfort. I felt myself slip out, quickly, a strange buzzing sound, and then I was outside the car looking at my body. I recall seeing the mess that was my bloodied, splattered corpse, the commotion of the cars and people who stopped nearby, the lady who was in the car behind mine, who got out of her car and ran over, then started screaming hysterically. But I was okay. It felt great in fact, to be…dead? Wherever I was, the discomfort of my body had peeled off of me like a heavy wetsuit. I can't describe what it felt like at that moment. No pain inhibited, distracted or drained me; it was as if my entire lifetime had been a series of transitions from one ache to the next.

There was a feeling of joy vibrating through me. I was preparing to go somewhere, to crossover, and I felt as though I should be leaving, but instead I studied my dead body, examining the mutilation, scrutinizing the damage that had cast me from that shell; it was like an animal corpse I had seen once in the streets near my home, run over so many times, there was barely any recognition that it had once been a living, breathing raccoon. I wanted to acknowledge my body for being my temporary home, like a pet, when suddenly I felt another presence, and I turned, because he was looking at me intently, and I could feel the friendly gaze, in that in-between place where I was. The stranger seemed, or felt, actually, friendly. He smiled and watched me, nodding hello. He was wearing some sort of dress clothes from another time, sort of dressed up for a poor person. I studied him, and the background of the world, where my accident happened, until the people running to and fro in the emergency of the car crash, faded. A rift opened up, a bright light flowing through. I could feel the warmth and the certainty of what waited for me on the other side. Home? I wondered about this stranger, but a sense of urgency moved me to turn toward the opening, and now to hurry through. I saw the stranger one last time and nodded back.

He smiled politely, and in the next moment he shouted and the scream of fear sounded inside of me. Terror passed through the in-between as a shockwave, violent like my car crash. I was grabbed from behind by stone claws – I could not move - and heard the snarling sound of the creature as I was thrown forcibly into a void, a dark rift that had appeared just opposite of the bright light; I screamed as I was tossed about, tumbling into pitch blackness. I was churned violently, caught in a mad vortex, other times falling, or twisting as a large ocean wave can only twist you. Then, as quickly as it began, it was over. I was stopped, standing upright on my feet, no inertia to keep pulling and dropping, past the gate opening; the light had changed from full daylight to blackness and finally to a gray twilight, like Seattle just before a darkly brewing rainstorm.

I knew exactly where I had landed. My mind shocked, I tried to look for the familiar, knowing it was in vain; the other person, the sweet, bright light that had opened up, even to see my ruined body. I stood there, seeing, feeling, tasting, and smelling this world with newly heightened senses, like being suddenly able to smell again and finding yourself among rotting corpses. The distant moans and cries floated up from the depths.

I collapsed, falling to the ground in a slump, and for a long time, I wept.

AngelFall – Books I, II & III

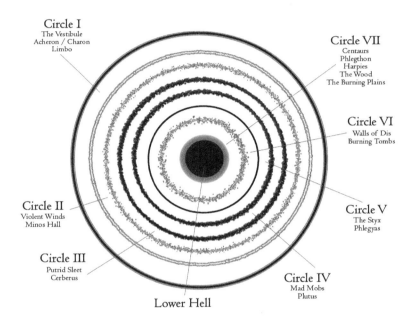

AngelFall – Books I, II & III

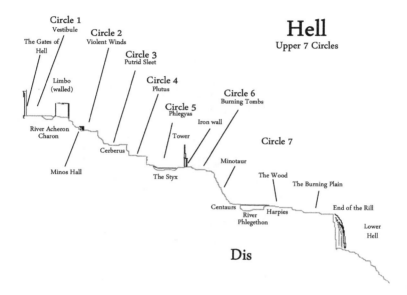

Chapter 1

Aristotle Finds a Secret Place

Aristotle crept low along the row of tombs. This place was always full of imps, Hell's vermin, which, while being relative easy to dispatch, could do a large amount of damage, and worse, give away the fact that Aristotle was out here, walking around freely. He was on his way to the inner ledge of Dis, the sixth circle, to study the Minotaur who policed the area between Dis and the seventh circle. Crawling along, Aristotle stood up hastily and looked over the glowing red-hot stone coffins. He spied a group of three more of the vermin off to his far left, throwing large stones and rubble forcefully into one of the open tombs, the crackling-fleshed inhabitant of that tomb cursing them amidst cries of pain. The sight of the roasting damned never got less sickening.

    Aristotle silently groaned his disdain of the creatures and ducked back down to continue his discrete crawling. Moving along, he unexpectedly detected a small darting shadow, ahead to the left. Aristotle froze, slowly moving his eyes back to the right, confirming his fear. Staring at him, not five steps away, was one of the beasts. It was as surprised to see him as he was to see it, and the shared shock bought him a crucial moment. The shadow from the left moved fully into view, and then its source, another imp. The second vermin did not see Aristotle initially, but looking toward its fellow, followed the focus of its glaring eyes. In a moment, hissing and snarling, the two creatures stared toward Aristotle, slowly, as wolves, eyes glaring in feral hatred, viciously snarling. Aristotle could do no more than pull his knife, ever so slowly, from the sheath attached to his ankle. He waited, hoping to dispatch them and run out of this place before the others were alerted, his current mission failed.

    Suddenly, the beasts stopped walking and sniffed the air, as their distorted purple ears twitched, then went still, and fear appeared on their deformed faces; Aristotle blinked, and the creatures vanished as if they had not been there. He looked around again to be sure, his eyes sweeping side to side and behind, and was surprised and briefly thankful, a moment before he became aware of the real danger. The imps were afraid of only two things in this place; demons, and Fallen. Demons made them cower, but only Fallen could make them disappear. Aristotle turned around again, without delay, and his fear nearly paralyzed him in his tracks. A group of Fallen approached one of the glowing tombs to his left, walking with their long strides and serious intent, almost spotting him before he skulked away behind a nearby stone slab. They walked past him quietly, moving further away. Curious, Aristotle looked around the slab to get a glance at the powerful overlords, always a rarest of opportunities; the group abruptly stopped and scrutinized one of the flaming crypts, scrutinizing each side and examining the markings carefully. They scanned the wider area, ensuring they were alone and unobserved.

A larger Fallen member then spoke in the ancient Angel tongue. Aristotle could not understand their language, but he could feel it. The speaking Fallen recited the musical syllables, concisely enunciating. Aristotle felt a twinge in his heart, and he saw something in his mind that was gone as mysteriously as it had appeared; a brilliant light, colorful, warm and healing, emanating from within himself, and then, the moment was over. He heard a grinding sound as the tomb slowly slid forward, opening up to reveal a roughly carved stairway that descended steeply into the underground. The Fallen disappeared down the steep stairwell as the tomb closed and resumed its ordinary appearance on the heat-distorted landscape, betraying no secret entrance. Aristotle, interest peaked, continued watching, until a long while later, when the Fallen re-emerged. He utilized the duration to practice the Angelic spell, singing it over and over in his mind. To his boon, he was not accosted by any of the vermin during the entire wait; no imp had returned to the area.

The group walked a short distance to a small clearing and suddenly became extremely wide, large wings seemingly exploding from their backs and pumping up and down slowly. Aristotle noted that their wings were invisible, as if they did not exist when not extended, but he could not determine how they could be undetectable; they were physically too large. All at once, the overlords launched from the ground, and Aristotle watched as they climbed out of sight in a fraction of a second, vanishing into the misty ceiling that concealed the heights. It was the first time he had ever gotten this close to any Fallen, and it was spectacular to watch their powerful ascent; he was relieved to have experienced the encounter unharmed. He inhaled deeply, unaware he had been holding his breath. He was shaking.

Aristotle carefully examined the tombs immediately surrounding the concealed stairwell, looking around for permanent landmarks, and any unique indicators to ensure his ability to return. Not daring to let the Fallen know he had found their secret spot, he etched a set of glyphs at the bases of the surrounding tombs, dulling his knife point and accidentally burning his elbow on the glowing rock. Aristotle exited, vowing to return and enter the mysterious hiding place later, when he was prepared and had his courage more intact. The punishment for his excursions would be grave, but the exhilaration of the treks became more addictive with each new danger he encountered and survived. And who else in Limbo had so much to write about in the afterlife?

He stood up slowly, scanning for vermin, and made his way out of the sixth circle. Aristotle headed back toward Limbo, abuzz with his latest discovery.

Chapter 2

Into the Undertomb

"Socius, once again I have an astonishing tale of adventure!" exclaimed Aristotle, over-dramatizing with his arms outstretched as if to welcome vast crowds to make his young charge smile. "You think you've seen everything, and then one day a whole new realm opens up." Socius sat down smiling, awaiting his faux-flamboyant teacher's story excitedly. Ever since Socius was younger, and smaller, Aristotle had enjoyed his youthful excitement at the details of his travels. The boy would smile from ear to ear, eager, rapidly questioning and impatient, and only recently had managed to be still enough to let his teacher begin. Aristotle usually scolded him lightly, teasing him until he settled down.

The adventurer took up his quill, dipped it in ink, and started writing as he related his tale to Socius.

Betraying his outer calm, the youth blurted out loudly, "Yes!" Aristotle's face became grim, falsely, then a frown of disappointment for effect. Socius resumed his most quiet appearance.

"I will now tell you of my latest discovery…and my next trek!" Aristotle smiled, and began to relate his recent discovery, leaving all the details in so he could enjoy his young ward's astonished facial expressions, adding a few more close calls than actually occurred. He did so enjoy entertaining the boy. Simultaneously, he scribbled down his journey's details in the blank logbook in his lap.

When he had finished logging and sharing the story with Socius, and had felt sufficiently rested, Aristotle set out from Limbo. He took several vials of Limbo's healing waters, natural waters that hastened regeneration markedly, useful in emergency situations. The imps would enjoy nothing more than capturing a fugitive and ripping him apart. Aristotle had been attacked many times by the small beasts, and found the waters worked very well when he was temporarily disabled by deep cuts, bites and scratches.

The waters were also good for bartering in lower Hell. Aristotle had given vials to the centaurian leader Chiron, and to the ferryman Phlegyas to allow him passage when needed. Although now friendly with Chiron, Aristotle continued to share the rejuvenating water vials.

Since he was also going to document his findings, Aristotle packed paper and charcoals for note taking, plus several candles (the underground would be dark) and an extra long knife. Aristotle could use a knife in each hand if he was outnumbered. He packed one last item, a crossbow, built by and for the warriors of Limbo for their battlefield games. He attached it by a loose knot for quick removal should he need it, preloading a bolt for quick, on-the-fly firing. Aristotle closed the bag, and slung it over his shoulder.

Socius said goodbye, as he did each time Aristotle exited the safety of Limbo, praying for his mentor's safe and speedy return.

* * * * * *

Aristotle arrived back at Limbo much later and into the company of his eager young charge. Socius, who somehow always knew when Aristotle was returning, was standing just inside the gate.

He was disheveled and exhausted, his mood more grim than usual, and he spoke to Socius solemnly as he logged his journey, explaining that he had found in the hidden underground a vault with many rooms concealed beneath the flaming tombs and red hot stone coffins of the sixth circle. He noted that this also helped to support his theory, made long ago, that the tombs and coffins were magically, not naturally, heated. After descending a long, narrow stairway, a hallway bent to the right, carved out of the stone with a rough precision, and led to another cavern with many rooms branching from it. The place was poorly lit, and Aristotle had been so afraid that he imagined he saw imps and demons in the shadows around every turn. Most of the adjoining rooms were pitch black, completely in darkness. The stone walls had many holes of various sizes and depths, formed from rock that had shifted and collapsed long ago; Aristotle climbed over the rubble and used some of them to hide in when he feared approaching unknown creatures. Other rooms had ornately carved wooden doors with special, intricate glyphs etched on them, but no handles or locks. He surmised they might open by magic, and attempted the spell he used to get into the undertomb area to no avail. Aristotle recognized few of the glyphs on the doors from the tomes that previously were kept in the Great Library of Limbo, before the Elders had them removed. The wood appeared to be from the seventh circle – it was a deep crimson color, and it smelled coppery like the river Phlegethon, though not as offensive as the boiling river.

Another large room with a high ceiling contained shelves with hundreds of books. They appeared to be spell and map books of very large size, far too bulky for the adventurer to carry while moving about discretely. While Aristotle was searching to see if there were any others that he could fit into his pack, he heard noises coming from another area, behind the last row of the large tomes. Startled, he hid in the closest crawl-hole he could find. When no malevolent creatures emerged from behind the shelves, Aristotle crept slowly toward the source of the sound. A small, curiously well-lit hallway appeared in the distance. Aristotle moved quietly, examining many brightly lighted stones that were inserted into the ceiling and walls of the hallway.

Socius watched the face of Aristotle change as he continued relating his tale; *this* was the cause of Aristotle's grim countenance when he arrived at the gate.

The end of the hallway was where Aristotle found the horror of the 'body room'; a gigantic hall with hundreds of large-sized male bodies, most with long hair, of muscular build; many were bloodied and mutilated, all were kept in an unconscious state, a long vine went into their mouths and down their throats. The smell was unbearable.

The body room had over fifty long rows of roughly carved stone tables with the unconscious men chained to them, dried blood that once ran down the sides in streams coming from under their backs or off of their mutilated torsos. The vines, which up close Aristotle discerned were filthy hollow glass tubes, ran from small metallic reservoirs over the heads and down the throats of the comatose captives, steadily draining a viscous, green fluid. Two workers, larger demons, tended to them all, busily keeping the containers from emptying by ladling more of the green liquid from a barrel into the slow draining reservoirs. They wheeled the barrel around, up and down each row in a never ending cycle, each row so long that the far end was out of sight. If the unconscious beings began to stir, they were beaten and ravaged by the angry workers, then given an extra dose directly into their mouth. They would become still soon after.

This large hall had many crawl holes. One particularly large hole near the hallway was suitable for Aristotle to hide inside, staying back in the safety of the shadows while studying the room layout. The two worker demons sniffed the air, then suddenly ran toward the hallway that Aristotle had entered through, frightening him into believing he had been discovered; they nervously began bowing and prostrating themselves. Fallen had arrived just moments after Aristotle had climbed into the crawl hole, and, as he watched, a party of lesser demons, who looked more human than demon and had accompanied the Fallen group, brought more of the large wooden barrels and placed them in a corner of the body room, taking empty barrels with them. The Fallen looked over some of the bound, unconscious bodies, examining them for signs of movement, their disdain clear in their expressions.

One of the Fallen approached a body, and for no apparent reason, began to shred it, ripping and clawing skin, flesh and bone, mutilating the unmoving giant as he roared in frenzied ecstasy. The workers stared intensely, appearing to enjoy the spectacle. Aristotle gulped quietly, not daring to move. Another Fallen restrained his fellow member, shouting until the violence ended as abruptly as it had started. The volatile Fallen group member breathed deeply for a minute, regaining his composure, then returned to his fellows. They observed the expanse of the large hall for a few moments, and finally the entire mixed party exited. Aristotle exhaled slowly.

Aristotle didn't know what to make of these large men on the tables, but he concluded that if they were being kept in this state, hidden away by Fallen, they must be a real threat. Why would they be hidden and kept unconscious? Hell was a public torture chamber, not a secretive dungeon. Unconsciousness was not painful, so what use was the undertomb area in the scheme of Hell? Hell had a structure, and this room did not fit.

Aristotle waited for the demon workers to resume the work they had interrupted earlier, far away across the room, so he could make his exit. It was during this waiting period that he came up with his plan, an experiment that might work if it played out optimally.

Aristotle looked up from his log writing, staring straight at Socius.

"Socius" said Aristotle, "why would the Fallen go to so much trouble to hide these men?"

Chapter 3
Aristotle's Plan

When the demons had resumed their duties, returning to where they left off at the arrival of the Fallen, they were far away, barely visible to Aristotle due to the combination of distance and poor lighting. Aristotle, thinking ahead, had passed another small hole in the well-lit hallway and had almost ducked into it. The entry hole was small and did not appear conspicuous, but Aristotle had noticed the interior was voluminous, easily capable of concealing more than two people. He quietly climbed out of his hiding place in the body room, and went to the body that was on the slab of rock nearest the hallway and furthest from the workers.

Silently, slowly, he removed the tubing, aghast that it went so deeply down into the throat of the still man. The heavy chains were held in place by a pin mechanism at the base of the slab on either side. Aristotle, with some difficulty, wrenched the pin out. It was extremely old and rusted, caked with the once dripping body fluids of the mutilated victim who lay unconscious atop the slab. He removed the chains carefully, without a single metallic clank, placing them on the far side of the semi-corpse. All the while, the demon-wary adventurer scanned the dark distance for approaching workers. Aristotle lifted the comatose man's shoulders up slightly and placed his hands under each armpit; the unconscious man groaned softly. Aristotle heaved once, and pulled the man partially over the edge of the rock slab. The man's head lolled to the side as his mouth began to drip the greenish liquid, a slow dribble, forming a pool on the stony floor.

Aristotle heaved again, and again, what felt like a hundred times, and the man was finally hidden inside the hallway crawl hole, concealed in darkness. He traced his steps and wiped the trail of dripped fluid from the stone floor, then returned through the orifice; he clambered in and opened one of his small vials of water, turned the being's head to face upward, then emptied the entire flask. The unconscious being choked, then moaned softly in a low, deep tone, slowly trying to awaken. The water was working its magic, and Aristotle grew hopeful as he pulled the wax off of another vial.

"Silence, my friend. You'll alert the workers." spoke Aristotle softly. "Drink again." Aristotle poured the second vial slowly, and the awakening man gulped down the water.

Socius interrupted. "Master, why do you sometimes say 'being' and not always 'man'? Are they not men?"

Aristotle conceded. "These are different – every feature of them is that of a man, but somehow augmented – they were bigger; taller, uniformly wide and muscular. Whereas we see various shapes and sizes in the people around us in Limbo, the sleeping men were very similar in their large size."

"But they are men as far as I can see, Socius – it's just - there is something more to them. I cannot grasp it, but I just …know. When I was there my terror at discovery and what might happen to me was so great that I would normally do everything in my power to run from the place; I have never released the damned no matter how much I pitied them for fear they would turn me in when caught by workers or Fallen; Chiron warned me of the dangers of this. Even when I re-emerged from the secretive vault, I didn't know why I decided to help him. It still doesn't make sense. But I know it was the right thing to do."

Socius nodded his head in understanding as Aristotle continued his story.

The unconscious man spoke briefly in a very low, dried out, *dead* voice, but his words were indecipherable. Aristotle named him in that moment, calling him 'Mortuus', as he was likened to death in his previous state.

"A bit morbid, isn't it?" interrupted Socius.

"Stop interrupting!" said Aristotle. Socius smiled, and Aristotle resumed his tale.

Outside, not far from where Aristotle and the awakening man hid, there was a noise. Aristotle covered the mouth of Mortuus, trying to look into his eyes to see if they were opened, but the light inside the cave was too low. Aristotle was afraid one sound would alert whatever was outside to their presence and suddenly he felt panicked that he would never see the light of Limbo again. He waited, anxious, but breathed deeply, quietly, until he could regain his sensibility. Mortuus stirred slowly, softly, but made no sound.

After a while, Aristotle heard the demons, still far away, in the back of the body room, both hissing and growling distantly as they continued their duties. Aristotle did not want to wait to find out what would happen when they discovered their loss. It was time to go.

He scribbled some instructions to Mortuus, along with a signed piece of paper for entry into Limbo, and left an extra vial of water and the extra long knife he packed for this journey. He felt a small cloth pack, empty, inside his own and pulled it out. The items he was going to leave were placed inside the small pack and secured around the forearm of the waking man.

A few whispers were all he could afford in the moment. "Find your way out Mortuus… get to Limbo. Farewell." Aristotle left, feeling like he had abandoned a child on a battlefield. But he had to leave; he had already gone far beyond his limitations and rules for wandering Hell. Half regretful, half afraid, he did something he hadn't done since before his own death – he prayed.

As he made his way out of the mysterious undertomb, he considered his actions. He knew the odds were against the success of the poor creature, yet he somehow felt vindicated inside. He made his way back to the surface and headed toward Limbo, genuinely relieved to be above ground again, even though it was Hell.

Chapter 4

The Mystery of Socius

Aristotle, upon finishing his tale logging, requested the boy make a copy for Limbo's Library. Socius soon began writing; he was always entertained and fascinated by Aristotle's adventures. The youth requested to join him on more than one occasion, but knew Aristotle would reject his pleas without a moment's further thought. Once Aristotle provided a prerequisite; after several centuries, his mentor *might* consider allowing Socius to come along. The word 'might' was emphasized by Aristotle, who then followed with '*might not*,' dashing the slight hopes of Socius. The boy had not been surprised whatsoever.

Looking up from his writing, he scanned his teacher with concern, as he silently noticed Aristotle's bloody feet, mostly regenerated, but in need of a wash to remove the caked-on blood. The blood was most likely the result of yet another imp attack. Aristotle had explained these creatures were like miniature, mutated demons in appearance, and were more populous in the sixth circle than elsewhere, probably, he joked, because they preferred cooked meat. Aristotle warned Socius that even though they were smaller sized demons, they were not to be underestimated; Aristotle had almost been incapacitated by a pair of them.

Directing his attention back to his copying, Socius stacked the pages in order, then picked them up and started toward the Great Library. The youth wondered if he would ever be able to journey into outer Hell alongside his teacher, or destroy the beasts using his own often practiced battle skills. He knew Aristotle would sooner keep Socius in a locked box than allow him to journey into outer Hell.

The boy meant a lot to Aristotle. The Elders would have thrown him into the Whirlpool long ago if Aristotle had not intervened and petitioned them for custody. Socius was a novelty to Limbo's souls at the time – he was the first baby NOT sent to the Whirlpool, and, in fact, the first baby ever actually seen by the

inhabitants of Limbo. The oldest inhabitants (who were not Elders) could not recall infants arriving in Limbo. The Elders, in their own words, thought that it was better for the citizenry to not see the children because it reminded them of their families and their lives before, a depressing topic for the Hell bound, and so they were said to take the infants discretely to the Whirlpool. It was fate that the newborn Socius had cried out when the Elder who was carrying him passed by Aristotle. Aristotle knew what he heard, and though the Elder had tried to take off at a fast pace, Aristotle pursued him, and pestered him to see the baby. The nervous, irritated Elder reluctantly uncovered his secret cargo, and Aristotle's heart was alight. Calling over other nearby citizens of Limbo, Aristotle sealed the fate of the child. Each of them smiled adoringly at the small wonder before them and recalled the joys of their own lives, or their own children or their nephews and nieces or their friends' children. On and on it went, as each stared into the bright eyes of the babe, with a lucky few getting a smile in return.
Aristotle was particularly enamored, and begged the Elder to let him hold the child. Annoyed, the Elder pressed forward, shaking his head and saying it was time to go, reminding the small crowd that this was why 'great discretion' was necessary.

But Aristotle would not accept this answer, thus beginning the events of Aristotle's Petition. Eventually, the Elder turned back toward the Keep, as the large crowd trailed.

In the long case of Aristotle's Petition, the Elders finally decided that Aristotle could be in charge of caring for the child, relinquishing all responsibility to him. They concluded that since Socius (Aristotle named him because he was a very 'social' child) had perished as an infant, he would remain an infant for all of eternity. They consented because, surely after years of caring for a baby who could not grow up, Aristotle would tire and allow the governing politicians to eventually perform their duty.

But Socius did grow up, very slowly, into a strong, intelligent, and eternally curious young man. He had been schooled by Aristotle and many of the other great teachers; warriors, artists, philosophers, scientists, linguists, and craftsmen. His innocence and charming persona endeared him to most of Limbo, with the major exception being the Elders, who never spared a chance to let anyone who would listen know that the boy should have been sent to the Whirlpool. Ignoring the grumbling of the Elders, Aristotle and the other mentors of Socius each took it upon themselves to create him in their own image, particularly the Generals Council. These senior warriors trained Socius in the use of weapons; how to fight hand to hand, battlefield strategies and situations, enemy logistical analysis, and basic moral issues for wars and battles. Socius devoured his training, playing with vigor at the war games and mock battles, even taking great damage at times but always returning after regeneration. His threshold for pain was immense compared to even the seasoned soldiers, his physical strength disproportionate for his boyish frame.

The other teachers in Limbo taught Socius to speak, read and write in their own languages, and educated him in their particular specialties. Mathematics in many forms, the natural and physical sciences, and various philosophies all were taught to Socius in depth. Deciphering the Astrochron, the only timekeeping device in Limbo, and the only connection to the living worlds' time began early, though Socius would not grasp the concept of why time was measured until Aristotle began his journeys to outer Hell, when he would mark the times of his adventuring teachers departure and wait eagerly for his return.

Socius learned quickly, far faster than the other students in Limbo. The teachers attributed the vast difference in comprehension to Socius' age and open-mindedness. After all, the dead were usually older and set in their ways. The boy had no such inhibitions, to his teachers' delight. They enjoyed his enthusiasm for learning.

Unbeknownst to the sages and their star pupil, the Elders monitored Socius' progress too.

Chapter 5

Elder Poison

Shortly after Aristotle's return to Limbo, he was approached by a familiar messenger from the Council of Elders, requesting his appearance at the Keep, Limbo's own version of a city hall. The Keep was a small castle-like structure that held large halls for gatherings of the people of Limbo, and smaller rooms that were the offices of the Elders. Prior to the occupancy of the Keep by the Elders, it was the original Library of Limbo.

The reason for this summons, Aristotle knew, was because he had traveled outside of Limbo into lower Hell, counter to the safety guidelines constructed by the Elders. The Elders were a group of eight men who had resided in Limbo since antiquity, when Limbo was still dark and barren of plant life, who served as the so-called voice of safety and reason for the citizens of Limbo. These men interfaced with the Fallen's messengers, lesser demons or their well-trained pet vermin, domesticated imps. They were the official liaisons between the people of Limbo and the Fallen, though none of them had ever seen a member of the Fallen in person. They loathed outer Hell, but did send messengers to Minos, the powerful, ancient King who presided in the Hall of Judgment just outside and down the path from Limbo. He was known to be friendly with three of the Elders. Like politicians, the Elders had their sycophants, clerks, and dissenters. They were safety-oriented, according to their own self description, but according to Aristotle, they were fear-oriented, and he commonly referred to them and their followers as 'the idiots.'

When Aristotle last appeared before the council, there was discussion of creating a special containment area to keep 'unreasonable wanderers' protected from harming themselves. Their reasoning - the welfare and safety of the people of Limbo; to Aristotle, it was their usual justification. It was a proposal for a prison, he knew, and stated this outright. Appalled and outraged that Aristotle would refer to their 'civilized' safety containment area idea as a prison caused a few of the Elders to swear. Aristotle merely turned away, dismissively, and walked out amidst their shouting; this infuriated the politicians, causing them to raise the volume of their oath shouting. He grinned as he heard the ravings continue behind him, finding their irritation to be very satisfying.

The Elders had split many of the people of Limbo along political lines, one which disliked and distrusted the adventurous Aristotle, and the other which approved and admired his courageous stance against their political smearing, and the sheer bravery of his journeying outside of Limbo.

The former group considered Aristotle as a pariah, echoing rumors 'leaked' by the Elders, that his travels would bring ruination to the people's privileged way of life. He suffered the accusatory stares of many in Limbo, knowing it was the work of the council, though the ignorance and weak-mindedness of the Elders' supporters was a great cause of annoyance.

On the other hand, Aristotle was well admired by those who were, like him, starting to tire of eternity in Limbo, questioning the 'gilded cage' of their existence in Hell. The journals of his wanderings and explorations, shared with all via the Great Library, were read more and more often of late, and many anonymous smaller groups had formed an interest in his 'Descriptions and Classifications' text, a book that described the architecture, plants, beasts and personnel of Hell, as far down as the seventh circle. It was almost as popular as the Chronicler's "History of Limbo," a relatively short book that described the origins of Limbo from the early Dark Times to the current.

Originally, Aristotle's friendlier groups had easily mitigated the damages that the Elders inflicted with their fear propaganda and malicious rumor spreading, but within the last few centuries, his supporters had been somehow forced into silence and hiding, their voices diminished. Disappointed, Aristotle grew more distant from the inhabitants of Limbo and increased the frequency of his journeys outside, attempting to forget the poisoning damage done by the Elders and the frustration with his previous advocates. Were it not for Socius and the other perks of Limbo, Aristotle would just as soon leave and stay among his centaur friends in the seventh circle. Most of the centaur population hated Aristotle just because he was human, but at least he knew whom he could trust among the Halflings.

The Elders, however, were treacherous even amongst themselves. This was evident on more than one occasion, but particularly the incident of the disappearance of the three Elders.

Chapter 6

The Missing Elder Affair

Little more than a century prior, three Elders had disappeared on a short trip to Minos' Hall, on their way to socialize with the ancient king, the judge of Hell. When questioned about the missing Elders, Minos provided no answers. It was easily possible they could have gone around Minos' Hall unseen, but not in character for them; they never, ever, went off the path to the Hall of Minos, lest they be taken for fugitives and carried away and tortured. Nor would they have changed course without informing the other council members or the guards who watched the gate. The threesome went to speak to Minos to get news of Earth and the living, for Minos was privy to such information and always had updates. The king was very gregarious, always enjoying having company to break up the monotony of the steady flow of the damned.

The three Elders had begun this tradition, ironically, due to the travel journals of Aristotle, though they would be loath to admit it. Reading Aristotle's travel logs secretly, they decided to make their excursion, for their curiosity of Minos was great. Normally, they were sternly against venturing outside of Limbo; they validated their need to visit the king as a practical necessity of diplomacy. The three were harshly rebuffed by the other Council members for disregarding their safety and the people's, saying this would certainly encourage more of the citizenry to make dangerous treks, just like that 'troublesome' Aristotle. Despite their detracting fellows, the three councilmen wove their web of justifications, politely and firmly, and eventually got the assemblage to see the reasoning of their diplomatic visitation request.

Then the time came for them to leave Limbo for their first visit. Nervously, each waited as the guards opened the large wooden inner gateway. One guard went inside the small pen that led to the outer gate, a massive iron door, and opened it. The remaining guards ran outside to the path that led down to the Hall, searching for fugitives or wild imps who would try to gain entry or attack the diplomatic envoy. Upon receiving the all-clear, the Elders stepped outside the large gate and onto the path. The guards returned inside, closing and locking the outer gate behind them. For the first time in millennia, the men were outside the security of Limbo. They nervously began the short trek, aghast at the power of the odors and sounds of torment, and immediately turned back. Prior to being sentenced to Limbo, when they initially arrived in Hell, each man had passed this way and entered Minos hall, not aware of where they would serve out eternity. The path brought back memories of their entry into Hell and the anxieties each had faced. Hastily, the trio of would-be diplomats turned around and banged frantically on the gigantic gate, shut just moments before. They were the laughing stock of their fellow Elders, and it was a long time before they regained the courage to journey outside again.

Eventually though, the Elders did make their trip, and Minos took quite a liking to them and their gifts of the waters, herbs, fruits and crafts of Limbo. In return for their kindness, Minos would share knowledge he gleaned from questioning the damned, who always came through his Hall before assignment to a location somewhere in Hell. To the discomfort of the three, the fear never left nor diminished, no matter how many times they visited Minos. Each Elder secretly sighed in great relief when they arrived back in Limbo.

When the Elders vanished, the citizens of Limbo were stunned. The great fear of the each inhabitant was to be removed from Limbo, the only place in Hell where there was no torment, and sent outside to an eternity of pain and suffering. Upon entry into Hell, each person who now resided in Limbo had walked from the Vestibule, been ferried across the river Acheron by Charon, the oarsman of that river, and walked past the gates of Limbo to the Hall of Minos to be judged; all had felt the horror of Hell. The anticipation of where they would be placed had been a torture unto itself, and many jokingly referred to the line into Minos Hall as the first torment of Hell.

Only one other resident besides Aristotle had ever ventured outside Limbo. Virgilius, a long term inhabitant, had disappeared many centuries ago. According to Virgilius, he had a premonition and was leaving to find the way out. No one ever saw him again. The citizenry assumed Virgilius went mad, and that reasoning enabled them to put the matter to rest. The three Elders' disappearance was an altogether different matter.

The trio were each the epitome of conservative, by-the-book personalities. Their disappearance, from a frequently navigated, short course was a whole other matter. They would not speak of escape or journey off the path. Virgilius was obviously 'crazy;' whatever happened to the Elders was cause for great concern.

The conjecture and rumors thereafter were powerful enough motivators to cause Limbo's people to place their faith in the Council of Elders, increasing their authority over the populace. Soon, a metal gate replaced even the interior wooden gate, and the number of guards increased. The council held a closed election, and the three lost Elders were replaced by others, unanimously agreed upon by the assembly. The new council had the unfortunate habit of agreeing unanimously, according to Aristotle and his supporters, on everything that was proposed by their fellow members. Meetings took place, motions were filed, and always with no dissension or argument, ratifying policies unquestioningly. At least with the previous Elders, argument was more commonplace. The three replacement Elders were silent, grim faced people; they seemed to unnerve the incumbent Elders when they entered the meeting rooms. Many onlookers, previously active in the politics of Limbo were put off by the newer Elders, and with the decline of the frequency of public meetings.

After a century, people rarely spoke of the missing Elders.

Chapter 7

An Earful from the Elder

Aristotle ignored the summons from the Council. It would only be another meeting destined to end in angry disagreement, further etching his disdain for them in stone. After drinking several vials of the healing waters, he was starting to feel better from the wounds suffered from his return trip. Twice, Aristotle was attacked on this trip; once by Plutus, the wolf-like guardian of the fourth circle, and again on the second circle by a pack of imps.

* * * * * *

Plutus was a constant threat while traversing the fourth circle, and actually seemed to be getting more daring. Prior to his last encounter, Aristotle had only to point his crossbow at Plutus, and the wolf-demon would cease his advance. This time Plutus slowly moved closer. Aristotle motioned with his crossbow, flicking it to his right to direct Plutus to move off of the trail. Aristotle would have to walk backwards to keep his gaze on Plutus, constantly turning around to check his path toward the next circle; the situation could have been precarious had there been any imps wandering this level. To the boon of Aristotle, Plutus would suffer no outside creature to wander within his circle; the adventurer never had encountered anyone except the wolf demon here.

"Back away hell dog!" cursed Aristotle. Plutus stopped moving forward. "I will shoot your hide full of bolts! NOW MOVE!!!" Aristotle focused down the shaft of his weapon, aiming at Plutus' chest; the wolf demons' glare betrayed his intention. Aristotle got nervous and Plutus, sensing his fear, became emboldened and stepped closer. Aristotle could stand the tension no more.

"THE HELL WITH YOU THEN!" he yelled as he fingered the trigger on the crossbow. The bolt disappeared into Plutus' lower left torso, sinking up to the hilt. He yelped, screeching, and fell to the ground on his back, frantically gripping the protruding shaft as blood flowed freely from the wound. Plutus looked at Aristotle helplessly, then back to the briefly protruding shaft, a mix of violent shrieks belting from him. Aristotle reloaded the crossbow quickly, and re-aimed. This was when Aristotle noticed the gold coins surrounding the writhing creature.

"What do you do with money in this place?" he shouted angrily at Plutus. He bent over and picked up three coins that were nearest to him and furthest from the wolf demon. They were heavy, with the head of a beautiful woman surrounded by grains and fruits on one side; the opposite side held the countenance of a powerful man, but with a small skeleton beside him. Aristotle placed them in his pack. Looking toward Plutus, he saw he needed to focus on exiting this circle. If Plutus freed himself of the shaft he might try to attack again. The adventurer did not wish another standoff with Plutus.

The wolf guardian's stare shook him up, more than he cared to acknowledge. Aristotle backed away slowly as the wolf demon's cries of pain lessened with distance. He hung his crossbow on his back belt and clambered up the wall to the third circle without hesitation; at the end of his climb he rested. Thankfully, the way was safe until Aristotle reached the second circle.

Aristotle always crawled from the interior edge of the second circle, staying low to the ground until the winds subsided enough that he was able to stand upright. The winds were at their worst near the ledge, diminishing in intensity as he neared Minos' Hall. Aristotle crawled forward, then stood upright and was walking and almost in full view when the pack attacked.

One or two imps did not concern Aristotle so much, but three, especially two being flyers, were considerably more dangerous. They had surely been tormenting the airborne damned of this circle when Aristotle came into view, oblivious to their presence. A shrill whistle from one of the two above brought a third wingless beast galloping across the grey landscape; the creature locked its teeth into his ankle as he yelled in pain. Before Aristotle could perceive the entirety of the situation, the ripping bites brought him down. Unsheathing his long knife, he frantically shoved the blade deep into the grounded imps' shoulder and twisted; after a sickening moment of feeling the bone and sinew with each twist, Aristotle dispatched the fanged creature into a screaming ball of black smoke. He twitched his body backward, pulling away as the loud pop affirmed the vermin's' demise.

The two flyers, enraged, fell upon him, and one grabbed the crossbow off of his belt, as the other distracted him with a frontal assault. The two jumped back into the air, and flew up out of reach. In the excitement of its new acquisition, the creature that had grabbed Aristotle's crossbow accidentally launched a bolt into its fellow imp, and the beast screeched in agony as it popped into a cloud of black smoke just before striking the ground. The misfired shaft that was buried inside it landed softly on the ground. The remaining imp, surprised and shocked at what had just happened, tried to use the weapon again, aiming at Aristotle. It grew frustrated after a few moments and flew high above Aristotle, then quickly descended, diving straight at him. The creature swung the crossbow behind itself, intending a long arc for a more powerful strike. Painfully rising to his feet, Aristotle fell backwards exactly as the flying imp would have cracked his skull with the weapon. Thrusting his long knife upward, the creature's insides were laid open and its entrails and fluids dropped out, intestines dragging on the dirt; it screeched and bounced twice before vanishing into a dark implosion.

Aristotle lay still, looking around for others that might continue the attack, and thanked the Gods when he was certain the encounter had ended. He was shaken badly, and his ankle and lower leg had been painfully ravaged; the skin was loose and hanging as the blood poured out of the deep puncture wounds. Higher up in the air, the tormented watched during their slight intermissions of being violently tossed in the chaotic winds. Aristotle rested a while, regenerating enough to get walking. He picked up the crossbow and bolt and reloaded, keeping the weapon readied as he resumed his painful trek toward Limbo.

* * * * * *

When Aristotle had finally regained his strength and composure in Limbo, he was visited by Alcander, one of the original eight members of the Council of Elders.

"Greetings, Aristotle. Were you planning on coming to see us?" Alcander inquired coldly.

"No." Aristotle replied curtly. Alcander considered Aristotle's demeanor for a moment, maintaining his composure as best as he could, his face slightly flushed.

"Do you know why we've called for you?"

"I'm in a hurry to leave, Alcander. Want to come along or do you have to be off somewhere slandering me? Or are you looking to show the people what a fine leader you and the other fear-mongers are?" Alcander reddened again, trying to maintain his composure. His voice betrayed signs of strain.

"I have news for you." Alcander's voice lightened. "You may be in danger. Do you know of the courier of Azza?"

Aristotle did. The imp was the messenger for Azza, a very powerful member of the Fallen who communicated infrequently with the Elders. It was different than the beasts that Aristotle had avoided or dispatched in his many trips; it was more of a trained pet, larger than the usual vermin but smaller than worker demons. This one was smarter, and so made into a special employee of Azza.

"You know I do, so why do you waste my time asking." returned Aristotle, his mood darkening. Alcander continued.

"The imp delivered a message not long after you returned." Alcander paused to study Aristotle's facial expressions. "Would you have any idea as to what the message is about?"

"I have no idea Alcander; get to the point." Aristotle spoke angrily, and was getting more impatient with each moment. Alcander was hinting at something, causing fear to build inside Aristotle, slowly igniting his rage.

"Azza has *determined* that someone is wandering freely through Hell…" said Alcander. Aristotle could detect the Elder's hidden glee at the news. "…and that fugitives have been helped by this wanderer."

"Do you have a point?" said Aristotle.

"Fugitives are NOT to be assisted in any way!" Demanded Alcander. He continued his talk, a sermonizing, righteous rant, and Aristotle stopped listening, relieved this was not about him. Aristotle had encountered many fugitives in his journeys, but none recently; the news relieved him and the dark mood dissipated. He continued his preparation, ignoring the droning council member.

Alcander finished some time later, frustrated as he finally recognized that Aristotle had stopped listening much earlier. Storming off, the Elder cursed under his breath, so as to not openly be heard losing his temper. Aristotle watched him go.

He began to make a mental list for the things he would need for his next trip. It was a long way to the seventh circle, and he had much to talk about with Chiron and Pholus, particularly regarding the undertomb area. He had a small amount of regenerating to do before he would leave, but at least walking was not difficult any more. He looked side to side, first toward the wall that shielded Limbo from Acheron, then in the general direction of the Great Library.

"Now where is Socius?"

Chapter 8
Last Instructions and Exodus

"Socius, when you finish copying my journals, I need you to be aware; there is the slight possibility that the being I awakened in Dis will appear at the gate while I am away. I left a signed message with instructions which he is to present to the guards. I'm hoping the Elders will not interfere when he arrives. Be discrete. Provide him with the waters he needs to regenerate – and he may need quite a lot – and some fruits, healing potions, maybe the formulas you and the others use after battles? Those will work fast. He may be badly injured when he arrives; in fact, I would count on it. Also, take this vial to Benjamin, and see if he can determine what this green liquid is. Be very careful and do not touch or drink it. I probably should have given this to him earlier, as soon as I returned. Ask Benjamin to write any information he finds out about the vials contents. He'll get busy elsewhere and forget what he found if he doesn't write it down." Aristotle paused for a second, looking at Socius as the youth studied the vial's contents.

"I will be visiting Chiron and Pholus in the seventh circle. It may be a long time before I return."

"I will ask Benjamin… about how long will you be out?" Asked Socius.

"I am not certain; probably more than one moon cycle. What is the Astrochron reading now? I can't read it at this distance, but you can." Socius' vision was quite keen, and a bit of an anomaly to many of his friends and teachers. The lad could see very far away with relative ease. Socius stared for a moment in the distance.

"The face of the Astrochron is turned toward the library – I cannot read it. The scientists must be studying it again. They just do not want to admit it is magically powered."

Aristotle turned to go. Socius hugged his teacher goodbye. Just hugging Socius seemed to make his ankle heal; what an energy this boy had. Turning away, he started toward the gates.

"Good journey." said Socius. The youth dropped his writing quill and walked toward the Hall of Science, in the opposite direction from the gate. As he walked, he became strangely uneasy, and a foreboding feeling came over him. Suddenly, he felt as if he was being watched, a feeling that seemed to originate far above him. Socius looked upward quickly; thirty meters up, on the top of the wall he thought he saw movement. He scanned left and right, as far as he could see in each direction, but detected no motion. The misty ceiling blocked further upward visibility.

Socius turned to face the gates, hoping to see if his mentor had reached the exit. Anxiety surged through Socius as he realized Aristotle had already departed from Limbo. The youth considered running and warning his mentor, but he shrugged off the fear that gripped his insides, justifying his uneasiness as merely aberrant thoughts, the usual worry he experienced when Aristotle departed. Socius continued his walk toward the Hall of Science and Benjamin; Aristotle would never heed a warning to stay in Limbo anyway.

Chapter 9
Changing Placement

Aristotle walked through the gateway. The guards, who were previously talking among themselves, opened the gate and turned to watch Aristotle as he passed by, eyes focused, curious and maybe a bit annoyed at his impertinence toward their leaders; the guards were respectful however, since most of them were friends of Socius. The boy defended Aristotle to anyone who dared speak ill of him, and had even swayed many to liking Aristotle. The adventurer continued to the outer path as the guards shut the gate behind him. Strangely, he felt more uneasy than usual.

It was always tense for Aristotle to leave the safe shelter of Limbo, and always just outside the gate he had to wrestle with his fear and keep to his planned course. It might have been easier if he had a friend come along, but Aristotle would not ask anyone to journey to outer Hell with him. Surely some of the youthful warriors would love to go; they were frequent readers of his travel journals. He would never ask anyone to leave the confines of Limbo. He could not protect anyone, and two adventurers were far more difficult to hide than one.

This was a journey people had to choose to make themselves. The Elders would certainly disgrace him to the rest of Limbo if someone, particularly a youth, was taken by the Fallen while in his company. Aristotle had once, for a brief moment, considered taking Socius. The youth would have jumped at the chance - had Aristotle allowed it. But Socius was the one person in Limbo whom Aristotle truly loved and cared about. Losing Socius to Hell would unquestionably destroy the adventurers' spirit beyond reparation.

It was out of the question.

Rare few citizens of Limbo would travel beyond the gate, and then only briefly. The gate guards were the only ones who even saw outside the gate regularly, and that was due to Aristotle's coming and going, especially since the disappearance of the three Elders. A messenger of Azza, a Fallen leader who occasionally communicated with the Elders, appeared at the gate infrequently, and passing newcomers to Hell got a peek inside Limbo's gate as they traveled down the path towards Minos' Hall if the gate was opened for any reason.

The guards did have some experiences with the wild imps. The creatures, on several occasions, entered or attempted to enter Limbo. During the earliest incident, no guards secured the gate; there had never been any need. A large pack of the beasts, approximately thirty to forty in number, wandered in, causing discord and injury to Limbo's frightened residents. The feral creatures' immediately met their demise, as the citizenry, including many warriors, had been having a small parade near the Keep; in fact, many conjectured that the music had actually attracted the imps to the interior of Limbo. The Elders initially tried to approach the pack, in true diplomatic poise, but the beasts responded with aggression, attacking and gnashing whoever they were nearest to. Everyone was reluctant to attack because of the Fallen; they did not want to provoke any ire or diplomatic rift if these were pets or workers of Hell's leaders. One warrior, Militus, a well-known pragmatic fighter and leader, highly revered for his battle strategizing, had no such inhibitions.

Grabbing one of the ceremonial weapons used in the parade, a decorated long sword, Militus stepped forward and dispatched two of the creatures; the warrior was not aware the creatures could actually be destroyed, but he relished the experience and he called his fellow warriors to join the offensive. The crowd watched in awe as the creatures disappeared into shrieking clouds of dirty smoke, a shocking death scene, yet morbidly entertaining. One imp could fly, and enraged, it flew at Militus, teeth bared and growling like a rabid dog. Just before the airborne creature reached Militus, a spear found its mark, and another cloud of shrieking smoke appeared. More warriors entered the fray, and in just a few more moments the entire pack was dissipated. The crowds cheered in awe and gratitude of their protectors, and the Elders thanked them publicly, but utilized the event to stir-up fear, talking of the coming retribution of the Fallen for killing their pets. The mood of the crowd, once high and joyous, darkened.

Word of the incident spread throughout Limbo, and the smiths and warriors began to craft weapons *en masse*. Crossbows and arrow production increased, as did hand weapons like axes, swords, knives and maces. The warriors arsenals were stocked, and every soldier trained intensively.

A need for more rapid regeneration necessitated the scientists to create special healing elixirs and potions, accelerating the rejuvenation of damaged flesh and bones so warriors could return to fight sooner. Their research also led to the creation an interesting powder that exploded when ignited by flame or struck forcefully against a hard surface. One naive blacksmith lost his left arm and a good part of the shoulder when he placed a canister of this powder too close to his forge. Fragments of the iron canister were pulled out of his body in various places, and the scientists thought he would require many cycles to regenerate enough to resume his smithy work. Because of this massive injury, the blacksmith was determined to be an excellent candidate for the testing of the most refined healing potions. His shoulder and arm was fully restored, as strong as before the accident. The scientists told him he would have to retrain his regenerated appendage, but this was not the case. The potion was a great success. The scientists and warriors felt as ready as they could be for the feared retaliation of the Fallen.

No retribution was imposed upon Limbos populace for destroying the marauding pack. When more imps showed up years later, they were dispatched by the guards, unless they had scrolls or items indicating they were delivering communications for the Elders. It was relatively easy to determine which imps were of the feral variety.

Outside the gate, Aristotle headed down toward the Hall of Minos. The odors once again assaulted his nostrils. The combination of smell and sounds seemed to be a torment of its own. Aristotle reached the roughly carved rock stairway that led down to the entrance of the Hall of Minos in the second circle. He stepped down diligently, around the line of new arrivals, but instead of going straight and inside, where the dead were judged and sorted, Aristotle walked to the left, off the regular path, outside and around the hall, giving it a wide berth as he headed into the windy violence. It was always so sad to see and hear the newly arrived souls who stood in line, crying or cursing while they waited for judgment and eternal damnation. It was one of the few places that really provoked Aristotle's anger at this God of theirs. It was unjust that punishment could be inflicted forever for crimes that occurred in the span of a single lifetime.

A well worn path beyond the left end of Minos' Hall marked the start of Aristotle's regular route to the lower circles. He did not know who created the trail, but it was intact, plain to see as far down as the fifth circle, disappearing into the spongy wetness of the fifth circle and the Styx. It was one of Hell's many mysteries, like the newly found undertomb area in the sixth circle. Aristotle thought about his recent discovery, excited that he would soon be describing it to his Halfling friends, Chiron and Pholus.

The winds picked up roughly, and he crawled along, avoiding the turbulence that tossed the souls above him so violently, sometimes against the rock wall between the circles, and other times against the each other. He would look down at the ground until he reached the inner ledge of this circle, then crawl down to the third circle using handholds in the stone wall. Aristotle edged along the path face down; he did not see the hellish demons or their Fallen lords flying toward him.

The brutal assault and capture was witnessed by many of the wind-bound souls as they twisted and tossed above the scene. A trio of Fallen watched as four angry demons mutilated Aristotle; the captured adventurer screamed and flailed helplessly, the sound amplified by his terror. One demon had a spear in Aristotle's back, impaling him facedown, while the others ripped him apart with large metal hooks, pulling and tearing in frenzied madness. Another demon twisted his right arm, pulling it upward behind his back until the bone snapped and his arm came out of its socket. As the vicious creatures savaged Aristotle's body, one of the Fallen spoke, barking out orders in a harsh voice.

The demons intensified their already maniacal blood frenzy until Aristotle was paralyzed from pain and blood loss. Finally, another member of the Fallen spoke, and the demons immediately halted their furious attack; two of them walked to positions by Aristotle's feet and head, respectively, and the demon who had impaled him removed his spear. The two demons by his feet and head sank their hooks into Aristotle, piercing his calves and neck. The pair began flapping their wings slowly. Aristotle shuddered as he was lifted off the ground by their metal hooks, leaving a dripping trail on the ground. The Fallen watched the pair of demons fly off, dragging the ravaged captive up, then over the edge of the circle, down and out of sight. The remaining two followed. The Fallen trio suddenly lifted off the ground and flew so fast and high that the wind appeared to be non-existent. Instead of following the demons, they flew straight upward, disappearing into the misty heights that was the ceiling of Hell.

Aristotle was captured.

Chapter 10

Awakening

He was aware of only darkness and pain. The voice was gone, and the cool moisture on his lips had dried up. For a long time he lay still, taking in the darkness, barely able to move. Then he slowly turned his head to each side as painful crunching sounds came from within his body. Slowly he moved his fingers until, more aware, his wrists, ankles, elbows, toes, feet and knees. Clenching his fists, he weakly touched his palms with his fingers, trying to regain feeling.

The blackness he awoke from was dreamless. Time passed slowly, and he was aware of his burning thirst. He could recall nothing except for a far away dream, across a chasm, someone had called to him. He remembered the voice. 'Get to Limbo' it said. Using all his willpower, he strained to rise.

He sat up. Looking around he saw a small hole of light. It was real. What had happened? Where was he? Who was he? "Mortuus." the voice had said. "I name you Mortuus." No more answers came, only darkness and a distant light. He fought long to get to a standing position. Grabbing onto some stone object, he lifted himself onto his feet, only to have his legs buckle beneath. He grabbed on again, weak arms and fingers, trying to grip harder with strength that was not yet restored, this time ready to hold with both hands and fight to stay on his feet. He worked, strained, pushed, and for awhile he stood up. Slowly, he picked up one foot, one leg, paying attention to put his strength into the leg still on the ground. Soon, he walked. The movements were jerky.

It was a long time before he could walk without holding onto something. The rocky ceiling cruelly reminded him of the low cave height. He winced in pain as he held his sore head, cursing silently at the unyielding ceiling.

The light was ahead. He walked there, crouching low. The brightness irritated his eyes. He squinted, lifting his eyelids in miniscule amounts, until he could see without pain. Something was tied around his forearm. He felt it, but was more curious about the light. He closed his eyes tight, then opened them again. Trembling, he looked outside the cavity of his awakening.

Panic set in and he stepped backwards into the darkness.

He had woken up in a nightmare.

Chapter 11
Emergence

Mortuus stepped out of the steep, narrow stairwell, emerging into a world of light, sound, and smell. It was horrific. He surveyed the immediate area, the sound of the tomb sliding into place coming from behind him. The stairway had disappeared.

All around were red glowing boxes of metal and carved stone in crooked rows, some in strange circles, and others stacked precariously high. They were tombs and coffins, each some sort of burial vault, placed across the mounded landscape; they glowed red hot. He could hear moaning sounds, and the smell of cooked meat was so foul it assailed his senses. The air was distorted by the heat, and he started to swoon, but he recalled more of the words of the anonymous guide – 'find the gates, then Phlegyas. Get to Limbo!'

The voice had left him a message, a crude map, a large dagger, and 2 vials of a clear liquid, all in the pack tied to his arm.

Mortuus, drank the vials of water as soon as he found them. After drinking the first, he could not stop himself from draining the second. The water refreshed him so that his strength came back and his thinking seemed to clarify instantly. But he wanted more. Aristotle had not considered that he would encounter anything like the body room, and so did not take nearly enough vials to slake the thirst of Mortuus. Mortuus imagined drinking many flasks, so great was his thirst, but unknown to him, a flask could not store these waters and keep their restorative properties intact from the infection which Hell had upon all things; thus the small, tightly clad glass vials were the only containers used by Aristotle that would insure the freshness and quality at the time of use. If the waters had been in a large flask, they would have become polluted and undrinkable soon after leaving Limbo's confines. Mortuus would have to get to Limbo before his burning thirst could be quenched.

Limbo, Mortuus thought, was his only hope; he would do whatever was necessary to get there. Checking the map and the instructions, he began to walk. He saw nearby a very tall wall of rusting iron; it was the only object besides the sticky muck underfoot that was not radiating heat. He would stay near this wall, avoiding contact with any encountered creatures, hiding as necessary.

Mortuus looked inside a metallic coffin that he passed; to his horror, a writhing, charred corpse lay in it, moaning in a low tone, the result no doubt due to the scorching of its throat. Mortuus reacted instantly, before he could think, reaching into the coffin and grabbing the convulsing corpse. He scooped the burning man out, tossing him hurriedly onto the ground on the other side of the burning box. His hands burnt, Mortuus ran around to where the body had landed, and watched as it slowly stopped writhing. Finally, very slowly, the corpse sat up. The eyes were gone; the orbs had melted inside the sockets, and were puddles that pooled in each reservoir. Mortuus studied the roasted body, noting that the skin was slowly healing. He looked at the face, and suddenly the eyes were there, glaring back at him. Mortuus was astonished. He continued to observe, understanding that slowly the rest of the charred flesh would be restored, healing itself to its natural state. Mortuus would have someone to walk with, and talk to, a companion he could ask so many of the questions he had, about this place and himself.

The burnt man spoke, the voice rasping through the heat damaged vocal chords. He leaned in to hear better, focusing his attention. The man was cursing Mortuus. Mortuus was staggered, stunned in disbelief! It continued its rasping oaths more clearly.

"Damn fugitive! I will not suffer your Hell, do not bother me in mine. You will get far worse, you fool!" said the man. "Now leave here and do not touch me again!" With that, the man clumsily climbed to his feet, barely able to walk as chunks of crusted, charred flesh fell from his body with each step; he looked around nervously. Mortuus was able to see the man was frightened, even through the melted facial tissues. Slowly, he climbed back into the red hot coffin, crying in pain for as long as his voice held out. Eventually, his throat burned back into its previously damaged state, and the low moaning emanated from the fiery box once more. Mortuus' shock at this point was unimaginable. He resumed walking, stunned and unable to comprehend what had just happened.

* * * * * *

During his trek to the gate, Mortuus noted the uneven landscape and the strange buildings; in some places the wall he was walking along merged into and became part of the buildings. He also observed the many strangely shaped creatures. Some were small and gnarled, white pallored with spotty-grayness to their skin, bobbing in their gait, with huge eyes and deformed appendages coming out from their backs or neck, while others were larger, clawed and muscular, smooth walking, and though not deformed, very much frightening in their manner. He saw a group of the smaller creatures were similar in appearance to a larger beast that they shadowed, walking behind the large one like pets as it strolled alongside the wall and into an attached building.

Mortuus observed that the smaller beasts were far less stable in temperament, and would screech, bite or swipe each other randomly, unprovoked; their tempers flared for no visible reason. He watched one pack of the beasts as a smaller creature started a fight with a slightly taller one, gnashing and clawing away violently, until the taller suddenly became a cloud of dark smoke, emitting a loud pop. The smoke that took the place of the dispatched imp was, for a moment, the exact same shape before it wafted off into the air. A much larger creature behind the vicious smaller one trotted over to the savage victor, enraged, and gave it a strong kick; the vicious smaller imp thudded against one of the glowing stone boxes, screeching in pain as its skin cooked and stuck to the surface. The wrathful large beast fell upon it, shredding it as it had done to its victim, until it too popped into dark smoke. The larger creature roared frighteningly in its fury, then turned and trotted away in the direction it had come from. Thankfully, this was the last time that Mortuus would see any of the larger beasts while in this circle.

Mortuus had startled a very small imp, accidentally sneaking up on it while he was trying to conceal himself from another that had been coming his way; the beast, which was about the most gruesomely disfigured of its kind that Mortuus had encountered, bit him hard and low on the thigh, shaking its head like a small dog. Grabbing the beast soundly around its neck, Mortuus thrust his dagger into its abdomen; it became a handful of smoke, and left him with sore eardrums from its high-pitched death screech. His thigh was bleeding and sore, just above the knee, causing him to crawl along until he had healed. Mortuus searched to see if the other imp had been alerted to his presence. To his relief, the creature continued on its course.

As Mortuus lay flat on his back avoiding more of the smallish creatures nearby, he saw them reach into one of the coffin furnaces and rip out pieces of cooked flesh from the tomb's occupant, scorching their miniature claw-like hands. The creatures would screech loudly as they burnt themselves, but the pain was not enough to stop their tormenting. The tomb dweller was screaming, for what a scream would be from its charred throat. The cries only seemed to inspire more sadism. Mortuus sat up again involuntarily when, to his horror, he witnessed the creatures consuming the stolen flesh! They were eating, as ravenous as wolves, dropping their charred food on the ground nearby to cool as they amassed more. Sickened, Mortuus crept away; he had no time to dwell on his revulsion. He knew he must keep moving to escape this madness.

Suddenly, from overhead came a noise, a loud and powerful flapping, too large and too loud for a bird. The sound moved quickly over the rows and piles of infernal tombs. The pounding reverberation echoed down and blasted off the rusted iron wall. A dim shadow passed over Mortuus. He could see, in the boundary of the mist above, a winged creature, like the large beasts he had seen earlier. It flew high and fast, beyond the wall and out of sight.

Mortuus resumed his crawl toward the gates, wary now of the overhead space up to the ceiling of mist. The smaller creatures that were just feeding seconds ago had vanished. Mortuus saw them much further off from the wall, slowly peeking out from their hiding places behind various tombs. They chose another interred victim, and resumed their abominable feast as the pained ravings resumed. Mortuus continued onward.

The tall wall eventually widened into a narrow building with a turreted walkway along its top. Mortuus kept scanning the area for signs of any creatures. Occasionally, he would look inside the glowing stone caskets, drawn to it particularly if the inhabitant was moaning louder than his neighbors. Each time he peered inside, he saw the same horror, affecting him as it had the first time. He considered this, and decided to stop looking inside no matter how morbidly curious he was. He quickened his pace and kept following the wall, more determined to get to his destination.

Finally, Mortuus noted a dimly lit object appearing in the misty gray distance, growing slowly larger as he kept walking toward it.

At first, it flickered silently like a faint star, then the pinpoint of light was gone. He increased his pace. A few moments later, the light appeared again. He was closer, and the source of light could be seen to be a large flame coming from the top of a very high tower! The tower was a thin, odd rectangular shape, deep black, with a small opening at its pointy tip. It rose from somewhere on the opposite side of the wall.

Just before the base could be seen, a large ornate wooden gate appeared in the wall. Next to it was a smaller wooden door, a miniature side access that appeared to open more easily than the larger.

"This is it," Mortuus thought; he had made it, and would soon begin his trek toward Limbo, relief for his thirst forthcoming. He was getting closer. Pushing open the small wooden door, he crossed the threshold to the muddy embankment that bordered a black-green swamp. As far as he could see, the water did not move; there was no current or waves, not even ripples. The watery landscape was dismal and stinking of stagnation. The air was very moist, causing him slight nausea as he breathed in. The metallic outer walls were badly rusted, though no holes could be seen; only a deep green slime clung in some spots nearest the stinking water.

He would not be able to drink. Overcome by this further continuation of horror, Mortuus bent over, vomiting vile green fluid until his stomach could only convulse in emptiness.

He almost retreated back through the gate.

Chapter 12
Styx and Phlegyas

Mortuus waited. After some time he could hear splashing from out in the distant darkness of this swamp, swirls of creatures that lived under the black water, swelling up randomly. Closer to shore, he noted bubbles rising up in a pattern, and an occasional movement, disturbing the greenish murk. Mortuus wondered what manner of horrific creature would live in such filth, when suddenly a head popped up, covered in slime; the creature looked around, but its features were not recognizable under its swamp mask. It quickly disappeared when it saw it was being observed from the shore.

The water looked shallow, with strange thin stiff weeds growing out in patches. The water was quite full of life; the denizens of this swamp could be seen moving through the patches of weeds, their secretive movement underneath the stagnant waters betrayed by the protruding stalks. As Mortuus watched, one of the swimmers popped up, and a group of others suddenly emerged from behind it, splashing frantically as they attacked. The stalked creature vanished in their midst, screaming as it made its escape, and the pack moved out of sight diving into the dark depths after their victim.

Mortuus grew worried, and began to reread his instructions again. The note had been very specific regarding this area. "WAIT FOR PHLEGYAS - DO NOT ATTEMPT TO CROSS THE STYX." He had no intention of trying to cross, though the waters did appear very shallow. Mortuus waited and distracted himself by examining the flaming tower. The tower was much larger than it seemed in the distance. A small doorway at the base, closed tightly and secured with a large, rusted lock, made it a bit more mysterious. While contemplating the purpose for this tower, Mortuus heard splashing sounds; they were not the normal chaotic rhythms as those made from the earlier attack. Looking over the vaporous swamp, Mortuus saw a small skiff, pushed along rhythmically by an oarsman whose back was toward Mortuus as he pulled his oars.

The oarsman turned, and seeing Mortuus, pulled his oars faster. The craft slid far up onto the muddy embankment. The oarsman stood; he was very large and muscular, his skin brown and leathery, aged, noticeable because he wore a small amount of clothing around his groin area only. He had an intense red-eyed glare, angry and focused as he jumped onto shore and pushed Mortuus to the ground with an oar; the surprised Mortuus had no time to react. Pressing him with the oar, Phlegyas spoke.

"Fugitive – where in Hell are you from? Tell me now or I will multiply your torment by calling the Fallen. Speak quickly and I will merely return you to Minos and your proper sentence." he said. Mortuus was still shocked, and could barely reply.

"I...I...I am no fugitive. I ...have come to seek passage to Limbo."

"You lie fugitive! I will call the Fallen and you will wish you had stayed in your own Hell-" Mortuus interrupted.

"I...I do not lie... Phlegyas. I seek passage ... and ...I will trade... for whatever you ask." Mortuus was stammering. Phlegyas softened his stance slightly, lightening up on his oar, but not removing it entirely. He considered the words of Mortuus. Mortuus sighed in relief.

"You will do whatever I ask, fugitive? First, then, tell me, how did you learn my name? No fugitive knows me by name, except one, who escaped me long ago. I do not speak it often, in fact the last soul to know my name..." He paused in understanding. "Ahhh. Aristotle." He nodded his head knowingly, understanding filling his eyes.

"You are in luck this time, fugit- ...Hmmm... Speak your name, friend of Aristotle." Phlegyas removed his oar from Mortuus' chest, placing it on the ground next to him and leaned on it, waiting, visibly interested in his new potential passenger.

"I am called...Mortuus. I journey to the first circle, to Limbo, to meet...someone. Aristotle? I will do what you ask to secure passage across the waters." said Mortuus. Phlegyas grimaced.

"Mortuus? You do not seem certain of your name? Strange, even for Hell. But we're all dead here, aren't we?!" Phlegyas laughed wickedly at his own humor, quickly becoming more serious. "You will not like my request, but you will not cross the stinking marsh without fulfilling it. If you attempt to cross by yourself, you will never leave. The muck which lines the bottom will suck you down. Those tormented who already reside therein will see to it you remain stuck. You may have noticed some who

have tried to escape their fellows while waiting for me; you will wish you had attempted a hundred of my tasks." Phlegyas stared at Mortuus. "How do you answer?"
    "I will fulfill your request."

Chapter 13

Phlegyas' Task

Mortuus was still, his heart beating rapidly, feeling like it was so loud it would surely betray his hiding place. He had returned far back into the previous circle with its glowing tombs. It had been disheartening to pass through the gates; the feel of the heat was even more repelling than before. His thirst intensified. The vicious little creatures all around were so far unaware of his presence. Phlegyas had told him this would be the sign that he was nearing his objective.

Mortuus had not seen so many of the beasts in one area. Some of the imps were busy looking into tombs while others had small meat hooks and strange, evil looking metal tools they used to harass the roasting occupants. They seemed to enjoy inflicting pain; the more a particular tomb dweller screamed, the more the imp was compelled to do the ghastly work. Cries and moans were strongest in this area.

Suddenly, Mortuus felt a stabbing pain in his upper back, his insides feeling cold metal; he had a metallic taste in his mouth as his body shuddered with pain, causing him to convulse and cry out loud. Spinning around in reaction, he saw the source of his pain. An imp had stolen up from behind and stabbed him. As Mortuus flailed wildly to remove the object, the beast jumped up and ravaged his arm and shoulder with its teeth and claws, laying open muscle and ligament. Mortuus panicked; it was all he could do to grab the creature by its throat and pull it off. A sharp pain on his left ankle increased his frenzy; two of these beasts were on him, and he knew he would soon fall prey to a swarm of the fiends. Mortuus squeezed the throat of the beast in his hand, breaking bones in its throat before shoving his knife deep into the creature and dispatching it into a smoking shriek.

The creature on his ankle was shredding it rapidly, exposing bone as it chewed hard and deep; it was so painful that Mortuus saw flashes in his head. He stabbed frantically and the imp screeched into the dark cloud of its death. Mortuus was briefly relieved; his time was short. He was in too much pain, almost immobilized by it, but he needed to run fast, to hide from the pack. When the imps heard the shrieking death of their fellows, all of them turned their attentions toward the source; Mortuus. They approached, growling like a pack of wolves backing prey into a corner. Mortuus searched for an escape route.

A building attached to the wall nearby was his only hope. He did not look back as he limped clumsily; he could feel their eyes on his back and their murderous intent. Mortuus needed to make it to the structure entrance. Though terrified, even the blinding pain coming from his wounds did not slow his run for safety. He reached the doorway, and, steeling himself for what horrors might lay inside, he entered. It was a thin, dim hallway, barely illuminated; a stone stairway led up to the wall turret far away. He stood in the slim wooden doorway, blocking the door so that it would not open more than enough to let one creature push its way through.

They would have to enter one at a time. Mortuus put his back to the wall and his good leg up against the door. He would have to make a stand and dispatch each beast as soon as it pushed through the entrance. If Mortuus let up, he would be devoured.

He held his ground, fearful of weakening for any amount of time. There were hundreds, each aroused by the hunt, and maybe fresh blood, he thought. Mortuus would wait for them to push their bodies against the door, letting it open until a single creature had pushed half its body through. Then they were easy to dispatch. Mortuus had only to shove his knife through the beast, the door would shut, and he would wait for the next one to begin the cycle again. He killed the imps quickly, at times so fast that his small hallway was filled with black smoke.

The ordeal continued on. His left arm and shoulder had been laid open by the first attack, and each movement resulted in pain. His back spasmed, and his ankle throbbed from the deep bites. It was a long time before imps stopped pushing through the doorway.

He was wary at first, afraid that they were hiding, trying to trick him into coming out; his biggest fear had been that they would just go to the far end of the hallway, climb the turret, and enter from behind. Thankfully, they were not so intelligent. He waited, catching his breath. Finally, when he knew it was over, he lay still in the hallway, weak from the blood loss and pain. He thought about this world he had woken to, the torturing and attacks, constant fighting, the filthiness and stink, and horrific creatures. He was weary and defeated, fatigued by the noise of pain and suffering that permeated everything. It was unbearable. Who was he and why was he here?

He lay there, contemplating, as his wounds sealed themselves and his skin regrew. He had only one chance.

He must get to Limbo.

Chapter 14

The Fugitives Trek

"Aetos, Darius – look, ahead, just beyond the depression in the mud. See the path?!" said Panos. Lying low in a shallow depression of mud and filth, three men were crawling, watching their surroundings for any signs that they had been discovered. They were covered in wormy muck, camouflaged from the other inhabitants and the cruel masters of this region. The foul smelling mud was cold, at first a welcome relief from their eternal run, but after a long period of time caused them to shake, uncontrollable spasms contracting their muscles painfully.

They had escaped their torment of running forever, herded into a rough formation by the flying, painfully stinging wasp-like creatures that were referred to as Hell flies by the people of this circle. The Hell flies no longer pursued the three. Now only the worms and chilled mud needed to be dealt with.

* * * * * *

Few of the inhabitants of the Vestibule had ever escaped. Once out of formation, the perpetrator was immediately assaulted by a huge mass of flies, far worse than the two or three at a time that would normally bite into their skin. The creatures bit out small chunks of flesh, the bite small but bloody, causing the skin to swell, and further bites in the swollen regions amplified the pain beyond what most people could endure. Most of this circle's inhabitants could hardly see, so inflamed and swollen were the bites around their eyes. Dripping blood and pus constantly clouded their vision, causing them to run into each other at times and fall to the ground. This brought on the attack by the shepherding insects.

The three men had endured the full wrath of the flies in the initial period of their escape, as they expected to. They knew that if in fact they were to have any chance of getting away, the flies would have to be distracted, and there would be a sacrifice. During their constant run, they had communicated with each other, no easy task when breathless. It took a long time to share their life stories, small talk, and occasional arguments and debates before they came up with the notion to break away; the idea was not originally theirs.

A few others had escaped long ago, one eventually returning. The returned escapee, named Philo, shared many stories about the lower circles and the horrors he witnessed. His was a terrifying story, of how he was captured by flying demons and tortured, then dropped into a river of pitch far below; devils guarded the pitch, and would rip apart any who they could fish out. Finally able to free himself, Philo returned to the Vestibule. He swore he would not attempt to escape again.

When the three men confirmed their decision, they plied Philo, seeking more detailed information about the depths and the dangerous creatures. The more information, the better their chances were. Philo was reluctant, shouting his disdain that they would even make the attempt after all he had told them, placing themselves into far worse torments of Hell. The men wanted the information badly enough to consider tripping up Philo and arousing the ire of the flies. They let Philo know their intentions. Finally, Philo spoke with them at length, but concluded his details with an ominous warning.

"Prepare yourselves for the boiling pitch. It is the fate of all fugitives."

The trio had narrowly eluded the flies. One of the members of their group, or as Darius had put it, their 'herd', was known for his ruthlessness, tripping others to get momentary relief from the bites, distracting the flies into swarming the fallen victim. Garum always got away with his bullying because of his large size. The last poor victim had not recovered before Garum threw him to the ground again; the flies shrouded him in a grey cloud as he screamed in pain.

The three men had not been bothered by Garum because of their size and their bond. It was known that Garum cowardly targeted only the weak loners and occasional newcomer; he would provide the perfect sacrifice for their escape.

Panos first suggested that the three try to escape the Vestibule. He reasoned that if Philo could get out, why not them? Certainly Philo was resourceful; his only problem, according to Panos, was that he went alone. If, suggested Panos, they were in larger number, the chances of survival could be greatly maximized.

Aetos, unconvinced, argued to remain. "We have the most lenient punishment in all of Hell according to Philo. You heard how the other fugitives regarded this place. Why do we want to go deeper and risk fire and boiling pitch? Wouldn't we be fools to undertake such a journey, when we have it as good as it gets right here?"

Panos was insistent, and pushed his point. "Truly you are wise, Aetos, but what about the fugitive that Philo spoke of?"
The other fugitive, whom Philo referred to as Occidio, had escaped the seventh circle, a river of boiling blood, policed by centaurs, large, fierce creatures with bows, arrows, and spears. Occidio was journeying toward the upper circles when he met Philo in the circle of the burning dead, (he had called it Dis), helping Philo during his first encounter with imps. Panos continued.

"Before Occidio and Philo were captured, Occidio spoke to Philo of a cave that was guarded, so guarded that even the centaurs were forbidden to approach. The centaurs are the assigned keepers of that area. If it is true that the Fallen were hiding something, then I ask why? Does that place hold secrets or forbidden knowledge? The Fallen reign over Hell – why the secret lair? My point is this, Aetos; There are things we do not know, and one of them might be a way to escape this place entirely. This may be a way out. Another point; what of Limbo? Occidio told Philo of the man, the old teacher, who visits the master centaur. This man was from Limbo. I believe that Limbo is behind the closed gate we passed when we arrived before Minos. Do you remember the gate?"

"I do not. I was weeping, anguished with the thoughts of eternal torment." returned a sad Aetos.

"Regardless..." Panos looked to Darius for support. "Darius, do you recall the gate, on the left side of the path, between the two great walls? After we crossed the river? The river is not far from us here."

"Aye." said Darius as he nodded his head. "I do recall the gate, but I need no further convincing. I will go. I'm curious also Aetos, and also afraid, like yourself... but I will not stay here any longer. Tell me your plan, Panos." Darius paused, then addressed Aetos. "Aetos, join us. Do not cast doubt. The risk is certain, but for a short time we will not run in constant torment. In my life, I laughed at the rebels who complained and fought the ruthless corruption of my country's leadership. They were fools, I was sure. I was content to labor for another, be beaten, and accept it as my just reward, and to make a goal of attaining crumbs from the taskmasters. A long time I thought I would go to a higher reward for being a good slave, taking the whippings in humility, obeying my cruel masters, and their crueler children. I put down the other slaves, keeping them like myself, complacent and waiting for mercy and freedom to drop from the sky. My masters told me I would see a grandiose reward for my servitude, in a greater place, all the more glorious for the pain I bore in life. And I believed, lazily unthinking, having faith like an obedient slave should. Yet, here am I, for eternity, in Hell. Now, I would fight alongside the rebels had I the chance again. My freedom, for even a few moments, is all I can see. For that alone I will gamble on this adventure."

Aetos dropped his head. He had been counting on Darius to support his position. Now he felt weak and ashamed for his cowardice. He had chosen to sit on the side lines in his life. He had no stories of his own to share; he had been from the upper classes of his society, the son of a son of a son of a wealthy nobleman. His life was about leisure, boredom and decadence, socializing within societal circles of the wealthy, even as the majority of his countrymen starved or were impoverished, and went to fight and die in the wars of land conquest. Aetos remembered it was always the aristocracy who started the wars for land, and the poor who fought. The patriotic soldiers did not return, or returned to the poverty they had left, and all were affected by the horrors they had survived. Aetos, in his sheltered station of society, knew no battles, only ceremonies. He provided large donations to the clergy, assured that his afterlife would be one of pleasure to rival that of his lifetime.

"I will join you." said Aetos.

* * * * * *

The three fugitives escaped and for the first time in hundreds of years, maybe even a thousand, they were free. Onward they crawled, the wall on their left, and the river distantly on the right. They had spotted a path in the distance, a trail that recalled the ominous memory of their arrival into Hell.

Chapter 15

The Way Out

The path was a well-trodden, sandy walkway. The trio stood up, happy to be off their stomachs, wiping the sticky mud off and detaching the worms that had bitten into their skin. Once on the path, they could clearly see the distant river, although they were much closer to the wall. According to what Philo had told them, they needed to continue past the path; there would be a rocky outcropping, a sort of oasis of boulders and rock, closer to the wall than the river; the rock gathering surrounded a small pool where they could wash and rest. The pool was fed from an underground spring, and trickled out slowly as a small stream that flowed into the river Acheron. Washing was important, Philo said, because if Charon, the ferryman of Acheron, suspected they were fugitives, he would allow them to board but might later throw them into the river. Philo stressed how much he had washed; multiple times before he would attempt to get into Charon's skiff.

The pool within the rocky outcropping was the only water source that could be used; Philo warned them exhaustively not to touch, wash in, or attempt to swim across the river; if they touched the river water Charon would smell it, and if they fell in, Acheron would become their eternal home.

Aetos followed the path with his eyes; it went slightly diagonal from the river to the wall. He surveyed the wall; the fact that it was the boundary between life and Hell made him shudder. During his running torment he had barely been able to see the river because of his swollen closed eyes. Now that the three were free of the fly bites for some time, their vision had cleared. Aetos looked at Panos and Darius; their faces were also showing signs of healing.

Aetos studied the wall, enjoying his newly improved vision. He looked left, following the wall. No running groups could be seen even distantly; the landscape was free of flies and people. Small and far away, where the path originated, a slight change in the pattern of wall stones caught his eye. It was a speck in the distance.

"It must be the gate" He thought, and then a light seemed to come into his eyes. "Why hadn't they considered trying to walk out?" Without a word, he began walking, following the path along its slight rise in elevation, striding toward the wall…and the gate. Panos and Darius looked at each other, puzzled for a moment before they were able to comprehend what Aetos was doing.

"Aetos? That's not the way." said Panos.

"Why can't we just go out the gate? Philo said nothing of any guards or that he even attempted to try to get through the gate. Can we try?" Aetos replied quickly, shouting as the distance grew between himself and the two men. Darius turned toward Panos, eyes locked in surprise. They smiled after a moment, at the previously reluctant Aetos' new display of courage.

"Very well Aetos, but I think the gates are guarded in some manner. Why don't we walk together." shouted back Panos. Aetos slowed for a moment, allowing the others to catch up to him. Panos and Darius hurried.

"Hmmm. It seems too easy, Aetos." said Darius. "Wouldn't Philo have tried this?"

"If he did, he did not mention it. Do you recall any mention of the gate by Philo? We'd be fools not to try; we're so close." said Aetos. The two shook their heads in agreement. Philo had not said a word regarding the gate.

They walked. It was a long, long walk, much longer than it appeared. When they got closer, they noticed the gate was just a large, single doorway of simple wooden construction, wide open; past the doorway they could not discern, except to notice there was no guard. Could it be this easy, they collectively thought. Why wasn't the doorway shut and locked?

They continued walking. The doorway remained far off. More walking, and no change in the distance. Aetos, seeming panicked, desperately broke into a jog, then a run, and then a full run. Panos and Darius watched as he stopped, far from the pair.

"How far is the doorway from you now Aetos" shouted Panos.

"There is no change Panos. As I ran I saw no change ever." Aetos said, hope deflated in his voice. "I don't understand."
Panos and Darius approached the disheartened Aetos.

"This is why Philo did not speak of the gate. There is no exit here. It seemed too easy because it is. This is only the way *in*." said Darius.

"Damn it." said Aetos. Then, suddenly he sparked up. "Why don't we go to the wall, farther down, away from the door, then just follow the wall back to the door. We have to reach it! " Darius nodded his head in agreement, interested to try out this approach.

"I'll stay here and observe. Aetos, go to the wall from the left. Panos, you go on the right. Walk toward each other. I will watch you both as you approach the doorway from here, which seems to be the closest we can get from this angle."

The two did as Darius recommended. Once they reached the wall, they turned and walked toward the opening. Aetos touched the wall, skimming it with his outstretched fingers, as if he was trying to ascertain that it was real while walking toward Panos. Panos plodded toward Aetos.

As the two of them walked at each other, Darius noticed that they reached a certain point and ceased to move. Their feet walked as if they were treading ground, but they could not get any nearer to the large door. The two continued walking, unaware the ground was not moving under foot. Darius shouted to each, informing them that they were not progressing. It made no sense. Finally they quit their march, and returned to where Darius stood, puzzled and frustrated for their efforts in vain, especially Aetos. They stood looking at the wall, then each other.

"Well. It does make sense. Magic is used to keep us imprisoned, a one way enchantment. That must be why Philo did not mention it. He would not have returned if he could have walked out." said Darius.

Aetos hung his head disappointedly. The three started off the path toward the rocky oasis, frustration dimming the joy of their hard won freedom.

Chapter 16
Paradise Found

The remaining travel portion of the three fugitives was uneventful, each silent since the failed attempt at the gate. Not long after leaving the path, the trio heard noises from behind them. Frightened they would be captured, they dove onto the ground, turning quickly to face the source of the sound. To their great relief, it was only a small group of new arrivals, walking toward the river and Charon's landing. The five newcomers, all men, followed along the path. Two were crying loudly; two walked silently, head hung in sadness, and one cursed at the weeping pair, berating them for their weakness. The entire party of five followed the trail until they were out of sight of Aetos, Darius and Panos. This scene brought back memories for each of the fugitives, as the three recalled their own arrival, and pitied the newly damned. They resumed their standing position and their trek.

The escapees arrived at the rocky oasis a long while later. It was as Philo had described; there was nothing more than a cluster of large boulders and rocks. The stand appeared in the distance to be a man-made structure, up until their approach. Inside the stony gathering was a hidden pool, very small and barely fed by an underground spring, revealed by the slight boil at the wall-side end of the pool. A shallow stream flowed from the opposite end of the pool and through the stony gathering out onto sticky sand, winding down and away toward Acheron. Small plants grew sparsely along the twisty stream.

The pool had a usable length that was roughly a meter and a half, but it was very shallow except for a small pocket near the spring. It was narrow; the pool could be easily leapt over from a standing position. The entire rocky formation sat in the midst of sandy hills, and appeared to have just dropped down from the mist ceiling above. Some of the rocks and boulders were split apart into small fragments while others stuck into the ground whole.

The three were very happy. They were relieved to actually find this oasis, as deep inside they were each afraid that Philo had lied to them. They could hide for awhile, clean up, rest and allow their bodies to fully heal. The mere thought of washing off the centuries of filth was immensely joyful.

Each man had been clothed in a burial shroud, tightly wrapped around his form. The white garb they began the afterlife in was now muddy brown and stained with the blood and pus that had oozed from them in their torment. The men removed the mud-caked wraps, and threw them into the pool. The pool, originally clean and clear, darkened to a muddy tea, while the trio searched for stones to pound the cloth. Aetos watched Darius and Panos clean their cloths, then imitated as best he could; Aetos came from high wealth, the sort that did no menial work. When the three finished their washing, they laid the shrouds on large boulders to dry. No shroud was as white as its original state, but each was infinitely cleaner. The men took their turns in the small pool, scrubbing their skin with wet, coarse sand from the pool bottom. Although painful, it was necessary to get rid of hundreds of years of caked on filth. Each escapee's bath took a long time; the wait for the stirred up sediment and filth from the last man to wash downstream was lengthy. Once finished, each man crawled onto the rocks, careful not to touch the wet sand between the stones. They waited on the rocks and enjoyed a long rest, enjoying the new feeling of cleanliness as they dried and healed.

"How do you feel about escaping now, Aetos?" said Panos, smiling. Aetos was examining his slowly healing fly bites. He spoke as he scanned the red holes on his arms.

"I am well" said Aetos, "but I still worry. Going to the lower circles still frightens me. For now, though, I feel like I could just stay here forever and -" Aetos stopped talking abruptly. He saw a shadow appear, out of the corner of his eye, for a moment, near the rocks at the stream edge. Panos started to speak when he realized there was something wrong. He looked at Aetos serious expression, and followed his eyes. Darius had already seen Aetos distraction, and he picked up a large stone. For just a second, Darius saw a strange, small creature; it looked like a twisted caricature of something else, more human, though its size and skin coloring was unnatural. Darius froze. This must be one of Philos wild imps, he thought. Grabbing his wet shroud, he wrapped himself in its wetness. Panos and Aetos did the same, then armed themselves by grabbing nearby rocks. Panos found a rock that was thin and sharp pointed. The three men crouched behind a set of large boulders, moving as quickly as they could in silence, eyes scanning everywhere, searching for the intruder. Inside, their hearts pounded in fear.

As they searched, the beast came out from behind a boulder right next to them, oblivious of their close presence. The three froze, quietly watching as the imp went to the pool edge, following with their eyes only. They slowly shuffled sideways, behind another boulder, their eyes glued to the miniature monstrosity. The imp sniffed the air, then bent down to the pool surface and started to growl; it was soon joined by another, appearing from behind a boulder on the opposite side of the pool. The latter beast was fully facing the three men; they could see its distorted features clearly. It leapt from its position, a standing jump disproportionate to the creatures' size. It turned to face the pool with the other, and bent down to inspect the water surface. Both creatures' backs were turned toward the hiding escapees. They were purple and grayish black, leather-skinned with well-defined, miniature musculatures. Their glowing eyes were an olive, greenish-yellow. One of the beasts had four arms, while the other had only two; the extra pair of arms hung limp, and extruded from the back and upper thigh.

The fugitives were not sure what to do. Philo made no mention of encountering imps in the Vestibule. But Panos, remembering what Philo said about killing the creatures, started to crawl up behind them; he worried that more were nearby and coming their way, and if they did not kill the two soon, they would be outnumbered. He shook as he approached from behind, crouched, almost crawling, silently. The imps were staring into the pool, curiously growling at its surface. Panos intended to surprise them, killing one in the least, in hopes his companions would join in. He raised the sharp rock, readying to beat the beasts. For a single moment, fear stalled the blow; Panos had hesitated too long.

The imp pair spun around, and Panos saw, too close, the raging yellow eyes glaring at him, their fangs bared for a split second before they were on him. The beast on his left ran straight into his legs. Panos knees were knocked out from under him so violently that he smashed his face on the rocks as he hit the ground. The other imp jumped on his back, bending down and biting into Panos' neck. The first creature was holding onto Panos' legs, biting and gnashing, tearing huge chunks of flesh from the back of the screaming Panos' thighs. Panos was yelling for help from Aetos and Darius, squirming violently to get free. The imp on his back suddenly was gone as Panos heard a commotion to his side. He pumped his legs frantically and suddenly his left leg was loose. He swung the free leg over and pinned the biting imp between them, squeezing tightly; the imp was clawing and ripping at his legs, attempting to get free, all four arms raking into his flesh. The pain was so severe that it caused Panos to tremble. He sat up quickly and grabbed the pinned imp by its throat. The creature clawed at his forearm. Desperately he searched for his rock, any rock, to start beating the brains out of the beast, anything to end this ordeal of madness. Panos found the sharp rock and jammed it into the imps' left eye as it twisted frantically. He held the beast flat on the ground, and leaned down into the makeshift weapon heavily. Blood began spurting out as socket bones broke; the skull interior split as the rock-knife plunged deep inside, mutilating softer tissues just before the creature popped into a dark cloud. Panos felt like he had been in a dream. Recalling Philos stories, he understood what had just happened.

There was a growling noise behind him; Panos turned to see Aetos fighting the two-armed imp. Aetos had come out from behind the boulder and tackled the imp before it could get at the neck of Panos. The imp had dug its sharp claws into Aetos' forearms, and was pinning them together, rending him helpless as it tried to bite and rend him. Aetos blood was trickling down from where the sharp claws pierced the skin of his arms. Determined, Aetos held on tightly, as if his life depended upon it. It was a stalemate, one not able to let go of the other, but unable to do more damages. Aetos tried lifting the small beast high, then slamming it down hard against the rocky floor to no avail; the creature easily caught itself, placing its feet on the ground. Panos, still shocked from his own ordeal, picked up his sharp knife-like rock and limped over to the pair. Summoning his full rage, the wounded Panos drove home his weapon one more time, deep into the back of the imps' skull. The familiar screech was a painful, welcome joy. Panos fell backward onto the uneven ground, distracted by the immense pain of his injuries.

Aetos sat down, gasping "Thank you Panos" between breathes. His heart was racing and he was shaken. So this was what they had left their torment for. He contemplated the other horrors which waited below in Hell. Yet they had beaten the beasts. Conflicted, Aetos considered their predicament. There were worse creatures ahead, and torments to match; the imps were easiest to deal with, according to their discussions with Philo. They simply smoked when destroyed. The others – much larger versions - must to be avoided. Aetos was unsettled. Panos was sitting up, examining his bloodied legs as Aetos lay still, breathing heavily; he looked around, suddenly curious.

"Where is Darius?" he asked Panos.

Chapter 17

The Stone Skull

Mortuus had rested and was leaning up against the wall of the hallway. Peeking out the narrow doorway, he scanned the grim landscape. The imps were gone, either dispatched or they had left for other interests. His wounds had mostly healed, and it did not hurt to move any longer. Mortuus was previously coughing up blood, his breathing impeded by rather large clumps of red phlegm. His thirst was burning very badly, worse than he could remember, at least since his awakening. He needed to motivate himself to complete his task.

Mortuus arose slowly, standing with some difficulty, intent on quenching his burning thirst, in Limbo. The object that Phlegyas wanted was nearby; Mortuus knew by the large number of imps he had just fought and destroyed. The object was an onyx skull, carved out of a piece of the tower that was on the shore where Mortuus had met Phlegyas; the oarsman had called it his 'art project,' explaining that when Hell was younger, he had much more time on his hands, and so occupied himself with carving whatever he could get his hands on. Carveable materials did not come his way so often, Phlegyas had said to Mortuus, so when he found the piece from the tower, it was a bonus. Mortuus listened although he was uninterested in the piece or its origin; he wanted only to gain passage across the Styx, and get closer to Limbo and its water. Phlegyas promised Mortuus he would ferry him to the other side of the dismal swamp, away from Dis, if Mortuus could only bring him the skull.

The oarsman's instructions were to follow the wall around the sixth circle, traveling to the left side of the entrance, until Mortuus found the area where many imps congregated. The imps were also looking for the skull, said Phlegyas, but were always distracted enough with their tormenting and morbid feasts not to find it. A symbol on the rusted wall, of an orb, surrounded by a ring, was the second clue for Mortuus. Once at the image of the orb, referred to by Phlegyas as 'the ringed Sun', he was to walk straight into the tombs, toward the opposite edge of the sixth circle and look for a tomb with an etching of a key on the side. It would be nearer to the edge of the seventh circle than to the rusted iron wall.

Mortuus found the ringed sun on the rusted wall. He walked straight from the wall image, deep into the circle until he saw a cluster of tombs in a rough pyramidal shape. Hundreds of the glowing burial vaults were in the area, many large and gaudy, but all without the specific key etching Mortuus sought. After exhaustively searching and walking, he noticed he was approaching a ledge as the number of heated tombs and coffins were becoming sparse. His curiosity had the better of him, and he walked to the ledge. Mortuus could see a rocky slope, with many large boulders lining the ground on a steep downward grade. Although the misty air made the visibility poor, he could see something, a large river, wide and red. He could not see the far bank, and a sickening, humid coppery smell assailed his nose, different from the normal stink of this circle.

As he examined this strange lower circle, a large creature appeared out of the mist, far to his right, but moving across the slope in his general direction, traversing the uneven boulders with relative ease. The creature was tiny in the distance, but at its current walking rate, it would be near Mortuus soon. He did not recognize the beast; it did not resemble any of the creatures he had observed since emerging from the tomb. Although curious, Mortuus turned back toward the tombs and continued the quest of Phlegyas'; he did not wish to delay his departure for Limbo. He resumed searching.

Much later, Mortuus found the marked tomb. It was only lightly etched; time had worn down the glowing carved rock. He had passed it many times, easily missing the symbol. Relief filled him, and he was glad to know he would not fail his quest. Sitting down and crossing his legs, he cupped his hands together, reciting the words that Phlegyas had him memorize. The oarsman had said it was magic, and was the only way to open the tomb and retrieve the skull from its underside. Mortuus would have to prepare himself, warned Phlegyas, for once he uttered the words, there could be danger; the skull was taken from the oarsman and hidden by Fallen. The incantation magic would pull strength from Mortuus, as magic required energy to work. Phlegyas would have fully explained to Mortuus, but realized Mortuus wanted only to get to Limbo; if saying a few magical words got him closer, so be it. Mortuus would do whatever was required to get across the Styx.

"Take the skull and return quickly." Phlegyas had said. "The tomb is surrounded with a spell of protection; once you remove the skull from its resting place, exit quickly. Run immediately, do not stop, until you are through the gate. Wait here, for I will return. You need not concern yourself about the dark angels; Fallen will suspect their little vermin pets have stolen the skull. They will vent their rage on the nearest imps and demons long before suspecting any escapee."

Mortuus prepared himself, closing his eyes and uttering the incantation clearly at the marked tomb; "Balukaa loch naskdu makhe." Nothing happened at first; for a brief moment he thought he had mispronounced the words. He opened his eyes just as the tomb was sliding sideways, loudly scraping a slab of stone beneath it. A small lid in the rock with a latch carved out of it was visible. Mortuus stood up, bending toward the latch; the latch was difficult to move, and pressing forcibly, he flipped it. The lid opened from both sides, revealing a shiny black, stone skull sitting beneath the surface. Mortuus, slightly weakened from the magic, grabbed the object, replaced the lid and stood quickly. The tomb closed automatically, sliding back into place.

Mortuus looked back in the direction of the gate, and peered ahead at the rusted wall in the distance. The thick air made visibility poor past a certain distance, but he could see where he needed to go. He saw nothing resembling danger, and began to run back diagonally toward the wall, then parallel to the wall. He looked around nervously as he loped through the randomly placed glowing tombs and coffins, moving quickly. Once, he saw what might have been imps, but he was moving too fast to stop and glance. He would deal with them as needed if they caught up.

Mortuus continued his fast pace until he saw the distant flicker of the tower, breathing a sigh of relief. He did not stop until he passed through the gate.
Limbo was near.

Chapter 18

The Mystery of the Skull

Phlegyas was a long time returning to the gate. The tower had flashed three times before the skiff emerged from the mist. Mortuus, waiting silently, watched the water dwellers partake of their violent frenzy several times. During one episode, they had actually come part way out of the stinking water with their victim, ripping, biting and striking brutally before the unlucky beast finally made his escape. Mortuus watched, stunned by the sheer brutality; he was becoming wary of their closer proximity, considering the possibility they could come out after him were he not so close to the gate. Finally the violence subsided; the watery commotion moved out, away beyond his sight, as the river resumed its still darkness.

Mortuus studied the skull that Phlegyas had sent him for, puzzled. This 'treasure' was hardly that; it had only a slight luster and smooth touch, but no real appeal. He scrutinized the skull's surface features, curious to determine why anyone, Phlegyas or Fallen, or imp, would desire it. The tower overhead flared, casting additional light on the object. Inspecting it more closely, Mortuus could barely see a thin, hairline circling around the top; he placed his finger on the slight line to feel the nearly invisible fracture. Holding the skull in his left hand, he tried to see if it would move in separate pieces. He twisted the bottom, where his grip was secure, trying to force the top, above the fracture, in the opposite direction. It did not work.

Mortuus looked at the detailed black face, teeth, the triangular nose hole, and the deep eye sockets and found nothing. He peered into the sockets again; they were the deepest and most likely to conceal other hidden openings or latches, or at least hold some clue. The tower flared once more, and this time the light it cast illuminated a slight depression in the top of the left eye socket, small and thin; it vanished with the light. Taking his dagger out, Mortuus felt the interior surface of the eye socket with the knife point, searching for anything useful. When the blade point touched the depression, he maneuvered the end twisting and pressing into it. All of a suddenly, he heard a faint 'click' come from the skull.

Mortuus held the skull steady, and noticed the line on the top of the skull had grown wider. He slipped his dagger into the eye socket again, and pushed upward; the top of the skull popped off and fell onto the soft ground.

A very large gem sat in the skull interior, bluish in appearance, though oddly shaped, an unnatural form. It fit perfectly snug inside the skull container, with no space between it and the skull to allow for movement when the skull was shaken. It was beautiful, sparkling and shimmering, like pure mountain spring water, reminding Mortuus again of his unbearable thirst. It emitted warmth that touched his heart, soothing him as he looked at it. He was sure the stone could not belong to this world, this Hell he had woken up in. The stone seemed alive, and Mortuus felt protective of it, wanting to free it from this place before it could be polluted. Maybe it was better off hidden. Phlegyas must have known the gem existed. What was the oarsman going to do with it?

Just as Mortuus had this last thought, a uniform, splashing noise from offshore indicated the imminent arrival of Phlegyas. He quickly picked up the top of the skull and pushed it back in place; it clicked together easily, concealing the treasure. Mortuus decided it was better to have Phlegyas believe he was unaware of the skull's content; his thirst was increasing in intensity. He must get to Limbo.

Chapter 19

Across the Water

Phlegyas was in a foul mood when he reached the shore where Mortuus waited; he had been detained forcibly on the opposite shore by patrolling demons and questioned intensely, then threatened with further violence. While Mortuus examined the onyx skull across the Styx, the two demons initiated their conversation with Phlegyas by cracking his skull with a large metal club. Apparently, Phlegyas appeared to be a fugitive to the pair. He had not seen the metal club until after being struck with it; he swooned and fell backward onto the muddy shore and they were on him, beating him savagely, until one of them noticed the skiff nearby. They stopped their blows, growling and yelling; defiantly, he cursed them out loudly.

Raising their weapon in a threatening pose, they commanded Phlegyas to tell them where he might have seen the fugitive. His head ached, swollen from their savagery. Phlegyas knew they would not leave him without some answer, and so he pointed in the opposite direction from where the pair of beasts had approached. They hissed and waved their weapon at the oarsman, resuming their fugitive hunt and leaving him holding his head until he could bear the throbbing enough to return to the other shore of the Styx.

He was angry at Mortuus for being late. When he reached the shore, he took the skull abruptly, motioning Mortuus to get into the boat as he touched his sore head. Mortuus stepped in timidly, wary of Phlegyas' mood, and not used to boats. He went to the furthest seat from the oarsman, and sat waiting to journey across the Styx, anxious to leave this circle and its horrors behind for good. Phlegyas took out a small water vial, like those Mortuus had been given by his benefactor. Mortuus' stared, coveting the vial's contents as his thirst burned. Needing distraction, he turned away and looked out over the swamp.

Phlegyas examined the dark skull carefully. He felt its weight, turning it several times as if trying to detect movement within. He held it up with his left hand.

"Lita bels scrinda." whispered Phlegyas. Mortuus turned around, curiosity brimming. While he watched, the skull began to glow from within, the luminescence in the shape of the hidden gem, revealing its presence. The glowing subsided moments later, and Phlegyas, satisfied with his treasure, opened a small panel on the side of his boat and placed the skull inside, then closed it up tightly. Mortuus, not wishing to engage Phlegyas in conversation, turned back to look out over the water as Phlegyas pushed off from shore. The water was foul, smelling of dead and decaying creatures. The uncertainty of the place enveloped him. He leaned to the right side, elbow uncomfortably placed on the thin starboard rail.

"Do not lean, or leave your hands over the sides." Phlegyas snapped his warning at Mortuus grimly. "The inhabitants of this swamp are very much afraid of my wrath…but not of you; if they drag you down into the filthy waters you will forfeit your journey to Limbo and suffer a lengthy violence at their hands, unable to escape." Mortuus nodded his head and pulled his arms in to indicate his understanding of the seriousness of Phlegyas' words.

"I am late, and of foul temperament because I was questioned by demons, and by that I mean they beat me very hard with a large club. Heed my words, Mortuus. The demons who questioned me are fugitive hunters. They wander freely, in search of fugitives to take to lower Hell. Rare few ever escape the lower circles." Phlegyas paused for a moment, scrutinizing Mortuus; he had just noticed something. Mortuus became increasingly uncomfortable at the length and intensity of Phlegyas' stare. The oarsman's face transformed into shocked disbelief.

"You are not a fugitive?" He paused, staring. "Why are you here?"

Mortuus was confused. He had some feeling, something bothering him inside.

"I don't know…what this place is or why I am here." He stuttered as a deep sadness erupted within him. "I don't know… I don't know … anything." His head bent down slowly. "I am going to Limbo because when I awoke, I was told to go there; I had… instructions. The instructions said to get to Limbo, and the voice said to get to Limbo. I…I haven't any idea…even who I am, but I need to get to Limbo." Mortuus paused, looking downward at the swamp.

"I'm so thirsty. I found some small vials of water…when I awoke; I was very weak."

"Ah. Yes, Aristotle…" said Phlegyas, understanding. The oarsman softened slightly. "I have some answers for you. Aristotle brought you the water from Limbo. It was he who awakened you, I know. Aristotle is the only one who travels here regularly, the only citizen of Limbo who ventures to the lower circles. But…where were you sleeping, and why? No one sleeps in Hell, outside of Limbo. Every pain is meant to be felt in its fullest intensity. None sentenced to torment may rest. There are no exceptions." He looked at Mortuus.

Mortuus was half weeping now. Overwhelmed with his thirst and sadness, he was trying desperately to hold back, to hide his pain. But his eyes leaked the truth in his heart; holding back only made it worse. He looked up with wet eyes as Phlegyas suddenly pulled in his oar and struck him squarely against the side of the head. Mortuus' ear rang just after he saw the flash in his head from the impact. Dumbfounded, he became angry and glared at Phlegyas, standing up to square off, not caring if it meant taking them both into the dark waters. Phlegyas swung his oar up between Mortuus' legs, causing him to drop and curl into a fetal position.

"Do… not… show… weakness… here" said Phlegyas sternly. "I do you great favor with my brutality. Do not advertise your softness to the creatures of the filthy swamp. As I said, I cannot save you from their grasp if you are pulled in." He paused, then turned to the back of his skiff and bent over. He arose with two vials in his hand. Mortuus, still coiled in pain, recognized them.

"These will help with your thirst, though maybe not fully. Aristotle brings these to me in exchange for passage. They do not just slake your thirst, they hasten healing. Limbo is the only place where you can get it.

Phlegyas handed the vials to Mortuus who immediately opened the vials and quaffed down the water. The water quenched his thirst; he felt his strength returning to him. He repeated this for the second vial. This seemed to also quell his rage at Phlegyas.

"Thank you." choked out the humbled Mortuus, sated for the moment. He sat up straight and waited to reach the opposite shore.

He wiped his face. Phlegyas stopped talking, rowing as Mortuus looked ahead.

This was a very curious situation, thought Phlegyas.

Chapter 20

Captured

Darius peered out from under the large boulder. He had tunneled underneath just in time. Only Darius had seen them coming, looking up at just the right moment and digging in before they discovered him. His heart was beating hard. Large and dangerous in appearance, they simply appeared from the sky overhead, dropping out of the misty shroud as if they had been waiting all along. Darius had never been more terrified.

The creatures were ragged and leathery skinned, monstrous winged demons, with twisted, human-like features, painted in a sickly gray- marbled coloring. For one moment, Darius saw them clearly; they were as caricatures of some human creature. Their huge wings beat thunderously as he scrambled to dig into the sandy wet gravel. His hands were raw and bleeding, but the escapee felt nothing but panic. Aetos and Panos were on the verge of dispatching the second imp when the demons appeared. Darius did not see the creatures fall upon his friends, but he heard, for far too long, their screams as the sound of flesh being hacked and ripped assaulted his ears. He could only churn the ground faster, but never seeming fast enough.

Darius overheard the creatures speaking in a strange language, harsh and deep, mixed with the common tongue; from what he could make out, they were aware of a missing third fugitive, Darius himself. They continued ravaging the unfortunate pair, until Darius could barely hear their muffled screams through wasted voices, exhausted from the lengthy assault. He heard the heavy, hollow arc of the giant wings again, pounding through the atmosphere so loudly he was sure he felt the beasts were on top of him; but slowly, the pitch diminished, slowly growing further and further distant. Darius cautiously peeked out, turning from side to side at first, then slowly crept around the boulder; he crawled out of his hiding spot tentatively, and searched the entire pool area, expecting to see his two mutilated friends still laying there, ripped apart. He grimaced at the thought of seeing the carnage.

The third fugitive looked twice, unsure of what he had not seen. He walked closer to the pool. Blood and gore everywhere confirmed the violence that had passed. Chunks of bloody cloth and human flesh were all over the place, even in the pool. Darius kept looking around, wary of the space above; where were his companions?

He did not dare call out, but instead walked out of the rocky oasis, down the stream that flowed to the Acheron. He looked up and saw, flying toward the river, a horror that made his stomach drop. He swooned and fell to his knees. The demons were carrying away the mutilated bodies of Aetos and Panos.

They were gone, consigned to the lower circles; they would be forever tormented, far worse than anything they had endured at the mercy of the flies. He thought of Aetos, whom he helped talk into making this ill-fated journey.

"What have I done, Aetos?"

Chapter 21
Cry Wolf

Mortuus' hands were covered with gravelly, stinking, wet grit. He had followed Phlegyas' directions to the path up to the fourth circle. The oarsman told Mortuus to find the partially visible path, to stay to the left; the fugitive hunters, the demons who had brutalized Phlegyas earlier, were walking in the opposite direction and they would eventually return full circle. One beast was a flyer, so Mortuus should look up occasionally.

"Head straight to the wall and then left," Phlegyas told him. "The pathway will become apparent."

Mortuus did as instructed, and soon was following the path. The difference between the path and the normal landscape was slight, and Mortuus suspected Phlegyas eyes were well trained to discern the differences. Intermittently observing the misty darkness above him, Mortuus walked until he saw a trickling stream of water flowing down the rock wall. The water flow had carved out a small crevice in the black rock and provided places for foot- and handholds that led up to the fourth circle. This was Mortuus' first movement upward, toward Limbo, and he was excited at the small-scale progress, though his excitement was inhibited by constant fear of capture.

The trickling water rolled over the black rock wall, carrying with it a silty grey muck that was slimy to the touch. The rock wall was coarse, leaving scrapes and scratches on his hands and feet as he clambered slowly upward. The scratches did not pain Mortuus initially, but the slime water agitated the wounds. This water source, according to Phlegyas, was the origin of the Styx.

"Do not drink of it, no matter how your thirst might burn." Phlegyas had said. "A nauseating sickness will fill you for all time, and you will know part of the punishment of the inhabitants of the Styx." Mortuus, thirsty as he was, would not begin to consider drinking from the polluted stream.

As Mortuus came within a few meters of the ledge, he began to hear blunt, bumping sounds. There were many voices, as if crowds of people were watching an exhibition. Mortuus reached the top, exhausted, long after he began the ascent. The ledge was gravelly and slippery, but manageable. He laid flat out to rest, the cliff on his right and the remainder of the fourth circle on his left. His thirst was becoming unbearable again. Catching his breath, he rolled to his left and surveyed as far as his eyes could see for the next likely obstacle; Plutus.

Phlegyas had insisted on telling Mortuus about the history of Plutus just as the skiff landed on the opposite shore. Mortuus was only interested in moving away from Phlegyas at this point, and so did not fully listen to what he had to say. Plutus was the designated guardian of the fourth circle, a wolf-like creature, stronger and more vicious than imps but less than the demons. Plutus had once been a proud and decadent man, welcomed, and even worshipped.

Plutus was a worker of Hell, like Phlegyas and others, but annoyed the Fallen with his wandering out of the fourth circle, assisting fugitives, and general disregard for Fallen law; thus, he had been transformed into the rabid wolf creature, with none of his own personality left intact. Plutus had become mad, a wolf demon, hunting and ripping apart fugitives caught in his circle. Vicious and merciless, none who encountered him could pass unharmed without appropriate weaponry. Fortunately for some fugitives, Plutus wandered his circle and did not always stay near the path that most took when traveling between the third and fifth circles.

Phlegyas was adamant.

"If he attacks, you must damage him badly; he will not cease hunting you. When you have disabled him, run, leave the circle as quickly as you can. Once he regains his ability to move, Plutus will stalk you until you exit his circle. Get to the inner wall and climb fast! Plutus will not be able to follow."

Mortuus observed large crowds of people in the distance, two groups, each rolling giant rounded boulders at the other. The crowds were screaming madly, so that even at this distance Mortuus could make out the foul oaths raging from their mouths. The two opponents were pushing as hard as they could, obsessively, until the boulders cracked loudly; the crowds then frantically pulled back their stones, until distant enough again for another approach.

Mortuus was slightly impressed they could move such large stones as quickly as they did. The two groups repeated their approach and reversal many times without hesitation, sometimes running over their own team members in the madness. They were thin, stringy people, skeletal in appearance, and their musculature was slight. They were sweaty, covered in the dust their activity kicked up. Mortuus looked at himself; a long bath would be wonderful.

He rolled onto his right side and looked out over the ledge, back down into the mistiness that concealed the Styx. He checked for movement that might indicate the fugitive hunters were approaching. Scanning until satisfied, Mortuus turned flat on his back. Moments later, low, rasping growls stirred him into action. His heart raced and his stomach tensed. Mortuus looked toward the sound; heading straight for him was the wolf demon Plutus. Phlegyas' candid description was accurate.

Plutus was on all fours, but switched back and forth between quadruped and biped, as if he was not sure he was man or beast. He was bearing down on Mortuus. His teeth were bared; terrible, sharp fangs protruded from his semi-canine face, a predator racing towards feed. Mortuus was terrified. He had hoped to avoid Plutus, and cursed himself for resting too long. Mortuus was cornered, backed against the cliff edge, with no option but to fight or flee back down to the stinking marsh. He would have to climb down hastily, knowing he would most likely fall off, becoming too damaged to regenerate before the fugitive hunters returned. Mortuus took a deep breath and faced Plutus, waiting for the violence.

Chapter 22

The Centaurs Unrest

Chiron inspected the red river. The humans were particularly emboldened lately, and he was focused on finding out why. Was the intensity of Phlegethon's heat growing? Surveying to his right and left, he watched as heads popped up, one or two at a time, disappearing quickly back under the crimson surface. The centaurs allowed them to emerge for breath so long as they did not linger for more than a few seconds. The rule of thumb for the tormented of this circle was to pop out for only as long as it took for a centaur to string his bow. Unfortunately for the boiling humans this was second nature for centaurs; they could let fly an arrow and restring before the first projectile hit its mark, and a centaur's aim was deadly accurate.

As Chiron surveyed the slow bubbling surface, he was aware of another Halfling galloping toward him, approaching quite fast. It was Nessus, who, upon seeing the master centaur began to shout.

"Master! Master!" yelled Nessus. "Master! I have news!" Chiron was curious. New events were rare; any odd occurrences and events broke the monotony of the centaurs' patrol duty. Nessus slowed his run. He had used most of his energy to shout as he ran at full speed toward Chiron. Trying to speak and catch his breath, he began again.

"Master Chiron," gasped Nessus, bowing on his front legs, the proper protocol for addressing his superior. "Master... I have news... I have news!" Chiron bowed back at Nessus, signaling him to return to his feet. Nessus did so, rising and breathing slightly less heavily.

"Report, Nessus." Chiron replied, somewhat coldly.

"Master, the demons, the flyers, returned again... carrying someone. You told me... to inform you whenever they were sighted... and so I am here. I would have... informed Master Pholus, but he ...hunts in the wood now, and has not returned for some time." Chiron appeared to be curious and irritated at the same time, his bushy brows squishing together in puzzlement. Nessus was still catching his breath.

"Pholus is hunting? How long has Master Pholus been away?" he asked.

"I have made the circle twice without observing him, Master Chiron." answered Nessus.

"Why is he hunting? I forbade all to engage the harpies. Was Pholus pursuing fugitives?"

"No, Master. The dogs attacked one of ours severely. To dispel the rage of the victim's regiment and distract them from seeking vengeance, Pholus promised them his own fierce retribution upon the hounds. He said he would throw the beasts into the river to return the favor…as a professional courtesy." Nessus grinned at this. "The guard who was attacked agreed this was a fair retaliation and his regiment conceded to Master Pholus. But, Master, I have other news for you."

Chiron was upset at the report of Pholus' abnormally lengthy hunt; he had a feeling in the pits of both his stomachs - that always meant trouble. Maintaining his composure in front of Nessus, Chiron kept his demeanor grim.

"Report your other news, Nessus," said Chiron.

"The demons carried someone from the upper circles. The guards who patrol the forbidden area informed me during my recent patrol. The flyers were carrying a human. They dropped the human onto the landing in front of the cave, and the workers came out and dragged the human inside. It was a mess." Chiron remained grim, not certain why he should be overly concerned.

"Why are you alarmed at this news, Nessus?" inquired Chiron. "The demons have their own agenda; we are forbidden to enter the area, and we have one less fugitive with which to concern ourselves. Why do you report this?"

"Master, I have made an observation." replied Nessus. "When you capture fugitives, you call the demons with the great horn; on a few occasions you met with strangers and called no one. The strangers that you did not report always wore finer, cleaner cloth than the fugitives you capt-"

"That is none of your concern!" interrupted Chiron angrily. Chiron had not considered Nessus would make this connection; he met with very few strangers he did not capture and report.

Knowing that Nessus observed these dealings could be a problem if any demons found out.

"-Master I..." stuttered a fearful Nessus, now beginning to bow. "I...did not...mean...to..."

"Pry? Create rumors? Hearsay!?!" shouted Chiron in a loud military roar. Chiron moved forward, looking at the top of Nessus' hairy head, Nessus bowed to show his apology.

"Finish your report, and quickly!" said Chiron, growing more uneasy, and determined not to show it to Nessus.

"Master, one of those strangers with whom you speak often - that was the human delivered to the cave mouth." Chiron stood speechless, glaring at Nessus. He turned away, and on all four hooves, began stamping the ground in rage.

"Nessus, do you lie? You were doing rounds – how could you have seen this when you told me clearly the guards had reported it to you? Do the guards know my business as well?"

"No, master; I do not lie!" Nessus bowed again. "I arrived at the moment they dragged the human inside. I recalled the cloth, clearly; it was the one."

Chiron was disturbed, for three reasons; the first, his friend and second in command was lost in the wood, possibly captured by harpies. Second, Chiron's human friend had been captured. Chiron suspected this would happen eventually but he did not like to think about it. Thirdly, Nessus knew Chiron was friendly toward a human. The master centaur had tried to conceal his social encounters from most of the herd; what had Nessus, the most untrustworthy centaur, said to his people? Had Nessus seen Chiron carry Aristotle across the river? Chiron could be challenged again, required to fight for his leadership. He considered his options as Nessus bowed low. Finally, after much thought, the Master centaur spoke.

"Nessus, get up. Tell me where Pholus entered the wood and have two companies meet me there. "

Chiron needed to find his friend.

Chapter 23
The Search for Pholus

Chiron started across Phlegethon. Looking carefully, he guided his steps evenly in the shallowest part of the river. His hooves were dense, with much resilience to Phlegethon's heat, but just above the hooves he was as vulnerable to the boiling liquid as any of the tormented whom this river had been designated for. It was a distant trot at slow pace to cross here; the required cautiousness upped the time to cross to the harpy side five-fold. The trees slowly came into view as he crossed, appearing gradually through the mist. Chiron searched for movement, seeking the dogs that he suspected of capturing his friend of many centuries.

On this side of Phlegethon, the harpies were resentful of the patrolling centaurs. They were extremely territorial and endowed with deadly talons, but would have kept to themselves had they not been attacked by the centaurs first. Since that initial incident, they would attack given any chance, particularly a lone Halfling.

There was not a great deal of knowledge about the harpies that the master centaur did not already know; the harpies were of a neutral sex, and ate only the leaves of the strange trees of the wood. This was in contrast to the myths of their being only females, half humans that craved flesh. They seemed to have an uneasy partnership with the dangerous, large dogs who roamed within the wood; the greyhounds patrolled within the forest, eating their fill of any captured escapees. Chiron had listened to many of these horrific encounters. The screaming was so disturbing that he once shot an arrow into the side of a feeding beast.

The dogs were also enemies of the centaur race, but were far fewer in number than the harpies, who lived high above in the treetops, just below the ceiling of mist. The harpies had once attacked a lone centaur who stumbled upon their flock as he ran through the dark wood in pursuit of a fugitive. The centaur was disemboweled and mangled so badly, Chiron thought he might not regenerate. The harpies had ripped the unfortunate creature apart.

Chiron and a small company of centaurs had found him in the midst of the ravenous harpies. Upon being discovered, the bird creatures shot up and flew away, though not without collecting many arrows in their hides. One harpy, slower than the rest fell to the ground, unable to fly because of the multiple arrows embedded into it. Several Halflings grasped the opportunity and stomped the creature into a gory mass of feathers and flesh, not stopping until Chiron recalled them to carry their ravaged companion back to the river's edge. Since that incident, no mercy was given or received from the harpies. Chiron soon forbade all the centaur companies to enter the wood. Pholus, his second in command, was the only exception, but the master centaur was now regretting not including his friend in his edict.

Finally, Chiron stepped on the opposite bank. This side of Phlegethon was far more dismal than his, he thought; the trees exuded sadness, and their mood filled the air, tainting everything with a feeling of depression and hopelessness. Strange, disturbing sounds, like low level moaning, came from the trees when the branches were broken; a thick syrupy fluid oozed out, blood-like though more viscous, and Chiron had surmised that the tree roots were getting the crimson coloring from the river water seeping into the underground. The centaurs, on the rare occasions they traversed the wood, were cautious, careful not to snap any of the tree branches, and even the harpies, who ate the leaves, were delicate enough to not cause the sap to flow. The greyhounds and occasional fugitives were mainly responsible for breakages. Escapees from the fiery plain, located on the other side of the wood, had their hiding spots given away by the pained trees, causing the harpies to locate and fall upon them in frenzied attack, in turn alerting the greyhounds, who came crashing through the forest roughly so that many trees would sound off in the choir of pain.

Chiron walked along the bank, scanning the trees for signs of danger. This was a situation where the Master centaur would have liked to have Pholus at his side. Pholus was the only other centaur with whom Chiron could have an intelligent conversation. The only other intelligent centaur was Nessus; Nessus however, was untrustworthy. Pholus was Chiron's trusted friend.

Chiron saw a herd far ahead, one regiment of approximately fifty Halflings, standing in ordered rows. He stepped up his pace, not needing to be concerned about the harpies or greyhounds, though he continuously glanced at the trees habitually. As Chiron approached the herd, the members recognized their leader immediately, bowing low on their front legs. Chiron returned the gesture, and bowed his head; the centaurs rose.

"Who is your leader?" commanded Chiron.

"I am the regiment commander. Tacitus reporting, sir." replied a muscular, older Halfling, who stepped out from the herd toward Chiron.

"Commander, I am informed by Nessus that your centaurs saw Pholus enter the wood at this location. Is this correct?"

"Yes." replied the commander. "My squad wished to avenge their brother but Master Pholus commanded them back, promising retribution. None entered except Master Pholus."

"Has anyone seen Pholus since his departure?" asked Chiron.

"I have inquired of all personnel whom we encountered in our patrol - we have made two turns around this circle since, Master Chiron - none have witnessed Master Pholus return from the wood." Chiron considered Tacitus' statements for a moment, then turned to address the centaur company. The second company had not arrived yet. He decided he would not wait.

"My fellow warriors" said Chiron. "I require a small company of five of your finest for a hunt in the wood. Choose wisely, then send the volunteers to the woods' edge, by that clearing." Chiron pointed toward a small opening where the trees were less dense. The centaurs of the company began looking at each other, excitement in their eyes, unable to contain the whinnying and snorting.

"We will rescue Master Pholus; he has not returned and I fear he may have been captured by the harpies and the oafish dogs." said Chiron. "Now, select your champions, Commander Tacitus, and send them to me in the clearing."

The Master centaur trotted toward the clearing, scanning the woods for pathways. After a few moments he looked back toward the centaur company. Already the five warriors had been selected and were moving to his position. Each had a quiver of arrows strapped across their back and a bow in hand, readied for battle. Since the incident of the centaur mutilation, the Halflings were anxious to engage the hated harpies. Chiron had known it would take little convincing to gather a squad of volunteers for the rescue task; he was more concerned his fellows would fight amongst themselves for a place in the search party.

Tacitus' hand-chosen squad approached. As they neared him, each centaur stated his name and bowed low, letting Chiron know the centaur was his to command, standard protocol for their kind. In the entire duration of the centaurs' presence in Hell, only one centaur, fittingly named Brutus, had ever challenged Chiron's position. Brutus was large bodied even by centaur standards, balanced out by a considerable lack of intelligence. The immature Halfling challenged Chiron's leadership, and the two fought hand to hand, in front of the entire race. Chiron ended the match quickly, tossing Brutus into Phlegethon, where he remained for five rounds; centaur code required the loser of any fight to swim around this circle five times, enduring the boiling river before he was permitted to exit. Brutus served his sentence, finishing the five rounds in the time it took a centaur on the bank to complete over two-hundred rounds. Chiron was not challenged again.

The company finished the introductory protocol, and waited in formation. Studying each of them as they stood in silence, awaiting their next orders, Chiron admired their warriors' stature. His people were crude in mannerism, but he detected great potential would have eventually surfaced had they had been permitted to exist and evolve. But this was not to be; they were hunted to extinction almost overnight by the humans. The extermination had been thorough and complete. Chiron addressed the five.

"Company, are you ready to enter the wood?" said Chiron.

"Yes sir!" shouted the five centaurs unanimously.

"Very well. Now hear my instructions well. Once we enter the wood, you will not break formation for any reason. Fugitives who we may encounter are the problem of the harpies and hounds, and not ours. We are for Master Pholus only. Do you understand?" Chiron knew the team would chase a human as vigorously as any harpy. Their hatred for the humans was legendary, one of the main reasons for their station on the banks of Phlegethon.

"Yes sir!" shouted the five.

"Very good. Weapons ready. Follow me."

The herd began the search, disappearing into the gnarled, bleak wood as Tacitus' regiment watched from the river bank, each centaur that was left behind envious to join this adventure and avenge the honor of their fellow. Unnoticed, high in a distant treetop, a lone harpy stared a hateful stare at Chiron and the five before flying off in the opposite direction, hidden by the tree tops.

Chapter 24
The Battle of the Wood

Chiron examined Pholus' mutilated torso. The bleeding had finally stopped, and the wounds were healing very slowly. The once fierce commander was still in pain, but significantly less than when he was found. Chiron had administered many vials of water, depleting the supply which he had stored for so long. It was a necessary sacrifice; getting Pholus back on his hooves was of utmost importance if Chiron was to free his friend from the forbidden cave. The hunt had been very successful. It was physically brutal on the regiment, but for morale it had been a sensational triumph, shared by all the Halflings.

* * * * * *

The search party followed Chiron straight into the forest until they reached the edge of the burning plain, a sandy Hell where fire balls fell at random, raining down upon individual groups of humans who endlessly wandered on the burning sand. The centaur party turned right, avoiding the sand, until they detected the scent of Pholus. They followed the scent, noting splotches of red drops, the blood of Pholus. It was as Chiron had feared.

Tacitus' five armed their bows, ready to fire. Some members of the wandering groups of the plain ventured nearer to the wood edge. They stared, curious for a better look at the Halflings, dodging the falling fire when possible. The fireballs began increasing in frequency, raining down more and more on the curious stragglers as they came closer to the plains' edge. This caused the centaurs to stamp nervously; they had an instinctive aversion to fire. The wanderers moved away from the wood side of the plain, returning to their original paths; the fiery precipitation decreased. The anxious centaurs calmed.

The band approached the rill, a thin stream in the center of a short levee that originated at Phlegethon and crossed through the wood and out onto the plain. The rill carried Phlegethon's steaming red liquid over the fiery plain, emptying out onto the next circle. Once the centaurs crossed the rill, the trail turned cold, perplexing their senses and causing some to anger; centaurs were not tolerant of failure, especially their own. The scent had been intensifying up until the rill.

The furious party would have dispersed in separate directions had Chiron not commanded them back into formation. Chiron was a seasoned veteran of battle strategy; he knew a trap had been set, and ordered the group to prepare for attack. Chiron's company snapped to immediately, the promise of battle grounded their emotion, strengthening them into their natural warrior-selves. They stood together, focused and ready. It was not a moment too soon.

Suddenly, breaking through a thick patch of the dark woods, eleven large greyhounds appeared, fangs bared and running at full speed, their violent intention clear. They were closing in before the band of centaurs loosed the first round of arrows, each large dog struck full in the chest by at least one projectile. The dogs slowed, and some slipped onto their fronts as their forelegs gave out from under them. One beast managed to reach the centaur to Chiron's right, despite the massive injury, latching onto the Halfling's front right leg and mangling it within seconds. Chiron grabbed the canine by his skinny tail, ripping the tail completely from its rear end. Yelping in uncontrollable pain, the dog turned on Chiron, who thrust an arrow into each side of it, just behind the shoulders, and used them as handles to lift it up. He tossed the beast over his head, and toward his tail end, then synchronously, reared up and kicked outward with both powerful hind legs, sending the flailing beast onto the burning plain. Yelping even more uncontrollably, it limped away as the heat began cooking its paws. A fireball exploded onto its back, then another, and its cries worsened, heightening in pitch, as the smell of burning hair filled the air. The beast ran away, cowed and in pain, deep into the wood, vanishing from the scene.

The hounds that remained were slowly turning away, painfully limping back into the dense wood. The downed beasts attempted to regain their feet, but the small herd of centaurs saw to their suffering. They pranced on the hounds' rib cages and legs, cracking bones and popping joints. Hound cries filled the air. Chiron called the centaurs back into formation, breaking up their bloodlust. The downed animals lay still, loud cries splitting the air, unable to move.

Chiron saw that the centaurs had exacted revenge upon the dogs, enough to satisfactorily report to their fellows upon their return. The Master Centaur considered the dogs mere work animals, performing tasks. The excessive cruelty his fellows exacted upon the pack was appalling, even after being so long in Hell. Chiron knew, however, that like everything else in this place, the dogs would regenerate. Perhaps they might be less quick to attack centaurs again after this fierce battle. The greyhounds, after all, were not the cause of Pholus' disappearance; they were only a distraction to finding him.

The harpies would have gathered in large numbers to not only defeat Pholus, but carry his large Halfling body off the ground. Pholus was one of the largest of the centaur populace, and the only way the scent could have been lost was for him to have been lifted into the air. The dogs would have dragged him, leaving an easy trail. Chiron called his group to attention. Danger was coming.

"Ready yourselves; we have been only distracted by the enemy." he said. "I have seen no harpy since we entered the wood and I believe they are amassing to attack us in such great numbers that we may not be able to defeat them. They have taken our brother, carrying him out of reach above the treetops. This is why you all lost the scent. At any moment we will be overwhelmed by those foul creatures."

The five centaurs, standing proudly after their victory, nodded in agreement. Each went to a dog and removed all their shafts with a single pull. The dogs yelped, but lay submissively, not daring to accost the centaurs. Chiron continued.

"We must return, back the way we came. I suspect the harpies are almost upon us; we will need reinforcements, and quickly! Run!" he commanded. The formation began to run along behind him, in perfect order, full speed. For a long while they continued, watching above, wary. Reaching the path through the wood where they had passed through, they turned in. The clearing appeared in the distance, and Tacitus' regiment watched from the edge of Phlegethon as the band approached. As the small squad of five got nearer, Tacitus' regiment stared upward, over the heads of the band. Pulling their bows upward, they raced toward the band and began to fire over the heads of the racing company. Chiron knew then what was happening.

The Master centaur's thoughts were cut off by the hissing screech of a harpy who fell to the ground just behind the group, gripping the arrow that had disappeared up to the hilt into its breast.

The band had reached Tacitus' regiment just in time. The harpies had followed them, and the flock was swooping in just as they came within sight of Tacitus' regiment; they were not a moment too soon! Chiron turned and looked up to see a harpy less than a meter away, ready to sink its talons into his bare back. An arrow thudded into the avian creature just before it reached Chiron; it screeched as the arrow carried it back and away from its intended victim.

The air was swarming with harpies. Chiron had only ever seen ten or fifteen together in all his years patrolling this circle. He had not considered they would be strategic or intelligent enough to plan an attack in such great number. The regiment and Chiron sent their arrows into so many of the flying beasts that to re-arm they had to retrieve arrows from the wounded. The harpies were extremely vulnerable on the ground, and the powerful crushing hooves of heavy centaurs stifled their furious demeanor.

Many centaurs were injured by the harpies, too. A harpy would land on the rear end of a centaur, and begin to rip the flesh out of its back; the victim had to roll over to stop the clawing bird beast. The few centaurs armed with spears were better able to handle this type of attack. The harpies could quickly damage the body of the unfortunate centaurs. Some centaurs were in so much pain that they ran into Phlegethon to shake the harpy off. This also seriously disabled the centaur, but the mutilation would stop. The centaur was strong enough to escape the heated river; the harpies had much greater difficulty, and shrieked loudly to their peers for assistance.

Tacitus' centaurs only minutes before had been complaining of their boring, uneventful routines. They awaited the return of their elite warriors, eager for new stories of their brethren's adventures, a welcome reprieve from the normal uneventfulness of their duties. Shooting humans was not great sport since they could barely move their boiled bodies to get out of the way; they were seldom interesting quarry. The only real enjoyment the centaurs got out of shooting humans was in revenge for their genocide, and after a couple thousand years, even that joy wore thin.

After a long bloody battle, the centaurs were victorious. The harpies were fast flyers, but the centaurs were master archers; their deadly accurate arrows thudded into feathery flesh mercilessly. Few harpies escaped without injury, and that was only due to their sheer numbers. The disabled harpies, those that could not run or fly off, were trampled into feathery heaps and tossed into the boiling river. The centaurs watched the mangled harpies flop around, screeching, unable to escape. The more mobile harpies crawled off into the dense thicket as the low pitched moaning from the fractured trees increased. A small group of harpies hovered high in the air, far from the clash, observing from the safety of the mist-edge; they had not joined their fellow avians in this offensive.

The centaurs stood or lay down to regenerate, many severely mutilated. Chiron visited each of the injured, thanking and congratulating them on their victory. Tacitus, massively wounded himself, beamed back at Chiron through his pain, overflowing with pride for his regiment's triumph in battle. The Master centaur bowed to Tacitus, honoring the wounded leader. Chiron thought of what might have happened had the harpies attacked the squad before they reached the waiting regiment. He stayed until the company was restored enough to fend off another attack.

Alerted to the events that had unfolded here, other regiment commanders sent messengers requesting orders from Chiron, asking anxiously; 'should they assist? Would there be war on all harpies?' But Chiron only returned the messengers with a simple answer – keep a look out for Master Pholus.

Chiron recalled his squad of five. The search for Pholus would continue. He had not forgotten his friend and the reason for going into the dismal wood in the first place. This time they were going to follow the rill from the river, straight through the forest to the plain's edge. Chiron had hoped that the harpies were seeing Pholus as a liability. If he was right, the harpies would release his friend on the plain side of the wood, even onto the plain if they were vindictive. Hopefully Pholus would be near the rill or the wood's edge; centaurs were naturally afraid of fire, Chiron included, and the soldier centaurs would be very difficult to coerce onto the plain for any distance.

When the small company arrived at the riverside of the rill, they turned left and followed, wary of their surroundings. The moaning was quieter here. The centaurs were cautious, careful to not molest the trees, even slightly. The rill was in a dark part of the wood, dense with older growth and many taller trees. This, thought Chiron, would be where harpies would find solace, high up in the dense tree stand. He looked high up into the trees, and was shocked to see several harpies, staring holes into the passing company, watching silently with deadly eyes of hatred. They were pressed against the trees, heads down as if they would crawl right down upon the centaur company as they forged ahead. Chiron turned to the nearest centaur, flicking his eyes up to point out the harpies' presence. He raised his finger to his mouth to motion the centaur to remain silent and tipped his head to continue forward.

The centaurs passed through the thick growth uneventfully. Although some trees were damaged slightly during their passage, the trees made no more than the smallest moaning noises. Finally, they reached the plain, where Chiron could see the company wanted to turn to the right or left. When he kept walking out onto the heated plain, staying on the levee and following the rill, the centaurs were suddenly immobilized, looking around at each other fearfully, some beginning to neigh and whinny, prancing away from the sand's edge. Chiron turned and motioned them to follow, but their expression showed conflict and confusion; they wanted to continue trailing their leader, but their animal instincts were stronger, and would not allow them to cross onto the heated plain, even from the relative safety of the levee.

Chiron conceded. He knew they would follow him if they could. He had hoped to push their limits, especially if the harpies dropped Pholus on the burning plain. But he had succeeded in pushing only his own limits, and now that he was here he would challenge himself to go further.

"Stay here then." he said. "I will return shortly. Keep a lookout for the harpies, and blow this horn when you have seen Pholus or if you are under attack." Chiron turned and trotted out onto the plain, staying on the levee as he fought his own instinct to return back to the wood edge. He looked left and right, seeing many groups of humans, some moving closer to better glimpse the oddity of Chiron, but staying near their individual pods. Fireballs rained down twice, crossing over the rill, though never hitting it directly. It was as if Chiron was watching a meteor storm. The human groups were struck many times by the raining fire, some more heavily than others. The victims were walking fast, or running, attempting to dodge the flame, but to no avail. Some would start to run forward when hit from behind, only to press straight into another fireball. The humans were all burned badly, their skin bubbling and red, feet blackened and swollen, oozing fluid as if they had been roasted on a spit. The sight repulsed Chiron, and he hurried onward.

As he neared the edge of the plain, he noticed the ground coloring change. The edge was blackened, darkening gravel becoming solid black stone. This must be what Aristotle had described.

Chiron recalled that Aristotle had almost ventured down to the eighth circle on two occasions; each of them had nearly cost him eternity there. Aristotle witnessed a strange creature that flew, a distorted reptile-like beast, he had said, but with furry forelegs and a large, stinging tail, not unlike a scorpion. The creature was larger than five centaurs, Aristotle told him. It patrolled the rim that was the border between the seventh and eighth circles, searching for fugitives. Like the Minotaur who roamed the rocky slope between Phlegethon and the fiery tombs of Dis, this creature was probably locked into its course by Fallen magic, and not permitted to fly elsewhere. The beast was one of the latest discoveries of Aristotle.

Chiron's human friend had a great sense of adventure. It was he who the Master centaur feared to be imprisoned in the forbidden area of the seventh circle. Chiron had been denied access to the cave, and the thirty meter radius around it, despite his assigned rulership of all Phlegethon and its surrounding banks. Chiron did tell Aristotle that he would one day be captured, prophesying Aristotle's torment at the hands of the Fallen. Aristotle believed his friend, but said he could not cease to explore; Limbo was a gilded cage, and Aristotle would not stay there, feeling trapped. Knowing he could not talk his friend out of his wanderlust, despite the peril, Chiron did not judge Aristotle. The Master centaur would leave his circle himself if not contained by the Fallen spells.

As he approached the edge, Chiron's inner eye came to life, awakening without warning. Suddenly Chiron was surrounded by Fallen on a dark patch of ice; a large group of centaurs stood in formation behind him, and a cold wind blew a thick, very fine icy dust in his face. Chiron could feel himself freezing up. He struggled to make sense of his surroundings, desperate for any recognition, but his eyes teared up into small ice pellets in the freezing wind. The Fallen were pointing at Chiron, glaring angrily. He could hear a distant horn, sounding three times; by the third blow, he was back, standing on the rill as he overlooked the edge of this circle, the red stream emptying out into the mist covered lower circles. The horn sounded again, and Chiron realized the squad was calling to him. Something had happened. He turned back, galloping as fast as he could toward the wood, across the fiery desert.

A short time later, Chiron was at the edge of the wood with the other centaurs. On the ground, encircled by the squad was his friend Pholus. The once fierce centaur was broken and mutilated. The avians had disemboweled Pholus. His face and human torso were clawed beyond recognition.

The harpies had dropped Pholus from high above, fleeing as he fell to the ground. He was immobile, his various muscle groups ripped out, blood loss maximal, internal organs ripped and chewed, legs and arms stripped to the bone. Pholus could not even moan, as his lungs were bloodied bags hanging out from his exposed chest cavity. Chiron was outwardly calm, but inwardly shocked and outraged.

"Quickly, we must carry Master Pholus back to the river's edge. Who will volunteer?" asked Chiron.

"I sir" said three of the centaurs at once. The other two, who were watching the treetops for harpies, turned, and made the same reply, each eager to assist their broken leader.

"Take him you two, and put him on both of your backs, you must walk together, closely" said Chiron. It would be difficult – centaurs were not built for transporting on the backs of other centaurs. "We return through the clearing where we fought; we cannot pass through the wood by way of the rill – Master Pholus is too large. I will lead, one of you will follow, then the pair, then another trails. Eyes forward and up."

They kept watch, scanning the treetops until they returned through the clearing of the battle. Tacitus' regiment carried Pholus and escorted their fellows to the far side of Phlegethon, near where Chiron had his medicines and waters stored.

* * * * * *

It had been more than thirty-five turns since Pholus was brought to safety. Now that the second in command was better healed, it was time for Chiron to reveal his plan.

"Pholus, you are ready to take over my command." said Chiron. "I am leaving."

Chapter 25

Plutus Attacks

Mortuus stood terrified. He had already been attacked by the wild imps and now faced Plutus, who was larger and far more dangerous. Mortuus was unnaturally weak, the fear in him paralyzing. Plutus moved closer, walking upright as he closed in on his prey. The crowds were loud behind the wolf demon, continuing on with their high energy madness, engaged and unaware of Plutus or Mortuus. Mortuus felt for his dagger, and wielded it between himself and the wolf beast. It felt inconsequential and useless. Plutus seemed not to notice, and glared unfalteringly as he approached.

Mortuus looked into the crazed, glaring eyes; the growling seemed to vibrate through his gut and make his insides rumble. He had to do something, or his fear would ruin his chances of reaching Limbo forever. Seeing only insanity in his attacker, he decided he would match the beast's viciousness. Mortuus grew enraged, hardening up as energy flowed into his shoulders, arms, and chest. Plutus lunged.

Mortuus thrust his dagger up, jabbing into Plutus but meeting only a sliver of flesh; the wolf beast was very fast. Plutus slashed, fully raking his sharp claws into Mortuus, whose face and neck were bleeding profusely. Mortuus swung his knife again, and Plutus ducked, then came up and bit Mortuus on the wrist, causing him to drop the weapon. Mortuus swung wildly with his free hand and struck Plutus in the side of the head. Plutus let go, shaking his head in disorientation. Mortuus saw the wolf demon waiver, and grabbed his throat with one hand and pounded his face with the other. He was afraid to let up, and so swung and smashed relentlessly. Plutus, weakened, slashed half-heartedly. Mortuus pushed him away, noting the lightness of the wolf demon. Plutus growled, still dazed, and slashed again, slicing Mortuus' forearm. Mortuus grabbed an arm and the neck of Plutus, and using all his strength, Mortuus turned him, pushing him toward the ledge from behind. Plutus suddenly understood what Mortuus was doing, and increased his clawing frenzy; the nearer Mortuus got to the ledge, the more Plutus tried to gnash and tear at him.

And then it was over. Mortuus collapsed to the ground, breathing and bleeding heavily, feeling the pain of the damage done by Plutus to his neck, face and arms. He had thrown Plutus over the ledge, hearing the wolf demon yelp in fear as he disappeared into the mist below. Despite his painful wounds, Mortuus did not linger. Plutus would return. On his way, he noticed a small, flat object, a metallic disc, with the imprint of a smiling person. He picked it up. Deciding to examine the object later, Mortuus walked swiftly. He followed the path, glancing back often.

Mortuus neared the wall to the next circle, passing through the crowds of angry people rolling their boulders. The wall had an easy set of handholds to grasp, and despite his injuries, Mortuus climbed quickly, and did not stop until he was near the next circle. He saw Plutus below, staring at him from beyond the oblivious crowd. In a rage, the beast attacked a nearby crowd member, slashing and ripping flesh from the victims' throat; he ran toward the base of the wall, shaking his victim's throat meat angrily at Mortuus.

Mortuus turned and climbed away from this horror. He reached the next circle, a frozen, stinking area; it was half raining and half snowing, only, the precipitation was putrid. The path was the least affected by the falling rot. Mortuus could hear growling coming from the distance, different from that of Plutus, it sounded like more than one beast. The grayness and weather blurred his vision, but he could see a single large creature, silhouetted in the distance. This must be Cerberus, he thought; Phlegyas had warned him of the beast, saying Mortuus should move to the second circle quickly. Mortuus, still bleeding and in pain, did not hesitate. He walked to the left, noting that there were bloated bodies laying in the stinking slush. They were barely moving, wallowing in slow motion in the frozen filth, and did not notice him pass. Many appeared mangled, as though partially eaten, but they barely bled. The ground was frozen mud and filthy sleet, and it was raining filth upon him.

Mortuus was a short distance from the wall to the second circle when he saw them. Something was flying over him, barely visible. It moved slowly across the dark gray misty ceiling. His eyes strained to pierce the mist and he saw there was more than one creature, flying in a close formation. There was something being carried between two of them. Mortuus struggled to see more, but could make out no better detail through the disgusting precipitation. The distant growling of Cerberus stopped momentarily. Mortuus moved toward the base of the wall, walking slowly to avoid attention. In the distance, the silhouette of Cerberus slowly moved closer. The growling resumed as the flying formation faded from view.

Mortuus scaled the wall. The handholds made this climb even easier, as the handholds were far better defined. Mortuus could hear the fierce winds, gaining in volume as he neared the top. When he climbed over the ledge, he crawled along the rocky ground, staying tightly pressed as he had been forewarned by Phlegyas. Stopping only for a short rest, Mortuus turned over onto his back and looked up in amazement; there were people, up in the air, being tossed violently to and fro by the wind. The whipping bodies were smashed sometimes against the ground, other times against the distant wall, and usually battered against each other, in constantly changing directions, as if they were riding the end of a whip. Mortuus heard their screams changing as they hurled in new directions. Their bodies were broken by the constant beating, and twisted in unnatural shapes to varying degrees. He was distraught witnessing their plight. The cruelty was overwhelming.

He rolled back onto his stomach and continued his crawl. Much later, Mortuus saw the next milestone toward Limbo, again per Phlegyas' counsel. The Hall of Minos was before him. He was instructed not to enter the hall, no matter what, nor speak to anyone in the line that formed outside on the path.

Nearer to the hall, the winds decreased substantially, enough for Mortuus to safely get to his feet. He breathed a sigh of relief, happy to be off his stomach, filled with excitement and joy.

He was almost there.

Chapter 26

The Gate of Limbo

Mortuus was unsure. He had made it; in front of him was the gate into Limbo. Mortuus pulled out his folded instructions, and separated a small sheet from out of the folds. Aristotle had written this note to allow him entrance into Limbo; Mortuus was to present the pass to the gate guard.

Doubt and fear stabbed at him. Would Mortuus find solace, friendship, relief from the pain of this world, this...Hell? He breathed in deeply many times, preparing himself for this next encounter. He had made it, all the way to Limbo, and soon he would get relief, answers, and especially, right now, water. His thirst burned inside him once again. Mortuus examined the door, seeking a handle to open it with. It was very tall and heavy looking, roughly thirty meters high, steel bolted to stone; it reached the full height of the wall.

On the gated side of the path, the wall stretched down toward the hall of Minos, then turned left abruptly as the path continued downward. To his right, the wall followed the path to the left. The wall formed a high boundary, carved rock sitting atop natural rock, separating the next circle with this one. The path Mortuus was on was narrow; a full stone wall with no doors or gates, created the other boundary of the path. The opposite wall was the same height, and the walls sandwiched the path, which was roughly as wide as five people standing tightly shoulder to shoulder. The narrow corridor went upward on a gentle slope; it curved enough that Mortuus could not see all the way to the end. But right now, he did not care for anything more than to get inside this gate to Limbo.

Mortuus found no device for opening the gate. Struggling to control his fear and nervousness, Mortuus knocked with all his might. He beat his fists against the huge metal gate, the sound seemingly absorbed and dissipated; he could hear very little of his pounding reverberate through the towering gate. Mortuus stepped back, waiting for a sign or movement from within, wishing he had a large rock or some tool to beat it with. Without warning, the door creaked open, faster than seemed possible for such a dense metal mold. A quartet of men approached, long spears pointing at Mortuus. They appeared to be afraid, as if he might hurt them. Behind the four spearmen, a row of archers with drawn bows stared intensely, looking like stone statues, ready to loose their projectiles. Behind the statuesque archers stood another gate which Mortuus assumed led to the inside of Limbo. Mortuus stared open-jawed at the rear gate; he was almost there.

The guards looked curiously at Mortuus, staring at him, his wounds and ragged garb. They were shorter in stature, nearly the same size as Plutus; they appeared pleasant and friendly, and had no stink of Hell on their person. In fact, their scent was fresh, like a forest, and their robes were clean and colorful under the light handcrafted armor. They scrutinized him, scanning up and down. Mortuus was suddenly self-conscious, aware of his appearance, the filth, his ripped and bloodied clothing; he was still bleeding from his encounter with Plutus. One guard, seeing Mortuus' sudden realization, smiled slightly. This guard took a liking to Mortuus, the way some people do for unknown reasons when they meet. Another guard began to speak, commanding Mortuus in a gruff masculine voice.

"Identify yourself. From what pit have you escaped? We do not allow fugitives to enter. Why are you he--?" he was cut off by another, who slowly walked up from the rear gate.

"I will handle this, Nigel. Return to your post. He is obviously no threat." said the man.

Mortuus examined him; he was more decoratively dressed, with no armor over his robes. His features were softer than the others, rounder and less chiseled. Mortuus did not like this man. The pit of his stomach clenched, and he felt suddenly nauseous. Instinctively, before the men could turn to leave, Mortuus held out the signed page of Aristotle, showing it to the man who had smiled.

"I have been invited...by Aristotle. He wrote this for me, to show you. Please, read it." He blurted the words out fast, desperately. This seemed to annoy the rounder man; he waved at the men to leave, impatiently.

"Return to your post Nigel! All of you - go!" he said angrily. But the men, including Nigel, looked curiously at Mortuus, then the round man, then each other, not knowing what to do.

"But should we not take him to Socius if Arist-"

"RETURN…TO..YOUR..POST…NOW, NIGEL!" yelled the man, each word enunciated angrily. His round face was distorted with rage, reddened at their disobedience. Reluctantly, they walked to the rear gate; the guard addressed as Nigel looked at the earlier smiling guard and nodded his head. They opened the rear gate just enough to pass through the opening. As they exited, a light breeze, soft and fresh as Mortuus had never breathed in this place encompassed him. For a brief second he succumbed, enjoying the fresh air. The gate clanked shut as the last guard passed through, and Mortuus was alone with the irritated round man.

"Stranger, only those assigned to Limbo may pass through these gates. I deny you entrance, regardless of what Aristotle has promised." he stated matter of factly. It was the coldest thing Mortuus had ever heard; his heart dropped instantly. He was stunned, wounded more deeply than imp or wolf demon ever could, the nausea resuming its presence inside him. He pleaded, softly.

"But I have the words of Aristotle, he has signed. Why would he have sent me all the way here? What…"

Mortuus stopped talking. The more he spoke, the more he could see the resolve of the round man, and the more futile his pleading became. The round man's face was expressionless, grim, and his intent was clear.

"You are a fugitive, sir" stated the man coldly. "so let me warn you. Fugitives are dealt with severely; I am sending a man to inform Minos of your whereabouts if you do not leave here. You will have only a short time to wander the landscape of Hell; cherish your time, for when you are recaptured, you will be tormented beyond your wildest nightmare." The round man's face seemed to twist into a hateful leer. "Do not provoke me and shorten your temporary freedom. Go…and do not return."
The man stared grimly at Mortuus, daring him to speak.

Mortuus turned away. He started up the path, moving with no purpose, stunned into silence. The gate slammed shut behind him, clanking noisily into place. He leaned against the wall and slid down to the ground, broken. He was alone.

For a very long time, he wept.

Book II

Prelude

Beginning Hell

I don't know how long I stood there. I had cried so much I couldn't cry anymore. My eyes were burning terribly, nearly swelling shut. I knew that I had to face the inevitable and I didn't want to. Ghastly sounds were constantly filling the background. It was like being outside a stadium for a big game, only, instead of cheering it was the opposite. Added to that was the horrific smell. There is no smell on earth comparable to the stench of Hell.

I wanted to tell myself that I was mistaken, that I was only in some sort of purgatory and I wondered, what happened to the part about the white light; about seeing all my relatives and the angels? I mean, I was not Good in life, but I was definitely not Bad either. Questions flowed from me along the lines of "Why me?" and "What did I do to deserve this?" I suppose this is common for everyone upon first arriving in Hell. It makes perfect sense, really.

I started walking, realizing I was tightly wrapped in some pure white, cottony material. Except for my head and neck, I was dressed like a mummy. I couldn't imagine I would have been buried in this outfit, but the cloth was comfortable enough and at this point, comfortable enough was okay by me. I was also barefoot, standing on a gravelly path leading towards a river. The path was pretty well-worn and distinguishable from the sandy muck that surrounded it. For the most part, the path was the driest area of wherever I was. I had not yet recognized that I was in Dante's Hell, because although the atmosphere was dark and dreary, it was more akin to a stormy day in Seattle rather than the pitch black of night.

A mist, lower than a cloud, floated high over my head. It was thick too, like a textured fog and it moved and swirled, never floating to the ground. I looked down the path, which veered to the left from where I arrived and I couldn't detect another soul anywhere.

On either side of the path were rolling hills. The mounds, bigger in circumference than golf greens, were scattered randomly and all composed of wet mucky sand. There was no visibility past those hills, not unless I went off-path and walked onto one of them. A person who thinks outside the box might have wandered off and at least taken a look. I certainly had the time and I wasn't in any particular rush to get to Hell, but I didn't venture or veer. I merely stumbled on, eventually coming to a rotted dock at the end of the path. It was on the river I had seen earlier as I approached. Had I not glimpsed the river earlier, I might have mistaken it at the dock for a lake because I couldn't see across it to the far side. Unlike rivers, the water did not flow in any direction. No swirl or eddy gave away the fact that this was a river at all. The mist floated on its surface, hiding the other shore and unlike rivers, this body of water appeared to be nothing more than a giant mud puddle that stunk of stagnation.

    I stood by the dock for a few seconds when out of the murk came a shadow of a figure looming tall and large. Terror gripped my insides because if I were correct, a grotesquely foul and filthy old man, his eyes on fire, would be pulling his skiff up to the dock shortly. I wanted to be wrong; I hoped for it, but the sound of an oar striking water began to slowly fill my ears with the dread of unwelcomed truth.

    Without warning, from behind me, a man sobbed out loud. I almost jumped out of my skin as I hadn't heard or seen him coming. He continued to sob even as I stood staring at him; as if he were alone and I was invisible. Which is as it should've been since I was too numb to spare any feelings of sympathy for him. I was simply too overcome with my own situation to care. And, there was no time for extraneous feelings anyway as just then, as I had been dreading, Charon's boat unmistakably emerged, pale in the mist.

    The ferryman's fiery eyes were locked on us and glaring, as if we two were the reason that Hell existed. I became acutely weak with fear and froze in place. I recalled my lifetime phobia of heights; its consuming and inescapable control over me and noted this was the same feeling. The greasy obscenity jumped from his boat, yelling at us to get in as he swung a giant oar around. We moved, the two of us trying to get the furthest away from the end of the skiff where Charon had stood. I sat at the front, just behind the newer arrival, who had managed to get in faster. Charon jumped into the skiff and with a single pull we were navigated far from shore. I did not look back, for to do so would have meant having to face that horrific apparition.

The dock and the landscape disappeared as we headed into the gloomy pother. The skiff slid across the river diagonally to the left from the dock, splitting the water surface like a speed boat as Charon paddled to the far shore. We were a few minutes on the river when we cleared the mist and glimpsed stone walls lining the shore at the far side of the river. It was strange to see. I had no recollection of walls in Dante's story, yet here they were, and they had to be nearly 100 feet high. I couldn't see where we were going to land or how we would enter the next circle, there was no apparent opening.

As I studied the wall, searching for a possible landing, the newcomer began to sob again, unable to stop himself. Charon howled a second before all went red. I saw a bright flash against my eyelids - the kind you get in a fist fight when punched in the eye, except this was far worse. The flash disappeared as the pain possessed me. My left ear and my head were throbbing in a tortured agony I had never before experienced. Charon had smacked me squarely in the side of my head with his big oar, out of anger for the sobbing man.

My skull should have been crushed and I should have been killed by that deadly blow. I should not have felt the aftermath. But of course, I was already dead, so the pain continued large and long. I could do nothing except move to get out of the way of the next strike. I pulled the sobbing man toward Charon, throwing him on the boat bottom, and sat in his spot, holding my head and keeping an eye on the ferryman the whole rest of the trip. The sobbing fool was also struck by Charon's oar, but still I cursed him for causing me to be punished for his wailing. Charon's blow seemed to be enough to silence the man's weeping.

Thankfully, no more incidents occurred during the trip. I held my hand against my throbbing ear until we reached the shore. As the boat slid into the bank I jumped out, eager to create distance between myself and Charon's oar. The sobbing man did not share my eagerness, or at least my speed. I heard his screams come up from behind me as Charon's yelling became a roar. I could hear the oar connect to the sobbing man and I covered my ear again, instinctively, heading quickly down a path between two enormously high stone walls.

I must have walked down the narrow path about a mile before I saw any change in the composition of the walls. On the left, a gate appeared. It was the height of the wall, though I could not get far back enough to see clear to the top. It was cast iron, and looked impractically heavy. I don't know how it opened; no handholds were present and it was a straight flat gate, all the way up. I thought to knock, but second guessed myself. Coming up behind me was the sobbing man, bruised and limping along slowly. Strangely, in my life, I could feel sorry even for guys I was fighting with, but for this man, and in this place, my compassion was not present. I stopped examining the large gate and moved away from him.

In just a few minutes I came upon a long, curving line of what I assumed were the recently dead that I could not see the end of. The line hugged the right wall which curved around slightly as the path gradually sloped downward. The people in front of me were dressed similar to me. Some were crying and some cursed while others said nothing. I saw no one making conversation or small talk with those around them. This was the path to our final judgment and everyone was focused on their imminent sentence to damnation.

It was a terrible, grim fate, and I had to wait in line for it.

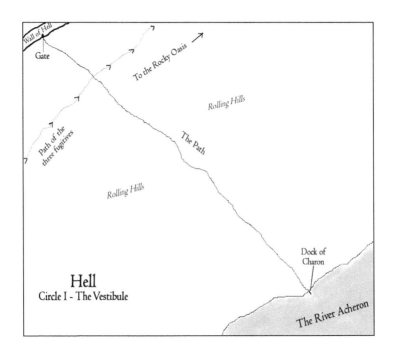

Chapter 27

The Two Fugitives

Darius sat, silently peering out from behind the boulders. He remained in hiding for a long time after his companions had been taken by the flying demons to what was assuredly a far worse fate than the torment they had previously escaped. Although no more imps or demons had visited the rocky oasis, the wait had provided too much time for Darius to anguish over his probable fate. When he emerged from hiding, Panos' and Aetos' gore lay before him, floating thickly across the pool and muddling in grotesque clumps on the stream drifting towards Acheron. Darius shuddered, trying not to imagine what lay before him.

Leaving this rocky oasis would be dangerous, but staying would insure the creatures' return. The fugitive wished he would go insane. At least that way, without the ability to rationalize, his horror might be diminished. Darius wondered if someone else would come along, another fugitive from this circle looking to escape Hell.

He had completely healed up from his wounds and regenerated back into the gaunt frame of the body with which he entered Hell. He was free of the Hell fly bites that had nearly blinded him in the Vestibule, but only somewhat free of the Vestibule's filth and dirt. Regardless of his having washed, Darius wasn't able to scrub himself free, yet Darius was content to be for the moment, safe and relatively healthy.

At long last, Darius gathered the courage to depart the rocky oasis. He planned to circle the perimeter of the boulder and stone outcropping, keeping an eye out for any approaching creatures or other fugitives. He would keep his wits sharp as he took the path from the gate to Acheron where the newcomers walked down to cross the river. No one would bother him there and he could enjoy the change in scenery, slight as it was.

Darius performed his perimeter check, and after many checks in every direction, he left the stony refuge, heading toward the path. The wall was a long distance away on his right side this time. He made it from the boulders to the path in a much shorter time than it had seemed when he and his friends were making their way to the boulders.

Darius paralleled the pathway, never stepping closer than a few meters. He watched the newly dead walk down the slightly sloping trail to the river. There were faces of myriad shapes and features but they all shared a single commonality: in their entirety, the faces expressed stories of guilt. There was the nuance of rage, victimization, and horrified shock; but as a whole, the stories were a countenance of guilt.

One man rushed over to Darius, pleading his innocence, and insisting there had been a dreadful mistake. But of course, Darius was unable to do anything about it. Darius looked at him, dumbstruck by the man's impotent denial, and his silence sent the man into a spasm of hateful cursing. After that, Darius moved further away from the path – close enough to continue observing but far enough away to discourage any more interaction.

When he reached the gate, Darius walked up to it, trying to negotiate a closer look at the opening. Perhaps there was some trick to it, some way to escape. Darius had heard of ghosts when he was alive, but he could not fathom how any avoided or circumvented Hell and visited the living. He wondered where he might go if he succeeded in stealing away. He did not relish the idea of hanging in the ether as a specter, doomed to wander the Earth as a frightening, unwelcomed stray; but better that than the eternal scourge of this nether world. Was there any way to get through the gate?

Darius checked from every angle available on his side of the wall. No luck. He walked toward the gate from each edge of the wall and from the path, over and over again. He tried to look through the doorway, but only once saw any glimmer of light. That was when a new soul had passed through. The soul, startled at first when he nearly bumped into Darius; gaped at him; taking in Darius' hardened face, his smell, his garb, his dark, haunted eyes; and then stumbled backwards in desperation, finally comprehending the gravity of his own plight. It was a dreadful moment for Darius, bringing back the grief and feelings of hopelessness he endured when he first arrived in Hell.

Darius left the gate when he was satisfied he had done all he could. Once again, his thin body paralleled the well worn trail back toward the river. Dwelling on his encounter with the newcomer, he felt lost and more alone than ever. He missed his friends greatly. Darius' head hung low, his weary eyes fixed onto the ground as he walked. Thus, Darius the fugitive was not ready for the next surprise.

Coming up the path approaching him, was a large, imposing figure of a man. Not certain why anyone would be walking away from the dock on the Acheron, in the direction of the gate, Darius leapt out of sight, scurrying towards the oasis. He was not going to wait for even a second to find out if the figure was a fugitive or a fugitive hunter. Darius ran for as much time as it took him to feel safe enough to notice he wasn't being pursued.

To his great relief, when he turned around for a quick glimpse, Darius saw that the stranger had not altered his course but was still headed towards the gate; oblivious to the presence of Darius. Darius watched the stranger with no small amount of curiosity, certain the man was mistakenly hoping to exit the gate whose mysteries had only just confounded Darius' every effort to unravel it.

Darius took in the sight of this larger than life presence; his strange, filthy apparel, his bruised and battered body and his purposeful but wounded gait. The man appeared young; perhaps he was no more than thirty years. He was more than two heads taller than Darius, with broad, strong shoulders which his dirty blonde hair rested upon. It was clear that this man had suffered a great deal of violence yet something in his demeanor suggested gentleness. This awakened a sympathetic response in Darius and he hastily retraced his steps, following the man until within speaking distance. Mindful to keep adequate space between them should he have to run, Darius was unable to keep his presence concealed. The stranger slowed, then stopped and turned around to stare at Darius.

Darius returned his gaze, examining the stranger's robes and especially his face. The man's eyes were bloodshot and swollen, carrying a weight of great sadness that seemed ancient and infinite. The pained, wraithlike expression of this man aroused no sense of danger in Darius but rather a great welling of compassion, and thus emboldened, Darius was moved to speak.

"Hail thee, stranger."

The man continued to stare at Darius.

"I am Darius." Darius nervously ran his fingers through his matted, reddish-brown hair.

Still the man made no change in expression. Darius continued.

"I have seen many come down this path from the gate, but you alone go toward it. By your garb, I see you have known much suffering and conflict, and so also, have I, in serving my sentence. If I do not offend you, please give me your name. I have been alone for a long time and I would at least share my story with you."

Still the man gave no outward expression of interest in Darius. But Darius would not yield and he pressed the gentle giant.

"As I have stated, I am Darius." Darius waited a few moments, readying to speak again. To his delight, he was cut off.

"I am Mortuus." replied the stranger.

Chapter 28

Chiron's Decision

"Pholus, now that you are mostly regenerated, I would like to speak to you about an urgent matter, a matter which took place when you were kidnapped by the flying beasts," said Chiron. Pholus considered Chiron's words, glad to be in the presence of his friend after having been inordinately and unusually punished by the cruel Harpies of The Wood. His insides had been ripped out by the avians, requiring most of Chiron's vital water supply to heal. Over time he would have healed by himself, but the waters of Limbo sped up the regeneration tenfold with each vial. Chiron was adamant that Pholus regain his strength, and Pholus believed he understood why. Now that he was intact, Pholus would have his suspicions confirmed.

"Pholus, I am going to Limbo." said Chiron. Chiron waited a moment, watching Pholus' face for any change in expression, expecting his surprise. Pholus merely moved his great bushy eyebrows and nodded his head in agreement. Now Chiron had the look of surprise that he had expected from his friend.

"Why do you nod in agreement?" exclaimed Chiron. Pholus smiled. He loved his friend, and he enjoyed knowing something that Chiron did not for just once. Chiron was the smartest centaur ever known in the world, even for the short duration that centaurs existed in it. Pholus, intelligent in his own right, could not hold a candle to Chiron's gift. The Master Centaur had trained kings and demigods; he had fought great monsters; he taught medicine, music, astrology, augury, weapon making, and mathematics to the sons of the ancient Gods; and he was highly regarded by the humans. Pholus was also wise, a maker of wine, but rarely mingled with the humans. He was perhaps the fiercest of the centaurs, but he was not Chiron.

"Chiron, my good friend, I am pleased to know a thing that you do not for once." Pholus grinned his horsey-toothed grin. Chiron could not help but return the favor.

"You have been building to this a long time now. Since the demons evicted you from the forbidden area, and after your last encounter with Aristotle. Change is happening, and I think you know it," stated Pholus. Chiron dwelled on Pholus' words for a moment.

"By the way, how will you leave this circle?" inquired Pholus. "Aren't the Fallen's spells still in effect? How do you plan on getting past the boundary enchantments?"

"I do not know Pholus; I will attempt to climb in a few moments. I need you to stay here and take command for now. If your fellows find I am not present, they may opt to leave on their own. You are my second in command, and it is you they follow dearly; not just due to ranking, either. During your absence, the others were united, if only for the moment, and fought alongside each other against a common enemy." Chiron continued. "They will speak a long time of the battle for the great and beloved centaur Pholus; of their proud stance and unity. Better, you will remind them of it while I am gone. They grow bored of the eternal task. Why would they not eventually tire of it, even as simple as they are? The harpies and greyhounds did us great harm in your attack and capture, but an even greater service in providing us the common enemy, and letting us forget for the moment our eternal sentence." Chiron hesitated, his demeanor softening. "I am sorry for your suffering, but I have exhausted most of my vital waters to hasten your regeneration and my departure. Should I not make it, or if I need to battle the Minotaur trying to gain the next circle, I will require your assistance."

"I will be there, my friend. Should you reach Limbo, give Aristotle my regards. I miss his visits." said Pholus. Chiron looked at his friend. He needed to tell Pholus the sad news.

"Pholus, Aristotle is the latest to be taken to the forbidden cave. Aristotle was captured by the demons recently."

The Master Centaur saw the look of surprise he had expected earlier. Pholus was shaking his head in denial. He did not want to know or believe it. Aristotle, who had wandered Hell so often and for so long, now was being held in the forbidden area cave? Pholus always shuddered when he thought of what those dragged into the cave endured. Aristotle was his only human friend. The fiercest of centaurs was beside himself, enraged at this news, then cold and deadly and calm. He looked at Chiron, then off in the direction of the caves.

"We will free Aristotle, Chiron. He is our only human friend in this place. We can amass forces, call out the demons before they can sound their horns and summon the Fallen masters, we'll have archers from all directions pointing…"

"No Pholus; it will not work." Chiron cut him off sternly. "The Fallen masters visit the cave after approximately two hundred rounds. One of our guards will watch the cave exclusively, and that guard reports to Nessus or myself. The cave has only one human occupant currently, by the count of the demons posted outside and around the cave. Something strange is going on. Otherwise, there would be no reason for someone like Aristotle, who is merely traversing Hell illegally, to be confined at that place."

"Will you just leave Aristotle to the cave?" exclaimed Pholus, incredulous.

"Do not worry" Chiron assured him, "I will not leave our friend to that fate. I just need time…and answers. Now, will you assist me in what I ask?" Pholus nodded his ready assent and Chiron continued, "In a few moments we will leave here, you to make your reappearance among your fellows, and command them away, and I to climb up to the Sixth Circle. We will go to the rockslide area, and keep a lookout for the Minotaur. You are well enough to walk now?"

"Yes" replied Pholus, full of wonder at what his friend was up to. He knew he could not encompass the thinking and strategizing that Chiron did easily in his head, and so, as usual, went with blind faith.

* * * * * *

Chiron had attempted before to escape the Seventh Circle, along with many other centaurs, by climbing to the Sixth Circle. A few of the centaurs had actually traveled the other way, deeper down into Hell, despite warnings from their fellows, and made it as far as the plains. The falling fire dispelled their attempts to escape via this route. Centaurs feared fire too much.

Back then, Chiron had begun his first climb toward the Sixth Circle in full view of the Fallen and their demon workers, who were stationed at various points above and surrounding the Rise. The rulers of hell attended the event, almost bemused, and their sycophants waited in feverish anticipation as the centaur leader made his way up the boulder-strewn Rise. It was soon after the centaurs had appeared in the Seventh Circle of Hell and they were, after surveying the entire territory allotted them, attempting to find a way out.

The Rise was the natural and logical place for the centaurs to make their ascent to the Sixth Circle. The area did not elevate vertically like the other areas around the entire Seventh Circle. The incline sloped upwards at a sufficiently favorable angle for the horse-bodied Halflings and was laden with huge boulders from an ages old landslide. The four-legged centaurs could navigate this expanse more evenly and their large hooves, stepping around the rocky terrain, could gain solid footing while using the boulders as supports.

On that infamous first climb, upon reaching a point roughly one quarter of the way up, a strange and terrible invisible force, met them, pushing the ascending centaurs out into the air, off the rocks of the slope and over the boiling river. The centaurs initially howled in rage and surprise, but began yelping and whinnying as they were dropped into the boiling river Phlegethon. Eventually, all the centaurs escaped the river, assisted by their fellows. But, feisty and arrogant, once they regenerated, off the climbing herd went for another attempt. Many centaurs had been dropped into the boiling Phlegethon more than ten times before they gave up their fool's quest.

The worker demons jeered at the Halflings for their arrogance, and a single demon slapped a nearby centaur on the hind flank, ignorant of the proud nature of the beasts. In retaliation, another centaur quickly loosed an arrow into the demon's backside, but as it screamed and screeched, its Fallen master, focusing intently upon the offending centaur, whispered incantations under its breath. The centaur spattered instantly onto the ground, in a concussion of blood and gore, leaving a twitching rack of skeleton, flesh and entrails. The remaining centaurs held their arrows.

The Fallen master had the other demons remove the arrow from the rear end of their fellow. The extraction took a large chunk of meat from the beast's buttock and it fell to the sandy turf in a frenzied shriek. When the Fallen and their worker demons finally departed into the mist, they left their injured coworker lying on the bank in the midst of its regeneration. The demon's last moments were in a surround of angry centaurs, their bows fully drawn. Its grotesque noise charged the millisecond, and then was silenced by multiple arrows through its throat. The first strike was followed by arrows to its head, chest, then legs and arms. No place on its body was devoid of arrows. The arrow fletching transfigured the beast into a feathery porcupine. The centaurs then grabbed the beast by the arrows, and heartily tossed it into the river, where it sank in the boiling abyss. The final iteration of the demon made its appearance in an explosion of red liquid bursting up from Phlegethon's depths. After which, only the arrows emerged flat against the face of the river. The demon was never seen again.

From that time forward, the centaurs did not attempt to escape. It had been thousands of years and sometime during those thousands of years, the Fallen stopped dispatching their demons to patrol the Rise.

* * * * * *

Originally, the Master Centaur had climbed up the rocky incline twice, and both times he was dropped into the boiling liquid. From this experience, Chiron knew the dangers of climbing the Rise. One of these dangers included having to watch out for the Minotaur, who often ventured down the slope looking for trouble. Aristotle told Chiron he had once or twice encountered the Minotaur, getting too close for comfort, but to the good fortune of the traveler, the half-bull beast was not especially burdened with great intelligence. The Minotaur could be easily deceived and Aristotle's strategy worked for him every time. When he encountered the Minotaur, Aristotle merely hid and threw stones in another direction, whereupon the half-bull beast would roar in a rage, and turn running like a fetch dog towards the sound; continuing until it was far away. It never seemed to tire of Aristotle's trick.

With exception of the more recent development of visitations by the Fallen to the forbidden area cave, which was located in the Seventh Circle, but far from the Rise, there was no regular presence of the Fallen or their demons around the Rise. However, there was still the danger of the confinement spell which had successfully thrown Chiron and the other centaurs from the slopes of the Rise into the boiling river below.

Chiron knew the potency of the Fallen spells, but for how long the spells lasted, he could only guess. In order to be successful with his plan, he would have to wager that the spells had run their course and were no longer in effect. It was a gamble he was ready to make.

Chiron and Pholus ordered the centaurs in the area away from the boulder-laden grade, then the Master Centaur instructed Pholus to keep a watch near the cave, and another near the rise so that Pholus would be informed when Chiron returned or if he had been captured. Chiron scanned the rockslide, looking toward the edge of the Sixth Circle and seeing no sign of the Minotaur, nodded to Pholus. He began his journey upward, toward Limbo.

Pholus watched steadily while Chiron made his way up the incline. He was relieved to see his friend still bound to the rocky slope well past the quarter way point and when Chiron at last disappeared beyond the mist, Pholus turned away, heading in the direction of the forbidden area.

Chapter 29

Socius Rebukes the Elder

Socius was beside himself. The gate guard, Philemon, had a moment ago informed him of the Elder Bracchus refusing to allow entrance to Aristotle's fugitive. Socius was in the main meeting room of the Keep, arguing with the Elder about the matter. Some of the other Elders watched, some were busy reading, pretending to ignore Socius while fully listening.

"You have no right to send anyone away from Limbo!" said Socius. "He had a signed parchment from Aristotle! Is Aristotle's word not good any longer?" The round-faced Bracchus smiled his controlled, condescending smile.

"I was doing what any good leader would do, Socius, protecting my people and their place in eternity…"

"What do you mean by 'my people', Bracchus? Surely you don't mean the people of Limbo as they never voted for you in any election." Socius smiled, counting on correct appearances to carry the day. He had stepped far over the line of decorum and he knew he must gain control over himself if he had any chance of rescuing the stranger from outside the walls of Limbo. "What I mean to say is, you were selected by a handful of Elders to your post. You should not burden yourself with speaking for the people of Limbo."

"And you should consider your words, Socius. Like it or not, I was selected by those who were *elected* by the good people of Limbo. I hold a position of great responsibility which I intend to oversee and influence to the utmost degree." Bracchus was moving his head to the side, ever so slightly, like a fat headed cobra with his hood up. "You, and Aristotle are of no consequence in these matters, and Aristotle has no sanctioned authority to invite fugitives to and endanger the safety of Limbo!"

"He is besotted with power," thought Socius, but he held his calm appearance as he bent his face toward Bracchus. "I see Bracchus. So the 'sanctity' of your appointment had nothing to do with your political ties to the other Elders?"

"It had nothing to do with my friends, Socius." Bracchus' face widened. "The welfare of my fellow citizenry is beyond question and my experiences; I would say my nature particularly qualifies me to this post."

"Yes of course, your experiences and your nature," mumbled Socius. He had several retorts to Bracchus' arrogance, but dare he say them?

It was rumored Bracchus had been a ruthless Governor of his province during his lifetime. A citizen of Bracchus' province also had been sentenced to eternity in Limbo. When he observed the climb of Bracchus into the council of the Elders, the man went into hiding and had only been seen since on rare occasions by very few, trusted individuals. Bracchus dispatched a small regiment to find the witness, but the search was fruitless. The man's story had reached Socius' ears as well as many of the guards and citizenry of Limbo. He stated that he had been a farmer who was taxed out of his land and home by the legislation of the wealthy Governor Bracchus. He and the other afflicted landowners began meeting with the local townspeople, discussing their options against the greed of Bracchus. When Bracchus got word of their assemblages, he had them executed publicly, without a trial, for treason. There was no reason to doubt the man, he had nothing to gain from telling either the truth or a lie in this situation.

"You are a stupid boy, Socius," remarked the Elder dismissively, "I am a busy man. I will thank you not to waste my time anymore."

"Truly, I am young in appearance Bracchus. But remember, I am several centuries old and the student of one of the great minds of all time. World histories praise him still. Is it not our privilege to follow his counsel and carry out his wishes whether we understand them or not? After all, can you say you know more than Aristotle?"

"You test my patience, *boy*. We have nothing more to discuss! Your fugitive will never be allowed into Limbo. That's the end of it," Bracchus looked around the room triumphant, and was caught unaware. "I wonder how *you* managed to get into Limbo then, Bracchus, since mass murder is such a severe crime?"

That was it. Socius' temper had got the better of him and the war of words found it's first quarry. Socius' immediate self recrimination was arrested by the enraged Elder who slapped the youth squarely in the face. "You will regret ever…"

Bracchus was stopped as abruptly when reflexively, Socius threw his palm into the abdomen of the chubby Elder. The deft maneuver of Socius launched the Elder across the room. Socius walked toward him, calmly looking down on the pained, frightened Elder. The other Elders were out of their miscellaneous poses of indifference, aroused now and calling for the guards to restrain Socius. But the guards had witnessed the entire incident and had already grabbed Socius by his arms. Ferris, the captain of the guards, approached Socius along with the Elder, Alcander.

"He has struck an Elder, Ferris. He should be thrown into the dungeon!" postured Alcander.

"The Elder struck first." said Ferris. "By your laws he should be thrown into the dungeon also."

"Bracchus is an upstanding member of ..."

"We all saw Bracchus strike Socius first, Alcander," nodded Ferris to the guards who surrounded Socius. "*Upstanding* members do not strike anyone. If you prefer to have Socius thrown into the dungeon, then I will do the same for Bracchus. You decide."

Alcander stood quiet, red in the face. "Let him go then!" he yelled, "But he comes into this building no more! Help Bracchus up."

The stunned Bracchus was heavy, and it took two guards to lift him from the stone floor. He was still very much incapacitated from Socius' blow. Socius was also released.

"Bracchus, if you wish to strike me," spoke Socius in an oddly ameliorating yet defiant tone, "Come to the fields when we have our battle games. Perhaps you could show me what you've learned about the lessons of power."

"Socius. You will leave now." said Ferris, who then turned to address the guards helping Bracchus. 'Take the Elder to his chambers."

"Bracchus had no right to turn anyone away," Socius repeated as he looked Alcander in the eyes.

"Do not return here again Socius. The next time I see you in here you will be on your way to the dungeon." Alcander grit his teeth angrily, but Socius ignored Alcander, and turned to leave. He had an idea brewing and needed to enlist some help.

The guards were generally always friendly toward Socius, though not as much toward Aristotle. Socius was a favorite among many of the people of Limbo, particularly the warrior types who had trained with him and enjoyed their battle games. Nevertheless, the guards were directly under the command of the Elders, and could not blatantly or openly disobey them. That is why, however reluctant, they were more inclined to obey the command of Bracchus rather than side with Socius. In spite of this, it was the guards who had dispatched Philemon to notify Socius of the stranger's arrival and subsequent refusal of entry.

Socius headed toward Elysius, a fragrant meadow of grasses and trees that scented the air with a perfume of earthy forest. The freshness never grew old here. Many of the warriors would regenerate in Elysius after each mock battle. The warrior leaders, the General's Council, were almost always present during and after these battles, working on game plans by creating or revising strategies and discussing prior battle weak points with their men. It was Socius' favorite place to hear their old war stories, too. Socius had come here since his early childhood, a way to escape from his less interesting lessons. The teachers always knew where to find him when he was late for tutoring. His frequent clamoring for the old timers' battle stories endeared him to the ancient warriors.

Once Socius arrived at Elysius, he saw Militus, one of the generals who had tutored him in the arts of combat. Militus sat in the middle of the field, reading a scroll from the Great Library. The familiar sight brought the resolve of clarity to Socius. Militus was the very one Socius hoped to find and he considered this meeting an auspicious one. Militus always had an open ear for Socius, and if there was anyone who could enlist warriors to assist Socius in carrying out his plan, it would be Militus. Seeing the boy approach, the old warrior smiled. Socius knew at this moment he would get the aid he required.

He only hoped the Fallen would not find the fugitive stranger first.

Chapter 30
New Friends in Exile

Mortuus sat, still lingering in depression and hopelessness, but lighter now. Darius, a friendly wanderer who appeared to be well into his forty years, had approached Mortuus on his way to the gate. Darius had to follow Mortuus nearly up to the gate before he could talk Mortuus out of making the futile attempt. Initially Mortuus was angry with Darius for interrupting his mood with what he deemed frivolous talk of friendship. Mortuus' recent rejection at the gate of Limbo still hurt and he was not interested in building up empty hope with equally empty chatter.

Despite Mortuus' rebuff, Darius would not be dissuaded and finally he was allowed to lead Mortuus to the rocky outcropping. Darius had encouraged Mortuus to clean himself before deciding on his next actions. As Mortuus followed him to the oasis, Darius talked about his two friends and how they had been carried away up into the air. This account piqued Mortuus' interest as he had earlier seen some of the same sort of flying creatures, though only one victim was discernible from his vantage point. He had wondered about the fate of the unlucky fellow.

Mortuus then recounted his own story of emerging from unconsciousness, and escaping from an underground passageway. It sounded to Darius as though his new friend had been hidden, but neither could fathom why anyone would be hidden and kept unconscious in Hell. There were too many questions, for both Mortuus and Darius.

The large man had no memory of anything before being woken up, and the awakening was so painful, he was loathe to discuss it. He wanted to get into Limbo and sate his thirst with more of the vials of water that had been left to him. Mortuus told Darius what he had sensed when the gates to Limbo had opened momentarily; the fresh, clean air, and the earthy scent that was on the guards. It was decidedly different from the rest of Hell; Hell's constant wailing and moaning coming from the depths; Hell and its ever changing, stinking odor that one could not get used to. Limbo also lacked the immediate and inexorable overwhelm of Hell's hopelessness.

Mortuus, his thirst burning, drank from the spring, cautious at first, and then ravenously. The water was refreshing, though not as restorative as the vials from Aristotle. When his thirst was finally quenched, he washed in the spring as Darius nervously kept watch at the perimeter of the rocky oasis. The water was the first that Mortuus had bathed in since awakening. It was rejuvenating, although he was initially distracted and then transfixed as his eyes began tracking the filth of lower Hell riding off his body, pressing obscenely against the clean water, and slowly drifting down the stream toward Acheron.

Mortuus, his body still bleeding slightly from his encounter with Plutus, shuddered. The pool was cool and seemed to draw out his pain and anger in the same way that it washed away the filth from his skin, his face and hair. He began feeling stronger and more relaxed. While washing his robe, he noticed his hands bore the marks of bruising and of abrasion. He noticed as well that his robe was heavier and much more sturdily woven than Darius' apparel. It absorbed a great deal of the pool water and took a long time to dry even though Mortuus had wrung it out several times.

Darius' garment was merely a death shroud; Mortuus had a full robe that became clean when washed. In comparison, Darius' death shroud was permanently stained from the mud of the Vestibule, his blood and other body fluids emanating from the constant attacks of the Hell Flies. No matter how many times Darius had washed his shroud, he could not rid it of its tormented memories.

During his cleanse, Mortuus was pensive, reflecting on his journey hoping to organize his thoughts. The cooling waters worked its magic, easing his inner chaos enough for Mortuus to think clearly until at last he knew what he had to do. His arrival at a decision, on the other hand, created another dilemma and that dilemma was Darius. What would his new traveling ally, this fellow fugitive, think of his decision? Would they part ways, and if so, how would Darius manage on his own? Mortuus could feel Darius had formed a certain attachment of fates, if you will.

"Darius, please come here."

"Yes, Mortuus," responded a curious Darius as he walked over to the pool, taking a last, quick glance skyward.

"Darius, I have decided to go back to Limbo." Mortuus examined Darius' face for signs of any change. "I will return and try to get into the gate again. I must. It is my only hope to find out who I am and why I am here. You know your identity, and your origin, and how you came to be here. I have no knowledge of mine." Mortuus turned intently to face Darius. "But what of you? Will you come along and journey out of your relative safety? I do not know if I can get into Limbo, but I was invited by the one who awakened me. He is called Aristotle."

Darius' eyes lit up in surprise. He had heard of Aristotle in his life many times – the great teacher, scientist, mathematician, and philosopher. He had died long before Darius' birth, but was legendary. Did Mortuus speak of *the* Aristotle as the one who had awakened him?

"Darius, why do you seem surprised? Is it some…"

"You say 'Aristotle', Mortuus? He woke you? And he is in Limbo, waiting for you? *The* Aristotle?" Darius could not contain his excitement.

Mortuus considered him for a moment. "Yes, I suppose. Phlegyas, the oarsman, regarded him quite highly as well. I do not know who *the* Aristotle is that you refer to, but I would guess this would be him," nodded Mortuus. "Aristotle was known by the guards of Limbo, too. They showed a bit of deference f…"

"I will journey with you." interrupted Darius, in a great rush, now quite enthusiastic. Mortuus was dumbfounded for the moment – he would have liked to have finished his statement, but he had his answer, and Darius was not angry or disappointed.

"Good." he smiled. "I would like to leave when my clothing has fully dried." Darius returned to the perimeter of the rocky oasis, scanning for trouble, and abuzz for their next adventure.

The pair of fugitives decided to follow the path to the river, starting from as close to the gate as they could get. They hoped that it would appear to Charon they had entered as all other newcomers did. Hopefully the ferryman would forget he had earlier transported Mortuus from the Limbo side of the river. If they walked along the bank to the landing, Charon would surely recognize them as fugitives, and deny them transport, and worse, inform the demon fugitive hunters of their presence in the area. It would ruin all their hopes of getting across Acheron and into Limbo.

Mortuus told Darius how Charon had denied him passage unless given something of value. He gave a good description of the small, flat metal disc that he found while crossing the Fourth Circle. The disc had an embossed picture on it and it was the only item he would part with because it was not given to him by Aristotle. Charon had eyed it in amazement, his glaring red eyes looking back and forth from the coin, (as Darius had called it), to Mortuus. Mortuus remarked that he was relieved he had picked it up before meeting Charon because Charon seemed at the time as if he would start beating Mortuus with his oar, such was his raging temperament. On the other hand, Darius' last crossing had been well over a thousand years prior, upon his death. Darius thought that his face would not be memorable to Charon, who ferried every single one of Hell's inhabitants since time immemorial.

After much walking, the two allies finally approached the landing, nervousness rattling their insides, causing great unease. Four men were waiting at the landing when they arrived; two were crying quietly, another was pulling his hair out in an angry display of rage, and the last one was cursing to himself loudly. The angry man looked around like a cornered dog, ready to strike at anyone who ventured too close. The four barely noticed the arrival of Mortuus and Darius.

The water's edge was muck, and the dock a rotting set of timbers. In the distance, on the vaporous river, they could hear the water moving in slow rhythmic strokes, though they could not see Charon or his vessel. The slowness of the strokes served to heighten the anxiety of the doomed group. Then, like a great monster appearing from the depths, the long skiff formed out of the mist, and the glowing red eyes of the old bearded one glared out, boring holes into each of the six waiting men. One of the new arrivals sobbed loudly, blurting uncontrollably as his horror was confirmed.

Darius also turned away, unable to look into the raging red eyes of the ferryman. It felt to Darius as if the ferryman could see his guilt plainly, maybe even remember taking him the first time. The Vestibule escapee thought he would change his mind and run away, back to the safety of the rocky oasis, alone forever, but safe from the first of Hell's monsters. Darius considered that he might even prefer serving his sentence; anything seemed better than facing Charon.

Mortuus, having dealt with Charon recently, was slightly less intimidated, but still found the experience frightening. He looked around to see the effect the monstrous glaring eyes had on the others. Disturbingly, Darius looked as if he was going to flee. Mortuus stared at Darius, willfully, silently trying to lock Darius's eyes away from Charon's, and stop his flight. Darius, mustering all his courage and willpower, looked away from the ferryman. He moved his eyes around, from the skiff, to the landing, then at the newcomers, who were now all crying loudly. Then Darius noticed Mortuus, staring directly at him. Mortuus had an unmistakable calming effect for Darius; he quickly regained his composure, keeping his eyes averted for the time being.

The skiff bumped the dock, and one of the weeping men was startled. Charon leapt out, his large oar in hand, and examined all the waiting men directly. His face, close up, was even more fearsome, as the wrinkles seemed to be hundreds of small scars carved into a shape that highlighted his glowing eyes. Holding his upraised oar in his right hand, he beckoned everyone to board the large skiff with his left. Darius looked away, then back at Charon. His eyes always seemed to be staring directly into Darius. Shakily, he got into the long skiff, and stepped uneasily toward the front. Mortuus was the last one to board, and stepped into the skiff carefully. He balanced himself clumsily as Charon began pulling the large oar through the water, propelling the craft and its passengers into the mist.

Without warning, Mortuus thudded flat onto his face after the large oar connected forcibly with the back of his head. The glowing-eyed ferryman was ominous as he stood over Mortuus's laid out form; the other passengers, including Darius, cringed at the front end of the boat. Mortuus was semi-conscious, blinded by the pain of the blow.

"Who are you that traverses Hell freely, fugitive?" roared Charon. "I remember every one whom I ferry, especially those that pay to go the wrong way."

Charon looked toward the front of the boat, glaring straight at Darius.

"You are no newcomer either, fugitive."

Chapter 31
Charon's Rage

The long skiff was far from the shore, the mist almost hiding the bank of the Vestibule. Mortuus lay across the bottom, his back uncomfortable and his head in throbbing pain, so much that he could not stand up. Charon stood over him and was swearing loudly. Mortuus could hardly understand him, as flashes of yellow pain were causing his closed eyes to throb. His ribs were bruised from the force of the sudden fall, and the gnarled old man-monster was raising his oar, preparing for another blow to Mortuus' skull. Mortuus lay unaware of the impending violence; his only thought, outside of the terrible pain, was that he had been captured.

"You would have been better off staying in your own circle, fugitive." said Charon. "The demons will make you wish you had." Looking down at Mortuus, whose face was vulnerable on the left side - the right side being pressed against the boat floor - Charon straddled over him to get a better angle for the next blow. The ferryman kicked Mortuus in the side with each step, almost breaking his ribs. Mortuus yelled and rolled over painfully to see the oar completely lifted up, ready for the downward swing into his skull. Before the stroke finished its descent, Darius' thin body lunged forward from the huddle of cowering men and took the full force of the blow on his left forearm. The bones snapped soundly and he screamed in pain. Charon, enraged at missing the stroke, roared at the insolence, swearing oaths at the grimacing Darius, who was clutching his broken arm and trying to push the bones back into the flesh. Darius knew this worker from Hell would surely destroy him, but decided he would not lose another ally without a fight.

Charon pulled back his oar and stepped forward toward Darius, still straddling Mortuus. He stared into Darius with angry intent. No passenger had ever taken a stance so much as mumbling angrily under their breath in Charon's presence. Charon answered that kind of dissent without prejudice; one blow with the great oar was a cure all.

* * * * * *

Impertinence occurred rarely, and was only the result of interactions with Charon's fellow workers, the demons. On one occasion, Charon had thrown two fugitive hunters, non-flyer demons, into Acheron. The beasts had appeared on the Limbo-side of the river, demanding passage to the Vestibule from Charon without payment. They hurled threats at the ferryman, cursing him and stating he would join the tormented in a lower circle if he did not transport them. Charon brandished his great oar as he stood his ground, threatening the demons with a bloody beating and a swim in Acheron. Furious, the demons advanced, but Charon, swinging his weapon as though it were a light wooden switch, promptly repelled the beasts back on shore, nursing their swollen heads and broken ribs. When they returned later, still bloodied, they tendered a single coin each to Charon. They boarded and were ferried across to the Vestibule.

When they had to make their way back to the Limbo side of Acheron, they appeared on the landing, now swollen and in foul moods from multiple Hell fly bites. Charon again refused them passage. They displayed their coins, but still stupidly arrogant, told Charon they would pay when they arrived at the opposite shore.

Charon transported them across Acheron while considering his options. A half second after the skiff landed, the ferryman beat the demons until they could not fight back. He picked up their coins, and then threw both far out into the filthy river. The demons sank beneath the surface like rocks and disappeared into the river depths forever.

* * * * * *

The ferryman had never experienced such insolence from human passengers prior to his encounter with Darius and Mortuus. Charon swung horizontally and missed, as Darius ducked, causing Charon to stumble and become even more enraged. He caught his balance, clumsily raising the oar above his head, sure not to miss the cringing Darius with a direct downward blow. But with Charon's rage distracting his attention, Mortuus was able to curl his legs up, unnoticed, right under Charon's groin. In an instant, Mortuus swung his lower trunk up so that his knees were nearly touching his chin and, aiming the soles of his feet at Charon's undercarriage, thrust his legs upward so hard that when they met their target, his legs cramped from the excessive effort.

The push propelled the thick-bodied ferryman in a trajectory high into the air and over the back side of the boat. He lost his great oar while in the air and it fell with a thud onto the swampy water and was taken under. Charon himself was in utter shock as he roared and flailed wildly, landing ten meters from the back side of his skiff, into the river of pain. The splash from his impact on the surface was disproportionate in its displacement of the water in that Charon landed flat, barely sending up a splash, then sunk like a big stone and vanished into unknown depths. No bubbles marked his entry into Acheron's filthy wash.

He was just gone.

Mortuus sat up, his head still hurting immensely. Darius, staggering and in pain, held his right arm gingerly; smiling weakly at his new friend. They had won, for the moment. Overwhelmed by the event they had just witnessed, the new arrivals stared at Mortuus, frightened he would throw them overboard next. Huddled together in the front of the boat, they did not move.

It turned out the skiff had enough momentum to reach the shore from Charon's initial few pulls of his oar. Several minutes later it skidded onto shore, and the newcomers jumped off hastily. They followed the path down between the two walls that defined the end boundaries of Limbo, disappearing from the sight of Darius and Mortuus, who got out of the boat much slower. The two sat on the rocky path for a long time, waiting for their wounds to heal and their pain to ease. They couldn't help but continue looking toward the river, not fully convinced Charon had been lost to Acheron. At length, they began to speak.

"How is your arm, Darius?" asked Mortuus first. "It does not appear swollen any longer."

"The pain is fading, though I do not believe my arm is nearly healed enough." replied Darius. Darius was thin and timid from his years living under the poor conditions of an impoverished slave. Besides taking the chance of leaving the Vestibule, his action in Charon's boat was the bravest thing he'd ever attempted and left him shaken up inside. It also had the odd effect of creating excitement in him. Though his arm was in the process of regenerating and therefore in discomfort, Darius was surprised at how well his meager body responded to the challenge. "I might be thin," he thought, "But I am sturdy!" He lifted his head and straightened his shoulders before turning to Mortuus. "Does your head feel better?" he asked.

"It feels better than it would have if that old monster cracked it with his oar again. Thank you for your intervention." His head was throbbing, and his vision slightly blurred, but it had gotten better. His nose had been broken and bloodied in his fall against the boat bottom, but no longer was it stinging.

"That was quite a powerful kick," marveled Darius, happy to be in a conversation of the winning side of a hard-fought battle, "You actually threw Charon from his own boat! You must have been some great warrior or athlete in your lifetime."

Mortuus smiled. His head was too achy to enjoy any boasts, but he mulled over Darius's words as they returned to him the pain of his memory loss. "I wish I knew about my lifetime, Darius. I wish I knew." He was reminded as well of their mutual goal to enter Limbo and knew he had to be more forthright about Darius' chances at the gate. Mortuus continued warily, "I have been thinking that maybe you will not be able to get into Limbo, as we spoke of. What will you do if that happens? I have to go in – I have to find out who I am and why I am here. But I worry for you."

Darius reckoned with this possibility sadly. He had already known it would be a long shot, but hadn't let that probability get in the way of his decision to join Mortuus. "I will wait outside the gate for a while if this comes to be. I may search for my friends or try to return to the Vestibule. It may be quiet and lonely, but I will not suffer the torments. If you should ever venture from Limbo, look for me."

"I will be sure to," promised Mortuus.

"It is well enough. Now, I do not wish to linger in anticipation." Darius felt his legs under him and rose with some discomfort. "Shall we be off on our next adventure?" His care-free determination, meant to supplant the woe of an impossible situation. In truth, Darius could not bear to be separated from his friend and left alone once more. Mortuus, his head throbbing, nodded and got up slowly. He could see the pain in Darius's face, but they both knew there was nothing more to say.

No sooner had they resolved to move on, than the pair, still sore and aching, froze. A small company of heavily armed men were running straight at them with dangerous intensity. Within seconds, the armed squadron had their weapons pointed directly at the faces of the two. The fugitives were forced down, back into their sitting positions; staring incredulously at the array of lethal weapons aimed at them.

They were captured.

Chapter 32
Chiron's Promise

Since his imprisonment in the Seventh Circle ages ago, Chiron had not the occasion to traverse Hell; the spell confining him and all centaur-kind left no possibility for travel. Now here he was in the Sixth Circle, trotting amongst the glowing tombs and coffins, headed for the gates of Dis. He surveyed the area, examining the heat distorted landscape as he searched for worker demons and imps. He was thinking about the failure of the confining magic that was used to contain the herds in the Seventh Circle when he picked up the familiar, dangerous scent of the Minotaur.

Chiron thought the creature might have spotted him exiting the Seventh Circle. The Master Centaur sniffed the air again, sensing the presence of the beast. This was the closest he had come in thousands of years, but how could that be, he thought. Was the Minotaur not confined to the slope area, and to the burial containers of the inner edge of the Sixth Circle? Chiron was far from the area of confinement for the beast.

The Minotaur was not a discrete half-animal, but similarly to Chiron, it had been imprisoned in its part of Hell by magical enforcement. Now the Minotaur was shadowing Chiron as he made his way toward the Styx and Phlegyas. The Master Centaur detected the Minotaur coming up from the back left. The odors of Hell were ever shifting, always to a new foul version that could not be gotten used to, but just past that odor, Chiron could perceive the wafting odor of the bull Halfling, a mix of stinking sweat both bovine and human.

The Minotaur was closing in on him. Chiron stopped and looked back, surveying the area when suddenly, from behind a stack of coffins, the Minotaur sprang up, apparently having burned itself on one of the red hot coffins; indicated by the way it held its hands on its hind quarters. Its position revealed, the bull-human stood erect, staring at Chiron across the separation of two rows of red tombs. It was enormously built, completely muscular, but with the head and lower body of a great bull. It was a fearsome creature, but awe inspiring to behold. Chiron stared at its face fully for the first time and noted something in its bull's eyes. Though they glared an angry red at the Master Centaur, it seemed that the creature was sad.

The Halflings studied each other and for a moment, Chiron was moved to compassion. Un-notching the arrow from his bow (he had automatically loaded a shaft as soon as he detected the scent of the Minotaur), Chiron approached the lone creature carefully, lowering his arms and replacing his arrow to clearly display his peaceful intention. The Minotaur scrutinized each step, growling in a low tone until the Master Centaur stopped two meters away.

"I am known as Chiron. Do you have a name?" asked Chiron. The creature was mute for an uncomfortable length of time as it weighed the words of Chiron. Finally, the Minotaur broke the silence with a deep and powerful voice that matched the countenance of the half-bull; the voice was gruff and booming.

"I am...Asterion. I am feared and hated by all who know me. Never before has anyone tried to address me. Why do you speak to me thus? There is no fear in your voice. I know fear, its smell, and I would have ripped you apart had I detected it upon your person. My enemies all had much fear, and they hated me for it. Do you not hate me also, Master Chiron?"

"You are half-bull, Asterion. I am half-horse. I have never hated anyone for being half-human. You are known for many atrocities during your time in the infamous Labyrinth, the killings of the innocents sacrificed. Your brutal violence is your legacy, but who are you now as we speak?"

"I am that monster of which you tell. But hear me. I was not always thus." said Asterion. "In my youth, my mother cared for me well, and I loved her very much. She was taken from me by her husband, Minos, her greedy, stupid husband, who threw me into a pit for many years." Asterion was beginning to speak angrily. "The dolt begat my birth by betraying Poseidon, who caused my mother to go mad and seek companionship with a great white bull. Thus, was I born, then taken away, and punished for my parentage and deformity. Once a day the fool king sent a tormentor to my pit, and he would beat me, saying "A beast must be beaten because he is only a beast." This occurred from my earliest childhood memory, everyday until I came of age. One day I fought back, killing the torturer and his guards, who had before this time laughed as I cried in torment, jeering at my suffering. Hungry and undernourished my entire life, I ripped out and ate his beating heart, and I grew strong. Thus, my placement was secured, and my reputation, in the cursed maze."

Chiron listened to Asterion tell his story. It did not much diverge from the life stories of his fellow centaurs. Most had tormented childhoods, and had been pushed to hatred and rage, eventually acting out with violence, killing or abusing others. Now the Minotaur stood here, telling his own tale, and it resembled the Halfling-kind story too well. The Minotaur had been, like all centaurs, persecuted because he was half-animal. Chiron's circumstances and intelligence were different, and so his path differed greatly, but they both ended up in Hell.

At the end of Asterion's story, the Halflings stood more comfortably in each other's presence. Chiron's compassion had been stirred; he spoke to Asterion in a more caring voice, instead of his usual commanding tone. The Minotaur was actually a very emotionally sensitive creature. Chiron could not fathom how Asterion had endured his life of extreme abuse to reach adulthood. The pair continued talking for a length of time before Chiron finally forced the conclusion of their meeting.

"Asterion, I am on my way toward the First Circle. I must leave you for now. If you wander this place, outside of your confinement area, you may be spotted and stopped, and maybe tormented like the humans. I would meet with you upon my return, and perhaps you will come and visit my circle, meet with my centaur kindred, and end your lonely patrol. For now, I must go. I have very important business needing my attention. I do not mean to abandon you, and I will make good on my promise that you join us. But please, return to your appointed patrol grounds for just a short while longer. And do not enter the Seventh Circle without my presence. The centaur regiments will not allow your visit, and I would prefer to see you unharmed."

The Minotaur was saddened, but looked into the intelligent Master Centaur's unflinching eyes. Asterion turned away, leaving Chiron. He headed toward the rocky slope and disappeared into the heat distorted Sixth Circle.

Chiron continued his movement toward the outer wall of Dis. He could finally see the wall. It was a dirty, dark, rust-stained metal, with a greenish mold growing on it. Here and there the buildings attached to the wall revealed doorways and steps to the turrets, or interiors that were on the top of the wall. In the distance, on his right, Chiron could see a flame, bursting in the air, barely visible through the mist. He saw many of the small creatures, which he recognized as imps; they cowered away upon seeing him.

* * * * * *

Long ago, the imps used to wander down on a regular basis to the Seventh Circle. The flyers, those imps with functional wings, would attack the humans who frequented the shallower portions of Phlegethon. It didn't take long before would-be victims of the little beasts learned to pull them down into the river, causing them to shriek and screech as the centaur patrols laughed loudly. Other imps attacked the centaurs, biting their shoulders as they flew from above while their ground-bound, non-flyer coworkers attacked the legs and hooves. Why the smallish creatures would attack the much larger, faster centaurs was a mystery. The packs of vermin were soon exterminated by the centaurs, who considered it great sport to 'smoke' the beasts with a single arrow. In subsequent encounters, the centaurs made it their policy to shoot on sight and the imps eventually figured out they were not a match for the much larger, stronger, skilled warriors. They did not visit the Circle of Phlegethon again.

* * * * * *

Chiron arrived at the gate of Dis, and was surprised by its large size, but then spied the small side door. It was a tight fit for his Halfling frame, but he pushed through. On the way in, Chiron saw the swamp that was the Styx, and the full size of the tower, from base to peak. It was a misty place; noises came from out of the vapors, screams and splashes of the human inhabitants, inflicting violence upon each other. Nearer to the landing, small trails of bubbles denoted the submerged existence of the tormented.

Chiron waited on the landing. He knew not to get near the swamp edge, at least not until Phlegyas arrived. He knew this from the stories of Aristotle. The oarsman would be very surprised to see the Master Centaur, and Chiron was concerned that Phlegyas might not be willing to transport him across the Styx. Chiron had no vials to exchange for his passage. He had used the last of the healing waters on regenerating Pholus from the harpy wounds. A steady, rhythmic paddling sound indicated that Phlegyas was approaching.

Chiron would soon find out if the oarsman would carry him over the Styx.

To his great relief, Phlegyas was overjoyed. The two had much to talk about, each quickly recounting their past attempts to abandon their posts, and each had incurred the usual consequences. Phlegyas had spent time in the swamp when he had tried to climb up the wall to the Fourth Circle. He had reached the halfway point when he was thrown far into the Styx, like the centaurs, who had been cast into the Phlegethon. Unlike the centaurs, he had been detained by the vicious inhabitants, and it took years to crawl out of the swamp. When Phlegyas emerged, he swore never to attempt escape again. Ever since, he remained the oarsman of the Styx.

Suddenly Phlegyas, reminded of the urgency and danger surrounding their encounter, motioned Chiron to get into the skiff, warning him not to get near the sides or the tormented of the swamp would pull him in. "We should get you out of sight, my friend, into the middle of this swamp, concealed within the mist. If the demons see you, they will attack, and worse, notify the Fallen." Phlegyas turned the boat outward, and pushed off the shore. Hidden by the mist, they continued their exchange of news and information and by the end of the journey across the Styx, had made plans to reunite again. Chiron explained to Phlegyas why he had undertaken the treacherous trip; their mutual friend had been taken into the forbidden area cave. Phlegyas was angered at this, but not so surprised.

"Aristotle was always taking chances by traveling through Hell." he said. "I told him on many occasions that it was only a matter of time before he got caught. I believe you also foresaw this happening - according to Aristotle?"

"Yes. I did, though it took no power of augury to divine his capture." said Chiron. "But why do they hide him? Hell is not secretive about torture, and there are many places Aristotle would find inescapable. What reasoning is behind this?"

"I have some information." replied Phlegyas. "Recently, I transported someone who Aristotle had awoken, a strange, large prisoner from another secretive torment."

"Awoken?" replied Chiron. "What do you mean, 'awoken'? Who sleeps in this place?"

"I mean it the way it sounds" said Phlegyas. "I do not know where the stranger was kept, except that it was a secret underground area of the burning tombs. Aristotle called it the Undertomb, and he told me only that the awakened prisoner would need transport if he made it to the swamp landing. The prisoner made it, much to my surprise and I transported him across, but while doing so, I learned that he had no memory of his past." Phlegyas stopped for a moment, looking at Chiron steadily, "Strange things are happening, my friend, many strange things; like your escape, Aristotle's capture – by the way, why do you journey to Limbo? Are you aware they may report you? I have spoken with Aristotle about the governance. They have become very bureaucratic. When I last spoke to Aristotle, I got the impression– "

"Wait, please." snapped Chiron. His inner eye had flashed - he quieted Phlegyas with a wave of his hands.

* * * * * *

Chiron was standing in a large room with older, well-dressed humans when a young man of roughly nineteen years of age entered the room. One of the elder humans stood up, looking at the boy, motioning him to remain silent as he gestured to another human to close the door. The man pulled the doors shut. The elder man addressed the young man.

"Well, Crucio?" asked the standing human expectantly.

"Yes, Elder." said the young man. "They have apprehended Aristotle behind the Hall of Minos. Demons flew off with him toward the depths."

"Then it is done." said the Elder. "You have served your people well, young man. You have the thanks of your leaders." The Elder smiled, approving of this young man's deeds. Chiron watched the boy leave.

* * * * * *

He was back, standing with Phlegyas again in his boat. He apologized heartily, and informed the oarsman of what he had just experienced.

"This has to do with Aristotle's capture." said Chiron. "The youth said he saw Aristotle taken – this has already transpired. I have recently had another vision, in which I participated, but it was somewhere else, a lake of filthy ice. A battle was imminent between the centaurs and the Fallen. By the dead! The past is always easier to see than the future." Chiron trailed off. "I must hasten my ascent to Limbo, Phlegyas."

"My friend, you will have to be very careful in Limbo – I imagine you will cause a great stir. Those Elders betrayed Aristotle to the Fallen. They are probably watching his young charge, Socius. You may want to warn him."

"I intend to." said Chiron. The Master Centaur stepped out of the boat which had grounded into the gravelly shore while he was having his vision. "I will see you again Phlegyas; it has been good meeting you. You have my thanks for your transport services."

Phlegyas watched his friend gallop away, heading for the point in the wall where he could climb up to the Fourth Circle. He then realized he had forgotten to tell his friend something, of utmost importance.

"Chiron!" he called out. "Master Chiron!" In the distance, the centaur heard the urgency in the oarsman's voice, and slowed to a stop. He turned, raising an arm to signal acknowledgement of Phlegyas. Phlegyas scanned left and right, assuring himself no others were present, and then stepped out of his skiff, running all the way over to Chiron.

"Chiron, I have a theory of the identity of the Awakened One," he said, out of breath.

Chiron's eyes revealed his interest, "Who is the awakened prisoner, Phlegyas?"

"I believe a better question would be *what*, Lord Chiron."

Chapter 33
Rage and Pain in the Pitch

Aetos was only able to scream silently; nothing else. He was sinking in boiling, black pitch. The demons that had ravaged and abducted him and Panos dropped him into a river of sticky, boiling blackness, maintained by tall, thin creatures that ran and flew in short jerky movements like dragonflies. The beasts patrolled the boiling pitch from the shore and in the air, and were constantly looking to skewer and rip apart humans who dared expose themselves. There were many in the pitch with Aetos.

Aetos' boiling was intensified by his anger at being captured. Out of his three fellow escapees, he alone had to endure the pitch. Darius had not been captured, and Panos had fallen earlier, accidentally dropped in a higher circle where flame fell on a burning plain. Aetos could feel it while he was being dragged through the air by the flying demons, dangling at the end of their meat hooks. He could see the flame forming below before it shot to the ground. The demons had flown just above where the fiery precipitation formed, but still under the misty ceiling. Aetos saw Panos drop out of sight.

During the flight, Aetos figured out, listening to their growls and rage, the demons were arguing amongst themselves. They swore violent oaths while in the air, tossing Aetos' immobilized form about like a dead fish on their hooks. Aetos was alone, isolated far from his two fellow fugitives; the thought, a torment that worsened the effects of capture.

Aetos had been dropped from high up. The demons had removed their meat hooks from his flesh and held him by the ankles. His exposed entrails hung down, dropping across his face, evidence of the earlier violence. The demons were laughing, joking how it would surprise the 'devils' when the human fell and pushed one of them into the pitch. Aetos was not the first, nor would he be the last fugitive taken to the pitch. This was the fate of fugitives that Philo had warned the three companions about. When Aetos was at last released he plunged quickly down, landing like a load of bricks onto the back of one of the thin creatures that had been hovering over the pitch. The beast did not know what hit it.

Nearby beasts, startled by the sound of the impact of Aetos and the creature onto the pitch, began shrieking in alarm; running or flying helter skelter, not thinking to look up. This chaotic behavior gave the demons a long and hearty laugh before they flew off, looking for another round of gruesome mischief. Aetos had no way to avoid his situation; the demons had ripped through his connecting muscle and ligaments almost completely. He was on fire, in the pitch, and there was nothing he could do about it. He could only surrender his body to the downward pull of the pitch while the screeching worker beast was being pulled out by his fellows.

It was a far cry from the tedium of his safely structured Earth life with all its inherited privilege. It was also a far cry from the vile Vestibule with its constant swarm of Hell Flies. He wondered, very briefly, what it all meant.

Aetos was only able to scream silently, nothing else. He was sinking in boiling, black pitch.

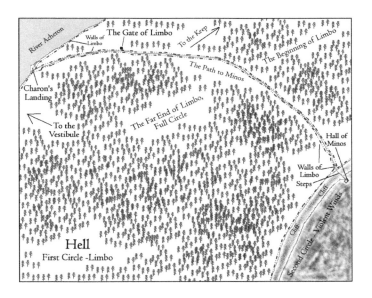

Chapter 34
The New World

Mortuus could not believe his nose. The air smelled beautiful. There was no feeling of gloom, decay or pain; hopelessness no longer weighed heavily upon him. The background noises were missing, too; the constant moaning, crying, and screaming from the depths no longer assaulted his senses. Since his awakening, he had been trying to get here. He would never leave. It was bright and colorful, and green grass grew, cooling his bare feet. Large trees and brush grew here, too.

The soldiers led Mortuus and Darius, surrounding them tightly to conceal their presence. The youthful one who introduced himself as Socius was at the head of this pack, and Mortuus, larger than any one of them, crouched in vain to conceal himself in the center. The soldiers were not pointing their weapons at Mortuus and Darius anymore.

* * * * * *

The fugitive friends had been shocked and afraid when they had been suddenly surrounded by the company of soldiers. Both thought these men were going to punish them for the incident with Charon, and turn them over to the demon fugitive hunters. When the youth, Socius, stepped up from behind the company, the soldiers lowered their weapons. Socius, introducing himself, asked Mortuus for his name. Mortuus pulled out the signed parchment of Aristotle and gave it to Socius. The youth smiled more brightly.

"I am Mortuus." replied Mortuus.

"Put your weapons away," Socius told the soldiers. He addressed Mortuus. "You were awakened by my teacher and mentor. I have much to tell you, but we must get back. The smells and sounds are unnerving my friends and myself. I now know why Aristotle would not allow me to accompany him on his journeys. He will flay me alive if he finds out I have left Limbo."

"Limbo?" said Mortuus. The boy did not hear Mortuus speak. Socius motioned the soldiers to help Mortuus to his feet. He turned toward Darius, who was staring downward sadly. Darius knew they only meant to take Mortuus, and he would soon lose his new friend.

"And who would you be?" asked Socius, peering into the hardened, weary face of Darius. The gaunt, older man looked as though he would cry. Mortuus spoke quickly.

"This is Darius. He has been helping me to get to Limbo. I arrived earlier, but was denied access. The guards were forbidden by another from within Limbo to allow me entrance. I was sent away. I crossed the river, where I met Darius. He showed me a pool where I could clean off and helped when I was attacked by the ferryman."

"Mortuus, you will have to slow down." said Socius. Mortuus' face reddened.

"That is all." said Mortuus. Socius' curiosity was peaked, but he looked confused. It was apparent that Mortuus wanted Darius to come along into Limbo. Socius knew the Elders would pick up on this, use it to cause trouble for himself and Aristotle. But the stench out here was unbearable, and the pain in Darius' face was too sad. Socius decided not to care what the Elders would do, and made up his mind. They would be dealt with later.

"Darius. You are a fugitive also?" he inquired. Darius was reluctant to answer. Socius felt his aversion to answering the question, and explained. "Darius, I am not the judge of Hell, and I do not have nor do I want the power to condemn, fugitive or not. Tell me the truth. *Are you a fugitive?*"

Darius looked downward, and sighed. He was sad and disappointed, but he would not lie to the likeable youth. "I am." Darius looked furtively around at the soldiers, who were curious to hear Darius's response. Surprisingly, he felt no judgment from any one. He continued, "I, with two others, escaped the Hell Flies of the Vestibule, which continuously herded and pursued us, causing us to run or be bitten by the swarms. We reached a pool, that which Mortuus spoke of, where my two friends were captured by flying beasts and taken away… on the end of meat hooks." Some of the soldiers grimaced at hearing this. "I saw both creatures descending at the last possible moment, and hid myself." He looked down at the ground, his voice choking, and he spoke in a low voice, "I was a coward. When I heard my friends screaming and being ripped apart, all I could think was to hide myself." The wiry man stifled his sobs. Socius and the soldiers watched this sad spectacle.

"*I* have never had to face demons, let alone fight them Darius. Aristotle has many stories of near encounters, and each time he has thanked his lucky stars to have escaped. The demons are far too strong for any man. I am sure ten men would hardly be a match for a single beast, let alone three men to two of them. I know if your friends were here, they would join us in Limbo. Will you join us, Darius?" Darius looked up wet eyed, unsure of what he had heard; Socius smiled.

"You would permit me entrance?" asked Darius, looking around at the soldiers and then back to Socius. "Are you sure? I-"

"I would Darius; *we* would." said Socius as he looked around at the soldiers; they nodded in agreement. He looked over to Mortuus cheerily. "What do you say Mortuus, shall we have Darius accompany us to Limbo?" Mortuus smiled broadly.

"Yes! Thank you, Socius, thank you." said Mortuus. He smiled at Socius and the soldiers. "I was afraid I would have to part company with Darius."

"You are welcome Mortuus. Shall we go? It is quite awful out here." said Socius. The youth smiled and began walking down the path. Mortuus and Darius stood among the soldiers as they started walking behind Socius toward the gate. After a short walk, they arrived at the gate, a large iron door on the left side of the path. The gate was locked, and one of the soldiers knocked on the metal, banging it loudly with the haft of a long sword. Socius motioned to the soldiers.

"Remember, the Elders need not know of this. As far as they are concerned, we went on an adventure beyond the gate, just as Aristotle does, though of much lesser ambition. We have traveled even less distance than the missing three Elders. We turned back because we could not take the stench."

"Whew!" shouted one of the soldiers. "That is no lie!" The rest of the soldiers laughed. Socius resumed.

"Our new friends should be hidden from the populace until we can get them cleaned up and blend them into Limbo's citizenry. They should become indistinguishable from our fellow inhabitants. Those of you who know the guard at the inner gate will need to get his complicity. Mortuus and Darius – stay to the center; the soldiers will surround you. We can get our friends some of the waters and healing potions." He turned to Mortuus and Darius. "Please follow my directions and keep a low profile until we get you cleaned up.

The politics at work here are less than benevolent, Mortuus. Be especially careful when we pass the Keep. It is the first, and worst, obstacle to your membership of Limbo. That is the castle where the Elders reside."

The guard opened the gate. Crouching slightly, Mortuus and Darius entered, surrounded on all sides by the company of soldiers. Slowly they made their way through and past the inner gate. They had made it; they were in. The company kept them pressed within as they passed the building known as the Keep, a large stone palace with many windows that fell just short of the walls in height. The Keep had five tall towers, each with four windows. A single tower in the center stood all the way up and pierced the mist. Its top could not be seen.

"Admiring the high tower, eh?" said the guard nearest to Mortuus. "That is where the Elders meet with Fallen. It is forbidden to enter without the permission of the Elders. What I would give to explore it all the way above the mist…"

The group continued to a place called the Fields of Elysius, out of eyesight of the Keep, and finally broke the tight formation. Socius left on an errand, and the soldiers, relaxed, placing their weapons down and breathing deeply, relieved to be back inside Limbo. They all sat on the grass, the smell of which made Mortuus's senses dance. A cool, gentle breeze flowed through the trees that surrounded the fields. Mortuus lay on the grass and breathed the fresh air. The soldiers smiled as they saw his childlike joy. They could not fathom what he had endured outside of these walls.

Darius, the once diligent and loyal slave remained silent, looking in awe at the brightness of the colors of everything, wondering how long his time in Limbo would last. It was brightly lit, though he could not tell from where the light came. Outer Hell was dingy and dark grey; everything seemed a shade of gray or black. Philo had said the depths were darker than the Vestibule, but he had not visited Limbo and seen its vivid hues. Darius hadn't breathed clean, fresh air for a long time. He was as overwhelmed as Mortuus looked and surprised that he might have caught a glimmer of the same insecurity he was feeling coming from his tall friend. The lifetime experience of being identified as no more than chattel had not prepared Darius to easily embrace this sort of kindness or generosity of spirit, this recognition of him as an individual. He was unworthy. He had always been unworthy from the time of his birth. And in his unworthiness, he was sure his wondrous stay would end with his eviction from Limbo. The only question was when.

The two were the center of attention, as, shyly, one of the soldiers asked a question of Mortuus. That seemed to open the floodgates for the remaining warriors. The soldiers inquired about the torments and wanderings of both Darius and Mortuus. None of them had been outside since arriving in Hell. Now they had actual inhabitants from outer Hell to ask personally. Mortuus and Darius could not have been happier to answer.

Chapter 35

Limbo's Newest Elder

Mortuus was large, with big, broad shoulders and a strong body that was wrapped in robes more refined and well-meshed than the death shrouds that covered all the new arrivals of Hell. His robes were indeed more similar to the robes of Limbo's citizens. Darius, in his ripped, stained shroud, was conspicuous as an escapee.

Two Elders, informed by a guard loyal to them about Socius and his warrior friends' exit from Limbo, went at once to Elysius, where they discovered why Socius and his warrior friends ventured outside of the gates. Raging mad, the pair began a shouting battle with Socius and Militus, who joined the group just before the pair of Elders walked onto the scene. Previously, the soldiers and Mortuus and Darius were talking amongst themselves and sharing their stories. Socius, upon seeing the Elders approach, motioned the two newcomers to be silent. Mortuus and Darius sat quietly as the fear of expulsion gnawed at them. They could not bear to consider leaving this wonderful place.

The Elders marched straight up to the group, eyeballing Mortuus and Darius disdainfully and speaking about them as if they were not present. The Elders were Alcander, one of the original Elders, and the more recently elected Morpheus. The Elder Morpheus was much taller and more stockily built than Alcander, and he moved aggressively toward Mortuus, scrutinizing him with an angry glare. Mortuus was reminded of something he had seen earlier, during his travels in the Sixth Circle, though in the moment he could not recall.

Unexpectedly, Mortuus, who was still sitting on the ground, caught sight of the Elder's form shifting from Morpheus the Elder to something not human. Mortuus, taken off guard and not entirely sure of what he was seeing blinked hard, but Morpheus, whose gaze had been locked onto the fugitive, caught Mortuus' reaction and within a split second, grabbed him by his arm and pulled his large frame to a standing position with unnatural strength.

Alcander, looking surprised, addressed Socius, attempting to distract attention from Morpheus, but it was too late for subterfuge. Socius reddened, seething with anger.

"What is the meaning of this, Socius!?!" Alcander was already bellowing with a false, pompous rage. "You went outside the gates —"

Alcander stopped mid-sentence. Morpheus was making strange, claw-like motions, as if he were trying to shred Mortuus' robes. Mortuus was flailing, attempting to wrestle his arm from Morpheus' grip, which he could not, and protect himself from Morpheus' bizarre attack. At the same time Socius, who had instinctively grabbed for Mortuus' free arm and was pulling it in an attempt move Mortuus aside, inadvertently left Mortuus more open to Morpheus' "clawing." Mortuus' robe was beginning to tear. Instantly seeing his mistake, Socius released Mortuus, and confronted Morpheus directly.

"Let go Morpheus!" yelled Socius, intervening, but Morpheus, in a move faster than Socius could see, backhanded the youth with such force that Socius flew into a grassy mound over five meters away. His landing was padded by Darius, who had been standing close to Mortuus when the altercation began. Socius got to his feet quickly, stunned, wobbly, and in shock from the Elder's ferocious blow. Darius had the wind knocked out of him and lay on the ground, gasping for air.

Militus leapt into action. He had observed the violence with which his favorite student was struck and reckoned something extraordinary and unnatural was occurring. Despite his apprehension, Militus hoped he could interrupt the provocation before it escalated further. He barreled towards the Elder, with a running tackle that dislocated his shoulder with a loud crunch. Militus went to his knees, holding his shoulder when the Elder sent a kick that propelled him up and backward nearly as far as Socius. The Elder had been barely phased by Militus' attack. Mortuus swung at Morpheus, missing as the shifting Elder ducked.

"Get the horn, Alcander! Quickly!" shouted the Elder. Only this time, his voice was changed to a low, rasping tone.

Mortuus remembered this sound and knew he was in real trouble. This was a demon, like the one he had seen in the tomb area, but somehow transformed. Morpheus grabbed Mortuus by his neck one-handed; he was growling and sneering. His facade now barely stable, he pulled Mortuus' head down and rasped intimately, "You will wish you had never awakened from your eternal sleep!"

Mortuus was choking in the iron grip of the masquerading beast. Out of desperation, he grabbed the offending hand causing his distress and pulled the fingers back, breaking them like dry twigs. The creature screeched in surprised rage and retracted its broken left hand, instantly swinging at Mortuus with it's right and causing a shallow, long gash to appear on his left cheek. Mortuus, emboldened by the way he was able to easily break the digits of the beast, swung hard, connecting his fist to the creature's chin. The demon elder fell backward with a heavy thud against a nearby tree trunk. It hissed at Mortuus in a way that left no doubt as to his true identity. Now everyone watching was aware Morpheus was a demon.

Alcander was beside himself. His anger at Socius was replaced by his fear at the untimely revelation that Morpheus was a demon. A demon had been in the midst of the Elders! How had this happened?

"Wait, stop, all of you. Stop, stop, by the Gods!" yelled Alcander, looking around nervously. Everyone was still; shocked in place. Their eyes were following Morpheus who had begun inching his way towards Mortuus, hissing and crouched like a hungry, wild animal stalking it's prey. The crowd was building, yet no one could be distracted from the scene before them.

"Morpheus! Stop this now!" pleaded a now sweating Alcander.

All eyes were on Morpheus, the Elder, who was growling like a feral beast at the giant fugitive. Mortuus stared back, preparing himself for battle. The warriors, at a gesture from Militus, made a semi-circle around Mortuus, Socius and Darius, and brandished their weapons; unnerved by this first time confrontation with a demon. The tense sensation of real, serious battle had not been felt by any of them in centuries

"Fugitives! You will be tormented far worse than your sentence. I will see to it. The pitch awaits you!" snarled the demon Elder as he looked past the guards, focusing only on Mortuus. "Warrior fools, you shall share their fate for your insolence!"

"What sort of Elder are you, Morpheus?" challenged Mortuus, "These people already know you are not human. Why don't you show them your true form; the one I see before me?"

Morpheus roared like an ensnared animal, but deeply and with uncanny resonance.

"Demon!" shouted Mortuus, calling the beast out, "You have no authority in this place; you belong here no more than Plutus!"

Morpheus snarled back his reply. "I am sent by the Masters to watch these humans. You cannot escape the wrath of the Masters, and you will not escape me."

In a sudden upward bound, the creature was revealed. His form changing dramatically as he became a flyer demon, with great wings suddenly appearing behind him and bearing him straight up into the air and away from the warriors. Downward, floating, then falling, came his robes, thrown from his form as he transfigured. The crowd beyond the soldiers gasped.

"No wonder," thought Militus as he held his throbbing shoulder. The revered old warrior shouted to his men, commanding them to engage the flying beast. The warriors raised their spears, and bent their bows, but before any shot could fly, Morpheus was gone, vanishing into the misty heights. The demon's speed was faster than they could target.

Militus, in pain, rushed at a nearby tree and slammed it with his dislocated shoulder. He groaned as his shoulder pressed back into the socket. The crowding spectators, growing more numerous, started to talk amongst themselves, and in moments they turned on Alcander, shouting oaths about his treachery, allowing demons into their governance, and some began demanding to know where the missing Elders were, and why had he taken part in the conspiracy to remove them. Alcander was crushed by their comments, red in the face with embarrassment and his inability to control the crowd. Militus had some difficulty silencing them but it was imperative to get the situation under control:

"Please everyone! We will address this situation. Please, let's quiet down," yelled Militus. The crowd, many of them warriors, became silent. Mortuus, discovered, was full of thoughts of expulsion from Limbo. He distracted himself by tending to his facial wounds, wiping the blood from his body with his robes. Darius was also preparing himself for his imminent exile to outer Hell.

"Thanks all, for your peace. At this time, I would address Alcander now. Alcander? Alcander! Come back here!" yelled Militus. Alcander was on the move, afraid of the enraged crowd.

Several soldiers ran after him, tackling him to the ground. They carried him back before the crowd, kicking and screaming.

"Put me down! Put me down! I did not know! I did not know!" screamed the pot bellied elder as they placed his feet on the grass, but held on to his shoulders and arms. He was desperate, frantic. Socius came up to him, looking him squarely in the face. "Socius, you believe me don't you? Please, tell them! Socius –"

Socius stopped Alcander's words with a wave of his hand, and Militus spoke.

"Alcander. You have brought a demon among us! A *demon*, Alcander! And you complain about two simple fugitives? What madness is this!?" Militus looked at Alcander's profusely sweating face.

"I did not know, Militus. I swear to you I did not -"

Alcander's attention was suddenly engaged by something above; his eyes were widening in fear. Socius and the others followed his gaze to the demon Morpheus, who was flying overhead and descending fast. Morpheus landed near Mortuus and the surrounding warriors. Murmuring inarticulately, he motioned his left arm and the warriors who wielded their weaponry flew backward as if hit by an invisible force field. They landed harshly, each dazed. Socius was readying to attack, and Militus reached for a spear on the ground with his good arm, keeping his eyes on the demon Elder.

"Do not move, any of you, or I will flay you before I drop you into the pitch." He turned toward Mortuus and hissed; long rows of fangs bared in his wide open mouth. "You will come with me now or I will make your punishment far worse than what awaits you!"

Mortuus, expecting to be given up by the crowd appeared sad and defeated. He did not wish to have his friends sent to torment. Now they would suffer for helping him, for allowing him into Limbo. At worst, he had expected only to be exiled. Never did it occur to him the good and kindly warriors, and Socius, would suffer.

"You have enjoyed your stay here in Limbo, then?" taunted the rasping demon, smiling hideously in derision. It's eyes were dark black, with thin red veins webbing around the interior as though holding the eyeball in place.

Mortuus's face dropped, and Socius, seeing his friend in such emotional pain, struggled to find a way out of the situation. The demon continued his jeering, moving closer to Mortuus.

"You will come with m-"

That was the end of the demon's cruel taunts. Mortuus struck the beast squarely in the face, causing it to crumple into a heap. Militus looked in stunned disbelief. The shock of the sight caused the crowd to freeze. From the back, one voice shouted.

"He beat the demon!"

But the demon slowly staggered to his feet and in a daze, moved toward Mortuus slowly.

"Hit it! Hit it again!" yelled another voice. And soon, most of the crowd, along with the warriors, was cheering Mortuus on.

Mortuus struck again and the crowd cheered.

Morpheus staggering, his wings beginning to stretch out slowly, involuntarily, stared at the ground as he fought to remain on his feet. Seizing the moment, Mortuus grabbed a wing of the demon, wrapping his free arm around its neck; he constricted the creature's throat with all his might. The beast struggled desperately, doing everything in its power to rid itself of Mortuus' grasp, but it was obvious he had been weakened considerably by the stranger's two blows.

Mortuus released the wing, and forced the demon's head forward, placing him in a choke hold that would have crushed the throat and neck bones of a human.

The demon thrashed violently, falling onto the ground and rolling over on its back like it was on fire; Mortuus would not relent. After that brief struggle, it managed to get back to its feet, and crashed Mortuus against the nearby trees; Mortuus hung on with growing strength. For the spectators, it was all they could do to stay out of the way of the titanic struggle. Alcander paled; Socius barred his way many times when the Elder tried to slip away from the scene. New spectators arrived, not understanding what was happening, but attracted by the noise of the crowd.

The beast continued to claw and gouge the arms and body of Mortuus in his attempts to free himself, but after awhile, it finally began slowing down, dropping to its knees. Its flapping wings suddenly vanished into its back, disappearing, as if into thin air, retracted in the purple-tinged skin of the demon. With a final push backwards, both men fell, Mortuus underneath, holding onto the demon's neck as if he would wrench it off. The demon's arms, still clutching the forearm of Mortuus, fell limp to its sides and lay on the ground; its dark eyes rolled up into its head. All was silent.

Socius and Militus moved forward cautiously as Mortuus kept his stranglehold firm.

"Mortuus. Mortuus." Said Socius. "I believe the creature is dead. I you think you can let go."

Militus also spoke, looking at the pair on the ground. It appeared to him that Mortuus had a stranglehold on a corpse. Militus kicked at the creature's legs, not really wanting to check its eyes, and getting no involuntary response he declared,

"I think it is dead, Mortuus. Why don't you let go? We -"

Before Militus could finish his sentence, a loud explosion, and a large amount of dark black smoke lay atop Mortuus, exactly in the space where the demon Morpheus had been. Mortuus lay on the ground, choking on the smoke, his back and forearms scratched and ripped, bleeding profusely. He coughed as he gasped for air and found only smoke. Socius and Militus fanned away the black smoke and picked him up by his arms. The warriors came forward with a look of awe, clapping him on the shoulders and back. Alcander, who was trying to slip away again, was grabbed by two of the warriors.

The gathered crowd, standing in disbelief, broke out at once, cheering, whooping and hollering at the demise of a real demon. Everyone wanted to get closer to Mortuus. Darius moved near to his friend, taking Mortuus' arm from Militus, who was still nursing his sore shoulder. Socius spoke to the overjoyed crowd.

"Mortuus, the Demon Slayer!" he exclaimed exuberantly as he held up the bloodied arm of Mortuus.

He wanted to celebrate this victory -- the likes of which had never been seen in Limbo -- as loudly and as exuberantly as he could. Excitement was abounding through him and the crowd, a high never before felt in this reality. The crowd returned his joyous exuberance before Militus moved toward the youth.

"Socius," Militus interrupted, looking serious, "We must go."

Socius could see the serious look in his eyes. Turning to the soldiers, Militus began mobilizing, "We need to help our hero, men. Have any of you vials from the three waters, regeneration accelerators, or any fruits? Give some to Mortuus - as we walk. We must hide him…you men," Militus waved to a small company nearby, "disperse the crowd. We need as little attention as possible."

"What? But, why? What is wrong, Militus?" asked Socius. "We should celebrate this moment!"

"Socius, hear me. We must go now!" said Militus, deadly solemn. "This demon worked directly for the Fallen. There will be trouble, and soon."

Socius nodded his head, chagrined at the folly of his youthful exuberance. Militus was right. What repercussions would come were wholly unknown – nothing this big had ever happened before in Limbo. They must move, and move *now*. Militus looked at the men holding onto Alcander and scowled slightly.

"Bring the bureaucrat."

"Where will we go?" asked Socius. "Limbo is large, though quite finite for flying creatures and Fallen."

Just then, a medium built, cloaked figure, who had been standing in the back of the crowd, stepped forward.

"Go to the Hall of Science – they can help you."

Militus nodded his head in agreement, then gestured to a man, an ogre-ish, older warrior type who stood near the cloaked figure. The ogre-man tapped the cloaked man on the left shoulder and then grabbed him by the scruff of the neck. pushing him toward the front of the crowd roughly. Militus and Socius lifted the stranger's hood revealing a curly topped young man with pale skin, a chiseled face and bright, intelligent eyes.

"Barak!" they exclaimed synchronously.

Barak was a student of the Chronicler, the chief Historian, and the Chronicler was the oldest known resident of Limbo; a legend who was highly respected and venerated, especially by the scientists. He had witnessed Limbo change from its dark, barren landscape into the current beautiful haven. The Hall of Science even had a statue depicting the Chronicler, though very few people actually knew what he looked like. Barak was his best known student because he often traveled back and forth from the Chronicler's homestead, near Basel, almost full circle from the gate of Limbo, to the Hall of Science and the Great Library. He was a friendly sort, sharing the teachings he learned from the Chronicler and always eager to discuss the known and unknown origins of Limbo and Hell itself with a willing listener.

"Greetings old friends. It has been a long time." said Barak. He turned to face Mortuus, who was examining his wounds after drinking several vials of the waters, happily given to him by assorted warriors and members of the crowd. Mortuus, though bleeding and in pain, was enjoying the water immensely. He shared a few vials with Darius, telling him these were what he had been talking of earlier when they were at the rocky oasis.

"Take these, demon slayer." said Barak, smiling, as he held out four small, blue fruits for Mortuus. "They are from the orchards between Terni and Porto, a long walk from here. Though not as fresh as when I picked them, they will still speed your healing greatly." Mortuus took the fruits, examining them curiously, and offered his thanks. He handed two to Darius, who didn't really need them and handed them back laughing.

"I think you need these more than me, friend."

"Fellows," Barak announced loudly, "You should get to the Hall of Science. There is much to learn about a newcomer who can slay a demon with his bare hands. And there will be trouble, I am afraid." He dropped his voice to address Mortuus. "You can remain in Limbo, Mortuus, but you must go now despite your injuries. Those fruits will accelerate your regeneration." Finally, as though checking off a list that he held in his head, Barak turned to Militus,

"Militus, I am returning to the Chronicler's cottage, and will walk with you. They will need to wash and get new robes, they carry the scent of outer Hell. Incidentally, how did you manage to get two fugitives past the Elders' guards?" asked Barak.

"It was the boy," deadpanned Militus, "Socius is blossoming into either a great leader or a juvenile delinquent." Barak smiled, as did Socius.

The group began their walk deeper into Limbo, much to the joy of Mortuus and Darius. Mortuus had been certain the fight would be the last of his time inside Limbo's gate. Darius was convinced likewise, that their moment of bliss was nearly over. But now they were headed farther within the landscape. Quietly, both walked and took in the peaceful scenery, trying to make it last as long as it possibly could.

Militus left a small company of soldiers at the fields, with two men designated to be runners; if there was trouble, one of them could be dispatched to warn the traveling party. Ten soldiers accompanied, two of whom forcibly escorted Alcander. The pair of fugitives walked and ate the small fruits they had been given. Mortuus sighed contentedly, unaware of how everyone was studying him as they walked; each proud to be near the mighty demon slayer and more proud that they had trusted their friend Socius to venture out the gate. It had been a day of daring and adventure for them all.

A small subset of the crowd stayed in the fields, talking excitedly about the events they had just beheld. Adventure had come directly to them; true excitement that they had never before or ever after would expect to see again. Oft times, all had shared stories of adventure and daring. Most were from moments of their lives. None had ever, in their lives or in the afterlife, come close to what they had just observed.

Now, in Limbo, the greatest story ever told would be, 'Mortuus the Demon Slayer.'

And it had occurred right before their eyes.

Chapter 36
The Walk to Bremen

It was a long walk to Bremen, a tiny village where the Hall of Science protruded up from its center, its four stories dwarfing the surrounding small huts and cottages. The path had started euphorically for Mortuus and Darius. Each had enjoyed the fruits provided by Barak, and everyone was abuzz with Mortuus' victory over the demon Elder. Everyone except, of course, Alcander, who was prodded along by his two guards; Alcander spent most of the time trying to explain that he had no idea Morpheus was a demon. Militus was so angry that he threatened to gag the ranting Alcander until they reached Bremen. To the great relief of all, Alcander finally conceded and remained quiet.

The soldiers who were escorting the group continued to ask question after question of Mortuus. All wanted to congratulate Mortuus on his victory, and they invited him to partake of their battle games, should he feel up to it at a later time. Mortuus replied that he had had all the battle games he could take outside the walls of Limbo, but he did thank them for their offer, saying it was an honor to be asked.

Socius filled in Mortuus and Darius about Benjamin. Benjamin was the chief scientist of Limbo, and had worked in the Hall of Science for many centuries. The Hall of Science was responsible for all of the agricultural and manufacturing development and processing. Benjamin, ever curious and always tinkering, had overseen many of the initial developments which led to making Limbo the green, beautiful countryside it had become; he was renowned for his work.

"Agriculture?" asked Darius. "What need have they here for growing foods in a large scale?"

"Not just foods," replied Socius, "but plants for dyes and regeneratives, and of course, wines. Some here have quite a taste for the foods, even though they do not hunger. It reminds them of their lives, mostly, and makes them feel normal. I, having been raised here, actually do hunger."

"That is a slight understatement," Militus chimed in jokingly. "The boy can eat! His appetite is legendary!" Barak laughed loudly at this.

"He is a growing boy, Militus," added Barak. "No others have ever grown here. Socius is truly one of the many wonders of Hell."

"What of earlier times?" asked Mortuus. "What existed here before the Hall of Science came to be?"

Militus answered, "It was darker, Mortuus. And these walls did not exist."

Mortuus looked at the walls to his left and right. They were never far out of sight unless the group passed through a well treed section of path, but even then there were always peepholes that revealed more walls. It was a constant reminder to Mortuus that Hell was never far away.

"When I first arrived, there was little to separate us from the outside," continued Militus, "The only benefit to being placed in Limbo was that we were not tormented. We could talk with each other, but always to the background noise and odor of Hell."

"How did you get the walls built? They are so high." said Mortuus.

"When the first plants and trees were developed by the scientists and then cultivated successfully, the Fallen erected the walls." said Militus. " In a matter of days, the walls, as you see them, were constructed. We saw no Fallen, nor any of their workers, perform the magic required to build anything so large, but we do know where they got the rock. Strangely, no one witnessed the construction either; we are certain it was Fallen magic. The scientists believe that the Fallen wished to contain the plants we had cultivated within Limbo. They believe the Fallen do not want to even allow a glimmer of hope to the damned."

"What do you mean, Militus?" asked Mortuus.

"The plants and trees here grow very quickly. Do you not enjoy their beauty?" asked Militus.

"I do. And if I understand your meaning," replied Mortuus, "Hell would not be a proper place of torment with beautiful plants and trees growing everywhere. The Fallen magic must be very powerful to achieve such great feats of architecture. Did they also build the Great Library and the Hall of Science?"

"No," answered Militus, "The Fallen do not care for our scientific or educational progress. We have much time on our hands, and so we are able to do quite a bit of building. The walls are the only gifts from the Fallen. They also keep out the fugitives. Once the walls were in place, the odors and sounds diminished; more so as we cultivated greater areas of Limbo. Did you notice the freshness of the air when you entered the gate?"

"Yes. I enjoyed the air more than I can say, Militus. I am still enjoying it. How does Limbo have this brightness? I see no source of light. Outer hell is only gray, or black and white."

"I can help answer your question." Barak interjected, "The plant from which most of the other plant life was developed actually glows from within itself. I do not recall the name of the plant, but the glow is very strong. It is believed the plant was discovered by the Chronicler himself and given to the scientists."

"Your curiosity is refreshing, Mortuus." said Militus. "You can get many questions answered better by Benjamin. He is an odd fellow, very quirky and very smart."

The group continued walking for some time before anyone spoke again. This time it was Socius who started the conversation.

"Darius, do you have any idea where your friends were taken to? Did the demons speak before they took Panos and Aetos?" said the youth.

"I was hidden in such a way that I could not overhear any of their conversation. It was all rasping and growls only." said Darius. But before we escaped from the torment of the Hell Flies, we spoke with another who had escaped and had been captured. His name was Philo. Philo, knowing we contemplated escape, repeatedly told us the fate of all fugitives is in the boiling pitch of the Eighth Circle. He somehow managed to escape the pitch and return to the Vestibule, swearing he would not ever attempt escape again. He warned us many times before our flight from the Hell Fly captivity."

"Your fate is the same, Darius." warned Alcander, a smug priggishness. "You should have listened to Philo."

"Still your tongue, fool Elder." snapped Militus. "Or I will cut it out."

"You too, Militus," the pot-bellied bureaucrat sneered, "In fact, all of you will share it. Aristotle already knows of what I speak. He disregarded our advice for the last time!" Alcander, used to his Elder's privilege for too long, forgot his place and was not aware at first of what he had revealed.

"What do you mean?" said Socius, who stepped directly in front of Alcander. "Tell me now, Alcander."

Alcander realizing suddenly what he had just said, clamped up, and did not elaborate. He choked and stumbled on his words, attempting to lie at first, then trying to take back his statement as the group closed in, curious and angry at his treachery.

"Aristotle has been taken." admitted Alcander weakly. "He would not listen to reason." Alcander hung his head, as if in defeat. "There is no coming back. The Fallen were very angry that Aristotle had been wandering for so long a time." And with that, silence ensued for a short while.

Thus, the trip to Bremen, which started happily, ended in mourning. Socius, beside himself with grief, walked away from the group and stood near a tree with his head down, shoulders trembling slightly. Everyone waited and watched sadly as his inconsolable anguish released itself in quiet paroxysms of despair. It had been hundreds of years and Socius never imagined he could lose the closest person to him. He had to reach for the tree to support himself when his legs began giving way. Everyone remained quiet until Socius returned. Militus, another father figure to Socius, stared helplessly, heartbroken at the great loss to this centuries-old youth. Militus had thought Aristotle a fool for his wanderings outside of Limbo, but he did respect the care and love that Aristotle provided in the upbringing of this most beloved student. What would the boy do now?

Aristotle was lost forever.

Chapter 37

Meeting Benjamin

They arrived in a field just outside of Bremen many hours later, still reeling from the revelation of Aristotle's abduction by the Fallen and their demons. The field would be a better location, according to Militus, as they would need to be as discrete as possible for the sake of Mortuus and Darius. The pair of newcomers still wore their ripped and stained clothing, and would stand out greatly against the common garb of the people of Limbo.

Militus left them and went to find the senior scientist, Benjamin. Socius kept to himself, unwilling to be consoled by the others. Alcander was laid down on the field by the guards that had carried him. Since the revelation concerning his awareness of and apparent collusion in Aristotle's capture, Alcander had been incapacitated, unable to keep up with the pace of the group. His face was bruised badly, his jaw broken, and he still spat out blood and teeth from the severe beating that Socius had given him. In the end, no one could pull Socius off of Alcander except Mortuus. Alcander had been screaming through most of the onslaught. Now he lay on the field, broken and injured. The guards had been careful to keep him far from Socius, who sat and stared into the forest surrounding the field. Mortuus and Darius sat with the soldiers and Barak.

"You will like the scientist," said Barak, addressing Mortuus and Darius. "He is the one to direct all of your questions."

"Why is it that we are meeting the scientist?" asked Mortuus.

"You have *slain* a true demon," answered Barak, "Something we did not know to be possible; and along with the mystery of your strange origin, it becomes more apparent that you were being hidden for a reason. We need to find that reason; what if your concealment was because you are a threat to the Fallen? We believe the scientist may have some idea of your identity. I am certain he will be very excited to meet with you."

Mortuus contemplated everything Barak was saying, but was doubtful. "How is it possible for me to be a threat to the Fallen, Barak?" he asked. "I beat the demon, but barely."

"You have been unconscious for many years, Mortuus. You have barely awoken, yet you had enough strength to best the demon. And, not just any demon; Morpheus was a high demon, one of the most powerful that exists. He was a magic user, so we know he has intelligence and great strength. You saw what happened when Militus tackled him." Mortuus nodded, recalling the demon's near indifference to the running tackle against him that dislocated Militus' shoulder.

"I look forward to meeting your scientist, Barak." said Mortuus. Just as he spoke, Militus returned from the path into Bremen. At his side was a strangely built man who walked oddly, his head slightly forward of his upper body. His eyes bulged outward from his head, and he examined each person in the group, scanning. His nose, rather large and pointed, began twitching as he sniffed the air around the group.

"My friends." said Militus. "Allow me to introduce you to Benjamin." The strange man nodded to everyone, and looked across the field at Socius and further away at the recovering Alcander.

"Why is Socius sitting by himself, Militus?" asked the scientist. "And is that Alcander, the Elder, lying out over there?"

"Socius needs some time to himself for now, Benjamin. And yes, that is Alcander."

"He appears to need some regeneratives.' said Benjamin. "I can go to my hut and –"

"Do not concern yourself with Alcander, Benjamin. I will fill you in later. We need to ask you about our two new arrivals." He pointed to Mortuus and Darius and introduced each.

The pair smiled at the quirky scientist, who sniffed the air again.

"You are fugitives?" asked Benjamin. Mortuus nodded, uncomfortably.

"Militus, we must get these two washed up. They stink of outer Hell." said Benjamin. "Let us go to the First Waters. They can drink and cleanse themselves. We will take the path around Bremen. Once they are properly dressed and washed, no one will suspect their origins."

As they made ready to head toward the First Waters, Benjamin queried, "I am very curious as to why you have brought fugitives into Limbo, Militus. I know you do not approve of Aristotle's venturing outside."

"Shhh, Benjamin." whispered Militus. "I will explain as we walk. Please, do not speak Aristotle's name again." Benjamin, surprised, looked inquisitively at Militus.

They walked to the First Waters and along the way Militus quietly filled him in on Aristotle's capture, and Alcander's beating by Socius. Mortuus and Darius, passing through the path against the wall, saw the towering building of the Hall of Science jutting high into the air and slowed to a halt, awestruck. Barak chuckled, enjoying their reactions to this architectural wonder and recalling his own amazement long ago, on his first encounter with the magnificent building.

They arrived at the First Waters following a few hours of walk. All were tired except for Mortuus and Darius, who continued to take in the splendor of Limbo, enjoying each moment. Neither had been there long enough to take any of the scenery for granted.

The First Waters was a large pool of water, flowing out of a rock face. The rock, the size of a small cottage, was partially covered in a greenish hue where the water touched it. The water moved quickly, and the swirls and eddies of the pool flowed in the same direction as the group. Mortuus, compelled by the beauty of the clear flowing stream, walked right up to the edge, wondering if this was the same water as was in the vials. One of the soldiers told Mortuus to drink his fill; the water in the vials was indeed the same, but straight from the source it would be far more delicious. Mortuus needed no convincing. He lay on his chest and drank deeply, beyond his needs. Benjamin and Militus stopped walking and turned to watch.

Mortuus finally turned over, and lay on the bank. He was overfull, but did not wish to leave. His awakening had been a Hellish nightmare of deep dehydration. Were it not for Aristotle's vials, he would have failed to make it to Limbo.

"Mortuus, we must go to the far end of the water." said Militus. "You and Darius will need to wash there. The current is much too dangerous here."

Mortuus, feeling stronger and more vital, stood up and followed. They walked along the edge of the water for another hour or so before reaching a quiet pool. The water flowed into another rock face, filtering between stones and small boulders and disappearing underground. This, explained Barak, was the end of the First Waters.

Benjamin encouraged the pair of fugitives to wash themselves in the pool. It was very cold, but felt even better than the pool within the rocky oasis of the Vestibule. Socius, who had been following silently behind the group, also disrobed and entered the cool water, diving into the deepest part of the pool. It helped to revive his spirits, and Benjamin, now aware of Aristotle's predicament, felt it to be a good sign.

Militus set the soldiers to guarding the paths into and out of the area. He wanted to have no interruptions or surprises while they consulted Benjamin. Alcander was taken to a nearby wooded area to be concealed for the duration of their meeting.

The pair finished their swim, feeling the most alive either had since being in Hell. Benjamin, Militus and Barak were sitting on a circle of mossy boulders, waiting as they dressed. Socius came out shortly after, and joined the circle along with Mortuus and Darius.

Benjamin began the discussion.

"My friends, I have heard most of your stories from Militus and Barak as you swam. It seems that Aristotle has awakened a giant, so to speak. Mortuus, do you recall anything of your former life before the sleep?" Mortuus shook his head as he answered.

"I recall nothing. It is as if I have been born as you see me, for I have no recollection of a living life." said Mortuus. "I have feelings sometimes, but nothing to attach them to."

"You will need to regenerate for a much longer time before your memories return." said Benjamin. "I was studying the sample vial of the green liquid you and the others were force-fed; your benefactor delivered a vial of it to me by way of Socius after he returned from waking you. I believe that it was what kept you and your fellows in the sleep, and most likely also had a hand in erasing your memories."

"Have you completed your study of the liquid then, Benjamin?" asked Socius.

"I'm afraid not, Socius, the vial disappeared from my lab without a trace before I finished my analysis. Based on the log of Aristotle, however, I can well conclude what the fluid did. I also was able to discern an herb, discovered and brought to me by

Aristotle that is known to slow regeneration; it grows along the edge of the Styx. It has a strong, unique odor when dried and ground. I believe the other components probably destroyed memories and kept you asleep, then this herb inhibited your brain from regenerating, thus enhancing the effects of the other components."

"But how did your sample disappear Benjamin?" asked Socius. "Are the assistants and other scientists not trustworthy?"

"I have my suspicions, Socius. There is another reason I did not bring you all into Bremen and the Hall of Science. But I will work that out myself. Now on to my next question. I have heard a commotion that something happened in Elysius recently. Would that be —"

"Mortuus destroyed a demon, Benjamin!" blurted Socius.

Benjamin studied Mortuus, his eyes scanning, searching his face.

"A demon? You destroyed one of them?" asked an incredulous Benjamin. "Was it a flyer, one of the smithies from the whirlpool area?"

"No. This one was disguised as an Elder." said Barak. That is why we brought along Alcander." Alcander was with the beast when it was found out by Mortuus. Mortuus saw right through the magic before any of us suspected."

"You saw through it? Is this verifiable, Militus?" asked Benjamin, growing more skeptical. "I would prefer more verif-"

"I saw it myself." said Militus. "Do you see my shoulder? I struck the beast with a running blow. It was as if I had charged against the boulder I sit upon. Socius and Darius were also witness to it, along with my men, who now watch the paths."

"Oh my. Oh no." said Benjamin, weakly. His face had turned a pale white. "They can change form? Then we are being infiltrated by the beasts. They will seek you as soon as they discover your absence, Mortuus. Oh my. They are among us." Benjamin's look of worry was infectious; the whole circle sat, grim-faced, looking at each other, no one knowing what to say.

'Why did no one tell me this as we walked?" asked the scientist. "The most famous event of our after-lives and you all held your tongues? No wonder your soldiers were so talkative the whole way. I should have walked along with them!"

"Things were still...delicate...after Alcander's revelation." said Barak warily. Militus nodded in agreement. Benjamin looked at Socius, who appeared somber-faced again, then decided to discontinue pursuing the subject.

"Mortuus, you must be taken to the Chronicler, but I would first have you meet Clavius." said Benjamin.

"Clavius?" uttered Socius. "Why Clavius? Where does he reside these days?"

"Clavius will test Mortuus." said Benjamin. "If Mortuus passes the test, and I am sure he will, Clavius will take him to the Chronicler. We are in dangerous times, and I believe I must go back to the Hall of Science and get some things. I realize you are skeptical, Militus, but I believe the time is nearing."

"You cannot be serious, Benjamin," replied Militus.

"Look at the signs, Militus," said Barak. "Demons living among us? Mortuus destroying one barehanded? What more do you require?"

"But where will we go? There is no escaping Hell," countered Militus, obviously troubled.

"Ahhh, yes. That has been the prevailing wisdom for thousands of years..." Benjamin, sniffing the air, blinked a couple of times looking upwards at nothing anyone else could see and continued, "But for those same thousands of years it was also 'true' that there were no beings who could destroy a demon barehanded either, Militus."

"Do your eyes lie to you?" Barak intervened, "You claim to be a witness. How come the demon did not use his magic on Mortuus as it did your soldiers?" Barak was recalling how the demon Morpheus cast a single spell that sent the soldiers flying backward. Militus grimaced.

"The demon could have cast that spell and many others upon Mortuus," advised Barak. It would not have worked. It knew this."

Worry swept across the General's face.

"Very well. I believe this may be the timing," conceded Militus. "But I do not know if we are prepared or if I am the best leader."

"You are the best we have, Militus, a noble and worthy leader, and all your men would follow you into the depths of Hell. The signs are here; we have been complacent long enough. The time to leave Hell is approaching." Benjamin turned to the group, resolved and with an assured authority in his voice.

"My friends, you must go now to Porto. Barak, take them to Clavius, and get them new robes. Stop by the Second Waters, carefully, and have them drink also. Now you must go."

And to Militus, "Gather your men, Militus. I would have you escort me to the Hall in Bremen." Nodding in the direction of Socius, Barak, Mortuus and Darius, "These four will travel alone; a small group will draw much less attention. Have your men bring Alcander also. We may have need of him."

To the four, Benjamin was somber but positive, "My friends, goodbye for now, until we meet again."

Militus whistled, and his soldiers returned within a few moments. He and the soldiers said their goodbyes to Barak, Socius, Darius and Mortuus, then ran to catch up with Benjamin, who was already far up the path. Alcander and his two guards followed the pack slowly.

"My god." said Barak. "I have never seen Benjamin this excited before. He is right; we must be on our way." The four began their trek to Porto, to meet Clavius, and then the Chronicler. They walked along in silence until Mortuus could stand it no more.

"Did he say *leave* Hell?" asked Mortuus.

Chapter 38

Panos On Fire

Panos lay writhing on the burning sand. His intestines and entrails had been ripped out of him, and lay beside him, baked dry in the oven-heat of this flat plain, until he had enough strength to gather and pull them back into his exposed abdomen. It was a slow process; the heat of the sand was intense enough to brown his back and sides where he had landed. On occasion, a falling ball of flame would strike his body, causing him to scream outright despite his lack of energy. The flame burned brightly for a few moments, and then hissed out, seeming to mock Panos's shrieks.

All around, Panos saw groups of people running across the plain, sometimes coming up close to him in their curiosity, but never staying long. They were naked, or only in blackened shards of clothing, always almost bare and blistered. They would run and rejoin their pack in short order, lifting their feet in an absurd dance to gain a moment from the intense burning. One passing man of small, thin frame yelled at him, requesting to know why he was here and how he had fallen from the sky. Apparently there were witnesses who saw the demons drop him. Panos had fully expected the demons to come back for him. When they did not, he was as relieved as a person being roasted on a burning bed of sand could be.

Many hours went by before Panos was able to sit up. The sand clung, sticking to his melted skin, and continued to burn until Panos could brush it off. As he did so well in his life as a traveler, Panos was looking around trying to orient himself to the environment. As far as he could see in the heat-distorted landscape, there was only sand and random falling flame. Knowing his pain would be reduced if he was on his feet, Panos stood up. His right leg, not fully mended from the fall, gave a loud snap, and Panos dropped with a yell to the burning sandy floor. He lay writhing again.

In his life, he had once journeyed across a great desert with nomadic traders, one of his many traveling adventures. He remembered thinking on his trip that Hell could not be any hotter.

He snickered to himself, though his face and body showed no signs of snickering. "I guess I was wrong," he thought.

He had to move. He knew it was the only way, so conjuring all his willpower, Panos began to roll and crawl like an oddly cocooned worm, turning his lean body over, and side to side, to permit temporary relief in the worst burnt areas. He needed to get off of this burning desert. But how?

One of the groups passed near him. The skinny man yelled out again.

"Get to the rill! It is ahead, far in front of us. Get to the rill!" The man's voice trailed off as the frail, burnt man, pointing into the distance ahead, was gone with his group. Panos began dragging himself in the direction of the group, wincing in pain.

He would get to the rill.

Chapter 39
The Miners of the Pit

"Socius, why would Benjamin speak of leaving this place?" asked Mortuus. The group, currently composed of Darius, Socius, Mortuus, and Barak, had just left the First Waters, and was proceeding toward Graz, the next small village clockwise in the circle Limbo occupied.

"I don't know Mortuus," answered the youth, "Benjamin is privy to many bits of knowledge of which I am ignorant, and this news is impossible to me as well. I have only left Limbo once, and that was to retrieve you. We almost returned without you; once beyond the gate we became almost paralyzed by the sounds and odor of Outer Hell."

"You would not want to leave after having been outside these walls. I am most grateful to Aristotle for awakening me, but I don't know that I would have ventured outside the gate, as he did." Mortuus shook his head pensively.

Socius had considered leaving with Aristotle to journey around on many occasions. Aristotle always abruptly dismissed Socius' requests. After his short departure from Limbo to retrieve Mortuus, Socius understood. Aristotle would sometimes answer "when you are ready, only a few thousand years more." And no one else in Limbo would even entertain Socius' suggestions on the matter.

"I requested to journey with Aristotle many times, Mortuus. He always refused me, and though I argued the point, he would not be persuaded." Socius was seized with sadness as the memory of his teacher in torment forever surfaced again; his face could not hide his feelings. "I'm not sure what I will do, now that he is gone forever."

"The demon spoke of the pitch, as have you Darius." said Mortuus. "Where is this area? Has Aristotle ever visited it in his explorations?"

"The pitch is said to be in the Eighth Circle." replied Barak.

"Aristotle was never able to travel beyond the Seventh Circle," Socius explained, "It is said to be occupied by the worst of Hell's workers, and a giant flying beast who patrols the outer wall and rim." Socius, pain on his face, trailed off. He was growing sadder as they spoke of Aristotle; Mortuus discontinued any further inquiries, and the group continued walking.

The landscape became abruptly rocky and uneven, although it remained green in small patches, where grasses found small holes and cracks of soil. Brightly colored lichens grew on boulders and strips of rock. The rockiness stretched on for awhile, and though the rock coloring was dark, the landscape was unusually brightly lit. The terrain gradually became more boulder-strewn, with smaller trees sparsely scattered. The walls on either side of Limbo were a constant reminder to Mortuus that Hell was eternally present on the other side of the facade.

Now the terrain flattened as they approached Graz, the next populated village. Mortuus and Darius peeked inside the doorways of several cottages and saw people talking around fireplaces and tables, others with books spread out, and still others who stared at the quartet warily. The doorways were carved with flowering vines, flowers, fruits, animals or geometric shapes. The village had a cobblestone path winding through it. Darius noticed the cobblestones were engraved, just like the doorways, in an ornate fashion.

"Barak?" asked Darius. "Why do the people of this village engrave their road stones?" Barak looked at the stones, considering the many shapes and wordings.

"In this village, many artists and art appreciators congregate. They desire to make everything around them beauteous," answered Barak.

"Even the cobblestones? I understand the woodwork on the doorways, but isn't it a bit tedious to shape and craft every stone?"

Barak chided, "Well, if you would be logical, there is little need here for a cobblestone path, Darius. The people did not have to bother themselves, but they created this path anyway. Though it seems overly decorative, we do have a lot of time when eternity is the measure."

Darius nodded in good humor to his companions' grins.

"Of course, of course," he muttered with a shy grin. "I knew that. Perhaps I will also have too much time to spend here, and I too will become an artisan road stone carver. This is what I wish for."

The carved stone path took them out to the other side of Graz in short order, where they continued walking through more rocky terrain, and two smaller villages; the first, Almere, on their left, and the second village, Rennes, on the right. Socius and Barak began talking just past Rennes.

"Barak, what was Benjamin talking about when he said we have been complacent?" inquired Socius. Barak was hesitant to answer, trying to decide what he should share with Socius, and what he should hold back. He was uncomfortable keeping the information from his friend, but there were some controversies that were too dangerous to share with anyone. Still, it was Benjamin that had opened this Pandora's Box, and Socius was a trustworthy friend. The events which had recently unfolded could only mean the change that had been foretold since the earliest days was in progress. They would consult Clavius to confirm this fact.

"I will tell you, Socius. I will tell you all just as soon as we see Clavius. For now, I will not alarm you and our guests needlessly. I ask for your patience until we visit Clavius." Socius, Mortuus and Darius were more curious than ever. "I promise to give you full disclosure *when* we get confirmation. Please save the questions which I see already on your faces." The three men, staring at Barak, were silent, stifling their many questions.

They soon approached very large piles of stone and small boulders, stacked directly in front of the path. Barak led them to the left, where it appeared the stone piles went all the way to the wall on the Acheron-side of Limbo. The path directly narrowed so that only a single person could pass through at a time, squeezing between smaller rock piles that had been assembled purposely to alter the trail.

Almost at the wall, an opening appeared on the right, and the men followed it to a giant excavated pit, rounded, with ledges of concentric circling paths. There was a slope from each ledge down into the ledge below it. A tiny building stood at the bottom center, and there were entryways into two tunnels visible from the location of the four. The rock piles were scattered all around the crater, blocking an easy trek through this area. A ledge went around from their edge on the right side, all the way around to a small opening that was the continuation of the path they were on. Moving toward the edge of the pit, Mortuus looked down to see that they were quite far from the bottom. It was perhaps the most uninviting scenery he had beheld since entering Limbo; a picture of man-made devastation that seemed a blight to even the barren rocky landscape. He hoped the area beyond the pit would return to the well-treed, grassy forest floor that he had come to love in his short time in Limbo.

"You see the ledge around the pit?" said Barak, addressing Mortuus and Darius. "We'll take it to the other side. This, by the way, is where we mine metals. This pit was created long ago, when the walls were constructed, and only now is it providing us with a good amount of metal ore. The ores are refined in the building at the bottom – it's bigger than it appears from our vantage point, and –"

"Barak, Socius, look! Demons!" warned Mortuus in a loud whisper. Barak moved closer, holding his hands up to signal Mortuus to silence.

Far across the giant pit, two large flyer demons had suddenly appeared from behind a large rock pile, and looked as if they were flying straight for the men. As soon as they neared the center of the pit, they dove, circling downward until they at last pulled their wings in and landed roughly, near one of the mine entrances. Mortuus and Darius looked at Barak, surprised to see him appear undisturbed by the menacing presence of the creatures.

"We will wait until they finish their business and leave the mine. It will not be long. Let's have a seat back behind the piles, where we came in." said Barak pointing backward toward the path between the piles. The men walked until they were hidden within the pit entrance, though Barak sat just near enough to see into the open area.

"For your information, those demons work in the smith shop adjoining the whirlpool building, which we are going to avoid. They come to the pit to take a share of the refined metals." said Barak.

"What do the demons do with metal?" asked Darius.

"The demons have a forge in their smithy shop. Some of our better blacksmiths have dared to venture inside to see what kind of instruments they create, but they were quickly chased away. It's said that they use magic to forge their weapons. I would surmise that is mainly because they have no skills of their own." said Barak. "As for the use, I expect their hooks and other crude torture devices are created from the ore."

"Who is required to mine the ore?" asked Mortuus.

"No one is *required* to mine" said Barak. "Believe it or not, our chief miner, Eruo, and his fellows actually enjoy the digging. Some folks like to get their hands dirty once in a while."

"He enjoys mining? Isn't that dangerous? Do they have cave-ins, or get trapped?" asked Darius. "I don't see the point of it." Darius had developed his own subservient philosophy of survival that he hadn't shaken in all his years on earth and in the Vestibule. It was along the lines of, don't do anything you aren't told to and find the quickest, most efficient way of getting through each task because there is no art or enjoyment to it. All toil, in Darius' mind, was duty, effort, burden, grind.

"Eruo has had a few troubles in the mines, but after many centuries, he's pretty well got it down. Some folks like the dig, some do it for the common good, others for a change of scenery. Limbo will get boring after you've been here a few years." Barak smiled and winked at Mortuus, forgetting the angst of Socius momentarily, "Lucky for you both that Aristotle felt the same way."

Seeing Socius' grim face, Barak corrected himself with a cough of embarrassment and looked out over the pit, motioning the others to come silently behind him.

"Look there my friends. The creatures carry a load of refined iron in their sacks."

The three men gathered around behind Barak, and saw far away, the creatures, each heavily burdened with a large sack, bigger than their bodies. The sacks appeared too big to be carried by the winged demons, yet, one by one, they flew upward with relative ease.

"Magic." said Barak abruptly. "We believe they have temporarily removed the mass from the iron. The magic will wear off after they return to the smithy."

"Amazing!" said Darius.

"How do you know of this magic, Barak?" asked Socius.

"Long ago, the Great Library contained many books on Fallen magic." said Barak. "No one could read or understand the tomes. In fact, the books were quite large and heavy, so rare few even attempted to borrow them. Then, one day, mysteriously, the tomes disappeared. No one ever learned how or why."

"Why could no one read the books, Barak?" asked Mortuus.

"They were written in the language of the Angelics." replied Barak. "None except for the Fallen can understand."

"Angelics?" asked Mortuus, his interest piqued.

"They are more commonly referred to as Angels," answered Barak. "The Chronicler believes Aristotle found the missing tomes just before awakening you, Mortuus." Socius became excited.

"The tomes in the room before the Hallway!" he cried, "Of course! But why hide them if no one can interpret the language?"

"Because someone deciphered the language." said Darius. "Or the Fallen believed someone had. Or could."

"Very good, Darius." said Barak. "Fallen magic can be very powerful. In the wrong hands, it could be used against the Fallen. We believe they came to understand this, and hid the books in their secret undertomb area. Another reason for their anger with Aristotle."

"So you have read the latest logs of Aristotle." said Socius. "How did you find out th-" Barak, still watching the flying demons, interrupted Socius.

"In good time, Socius." replied Barak. "We must get past the pit before the beasts return."

The group crossed the pit via the narrow ledge around the top. The rocks were small and bothered the feet of those who were barefooted, namely Mortuus and Darius, but they did not complain. Barak kept a quick pace, constantly scanning ahead for demons. When they had almost reached the far side, two men, miners, shouted up from the bottom of the pit, waving at the group to wait. The miners climbed fast, using handholds to scale the walls straight up to the ledge where the four men stood.

"Hail thee Barak! What news have you?" asked one of the miners. Barak nodded his head, chuckling. Abreo, a short, plump, round-faced man, dirty from the mine dust, approached like a pre-pubescent boy, innocent and friendly, smiling white teeth emphasizing the dirt on his face. Barak was reminded of a dog he had loved in his life, which would wag its tail furiously at the sight of any newcomer. Behind Abreo, a taller, more serious looking miner, also covered in the dust, walked toward the group, eyeballing Darius and Mortuus suspiciously. He was a grim sort, and contrasted sharply with his fellow miner in gaunt appearance and behavior toward the transiting group. He had immediately altered his gait upon sighting the garb of Mortuus and Darius. It made the pair of newcomers to Limbo self-conscious.

"Hello Abreo, Exaro." said Barak. "We need to pass through before the demons return. May I speak with you of your news later? We must avoid the flyers." said Barak.

"They will not return for some time, Barak. They have cleaned out all of our stockpiles. At least they believe they have." said Abreo, smiling mischievously and winking.

"Well, good news then. What other news have you, Abreo? I know you well enough to see it is you who have information to share. You may go first; I know I can hardly get a word in when you have something on your mind. Speak to us Abreo."

Abreo was looking at the other three men, particularly Mortuus. "Oh yes, introductions first. Abreo, Exaro, these are our friends Darius and Mortuus, and you know-"

"Socius! It has been forever! Look how you have grown! He is getting big, isn't he Exaro? I think it's been almost a century since – " The chubby miner was cut off by his associate.

"Far longer, Abreo." Exaro teased. "Why do you wait so long my friend? I know you do not like the underground, or the company we keep..."

Barak whispered a clarification to Darius and Mortuus. "He means the demons."

"...But we'll come out for you if you visit once in a while." Exaro looked at Mortuus and Darius, studying them again.

"Newcomers?" Exaro prodded as he examined them toe to head, stopping and staring abruptly at Darius. "Why do you wear the robes of outer Hell? I..."

"Exaro, mind your business." quipped Abreo, seeing the discomfort on the faces of the four men. The mood changed to uncertainty, and Abreo was doing what he could to remedy it. He was also curious about these men, but his desire to know did not supersede his desire for good manners. And he wanted badly to share his news, above all.

"I'm sorry - we cannot stay and talk my friends." said Socius. Barak was looking at him and nodding. Socius did not want Mortuus and Darius put off by these old acquaintances, nor did Socius want any information about the fact that they were not proper inhabitants of Limbo known outside of a few people. "We have to move on - we have business past Basel."

"Wait my friends." pleaded Abreo. "Please excuse Exaro's...abruptness. I have news that I would discuss with you. It will not take long. Then you can continue on your journey. But please stay, just a bit longer."

"I am afraid of your demon guests returning, Abreo. Really, we should be going," said Barak, "But I promise to return and visit for as long as you like, later." Barak was using this as an excuse to get away before the unwanted questioning continued. Mortuus and Darius stood, not knowing how to act in this uncomfortable situation. "I give you my word-"

"Hear me out, Barak, Socius. Believe me, there will be no demons, not for a long time. They took a great share of our latest work just before you arrived. Your friends are welcome, by all means." Abreo turned to Exaro, and shot him a glance, indicating he should affirm Abreo's assertion.

"Stay, friends. Please. You should hear this." said a more softened and duly chastised Exaro. He looked pleadingly at the four.

Socius nodded at Barak, who reluctantly agreed. All six men sat on the ground. Smiling and anxious, Abreo told his news like an anxious gossip. His manner was solemn, but his countenance could not portray such seriousness, like a small child who describes an event with importance far beyond his years. It was an endearing quality of Abreo's, and he had no clue whatsoever it existed.

"Many centuries ago, as you know, we began mining f-". Exaro cut him off sharply.

"To the point already, Abreo. Barak can listen to the Chronicler if he needs the entire history of Limbo." He was a no nonsense sort, and he knew his friend would recite the history of mining in Limbo from the beginning of time if he was left to his own devices. Abreo gave a mock salty look in his naturally humorous way, then restarted.

"We speak with the demons on occasion to find out what they know or what they may be up to. On this last visit, they were quite anxious to take as much iron as we had, not that they usually leave us much anyway. Did any of you notice the size of the load they carried?" The four nodded. "It was quite large," answered Barak.

Abreo continued, "They are in chaos. It seems that they have a secret area in the tombs. That's the Seventh Circle, by the way."

"Sixth," corrected Socius.

"Right. The Sixth Circle," said Abreo. "They have an underground where they keep prisoners isolated and unconscious. This area is unknown to most of the demons, and is visited by Fallen regularly."

"How do you know of this?" asked Socius.

"Eruo," replied Exaro, "He speaks with them." Abreo nodded in agreement as the four men appeared to be in shock. Abreo spoke again. "On this visit, they were angry, speaking of the 'wrath of the masters' that came upon their fellows who work in that secret underground. One captive escaped, and they only very recently found out about it. The Fallen were so angry, they destroyed their own workers. Probably through some sort of magic I suppose. They relocated several workers from the whirlpool building to replace them. To top it off, they have upped the expected quotas of weaponry from the pool house smithies."

"Demons," whispered Barak to Mortuus and Darius.

"Yes, worker demons. And that is why I was so certain they would not return while we spoke, Barak. They have more than enough metals and far fewer hands to forge their weapons. That last pair was as bedraggled looking as I've ever seen them." Abreo took a deep breath as his story came to an end, "...And that is all I needed to tell you." Looking around at his guests, Abreo proceeded carefully, "I must say, you ventured past our pit at quite an interesting time." He spoke slowly and deliberately, "I will not question it, and nor will Exaro," Abreo said, nodding in Exaro's direction, "I will only say I am quite curious... and... I would like to hear your new friends' stories sometime." Abreo was running out of hints, but his curiosity was overwhelming, "Pity you must be going. This giant one looks to have quite a good story. I have never seen such robes either. I don't believe any of the weavers in Porto carry such fine threads."

Mortuus and Darius glanced at each other, waiting for either Barak or Socius to make a move. These were their friends, after all.

"And now you are being rude, Abreo." said Exaro. "We must let our friends continue their trek, though I, admittedly, am also curious. I will not, however, hold you to remain longer if you desire to leave. We do enjoy the company, and Abreo was getting unbearable and really needed to share the news."

"And it is good you have shared this news, Abreo. Barak, I think we need to trust our friends." said Socius finally. "May I share our news?"

"Very well," said Barak after a few moments.

Socius began recounting the story of the newly arrived pair, and everything he knew since Aristotle awakened Mortuus. Very early on in the telling, Abreo and Exaro were both pleased that they had persuaded the group to stay.

It was a long tale, uninterrupted by flying demons.

Chapter 40
Clavius' Secret

Abreo and Exaro were beside themselves. After listening to Socius, and confirming his recollection of events with Mortuus and Darius, the two miners quizzed the pair intensely. Abreo asked Darius about the gate, as he had a longstanding belief that if any newcomer had just turned around he might be able to go back out the way he came. Exaro scoffed as Darius told of his attempts to exit. Both miners were in complete disbelief at the story of Charon's drowning until hearing Socius' eyewitness account of seeing the empty skiff. Abreo got excited over the incident of Mortuus and the demon Morpheus, clapping his hands in a victorious display.

"He does not much like demons." said Exaro as he pointed at Abreo. "One of them kicked him around when it thought he was hiding extra supplies."

"Of course, I *was*," replied Abreo. "But we always do. This one just decided to have a problem about it. I felt like I had been trampled by a herd of bulls. It broke most of my ribs. I didn't think I'd ever regenerate again, but you killed it by strangulation? Impossible! They are too strong! And, how did you hang onto the beast for so long? Shouldn't he have ripped you apart long before it expired? What did –" Abreo was nearly rabid in his excitement, firing questions at Mortuus fast and furiously. It took the better part of several hours before the four men were able to get on their feet to resume their journey. When they were finally on the way, Barak made a last inquiry of the road ahead.

"Abreo, is there any trouble likely when we pass the whirlpool building? Anything we need concern ourselves with?"

"Nothing I am aware of." said Abreo. "There should be fewer flyers since they lost a portion of their staff, but they may have Fallen visiting. Send someone ahead or take the far path." He stopped for a moment, twitching his nose almost imperceptibly, like a tiny mouse. "You may want a change of garb for Darius also; he's very noticeable in that death shroud, and Mortuus, your robes could use replacing. They are clean but raggedy for Limbo and there's no place between here and the whirlpool to re-clothe either of you."

Darius and Mortuus were nonplussed. They had heard this warning about their clothes many times, feeling more and more vulnerable each time someone pointed it out. Abreo didn't take notice of their discomfort and continued, unabated, and pleased with his solution to the problem, "You will all have to keep your eyes open. Once you reach Porto, you'll find more than a few weavers. And, in Porto, they enjoy dressing newcomers in their fancy clothes."

Exaro chimed in, "And Abreo should know this since he wears the fancy garments himself when we are not at work in the mines. You four must stay to the path against the inside wall when you pass the whirlpool building. The demon's smithy is located on the Acheron side of the pool. Do not forget they can fly! Look upward…often! But never fear, chances are, they will not expect to find their fugitive right under their noses."

"Or you can just destroy them, demon slayer." laughed Abreo.

"Wait until I tell Eruo!" exclaimed Abreo. "Maybe we will strangle one ourselves!" He smiled and winked at Socius. "Goodbye my friends. Thank you for the wonderful news. Stop back on your return if you like. I will provide a wonderful tour of the mines should any of you be interested. You will not believe what we have been doing down there these last few centuries."

With a wave, the four turned and resumed their trip. The two miners stood watching as they departed, then returned to their mining. The four followed the twisted path around various rock piles on the far side of the pit until the way at last became straight and open and led out to rocky, flat terrain similar to the path they had taken to the pit. Here, they had the advantage of being able to spot anything approaching for a long distance and they were relieved to know, via Abreo and Exaro, the demons would not be passing overhead for some time. Mortuus saw green in the distance. The group was near to the wall on the right. For one moment, Mortuus thought he could hear a loud wind.

After a long walk, the four men arrived at the edge of a stand of trees, and soon were surrounded by full forest. Short green grass, bordered with taller grasses highlighted the way, and the smell of the forest's freshness permeated the air. Mortuus imagined he could remain here for eternity very easily. At the same time, he brooded over Benjamin's talk of escape. It was far better here than outer Hell. Why would Aristotle even have wanted to venture outside? Why would anyone want to escape Limbo for the outside?

More questions surged within the thoughts of Mortuus. What had he done to deserve his specific punishment? Why had he been placed in an 'eternal sleep'? What memories had he lost; why would they be wiping his memories? And, why would they want to hide him and the others, as Socius and Barak suspected? Others? Like Mortuus? Surveying the landscape, Mortuus decided he would not trouble himself over these questions he could not answer. For now, the trees, the grass, and the other scents of Limbo were all he needed. Answers could wait until he had his fill of this place.

The whirlpool building was visible in the distance. It was longer than the Hall of Science was high. The group emerged from the wooded path to see a large reservoir, a giant bubbling lake tightly lined with trees. Sparsely jutting out from shore were rocky ledges. The pool was so large it seemed that it would be impossible to swim across, though unlike Acheron and the Styx, no mist shrouded the far edge. The four men went to the nearest opening in the trees, keeping constant watch for flying demons that might be traveling overhead.

"My friends, welcome to the Second Waters. Please help yourselves," said Barak. Mortuus was not thirsty, but the sparkling water did entice. He and Darius drank a small handful. One taste and the pair began drinking ravenously. This water had a strange effect. The pair finished and stood up in some confusion, not understanding why they felt disoriented.

"Did you enjoy your drink? This is a cleansing water." said Socius. "The First Waters are generally considered potent for regenerating. Drinking of the Second Waters seems to enhance the effect of the first. Many newcomers feel lightly intoxicated. This will wear off, and after you will feel more at ease within yourself. It is believed this water diminishes the stress of a person's lifetime, though there is no discernible proof. I was an infant when I arrived in Limbo, so I cannot say for certain."

"You see the building on the far end of this lake?" asked Barak of Mortuus and Darius, "That is built across the top of the whirlpool."

"Why would they erect a building over the whirlpool?" asked Mortuus.

"I am curious about that also." added Darius.

"These waters feed the whirlpool." said Socius. "Do you know of the concept of reincarnation?" Darius and Mortuus both shook their heads. Socius continued. "When infants die they are immediately brought to the whirlpool. We call it the Whirlpool of Reincarnation. The infants are placed into a basket, and are floated into the whirlpool. According to the legend, the children return to Earth, reborn into a new life. It is a great point of interest in Limbo, but we know no more than what I tell you. Many here would gladly throw themselves into the whirlpool, but only infants are permitted since they have been unfairly taken from life." Mortuus and Darius listened with fascination.

"They return to another life? You mean they escape Hell? How do the infants get into Hell? Why would children be brought here at all? Who walks them to the gate of Limbo?" queried Darius, disquieted at the thought of such innocence being subjected to Hell.

"We are not certain how they get through Hell, nor why they are even brought. The Elders tell us they simply appear within the Keep. They are charged with bringing the infants to the whirlpool. The workers allow only Elders inside the building, but they are not permitted to wander. The building is guarded by Fallen magic, and only Fallen and certain demon workers may enter. Many people have tried; most have been dissuaded by the demons and magical traps."

"Have any succeeded?" asked Mortuus.

"We do not know. None have returned who have attempted. For all we know, they may be stuck under the water forever, or have been carried to outer Hell."

"But they push a baby into a whirlpool, regardless? Without knowing for sure? That is too horrific!" Darius was visibly outraged, surprising Mortuus, who had come to know him as a basically steady fellow, unassuming and almost stoic. This was more emotion than Mortuus had seen from him since they met. "As for grown people to make the attempt, I understand. It makes sense," Darius continued, "I might try, but only after I tired of Limbo." And, with that he folded his arms across his chest, frowning.

"How many attempted before the Fallen decided to build a structure over it and heavily guard it?" Mortuus asked in a calming tone.

"Roughly five are commonly known about, Mortuus," answered Barak, "And that is confirmed by the Chronicler, so I expect it is accurate. Many believe that we would return to a new life, start over again, while others believe that we would be rejected by the reincarnating magic and transported to the lower circles. Limbo is not so bad, as you have seen, but after many centuries it may become tiresomely predictable. Those five who attempted to escape did so when Limbo was still dark and barren, and no walls yet existed. There was no direct torment, but the sounds and smells of outer Hell permeated our being, and the eternal darkness weighed on us, making our mood always gloomy. Now we keep ourselves busy with arts, education, games, hobbies, crafts, and storytelling. All citizens are aware of their great fortune. Rare few exit the gate you fought so hard to enter."

"How do people enter Limbo?" asked Mortuus. "I saw no one at the gate when I passed. And I waited there for a long time when I first climbed to this circle."

"Everyone who is a proper citizen of Limbo enters through the mirror of Minos. When the people enter for judgment, they are required to look at their reflection; in fact, once they enter the room where the mirror is located, they are naturally compelled toward the mirror. Then the individual is transported to their eternal placement, be it here or in outer Hell. I know you do not remember, Mortuus, but Darius, you must recall that fateful trip. Can you tell us what you experienced? I myself stared into the silver glass, dreading what I would see. The image in the mirror looked back; it was me, but it smiled…and then I was standing next to the Keep. I sat there until a guard came over and asked if I was okay. I said I did not know where I was, and so he explained, understanding I was a newcomer. I cannot tell you how relieved I was."

Darius winced at Barak's story. His encounter with the mirror was an entirely different experience, and part of his torment had been remembering it as he was chased and stung by the Hell Flies. Darius swallowed, a little reluctant to tell his story, but also drawn toward it as if it were a confession he needed to make.

"My version is very bad, Barak. You remember I was sentenced to the Vestibule. I saw my entire life, in but a moment, and the pain I had caused upon others. Each second I felt all of the transgressions I committed upon others, as if each was being inflicted on me. I experienced everything firsthand; I was each person whom I harmed." Darius stopped speaking, an expression of pain on his face. "The recollection makes me cringe."

He looked quickly into the eyes of his companions. He was not that eager to reveal his shame, but when his gaze met that of Mortuus, Darius was calmed and his reluctance subsided.

"You see, I was a slave," he went on, "My people were conquered, and the survivors were enslaved just before my birth. I was raised as the property of a wealthy aristocrat, and imbued with the values of a proper servant. I endured much abuse, never complaining and always eager to give more. I became the best slave, my master's favorite, and I played this role to the point of informing on my fellows. It was as any virtuous slave would do. Those who I turned in, who only wished to escape from their lives of captivity and daily abuse, would, at worst, be put to death and in the least, be beaten severely."

He took a quick glance around and, seeing no look of judgment on any of his companion's faces, but rather, interest, and maybe even empathy, Darius went on, "My life wasn't much better for my 'virtue.' I still toiled and slaved like everyone else, I was still beaten on the whim of my master or his wife and children, but I was relatively safer from scrutiny, which allowed me brief moments of sanctuary. And I could occasionally expect table scraps and cleaner clothes since I was required to be in their presence more than the others."

Darius was now looking down at his bare feet; his toe had dug a tiny indent into the gravelly loam, "My guilt, which I attempted to banish from memory, weighed heavily on me by the vision's end. I loathed the person who stood before me. I thought it odd that my image was sobbing, loudly, though I was not. A moment later, I stood in the Vestibule, and was collected into a herd by the vicious insects." Mortuus and the others looked at Darius's saddened face, seeing clearly he was still haunted by his experience.

"We shall add your story to the collection of the Chronicler, Darius. His students study every individual's personal entrance into Hell and Limbo. Up until now we have only information on how we enter Limbo," said Barak. "The students will greatly value your personal story. We will endeavor to keep your identity a secret, however. The Elders Council and their followers are not so open to your presence."

Socius interrupted. "How many students does the Chronicler have, Barak?"

"We do not keep count. Some attend at the behest of the Elders. Others do not attend consistently. A rough guess would be about one hundred." Barak paused, freezing in motion. As the group watched, a lone man came jogging down the path. The man, seeing the group, waved hello as he passed by and continued down the path. Barak had a sudden look of concern on his face. Socius saw this, and studied the runner, who was moving away from the group.

"It is time to go." said Barak. "That runner was sent to alert others whom the Chronicler trusts that something is happening. He has been newly assigned, and was stationed by the Keep. We shall follow the path away from the whirlpool building as Abreo suggested. We arrive in Terni next."

The group of four continued their walk. Darius and Mortuus nervously watched the building, slightly on their left. The path split off to the right, veering away from the building and toward the inner wall. The largess of the building disappeared as the path became tightly clad within dense tree growth, though occasionally it became visible through small gaps.

At length, the men noticed the building passed into the distance behind them. They walked by individuals and small groups of people sitting in patches of grass on their left as Barak and Socius scanned overhead for flyers, just to be sure. Mortuus saw why they decided to take this path; there was only a sliver of visibility overhead due to the thick forest canopy. They journeyed uneventfully until they reached a tiny village that appeared out of a clearing. There were only two dozen buildings, all built off of each other. A winding path of plain cobblestone trailed through and led to more thick forest on the other side of the buildings. Another path merged smoothly near the center of the village.

"Welcome to Terni." said Barak. "If you like wood and jewelry crafts, this is the place you visit."

Wooden tables lay at the center of the village, spread out. Inhabitants of the area sat around these tables. One group was carving ornate shapes out of chunks of wood. Another was crafting small jewelry items, which Barak told Mortuus and Darius were all from the metal mine. One short man, of thin frame and somewhat skeletal appearance, was pounding glowing iron with a small hammer against an anvil, heating the small sliver over a red hot forge, and then pounding it, repeating the cycle many times. The glow and heat of the forge reminded Mortuus of the burning tombs in the Sixth Circle. Small, multicolored stones sat in a large bowl on a wooden table next to the thin man's forge and anvil. The man looked up for a moment, studying the visitors faces, then returned nonchalantly back to his work.

"Barak – what are those small stones used for?" said Mortuus as he pointed toward the wooden table. Barak looked over at the table, examining the tiny, colorful stones.

"They are for decorating the jewelry." said Barak. "Those stones are a byproduct of the mining that Eruos, Abreo and Exaro do. That man probably extracts the stones, or has another do it, from the large piles of rocks all around the mining pit."

"I see." said Mortuus. "I will bet he makes very nice jewelry with those. They remind me of a larger stone I found for Phlegyas."

"Phlegyas?" replied Socius. "I do not recall you speaking of the oarsman, at least not regarding any stone."

"I did not have the time earlier to speak of Phlegyas."

"I am interested to hear," said Socius. "Did Phlegyas require you to do something for him? I recall Aristotle having to perform a dangerous quest for Phlegyas before the oarsman would transport him to the far shore. It must be his test as to whether he will trust you."

"I had to find a tomb," said Mortuus. "It had special markings and hid a carved stone skull underneath. It opened by use of magic incantation. Phlegyas taught me the spell, and had me repeat it many times so I would not forget. The spell made me feel weak. The skull lay in a place of that circle -"

"The Sixth Circle." said Barak.

"Yes, the Sixth Circle. The area was swarming with imps." said Mortuus. "I almost failed the quest. I was savagely attacked by one and sure that I would be found by the whole host of the others. Thankfully, a small building nearby served to conceal me as I slay the small beasts, one at a time. I remained until I had regenerated enough to continue my search."

"Phlegyas sent you into a pack of imps!?!" exclaimed Socius. "Aristotle told me that his quest was similarly dangerous; Phlegyas eventually accepted the vials of water for passage. After many years, Phlegyas required only news from Aristotle's travels. The oarsman especially liked to hear of the Master Centaur, Chiron."

"That must be why Phlegyas had a small supply on hand. He gave me a few vials when I returned with the skull."

"Of what use was the stone skull to the oarsman?" asked Darius. "Was it beautiful, or –"

"I would guess it had magical properties." said Barak. "The Chronicler has spoken of magical objects on very few occasions. They are believed to be hidden in outer Hell by the Fallen and are quite rare."

"Why do the Fallen not keep the items at their homesteads, wherever it is they reside? Where do Fallen reside?" asked Mortuus.

"No one knows," replied Barak. "They are very rarely seen, and only fly upward through the mist. Aristotle witnessed them on a few occasions; the centaurs have had encounters with Fallen also, though long ago. Our closest contact is with Azza's imp. Azza is the name of one of the Fallen. His imp only passes messages to the Elders Council." "What did the skull look like, Mortuus?" asked Darius. "Did you notice anything strange about it?"

"The skull was a container for another item. I discovered it as I sat waiting for Phlegyas. I did not want him to know I had opened the skull. Phlegyas did not speak of it, and at that time I did not care for anything except to get to Limbo."

"What was in the skull?" asked Barak.

"A large gem, about the size of a hundred of those small stones," said Mortuus. "It was clear and beautiful, like the First Waters. The feeling I got when I touched it was strange. I felt that I had to protect it, to save it from this place. Have any of you ever felt such a thing?"

"No," said Barak, "But your reaction is intriguing."

"I have many questions for the Chronicler, Barak," said Mortuus.

"You will get answers in time," Barak assured Mortuus, "We need to increase our pace. I had forgotten that a few close friends and supporters of the Elders Council reside in this village. Let's hurry to Porto and get you two proper clothing. Clavius awaits."

"Who is Clavius, Barak?" asked Darius, whose demeanor had become lighter since his drink at the Second Waters and the subsequent telling of his life experiences.

"Clavius? Well, he is a scientist-miner-loner, Darius. Clavius was once one of the senior scientists, on the lines of Benjamin; then he just up and resigned suddenly, no one knows why. After, he went to work in the mines with Abreo, Exaro and Eruo. He was there for many years, but would provoke the demons often. At first he attempted to converse with the beasts. They were not friendly to his questioning, and so he backed off. Later, he was caught eavesdropping on their conversations. They beat him severely on more than one occasion for that transgression. Eventually he quit working in the mines too. Abreo said he was a natural at mining and that they were sad to lose him."

"Hmm. What a strange thing to do, talking to demons," thought Mortuus out loud, "Why are we going to meet Clavius again?"

"Clavius has accumulated a certain specialized skill," Barak answered simply, "But we are almost there, my friends. You will see what I mean soon enough."

They passed into the wooded area and reached the small village of Porto in the same amount of time it took for them to get from their whirlpool stop to Terni. Barak, increasingly concerned, and angry with himself for forgetting about the Elder's friends in Terni, urged the four to move quickly.

"This is Porto. We will find Clavius so that Mortuus' origin can be confirmed. Socius, you will find proper clothing for Mortuus and Darius. There are many weavers and tailors here. If you can, find a larger pack for each as well." Socius nodded and disappeared between two cottages. Barak motioned the pair to follow. They walked through the grouping of cottages until they reached a small, unkempt homestead, unoriginal in appearance. It seemed plain, not noticeable.

Barak knocked three times in a rhythmic order. Immediately after the third knock, the door opened, and out stepped a small, squatty man, looking as if a giant had been compressed down to a fifth of its size; the wide square frame and head a caricature of a full grown adult. The strangely built man looked at Barak, then eyeballed Darius and Mortuus, scrutinizing each from head to toe. He gestured the men to come in hurriedly. The windows were shuttered closed; the darkness was unsettling for all three visitors.

"Do not speak until we are in, my friends," whispered the compacted man in a deep, gruff voice. Mortuus and Darius were puzzled, but knew there was always more than meets the eye in Limbo. A clicking noise crossed the cottage, followed by a grinding sound, emanating from underneath the three. Mortuus was reminded of the Sixth Circle and the tomb with the skull hidden under it. Suddenly, an opening appeared in the darkness, and a stairwell was revealed which went down into a well lit hallway. "This way, please, hurry," said the square man.

The three men, followed by the dwarfish man, climbed down the steps. The stairs were steep and narrow, and each man stretched out his hands to hold himself upright between the side walls all the way down.

"You should consider installing a handrail for people to hold onto, Clavius," said Barak. Clavius did not answer. He was intent on getting the three inside. The descent was far deeper than it initially appeared. They heard the grinding noise again, though it was louder, and over their heads, and they knew the passage was closed.

"Darius, Mortuus, I would like to introduce you to Clavius. Clavius, this is Mortuus an-" Barak was cut off.

"Keep walking Barak. Introductions come later," ordered Clavius. The hallway at the bottom of the steps continued far out of sight, lit with an unseen source of light from the ceiling. Mortuus was growing anxious as he was reminded of the undertomb he had escaped after his awakening. The hallway was carved out of solid stone, with rough walls that had no doors or indication of any openings, but soon, after only a minute's walk in the seemingly endless tunnel, Clavius stopped. Turning toward an indistinguishable section of wall to the right, Clavius abruptly, and very loudly, cleared his throat.

"*Ostendo!*" trumpeted Clavius at the plain rock wall. With a low rumble, a crack appeared in the wall, then an outline appeared in the shape of a semicircle. The piece of wall pulled away from Clavius, forming a deep depression.

"Amazing!" Darius murmured as he bent his head to look at the new opening. The rock piece that pulled back was sliding to the right, disappearing from view behind the wall. The opening was large enough for all to enter at once. The inside entryway opened to a giant cavern, complete with stalactites and stalagmites, crystalline and icy in appearance. A small path went down a slope to the cavern floor. The path was twisted and hidden partially by the columns of stalactites hanging down and meeting the stalagmites, as if the cave was a giant fanged vampiric mouth. A rectangle of bright light marked an opening at the end of the path.

"Clavius, how did you find this place?" asked Mortuus.

"My friend, when you have centuries, you get a lot of work done. I used to toil with Abreo and Eruo at the pit. Once I learned the spells the demons used for excavating rock, I used it repeatedly to create this long hallway. The Fallen have no idea that a human can perform their magic. Having a lot of strengthening and rejuvenating potions helps too," smiled Clavius.

"Where does the hallway end? I would like to see how far it goes."

"The hallway length is an illusion. The tunnel ends not so far away as it appears, though the lighting creates the illusion of great distance. There are traps set to capture anything that tries to go all the way to the end, so if Fallen or demons get in here, they will not find us too easily. Weapons are also hidden inside the walls."

"Amazing," repeated Darius. "What is that light at the end of the path? Is that where we are headed?"

"Yes. That is my laboratory," replied Clavius. The group followed Clavius down the slope and across the floor of the giant cave.

"Do you need to close the entry way?" offered Barak.

"Socius can do it when he gets here. I am tired. The magic has taken much of my strength. Next time I'll use the wall lever instead of showing off," smiled Clavius, a little weary looking. "Gods, I am exhausted."

Mortuus and Darius, their interests greatly aroused, examined every step of the path, and the whole cavern. The stalactites shimmered where the light from the opening struck them, sparkling like miniscule diamonds. The crystalline outside made it look as if snow had fallen. The two newcomers stopped for short intervals of sightseeing, but were hastened along by Barak and Clavius if they slowed. Soon they had crossed the canyon floor and were at the steps to a large, well lit, doorway. Mortuus grew nervous, more anxious because of what Benjamin had said. Soon he would have knowledge of himself and his origin.

He was as frightened as he was excited.

Chapter 41

Panos on the Rill

Panos made it to the rill. It was a difficult climb up the side with his mangled, baked body, but as he slowly moved his body off the burning plain, he regenerated, and the incredible pain began to diminish. Once Panos was fully off the scorching sand, he lay still. Feeling the pain slowly ebb away, he crawled to the flat top of the rill. A hot, red, coppery smelling stream ran through it. It had eroded a deep furrow into the rock. Panos lay on his back, looking around for the demons that dropped him earlier. He did not know that they were loathe to come down to the fiery plain. He would have been easily picked up if they had the courage to pursue him under fire.

When he had enough energy, the fugitive from the Vestibule sat up. He had lain at the top of the rill, staring upward long enough to ascertain he was not being pursued or watched by any sky creatures. He thought about his friends; the demons still had Aetos and Darius, for all he knew. Panos stood up, letting the blood flow to his regenerating legs. He knew the demons had flown to the lower circles, and so decided he would follow the stream and go toward the source of the flow. His plan would take Panos back and away from where demons take fugitives - the boiling pitch according to Philo. The red stream must be flowing down to the lower circles, he reasoned. Philo had been right; Hell got worse farther from the Vestibule. Panos wanted to go back, to have just one more bath in the pool. He imagined feeling the coolness of the water again. Next time he would be sure to watch out for the flying beasts. He was lonely and saddened about the loss of his companions, and hoped they had a way, like him, to make it back.

Panos had few friends in his life. He had been a traveler, nomadic and adventurous right up to his death in his late twenties. His parents forced him to assist them in their duties as Innkeepers, and he had received many slaps and tweaks to his ears when he was caught plying the customers for their tales and experiences in foreign lands. He had caught the wanderer's disease, his father had said, an incurable ailment that would leave him no lands or stable source of income in his later years. Determined to cure his son of this wanderlust, the Innkeeper placed heavy burdens of work and chores on Panos, forcing him to work to distract him from socializing with travelers who were passing through. One day, when Panos had reached an age of young adulthood, a band of traveling merchants staying at his father's inn hired him to assist them on the road. Panos disappeared quietly, leaving his parents only a note as to what he was doing. By the time they found his note, he was on a ship far out to sea.

Panos traveled far and wide, seeing the known world of his time, usually as a deck hand or merchant's assistant. He had few friends, as he did not settle down, and would likely not ever see those he met again. Before his death, at the hands of a small group of simple bandits, he had been considering returning to his parents' inn. Panos' wanderlust was waning, and he longed to return to family and friends. In eternity, they were Aetos and Darius. And now they were gone. Did he dare hope again in the land of hopelessness?

The walk was painful, as Panos was not yet fully regenerated from the burning. After a while he saw what looked like trees, far off in the distance. He was sure the heat of this plain must be creating a mirage; how could there be trees in this miserable oven? He eventually realized this was the Wood that Philo spoke of. Panos hastened his pace, scanning the horizon with each agonizing stride. He reached the tree line, the boundary where the burning sands ended and the dense tree growth began.

There was a distinct line which marked two different soils; one soil was heated causing the air above it to distort, the other was a hard, dark clay. This dirt did not appear able to support plants, yet the trees and brush were growing on it plentifully. Panos had not seen a real tree in many centuries and these were a welcome sight indeed. He scanned the forest, wanting to take in all the pleasantness yet realizing there was something odd about the Wood. He cautiously scrutinized the surrounding area. That was when he noticed a movement. He crouched low, and moved back toward the plain, on the rill. The movement stopped, but Panos stayed low.

Then Panos saw it clearly. It was a large beast, not like the demons who took him and his friends. This creature had a beak, like a large bird, but the face seemed very human. It had no arms, only wings at its side and large deadly, talons. It was perched high atop one of the trees, eating leaves. Panos watched as the beast snapped a small branch. The tree made a low moaning sound, as if being tortured. A red liquid flowed from where the branch had broken. The winged creature, disturbed by the noise, decided its meal was over and flew off, oblivious to Panos observing. The fugitive suddenly recalled that Philo called these creatures harpies.

Not wanting an encounter with such a beast, Panos moved further back on the rill, walking slowly, until he was distant enough to feel safe. He noted on his right, a clearing that appeared to pass through the Wood. Panos might have to walk for a short distance on the sands, but he knew he could return to the rill if he got chased by the bird demons. They surely preferred the trees to a burning desert and fireballs.

Panos did too.

Chapter 42
Pholus-At-Large

Pholus reached the forbidden area shortly after Chiron's departure up the rocky slope. He was excited, for he had witnessed his friend and leader of centaur-kind ascend the slope to the Sixth Circle in safety. The Fallen spell of restriction had, for some reason, dissipated. The only remaining concern for Pholus was the half-bull, half-human creature known as the Minotaur; the patroller guardian of the slope and inner perimeter of the Sixth Circle. The beast would rend into pieces any creature that dared get caught.

When the Master Centaur had disappeared from his sight, Pholus trotted toward the forbidden area cave in a relaxed pace. He was enjoying his reclaimed mobility and strength after having regenerated from the mutilation of the harpies. In his mind, Pholus began to entertain the idea of leaving the Seventh Circle. Chiron must be overjoyed, he thought.

The forbidden area was far off, on this side of the river Phlegethon. On the way, Pholus stopped to meet with his commanding officers and their companies. No news, as usual, and even less now that the harpies had been defeated soundly. The herds, however, were happily surprised to see Pholus fully recovered. All had known of his abduction and abuse by the harpies, and more than one of his commanders stated their curiosity at his rapid regeneration.

Chiron's Second in Command noticed many of the companies had busied themselves shooting humans who boiled in the river out of sheer boredom, for sport, and always, for revenge. The silence since the defeat of the harpies had created a great vacuum within the herds, and the many centaurs that had not been able to participate in the battle were restless; eager for any sort of excitement. Humans were the base enemy of all centaurs. No Halfling had ever been unaffected by human brutality and prejudice, and most had met their end at the hands of the marauding hunting parties. Some had been forced to watch their families die, a final act of cruelty that pained them even more than being flayed alive. Pholus, not having shared the experiences of these centaurs, understood their angst, and did not hinder their brutality. The humans were, after all, in their own Hell.

The centaurs had been placed forcibly into this place by the Fallen, and patrolling the Seventh Circle was the duty they had been assigned. Pholus passed a small herd of centaurs, who stopped to bow and salute, then continued on with their targeting game. He would be nearing the forbidden area shortly.

He knew he was near the forbidden area when an imp appeared in the distance. Only within the confines of the forbidden area did the creatures have safe haven in the Seventh Circle. It was here that Nessus stood watch. Nessus, seeing his superior trotting toward him, looked surprised as he bowed to Pholus.

"Report, Nessus," ordered the Second in Command. "What news since last you spoke with Master Chiron?"

"Master Pholus, Sir, there has been little activity to report since I last saw the teacher taken inside the cave."

"Who took the human into the cave? Was it the Fallen, or their workers? asked Pholus.

"Workers sir. There were two flyers, quite large as demons go. The flyers dropped the human, and workers from inside the cave came out and carried the human inside."

"I see," Pholus wanted to storm that cave ever since it had been declared off limits to the herds. This circle was their only place in the afterlife, and an important portion of this circle was denied them, just as humans slowly denied centaur-kind pastures and forest lands during their lives, legislating the herds to live in obscurity. Pholus's mood grew foul.

"Nessus, you will patrol the rocky slopes, where the Minotaur dwells. I want to know when Master Chiron returns, and I want you personally to come and inform me. Do not send an underling, and speak to no one else about this matter. Do you understand?"

"Yes sir," said Nessus. He trotted away slowly, then galloped, and did not look back. Pholus turned to face the cave, watching a pair of imps as they fought with each other. The usual moaning from the Wood across Phlegethon filled the background, punctuated by the occasional shriek and the hollow flapping of the harpies. The foul odors of the burning plains wafted past intermittently. Pholus realized that the tormented of this circle knew about the special area forbidden to centaurs. Special humans were brought to this place for torturing by the demon workers. Pholus grimaced as a new set of screams emanated from the cave mouth.

Abruptly, three of the Fallen flew onto the landing in front of the cave. They looked like semi-giant humans, and as soon as they landed, their massive wings disappeared into their backs. The imps that were fighting at the cave opening scurried away in alarm as the masters of Hell stormed the entrance. Pholus had only seen the Fallen once before but he was no less awed. It seemed, if Pholus read their body language correctly, that the three were antagonized and agitated. The cave seemed to shake after they entered, and the screaming resumed, unbroken for an extensive period of time. Pholus shuddered, then nearly jumped out of his skin as a hand touched his shoulder.

"By the Dark Gods!" he yelled, throwing his arm up defensively. A small, young centaur, humorously known to the herds as 'Titan' jumped back, away from Pholus.

"Titan, what is it!?!" yelled Pholus. Pholus saw Titan cower. He took a deep breath and softened his words.

"Titan. What do you need? I am very busy now."

"Sir" said the Halfling youth, nervously. "I have news from Master Nessus. The patrols have caught a fugitive."

"A fugitive? Which company?" asked Pholus.

"Commander Equus, sir. He said they caught a human in the midst of the woods, near the clearing. He was being attacked by the harpies. The human had almost gotten through, when they descended on him. The company watched the attack, but decided they must capture the human themselves. They did not clash with the harpies; the avians flew off as soon as Commander Equus and his regiment started toward the flock. The human was shredded badly and fares poorly."

"And so what do they need me to do? They have a strict protocol for these matters. Did they not sound the horn to alert the demons?"

"They said that they would have alerted the demons, but they believe the human is from the upper circles, not the lower. Commander Equus remarked that the human carried the scent of the Vestibule."

"The Vestibule? How did a fugitive get all the way down here? How did he cross the river without us knowing?" Said Pholus.

"He cannot speak yet, Master Pholus. The harpies have damaged his face, mouth and throat quite severely. He will not be able to speak until he has regenerated. Do you have any orders for me to return to Commander Equus or Master Nessus, sir?"

"Detain the prisoner until I arrive. He is not to harm the prisoner. Understood?"

"Yes sir," Titan retreated quickly. Pholus turned back to the cave just in time to see the three Fallen emerge from the cave opening. Their faces were twisted in a spasm of indignation and fury as they walked far enough apart to open their wings. They flew up vertically, with a single flap of their huge wings, vertically, and disappeared into the misty ceiling. Pholus, reputed to be the fiercest of the centaur race, felt veritably insignificant as he witnessed this.

The vermin imps came out of their hiding place and resumed their fight in the front of the cave entrance. Pholus watched, expecting something to happen, and sure enough, the imps abruptly scattered again. Pholus checked the entry way, then looked upward toward the mist, then back at the opening again. The cave darkened a moment before no less than seven demons emerged from the interior, all flyers, each carrying with it iron weapons and metal tools of torture.

"They probably used them on Aristotle. Filthy beasts!" thought Pholus. The flyers spread their wings and ran into the air. They proceeded along and up the incline to the airspace of the Sixth Circle. They were not strong flyers, like the Fallen, but they were all gone a few moments later.

Pholus, hoping his friend's torture session was finished, decided to see to Commander Equus and the human captive. He trotted deliberately toward the shallows of Phlegethon, glancing skyward for Fallen or flyers. He would see to Commander Equus' prisoner from the Vestibule. Surely they must be wrong. If the stranger was from the Vestibule, so far above, how did he get through the river?

Hell was becoming a very chaotic place.

Chapter 43
Old Friends

Chiron could not believe it when he saw his old friend. Reduced to an animalistic state, the sadism of the Fallen was apparent in the twisted appearance of Plutus. Aristotle had described to the Master Centaur the details of Plutus disfiguration, but oral description did not register as deeply as being in the presence of Plutus himself. Studying the rabid, mutated deformity made the pain penetrate into his core. Plutus had been a friend of Chiron's from long before their exile into Hell, and Chiron had hoped to one day meet his old acquaintance again.

Chiron stood near the edge of the Fourth Circle, in the same spot as Mortuus had much earlier. He had had a very difficult time climbing the wall. Centaurs were not built for scaling vertical walls with small footholds. Plutus, catching a scent out of the ordinary coming up the wall, arrived near the ledge just as Chiron clambered over, exhausted and sweating. Chiron stood up to behold his old friend, malformed and twisted, growling. He readied his bow.

Chiron stood his ground and looked into the eyes of this wolf-form of his old friend. They were glazed red, an angry hatred for all that passed through the Fourth Circle. It was the Fallen magic, thought Chiron. He looked deeper, and saw no hope for communicating with Plutus; the friend he knew was buried deeply within the psyche of this beast, unable to take control. The Fallen had imprisoned Plutus within himself.

"My friend" said Chiron, knowing his words were moot, but in hopes of somehow reaching Plutus. "I will return this way to free you from the prison you reside within. If you have any will, permit my passage. You have my word I will do whatever it takes to free you." He stared into the eyes of Plutus, who was edging slowly forward, red eyes glaring. The Master Centaur pulled his bow back, aiming directly at Plutus' chest. "Do not make me release, Plutus."

Plutus knew a bent bow meant pain. Though the bestial creature wanted only to attack, rip, and shred, he moved out of the way of danger. Plutus sidestepped off the rough path between himself and Chiron. He had not so long ago felt the shaft of Aristotle, unbeknownst to Chiron, though his feral mind barely remembered it. Chiron, relieved he would not have to shoot his friend, slightly relaxed. He lowered his bow, and unknowingly provoked the wolf-demon to attack.

Plutus sprang at Chiron, who, in surprise, stumbled backward. Chiron's back legs hung over the cliff. He struggled tenaciously to get back on all four hooves solidly while Plutus was in his face, biting at his throat and clawing any flesh that his deadly claws touched. Chiron became enraged, forcefully shoving Plutus away and regaining his foothold on even ground. Plutus landed on his feet and dug in, jumping at Chiron again. In that short moment, Chiron's legendary archery skills brought down the wolf-beast. With a single arrow going from under his carriage, straight through his right shoulder, and out his back. Plutus stopped a moment to growl and yelp in pain, giving Chiron the opportunity to ready another arrow. Plutus was struck down by the force of the arrow shaft, which stuck out from his belly. He ceased his attack, as the acid from his stomach began leeching into his other internal organs. Plutus lay where he landed, crying in pain. The injury would cause him great discomfort for the remainder of his curse.

Chiron touched his own throat and face, feeling the burning pain of the lacerations. Blood was pumping out of his neck, weakening him too quickly. He saw the wall to the next circle in the distance and decided to run for it. He galloped hard, his vision blurring with the increasing blood loss, and leapt over a group of humans who were pushing a giant boulder in their mad spell. Chiron's blood spilled onto the humans as he flew over them. The Master Centaur placed his hand flat against the wounded area of his neck to stem the flow. He was approaching the wall fast, and hoped the handholds to the Third Circle were more centaur-friendly.

When he reached the bottom of the wall, a slight slope provided a far easier climb. The rock had been chiseled and arranged to ease the ascent for bipeds, but it was good enough for four-leggeds. At the middle of the climb, Chiron lay out on an adjacent rock ledge, his hooves jutting over the Fourth Circle below him. He could see the feral Plutus far off, struggling to remove the arrow. Plutus's cries could be heard from even this great distance. Chiron, pushing his hand against his neck, felt the bleeding had slowed a little. He pulled out his last vial of water and drank deeply. The cool liquid was sweet and began its healing work immediately.

As he rested, observing the madness of the mobs below, he contemplated the future of Hell.

Chapter 44
Meeting the Father

Chiron kneeled his way across the windy landscape of the Second Circle. Above, tormented humans were cast about by the high winds. Violently and mercilessly twisted, they smashed against each other, and splattered against a far off cliff, the edge of which lead up to the First Circle. The winds were threatening his foothold and it was an unbearable trek. Centaurs have great difficulty kneeling for long periods of time. A few humans above, who were stopped momentarily as the wind shifted direction, had obviously never seen a centaur. If Chiron stood up on his hooves, he would have been swept up with the blustering crowd above.

Chiron grunted through the discomfort, continuing to hobble across the Second Circle. He could see the Hall of Minos ahead, just as Aristotle had described it. It was a large, stately building, once white and marbled, now dirty from many millennia of dust and wind. It stood small against the background of the rocky heights of the First Circle. By Chiron's standards, having been in the Seventh Circle for thousands of years, the Hall of Minos was huge.

The sight of the pillars took him back to his life in the ancient world, when the sun shone and night fell, and for a moment he could even remember the smell of the daylight. As he got closer to the building, Chiron apprehended a shadow, moving quickly toward him. He stopped moving, checking the wind to determine if it was powerful enough to sweep him away. The winds had been slowly diminishing as he neared the hall, but the shadow disappeared suddenly. Chiron waited, sniffing the air. Centaurs have a highly developed sense of smell, and on the occasion where there was danger, it was very helpful. Chiron strung his bow, and pointed it up, searching left and right, before the creature struck him from behind.

The beast ravaged his right shoulder, leaving several bleeding bite marks. Chiron dropped his bow. The beast had a hold on his upper right arm. Chiron reached with his left arm and tore the creature off, swinging the rabid beast around so he could confirm what he suspected. He pummeled it, unleashing his rage, as it squirmed and tried to bite him to escape his grip. It was a small, two headed imp, with tiny wings, and apparently must have flown quite fast to get behind him in the torrential winds. Only a severely unintelligent creature would try to attack a centaur, twenty times its size and as much stronger. They were vicious, stupid little insects to the centaurs, and the centaurs would not suffer their existence. This one would wander no more.

Chiron grabbed a hold of the small wings, holding one in each hand, and pulled. The beast shrieked loudly, though this was not enough to dispatch it. Taking the long knife out of his sack, Chiron thrust forward; the flailing imp became a shrieking puff of smoke, and was dissipated into the wind. Chiron replaced his weapon and rubbed his back, neck and arm where the imp had clawed into it. This wound was an irritation compared to that inflicted by Plutus, but caused Chiron to stop a few moments. The Master Centaur searched the air for more beasts as he checked his pack needlessly for a possible last vial. No water remained; Chiron would have to wait until he reached Limbo. He was almost there.

Chiron walked around the Hall of Minos and, noticing the long line of people, he trotted alongside, moving closer to the humans. The humans, believing they were in for the first of Hell's punishments, recoiled in fright. Chiron looked at them pityingly.

Far up the line stood a pair of imps. They had come around the other side of the Hall, and must have been in the same pack as the imp Chiron had just destroyed. The pair headed straight toward a horrified human. The closer they got, the more the man cowered. He tried to hide within the crowd, but everyone moved away from him as the beasts attacked. Chiron decided he would tolerate the beasts no longer.

He drew his bow. In a moment he would dispatch both creatures. But before the arrow was loosed, a thundering voice came from inside the great hall; a great booming voice that unnerved Chiron, and caused the humans to cry out in fear.

"Stinking hell spawn!" roared the voice. In a moment, Chiron could see its source. It was a large human, as tall as Chiron, muscular in build, and olive skinned. He walked proudly toward the cowering, savaged human. The imps were in a feeding frenzy and had not noticed the immense human bearing down upon them.

"Get off. These are not judged yet. Leave now or I will-" the voice stopped abruptly as the human saw Chiron. His surprise was great, so great that he stopped his motion toward the imperiled human.

"What is this?" he roared at Chiron. "Why are you here? Centaur-folk are not judged in this place." The human, whom Chiron assumed correctly to be Minos, stood in front of the Master Centaur, studying him.

"I am Chiron, of the centaurs of Phlegethon. I travel to Limbo with news for the citizenry therein."

Minos appeared puzzled. "And I am Minos, Judge of the Dead, Lord Chiron. This is my great Hall, where the dead come for assignment of their torment. How is it you travel freely through Hell, Master Centaur? Very few do so, and rarely are they not demon-kind. Never are they workers who have been assigned to any circle." Minos drew in closer and lowered his voice, "Have you learned to dispel the Fallen magic? You must have to have countered the spell that bound you to the Circle of Phlegethon."

"I have not used Fallen magic, King Minos. I have no training or ability with it. But it seems the spell which confined me and my kind to the Seventh Circle has been lifted, or diminished. I can provide no other explanation."

"What news have you to speak of to Limbo's untormented?" asked Minos, as he looked at the wounds on Chiron's back and neck.

"With respect, King Minos, that is private business."

Chiron was stern. A noise from behind the line reminded the two workers that the problem with the imps was still in progress. Chiron, in the blink of an eye, shot off an arrow into the neck of one of the creatures, which had climbed up onto the shoulder of the screaming man and was clawing the hair off of his head. The creature grabbed the arrow sticking out of both sides of its neck, unable to shriek, and then became a black cloud, as the arrow dropped through the smoke and onto the ground. Minos, in admiration, motioned to Chiron to let him take care of the remaining imp. As Chiron watched, the large human waved his arms, then spoke.

"I will show you something I have learned, Lord Chiron. *Bascaria – batah*!"

Chiron watched as the imp, terror on its face, went motionless, and then disappeared into a puff of black smoke as his companion had. It was effortless, and Chiron nodded his approval to Minos. The King smiled proudly. The attacked man sat on the path, still screaming, even with the beasts gone. Minos stared at him, and the small human stopped at once.

"That was Fallen magic. The hand waving was for my own dramatic emphasis," said Minos. Chiron smiled, and Minos turned back toward the hall. "Chiron, I would ask you to stay a while. I would like to speak with you, maybe even give you some knowledge to use on your trek. But I need to sit; the Fallen magic causes me to tire. Please, come into my hall. I have had no company for some time. Will you be returning to Phlegethon when you finish in Limbo?"

"Yes. I will return. I will come into your hall also."

"Very good. I must keep this line moving or the people will be backed up all the way to Acheron, and then I'll have to deal with Charon. He is so unsociable. We can speak while the crowd continues," said Minos.

"I believe I will enjoy a visit. This is the first time off my post in millennia," said Chiron. "I would also like to talk to you about your son." Minos turned quickly in surprise. He did not believe he had heard the Master Centaur correctly.

"I am sorry. I do not believe I heard you. Did you say my *son*?" asked Minos. "Do you know my son? Are you sure?"

"Asterion. I believe him to be your son. Am I incorrect?" asked Chiron.

"You are certain? My son is…" Minos paused, concerned as to whether he should continue.

He is Minotaur." said Chiron. "Half-human…like me."

Chapter 45

End of the Line

I stood in line for many days, or at least it seemed I did. The line moved slowly, and for awhile more people came up behind me and took their places in the back of the line. Curiously however, within a day's time, I noticed an end to the line coming from Acheron. That is, people stopped coming from the dock. The sobbing man was there but did not speak. He only leaned against the wall, grunting every so often, and breathing in short shallow gasps. I suspected he had broken ribs, but I was not going to ask him. He should have been faster getting away from Charon. I was still angry with him for that. Otherwise, like everyone else in line, I waited for eternal torment.

I thought this line must be the finale before meeting the judge of Hell. Minos was, according to Dante, the decider of the fate of all sinners. I was almost sure this was Dante's Hell, but I wasn't absolutely positive since there were no walls in Dante's Hell. Or at least, I did not remember the walls. I was sure there was only a path through Limbo before the line into the Hall of Minos. I guessed that Limbo must have been walled off to keep the sinners out, since there was, according to Dante, no punishment there; certainly it would be a great place to wander into. I wondered how many people had 'accidentally' done that. But then again, no way would it be easy, right?

The line was about the worst I had ever been in. The worst, in life was at Disney World when I was nine years old, but that was because I was too young to wait. Here, I felt that impatience again. I did not want to move forward, but I didn't like waiting either. I looked at the sobbing man. He was standing better than before, having no trouble breathing. Perhaps Charon had not broken his ribs? Maybe he had some anxiety issues that caused him to breathe with difficulty? I looked behind him. The end of the line contained the same faces I had seen before. Was no one else dying?

I finally came to a place where I could see ahead. I saw a darker atmosphere in the far distance, and could hear the sound of high winds. Now I was certain where I was. A little while later I saw the destination of the line I spent so much time in. It led down into the Hall of Minos.

The Hall of Minos was a Parthenon type of architecture, with large columns. There was a thin path of steps rising slightly and leading into the structure. The building was lit up, though I saw no torches, light fixtures, or any other light sources. It was still in the distance, but I could see my path would soon become a crudely carved stairway. I glanced around, my eyes hungry for new scenery. I had seen only walls and miserable people for too long. I took in the new sights, searching for whatever lay ahead.

Down the path, toward the hall, there was some commotion. The people were making that noise a crowd makes when everyone becomes frightened or alarmed. Anticipating danger, I anxiously strained to see what had made them cry out. In a few moments, I saw a creature, coming out of the darkness, from the left side of the building. I squeezed my eyes shut, then slowly opened them.

Moving toward the line was a huge centaur. Where in Hell was I?

Book III

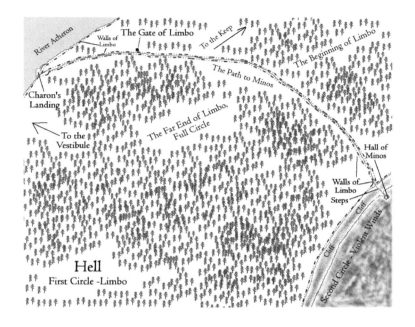

AngelFall – Books I, II & III

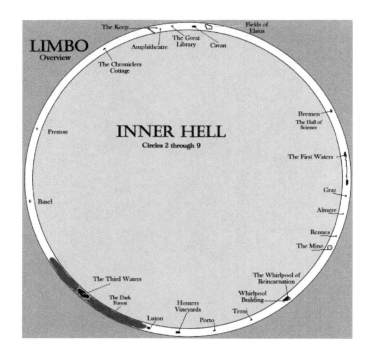

Prelude

A Fateful End

I stood there, watching in surprise. I was in a very long line, the line that leads into the Hall of Minos, where I was to be judged and sentenced for all of eternity. I had gathered this much since entering the place, having been a once ardent fan of Dante's Inferno, though a few things were off, like the high walls on both sides of this path. I did not have time to think out or consider the differences, because even if I was not in the Inferno, I was surely in Hell somewhere. And that weighed upon me beyond comprehension. The sounds of thrashing, violent winds grew ominously louder, and I felt the foul air brush against my face. Far ahead, where the line neared the Hall entrance, a huge centaur had appeared out of the darkness, trotting toward the line, where a commotion was scattering the once orderly, almost sluggish line. I could not see at first; the people ahead stood in the way and the drop was too shallow to catch a glance. But as the crowd began to part, I finally spotted a lone man at the center of the crowd. He was shrieking in anguish and terror as a pair of toddler-sized, discolored creatures, maybe three feet high, tore away at his flesh with claws and rows of razor-sharp teeth.

The centaur was huge. If he were all man or all horse, he would be considered large, from head to haunches. His musculature was that of a body builder, only naturally built, not of the steroid variety. The centaur was bleeding from its shoulder as he walked straight at the melee. In hand, the centaur had a large thick bow, and was stringing an arrow while keeping his eyes locked on the hideous blood frenzy. Just as I thought he was going to shoot off the arrow, there was a loud noise that came from the building; like a roar, only with a human-like voice. the air trembled. I was reminded of my Uncle Rich, who had a booming timber when he spoke. Uncle Rich had a unique sound I'd heard rarely in my life. This new voice, however, was seriously frightening. The whole line, previously panicked and reacting to the sight of the blood fest, got very quiet, very fast, and only the sound of the blowing winds from behind the hall could be heard. Even the centaur, intimidating as he was, stopped and lowered his bow. Then, out of the building and down the steps came a human who was as muscular as the centaur. He looked to be in his fifties, darkly tanned, with huge arms and torso muscles, extremely well defined, and a powerful, square jaw and weathered face. Like the centaur, he was shirtless. From where I stood, I guessed he was about six foot eight, but I recalled meeting a professional basketball player once who was the same height, only the basketball player was nowhere near as wide and muscular as this guy. I watched just as quietly as everyone else, the man approach the centaur, wondering if I should expect a fight. If they did fight, I wanted to be out of striking distance. I was still recovering from getting my brains bashed in by Charon.

Before he became aware of the centaur's presence, the big man had shouted at the small beasts, stopping short in his surprise. The strong winds from behind the Hall were incredibly loud, increasing and decreasing sporadically. I could hear the two exchanging words that were too muffled to discern. They spoke briefly before the centaur finally turned back toward the man who was being attacked by the rabid beasts. The centaur raised the large bow but I did not see him aim or fire. I saw one of the beasts that had climbed onto the screaming mans shoulder, suddenly grasping at its own throat, trying to remove an arrow which had magically materialized there. The centaur had moved that fast, and that precisely. A few inches less and the beast's victim would have had the shaft through his head. The pierced beast stood, frantically trying to pull the arrow out when in seconds, still holding its shape, it transformed into a black cloud; another second later and it was gone, the blowing winds dispersing the smoke rapidly.

At that point, the powerful man said something to the centaur, then waved his arms as if performing a magic show trick with great flamboyance. He spoke words, again, which I could not make out. A strange light went off in my head and the second creature became a smoke cloud, dispersing in the wind. The centaur seemed to relax a little, and the crowd, recognizing the disturbance was over, was eager to move away from the still screaming man and return to their previous, orderly line. Everyone continued to gawk at the commanding pair until they disappeared into the Hall.

No longer bored with this line, I stood in anxious anticipation, as if a giant wave was coming at me. I remembered I was fast approaching my sentence.
Eternity was near.

Chapter 46
Fatherhood

Chiron's visit with Minos lasted a long time, and only after deciding he could trust the thunder-voiced human would Chiron divulge his reasons for traveling to Limbo. Originally, he was afraid Minos would be a cantankerous old fool, untrustworthy and too pompous to deal with; instead, the two hit it off as if they had been old friends. Each shared his stories from life, and each had details to tell the other about their experiences of Hell. They sat in the Great Hall, in a section that was behind the pillars, and out of sight of the line of new arrivals. A doorway off to the right of the pillars contained a large throne, and Minos sat while Chiron stood on all fours. There were chairs for company, but none that would accommodate a Halfling form. The large room was empty except for three chairs, a large mirror, ornately decorated with gold carvings of winged humans and strange, beautiful beasts, and the two new friends. Chiron was impressed by the workmanship of the carvings, and mysteriously compelled to look into the mirror. When Chiron moved in front of the mirror, Minos gave him an ominous warning.

"Do not get too close to it, Lord Chiron. I do not know what effect it would have upon you, being a centaur, but I prefer not to lose your company prematurely. It is enchanted and would send you away from here should you look into it too long." With decided urgency, Minos commanded. "Please come away from it for your own good."

Chiron did as he was told, not wishing to be transported when he was so near to Limbo. As the pair conversed, newcomer humans came into the room and walked to the mirror. Chiron watched as the people would stare into the glass, mesmerized for a few minutes, and then vanish. After, Minos would roar "NEXT" and another human would enter the room. Minos turned back toward the conversation as if nothing had happened.

"And how is it you know Aristotle is being held in the cave near you?" asked Minos.

"My commander, Nessus, informed me. I ordered him to watch the area, as he is the least distractible of all my sentries." Chiron seemed to be bothered as he mentioned Nessus, and his discomfort was visible to Minos.

"My friend, who is Nessus, your fellow centaur? Why do you seem pained at the mention of his name?"

"It is nothing, Minos," said Chiron, but his body language, at least from his human torso up, spoke otherwise.

"You distrust Nessus. It is obvious, my friend." Chiron knew he was cornered in the conversation, and decided to open to the ancient king.

"I confess that I do not trust Nessus, nor does my second, Pholus."

"What has he perpetrated to earn your distrust, Master Centaur?"

"I am loath to speak of it, Minos. I haven't any real proof, only hearsay and my own intuition. I would not speak of it harshly until I do so."

"Surely you can speak of what evidence you have, be it hearsay or feeling, without slandering your fellow." Chiron, thinking about Minos' words for a moment, decided it would not be unfair to express his own reasoning and doubts.

"Very well Minos. It will do me good to be rid of it after so many centuries. There are two issues I can speak about, and, as I have said, they are based on hearsay and circumstance. First, I believe that Nessus desires my position as head of the centaur race. I hear stirrings from time to time, and once I was even challenged to physical combat by an oaf who is so lacking in basic intelligence I know he could not possibly have imagined a challenge of his own accord. Furthermore, investigations were initiated whenever these stirrings rose in intensity, and each time Nessus' name came up somewhere in the controversy. Yet, when I question him, he always has a solid alibi, and proclaims his innocence and lack of knowledge."

"You believe he is after your position?" asked Minos.

"Yes I do. And I would gladly hand it to him if I could leave this place."

"Why don't you let him have it now?" asked Minos.

"I knew of Nessus in life, Minos. He may have betrayed his fellow centaurs to the humans who slaughtered our kind in order to save his own skin; which leads me to the next item for which I do not trust him. I believe Nessus reports to the Fallen." Minos looked surprised.

"What evidence have you?" asked Minos.

"The harpies. In my circle, the harpies hate only one thing more than they hate my kind, and that is the Fallen. When Fallen appear, harpies disappear. It's as if the harpies can sense or smell the Fallen; they always disappear just before the Fallen arrive."

"How does this tie into Nessus?"

"Nessus stays on the far side of Phlegethon, usually observing the forbidden area cave. On one occasion, he was required to cross over to meet with Pholus, my second in command, and I. When we travel to the wooded side of Phlegethon, the harpies are always present, watching from a distance. When Nessus was coming to meet us, I had noticed the harpies, in fact a few of them, sitting in the tree tops; they ate silently, eyes on the herds warily, but disengaged. As Nessus was approaching, however, I detected many sharp movements out of the corner of my eye, and the harpies quickly vanished altogether. It took me awhile to put it together, but it makes sense to me that Nessus, in his duty as watcher of the forbidden area, has consorted with Fallen. I believe this is the case."

"It is a terrible thing to – NEXT! – not trust your subordinates. My palace was full of treachery between the servants, and between the nobles, who often attempted to manipulate me to distrust their peers. I was foolishly coerced many times, even having one of my servants beaten for a crime he did not commit. I almost executed a noble for the same reason."

A large man entered the room and walked to the mirror. Chiron could see the partial reflection of the man, and as the man began having a tantrum, cursing and trying to pound the glass, Chiron noticed the mirror's reflection steadily blackening and flowing like liquid; Chiron could smell the unmistakable stench of the Styx coming from the mirror. The upset man vanished, and the mirror returned to normal. Minos did not seem fazed by the incident, and continued his story.

"NEXT! When I learned of this treachery, I spoke no more to my servants and instead hired a master who would manage them directly. The perpetrator - JUST WALK OVER TO THE MIRROR

- who fooled me into beating the servant was released. He jumped to his death shortly thereafter. It was a shame. They have such small lives."

The next man, small and skinny, moved so slowly that Chiron thought Minos would go over and throw him at the mirror.

"MOVE!"

The king kept talking, and the man finally reached the front of the mirror in tears as he anticipated his torment. Chiron saw the mirror change quickly, only this time it looked like the place he had seen in his vision, the icy area. The skinny man cried out and bowed his head, and then was gone instantly. The mirror returned to its normal state.

"NEXT!" roared Minos. The individual humans continued to enter the room and evoke the powers of the mirror. In some cases, Chiron saw the moaning woods that bordered his river. Other times the red river itself appeared, or the fiery plain beyond the wood. Another time it was the tomb area, and many times there were areas he did not know. In each case, scents and odors came from the mirror which Chiron knew emanated from the site shown to the human. All the smells were different, and usually foul. In just one case there was a scene and a scent that was so pleasant that Chiron could not help but stop listening to the king. He had detected a trace of the scent on Aristotle once, but it was so polluted with the odors of outer Hell that the Master Centaur could not tell if it was real or he had imagined it. Minos smiled as he saw Chiron's distraction at the pleasantness.

"Limbo," said the smiling king. "It is very rare; the last one happened many hundreds of years ago. Smells wonderful."

Chiron sniffed loudly, taking in the smell of fresh forest and field as the man disappeared. The scent disappeared immediately, disappointing Chiron momentarily. The two masters continued their seemingly endless chat, where, after much talk that
wandered far from the original subject, Chiron became comfortable enough to discuss the matter of Asterion with Minos. He had been uncertain earlier on, but the king seemed genuinely happy to see Chiron, and opened himself up to the point where the Master Centaur knew Minos could be trusted.

"Minos, I would speak to you of your son." The king looked away, suddenly distracted by the mirror and its next victim for the first time since the centaur's arrival. Chiron could feel Minos cringing, though he continued. "I realize this is an uncomfortable topic, but I am compelled to speak of it, as I have promised. Minos, I have met your son, in the Sixth Circle." Minos grew pale and suddenly acted as an adolescent, shying away from an accusing parent. Chiron, originally fearful of how the great judge of Hell would respond, smiled to himself.

"He is not my son, Chiron. I have been made aware of the presence of Asterion in the tombs – I caught a fugitive, who told me many things about the circles and creatures below before I summoned the Fallen." Minos was scowling at the mention of the Fallen. "Asterion was the son of my wife and the accursed bull-"

"He is *your* son, Minos. I can assure you of that." Chiron was direct, and looked straight at Minos, who was now reddening.

"And how is it that you know this, Chiron?" Minos' anger stirred, but he kept his voice in check. "I have no bovine lineage to speak of and my advisor informed me that my wife had been with the bull-"

"Could your advisor have been lying to you? I saw Asterion, and I know he is your son. We centaurs have senses that are far more acute than that of humans, Minos. I can detect familiar scents, my eyes are sharper, and I can see his parentage clearly, especially after seeing you. I know he is your son. Have you ever consulted with anyone outside of your advisor?"

"My advisor was highly trustworthy, Chiron. He saved my life once, when we were children. His parents were of noble lineage, and he had the deepest regard for my wife. I would dare say he loved her himself! Were I not king he would have certainly married her first. Reporting that she was with the bull was so very difficult for him, I could tell just by his stammering, his pleading for me to forgive him for having to report such an aberration of behavior." Minos looked at the floor briefly and then straight ahead with determination.

"Still, I took care of the beast-child, and I give my regard to you; I only say 'beast' because that was his nature, not because he is a Halfling. The child ripped out my advisor's heart one day, and devoured it in front of his dying eyes. The advisor was charged with taming Asterion for public appearances, for his own good. Asterion would have no kindness, only blood. I had very little choice; either slay him or condemn him to spend his life in the labyrinth. I chose the latter."

"And you trusted the advisor with the boy?"

"He was the bastard son of the bull and more feral than other Halflings. My advisor assured me he had no intelligence beyond the ability to hate and to kill humans! The child murdered my friend and was found over the body, eating the man's heart! And this even after my advisor had given him much care and personal attention."

Chiron shook his head knowingly. He was hearing all the same rhetoric used to justify the extermination of his kind, and the anger and disgust he felt was being rekindled. Minos was highly irritated by Chiron's head shaking, and burst out in anger before he could control himself.

"Do not shake your head at me! The child was a killer!" Minos took some deep breaths. "Why do you not you believe me, Chiron? I realize you were persecuted in life for your parentage, but you were not of wild, violent disposition. Look how well you did for yourself – you are highly respected by kings and gods alike. Asterion was not near your temperament or intellect."

Minos trailed off. He was not happy to have lost his temper, and over the thousands of years he had much time to consider a number of issues in his lifetime, including the matter of Asterion. Questions had surfaced again and again, but the king kept telling himself he *had* taken the appropriate measures, he *had* done the right thing, he *had* done the best for all concerned. But now it was evident to Minos that the subject of Asterion was not fully resolved within him. The mere mention of the bull Halfling had unsettled him beyond the many reasonable facts he had been ruminating over for millennia.

"Minos," Chiron paused, looking into the pained eyes of the former king. "You do not know the persecution I went through in life. I was nearly slain by humans on many occasions, and were it not for my special parentage, I would have perished long before making a name in the world of the living. I will speak to you plainly, and I would have you listen. I respect you, and your position, but I must impose what I understand to be the truth. Will you listen, and listen only, until I finish?"

"Of course." replied Minos quietly, held in the eyes of the centaur.

"I have another sense, a sense of character assessment, which I have had since birth. This sense of assessment has helped me dealing with many humans and centaurs alike, and I trust and regard it highly. Many times while growing up, I was warned, and I disregarded this sense for what was before my eyes. I gave more weight to what I saw rather than what I sensed. This led to betrayal by those whom I trusted, and I so wanted to trust."

"When I finally began to trust in my ability, the world changed for the better, minus the attempts on my life by those who were threatened by my ability." Chiron paused again, and looked at Minos so that the king could not pull his gaze away, pinning him with his eyes. "Asterion is your son. Not of the bull, or of anything other than some malevolent magic aimed at you and your wife. I sense the magical and I know Asterion is a human child, cursed at birth or just before, and transformed into the Minotaur. The spell was singular and irreversible in effect. You must have had a great enemy. This is powerful magic that can hold from birth and throughout even death."

Minos was squirming with the discomfort and shock of this revelation.

Memories of situations where he had questioned his advisor-friend, and was given answers that seemed to conflict flooded his mind. Minos never bothered to inquire more deeply because Asterion and his deformity had always pained the great King. He had been awaiting the birth of a beautiful son, and the monstrosity that birthed from his wife's loins horrified and wounded him greatly. He did not know of the incident of the bull and his wife until his friend, the advisor, reluctantly spoke of it. Until then he had been terribly saddened, but coped as best as he could because his wife kept the child close to her, caring for it tenderly. Eventually, the advisor persuaded Minos to conceal the half bull from the eyes of the nobles. Minos' wife wept for weeks, and after a month threw herself from the palace walls. The king recalled with no small amount of guilt how his hatred for the child grew uncontrollably after that and how he completely relinquished the child to the care of his advisor, who convinced the king to banish the child from memory.

Now the legendary Chiron was confirming what Minos had been seeking to bury and deny. It felt true. The king was stunned. What else did the Master Centaur know, he wondered.

"Minos - Asterion was a wild, unmerciful killer who fed on his victims." Minos didn't move a muscle. "Asterion was *raised* to become a killer... made into a killer...trained and brutalized by someone, who I now know was your advisor. Have you ever seen a dog raised to attack and kill? Dogs are domesticated, and will do what they are trained to do. If the dog is beaten, it becomes mean, and lives only to survive. Asterion was treated similarly, and lived to survive."

"I spoke to your son. He followed me into the Sixth Circle, and I do not know if he intended to attack or only wanted to study me. He could not believe my kindness toward him. He shared his stories, the only stories he knew, stories of his upbringing, beatings and captivity. Your advisor treated him so badly that he wanted only to die. He wished to die. But in his rage, your son destroyed the man who destroyed his soul. For this, he was sentenced to the labyrinth by you, and was given a reputation not of his own making." Chiron stopped. Minos had just enough energy to look away.

"Interestingly, we were on the topic of distrust of those whose loyalty should be unwavering. Tell me, Minos, what was the name of your friend, the advisor?" asked Chiron. The king spoke softly, as if he did not want to be heard, but his reply did not escape the sharp hearing of the centaur.

"His name was Garum."

Chapter 47
The Missing Ferryman

The centaur could feel it; the anguish that had been trapped inside of the king - now judge of the dead - welled deep and, surging like waves, overflowed like a slow, powerful tsunami. The enormity of his anguish caused Minos' body to convulse spasmodically. Chiron stepped away, trotting outside the room to allow the proud king his privacy. Hell was the land of tears and anguish, guilt and regret. It was a human land.

Chiron stopped short. The line to the great hall was gone. Formerly filled with the newly arrived humans waiting for judgment, it was now vast and empty. The quiet was not natural for this place; most would be weeping as they got closer to their eternal sentence. The hall had an eerie low tone; only the wind could be heard as it whistled across and around the back of the structure. Chiron wanted to tell Minos, but the king needed this time alone. Chiron stood quietly, inspecting his wounds that had been inflicted by the imps behind the Hall earlier, to see how they had healed since beginning his conversation with Minos; it had been quite a while. They had closed up and only the dried blood that had flowed from the lacerations indicated that any damage had occurred. He wiped the crusted blood away mindlessly when, in an instant, the silence was broken by Minos, roaring through his sobs.

"NEXT!" Silence, then after a short pause. "NEXT!" Chiron watched as Minos stormed out from the mirror room, swollen red eyes glaring at the empty hall. "What is this?! No!" Minos looked around, behind pillars as if the people would be hiding from him. "Where are the people Chiron? Chiron?" The king stared at Chiron as if he were hiding the people himself.

"The Hall was empty when I arrived, Minos. I do not know why. The line must have finished as we spoke." The two walked to the steps and out onto the path leading up to the First Circle. Minos was looking around frantically, in complete disbelief.

"This has never happened. I am not sure what to do!" Minos looked into the air, walked around behind the hall, and returned back to the front steps, frantically searching for what could have happened to the line. "I am afraid I will have to summon the Fallen, Chiron. You must leave this area."

"Minos, can you withhold your summons, for just a short time? I would investigate further were I you. Perhaps talk to Charon, despite his temperament. He may know something we do not."

"Yes - yes" said the frantic judge. A very good idea. I would walk with you up to the gate. They would not let you in alone I fear, but I have friends there, and they will not deny me entry. If they do not allow you entrance, I will intercede. Let us walk. I am growing more concerned"

The two quickly walked up the steps to the walls that formed the corridor of the path. Soon they came to the gates, as Minos continued speaking.

"I would help you further were the burden of my fear lifted; I am not finished with our conversation, but you have given me some release, and I would speak with you longer. Would you walk with me to Acheron, and stand with me while I question Charon? Your presence may help to stifle his gargantuan rudeness and temper. You have nothing to fear as long as you do not touch his boat or his person. I will properly introduce you as a co-worker of Hell, and he will not threaten you. He suspects everyone as being a fugitive, though I have heard he will transport anyone for an object of worth. I don't know why since he has no use for valuable objects. Perhaps old habits die hard."

Chiron considered the request of Minos and recognized he might not be able to venture outside of the Seventh Circle ever again, he wanted to see more. Thousands of years of boredom made his decision certain.

"I will assist you, Minos. Let us go see the ferryman." Minos smiled briefly, and the two set off up the path to the river Acheron, reaching it after a long walk. When they arrived, Minos' shock worsened. Sitting on the shore was the skiff of Charon, but there was no sign of the volatile ferryman to be found.

"Perhaps Charon has taken a break, or is off on his own journey?" offered Chiron.

"Charon has no adventuring spirit within him, Chiron. He is a creature of cold habit, never changing, intolerant to any new difficulty or challenge. It is what makes him a miserable old fool, and he clings to it steadfastly." Minos paused in thought. "Would you like to come to the far shore, Chiron? We can take the skiff and-"

"I would not be comfortable in this 'skiff' Minos. I was able to cross the Styx by way of Phlegyas, but only because I had no other choice. I believe I should return to my task before I am discovered by those who will soon be missing Charon. I must leave now for the gate."

"Wait my friend. I will help get you passage into Limbo as I said." Minos looked furtively around, "I would warn you also, you must not tell the Elders of the problem with Charon - I suspect the leaders of Limbo have too much loyalty to Fallen, and I would still prefer to solve this riddle myself, before we are overrun with their worker demons and imps." Minos looked straight at Chiron, seriousness in his eyes. "Chiron, that spell I cast on the imp earlier - it is forbidden. If the Fallen were ever to know that I had used their magic, I would be sentenced to one of the punishments in the depths far below, maybe in your forbidden area, or deeper. Do not use the spell in front of anyone you do not fully trust; I believe in your sense of character and I would trust you to rely heavily upon it. That incantation is the only other way to destroy the demons and vermin imps, though for demons it may not be as subtle as you have witnessed. I do not casually cast this spell. I have had no company for some time, and thought to impress you with my knowledge. I am a fool for showing off. The spell will work only on the demons and imps and not humans or any other creatures of Hell. Have a care, Chiron. It may come in handy in your travels. Now, let us go."

Back they walked along the path until they reached the giant iron gate of Limbo again. Minos motioned Chiron to stand back while he knocked loudly on the great metal doorway. In a few moments, a plate slid away and the eyes of a guard looked out at the king. The eyes stared and grew large as he saw the formidable size of the powerful judge of Hell, then appeared to consider before finally speaking.

"Greetings sir. You are King Minos?"

"Yes, I am he, my good fellow, though king no more…for quite some time. I do appreciate your respectfulness, however." Minos smiled. He was happy to socialize, especially if it would further

Chiron's chances of entry into Limbo. A little charm could spare a thousand soldiers, his mother would say.

"Your highness," said a deep voice from the gate, trying to emit respect in his tones. "Pardon me for not opening the gateway. We have recent orders to inspect our guests first. We are honored."

"Greetings to you my friend." returned Minos. "Please open the gate. I would ask a favor of you, friend guard."

"Yes sir!" replied the guard's voice; he had stepped away in order to open the gate. The plate slid back into place, just as the gateway opened wide. The guard looked at Minos, and was smiling when he saw the large form of Chiron standing at the side. "Your highness! What is -" exclaimed the stunned guard. Minos noted the shock of the guard, and seized the moment.

"My friend, this is Master Chiron, leader of the centaurs of the Seventh Circle and a proper worker of Hell, as am I. He is also a friend to Limbo's citizenry. I came to ask you to allow him entry – he is on a brief task, and will only remain within your walls temporarily." The guard stood staring at the Master Centaur, mouth agape. "Will you permit my friend, Lord Chiron, entry into Limbo, friend guard? I will assume full responsibility."

"Yes, your highness, sir. It would be our great pleasure to entertain any guest you send us and we are much honored to have one so well known and revered! I do not need to inform the Elders, they will find out soon enough, and it will be to their delight, I assure you." The guard turned to Chiron, bowing his head in reverence. "Please, enter Master Chiron. I will accompany you personally, and take you wherever you wish to go. Which Elder is it that you seek?"

"I seek Socius, ward of Aristotle." said Chiron. The guard smiled.

"Socius? We all know of Socius - he is friend to many. Please, Master Chiron, enter and enjoy our air and environment." The guard turned to Minos. "Your highness, you are also welcome. It would be a double honor for us." Minos smiled at this.

"I will visit my friend, though not this time. I have my own tasks which I cannot ignore. Thank you for allowing my friend. May the Gods honor you." Minos waved to Chiron, and then started back toward his hall.

"Goodbye my friend." said Chiron as he watched the king leave. Minos was going back to his hall to investigate before summoning the Fallen. Chiron would have liked to see the reaction of the Fallen himself, but since he was out of his assigned territory, it would be a very bad idea. They might transform him into some monstrous mad centaur-demon, as they had turned Plutus into the wolf-demon.

Chiron watched his new friend disappear down the path. The guard waited, smiling, and the inner gate was opened by his fellows, revealing a grassy, green, earthy smelling Limbo. The other guards, like the gatekeeper, stared in awe at the massive centaur. None had ever seen a centaur, and now they were being visited by the master of all centaurs, the legendary Chiron. They stood agape as he walked regally past them and into Limbo. People who had been engaged in conversations with each other stopped and stared in disbelief of their own senses. Chiron saw all their shocked faces, but was involved with the scents he had barely experienced before when he stood in the mirror room of Minos' hall. He was enraptured as his nostrils snorted and breathed the earthy scented clean air of Limbo.

"Master Chiron, I see you are enjoying our fresh air. Please follow me." said the guard. "As I promised, I will take you to Socius personally."

"Thank you friend. I will enjoy your environment as we walk. Is it a distant journey to where Socius dwells?" asked Chiron. He would prefer it to be very long, as he took in the sights and smells.

"Master Chiron, Socius normally dwells nearby the gate, particularly when he awaits Aristotle, but he has recently taken a journey to the far side of Limbo, and we will have to walk for a long distance. We can stop at the First Waters along the way; they will refresh you unlike any other." The guard could not believe his luck. Here, walking along with him was the legendary Chiron. In the childhood of his lifetime, the warrior had been told many stories about the ancient heroes and characters. He was in a haze, a dream state, and he thought he would be better off not to awaken from it. If he would escort the great Chiron, let the way be long.

Chiron smiled. He had not been certain that he would be welcomed, and now he was being escorted into Limbo as an honored guest. The trees were real - different, but real, unlike the bleeding, moaning trees the harpies lived in and fed from. As he walked near a large tree, he sniffed the air to lavish the scent of it. A centaur's sense of smell, far keener than a human, allowed Chiron to smell not only the leaves, but the trunk, the bark and the oils produced within. It was remarkable and healing just to be inside of

Limbo, an aromatherapy he had taken for granted in life. Chiron wanted to take his time and dwell in this intoxicating atmosphere, but he would do what he came to do, above all. Surely his exit would be a sad occasion.

"Guard," asked Chiron. "I would prefer to not be involved with the Elders at this time. Is it possible we can circumvent the structure known as the Keep? I am in urgent need of speaking to Socius, and then I must exit Limbo in haste. I hope your leaders will understand. Should I be able to make a diplomatic journey and return, I will follow the proper protocol. For now, I must get to Socius as soon as possible. I would be discrete, though I see that is no longer an option." Chiron looked around as the few people in the area had all stopped their conversations, agape as he stood with the guard. Even the guards behind him had not closed the entry way into Limbo because they did not wish to lose sight of the Master Centaur.

"Lord Chiron, it is my honor to escort you as you wish. We can move in less popular pathways to reach Socius, and I will ask other guards to assist so we can pass through without interruption." said the guard. Chiron smiled and nodded his head.

"That would be my preference, friend guard." replied Chiron.

"It is my honor, sir. And please call me Nigel." said the guard.

"Thanks to you, Nigel. Lead on." Chiron and the guard turned to the right, and walked a narrow path toward the wall that bordered the Second Circle, and he could hear the winds faintly with his keen centaur hearing. Soon, they were alone on the path, and concealed by more medium sized trees. Chiron saw only trees and wall, and he delighted in the environment as they journeyed. He thought of his human friend, and asked questions of himself. Why would Aristotle ever leave Limbo for outer Hell? What had he found that threatened the Fallen? What could possibly have happened to Charon? He did not distract himself with the thoughts for long, however. Chiron wanted most of all to spend his time enjoying the refreshing air and scenery, savoring his temporary bliss.

He felt renewed.

Chapter 48
Panos and the Centaurs

Panos could barely see. The strange demon bird creatures had swooped down on him just as he spotted the red river. They had pinned him down, shredding his chest and abdomen and disemboweling him viciously strokes with their razor-like talons. Panos had immediately feared he would encounter trouble from the herd of centaurs he'd seen standing in the distance when he emerged from the moaning trees. He had not seen the bird demons coming.

Now, Panos lay on the ground, surrounded by the Halflings. He could hear them talking, but could not yet see; he was blinded in one eye, which had been ripped out by the bird beasts in their frenzy, and blood flowing from the other wounds on his face interfered with the sight of his remaining eye. Panos wondered if his eye was gone for good or if it was still hanging there. He heard the deliberate trotting of one of the centaurs coming toward him, and then a commotion of hooves in slight movement, as if giving way to the newcomer.

"Greetings Commander Pholus!" said Equus, the leader of the herd that had inadvertently rescued the human from the harpies.

"Equus," replied Pholus, approaching the bloody mess that was Panos. Pholus looked down at the mutilated human, sniffing the air around Panos, analyzing it to discern his origins.

"Then it is true, Equus. I could hardly believe it when Titan informed me. We will have to wait for the regeneration to complete before we get any information from this fugitive. Do not blow the horn; we need to find out how and why this human is here." Pholus studied his wounds. "They have really mangled his face, nasty, crude beasts. They are still angry at our battle victory, and apparently have taken it out on the human."

Pholus threw this out for the benefit of the herd as a reminder of their recent battle. He knew they would take it well, and predictably, the centaurs cheered in unison, taking in the compliment to their battle prowess. "At least the harpies were smart enough to flee when your command arrived. They may have some intelligence to them after all."

"Master Pholus, should we not report this to Master Chiron?" asked another centaur. The herds were not aware that Chiron had journeyed to the First Circle to get answers about his human friend, Aristotle. They did not know Aristotle was being held and tortured in the forbidden area.

"Yes, Equus. I will inform Master Chiron," replied Pholus. "Have Titan report to me at the forbidden area cave when this human can speak, but do not question him until I arrive. I would hear his answers firsthand." Pholus looked at Panos, who had been listening intently. The weakened human had lost the ability to move his arms. The muscles in his arms had also been shredded away, and so he could not even wipe the blood pooling uncomfortably on his face. "Equus," said Pholus, "Do not allow any harm to come to him. We need answers before we contact the Fallen. There are strange occurrences happening in Hell and we must be cautious for now." Then Pholus turned and headed back toward the shallows. The herd resumed speaking among themselves.

Panos sighed in relief as he heard the centaur trot away. He would have some peace while he regenerated. He was grateful for that. Exhausted and in pain as he was, he marveled at being in the presence of what he had always believed were but mythical creatures.

Centaurs had held Panos' imagination even while he lived as a boy in the old countryside. Yet once he regenerated and answered their questions, Hell would come for him once more in the form of the Fallen. Panos tried to relax into his regeneration aware of one important thing.

He must escape.

Chapter 49

Identification

Mortuus could hardly believe what the dwarfish Clavius had just told him. He swooned, unable to digest the news. Clavius was shouting something to the laboratory assistants, but it was indecipherable to Mortuus, who could not grasp spoken language in this moment. Words were sounding like grunts and groans in the ether. Socius and Barak had already jumped up on either side of Mortuus, each grabbing an arm and supporting his large, limp frame as best as they could. Darius moved behind Mortuus, propping him up with both hands. Clavius' two assistants exited, running into a small hallway.

"Mortuus! Mortuus!" everyone was shouting, trying to bring their friend back to balance. Mortuus had gone limp for a second. Barak strained to hold him up; Mortuus was quite heavy. Just as quickly as his legs had buckled under him, Mortuus willed himself to consciousness as if fighting off sleep.

"Clavius, you are certain then?" asked a groaning Barak. "I have heard this theory, but I have not seen any evidence to conclude that Mortuus..." He was loath to say what Barak had just told them.

Mortuus was one of the Fallen.

Barak had been astounded when Mortuus destroyed the demon, but automatically attributed it to two intersecting trajectories; one, the fact that the demon was in an unusually weakened state because it was under the spell of transformation, and two, that Mortuus was unusually large in frame. It was a great victory, but certainly only an extreme human accomplishment, so he thought.

"There is plenty of evidence. You related the first sign of it to me, and the runner, whom you recently saw pass the whirlpool house has confirmed it. The theory is sound. The Chronicler had sent the runner to find Mortuus before the demons could," Clavius spoke firmly. Barak tried to rationalize all the various bits of information pertaining to Mortuus that he could think of in a logical manner. He didn't want to believe Clavius' theory, but the pieces began to come together when he considered the runner who passed them by the Whirlpool building.

"The runner? I almost forgot him," said Barak.

"What evidence did Barak give you first?" asked Socius, as he let go of the recovered Mortuus.

"The demon," replied Clavius. "Mortuus is the first ever known to have beaten a demon, and I do not mean just to get away from it; Mortuus *destroyed* it, singlehandedly. No human, not one, could have held on to that creature's neck without being annihilated, let alone squeezing it hard enough to stop it from breathing. The demons are very powerful creatures, second only to the Fallen. Restricting its air flow is the only way to destroy it without using magic." Clavius' assistants returned, holding large vials of clear water, and a basket full of very strange looking fruits. Mortuus examined the doorway to the hall. It reminded him of the underground where he had first awoken into this Hell nightmare.

"Drink the water, Mortuus," said Clavius, "It will aide you in your recovery." Mortuus was still dazed from the revelation of his identity and its mystery. "Thank you" he croaked, surprised that his voice had left him. Clavius continued talking.

"Demons are very dense creatures as well. You said that Mortuus was able to hit it and cause it to falter, Barak. Socius, you were struck by the beast. No human could have sent you flying. Luckily you did not have a broken jaw or worse. Yet Mortuus struck the beast, and it fell! No other but one of the Fallen could have caused it such harm." Barak's resistance was giving way as Clavius spoke.

Clavius turned to Mortuus, who had just drunk a vial of the water brought in by the lab assistant.

"Mortuus, do you recall anything of your past? You have been to the first and second waters. Have there been any shadows or feelings of memories…anything at all – which you can remember?" asked Clavius. "Any information, small as it may seem to you, would be helpful."

"I have tried to remember, Clavius. I had a sense of a past while at the first waters. But I could not connect to it. I am only aware that memories exist out of reach. Otherwise, there is nothing," said Mortuus. "Are you certain of my…identity?" he asked tentatively. He had also been grappling with logic and reason. "I mean I was slashed up pretty badly by the demon. I have only healed so quickly by the grace of the waters," he offered almost hopefully.

"Well, let me ask you this Mortuus; when you looked at the demon while he was disguised as the Elder, what did you see?" coaxed Clavius.

"That was different. I saw a man shift into what seemed to be a beast, shift back into a man, then back again." replied Mortuus. "It shifted as the air does, in the Sixth Circle; like the heat above the glowing tombs, constantly distorting the air."

Clavius nodded, satisfied that his theory was fact, and Barak had to acquiesce.

"There you have it, friends. Only a magical being could discern the transformed demon; Mortuus *is* one of the Fallen," stated Clavius definitively.

"Only the Fallen can see through the spell?" asked Socius.

"That is correct."

"Then what was Mortuus doing in that underground dungeon with other Fallen? Why were they all in a deathly sleeping state? Why are the Fallen keeping other Fallen imprisoned and hidden away?" Barak questioned.

"And by what means are they kept asleep?" mused Socius.

"I do not have all the answers, my friends," answered the dwarfish Clavius, "But obviously, Mortuus and the others were kept there in an immobilized state because they were not wanted conscious by the others. Since the Fallen have been banished here, I would imagine that Mortuus and company fell from the grace of their fellows, and were somehow rendered unconscious to keep them under control. I know they are very upset, and are no doubt searching for Mortuus as we speak."

"Your old friends from the mines had quite a bit of interesting news in that regard," offered Socius.

"Oh?"

"The demons that guarded the sleeping Fallen were replaced with some of the smithy demons. The Fallen were so angry they destroyed their underground workers, and the remaining smithy demons are angry because they have to do extra work with fewer workers."

"They will most likely get a lot more work done since they have less 'friends' to fight with. I bet they increase their quotas considerably," chuckled Clavius.

"They have to. The Fallen are arming the fugitive hunters and sending them out to search for Mortuus," said Barak.

"Threatened, you mean. They are not used to fear," noted Clavius. "This is a good sign."

The assistant with the basket moved closer to Mortuus. He seemed to enjoy watching Mortuus quaffing the large vials of water. He held the basket up, urging Mortuus to take the fruit. Mortuus shyly looked around at the others in the room.

"Yes, Mortuus, eat the fruit. It has medicinal qualities and will speed up your regeneration." said Clavius. Socius and Barak watched as Mortuus inspected the fruit.

"What fruit is this, Clavius?" asked Socius. "I have never seen its like before."

"It is from a special tree, Socius. I was given it when it was a small sapling by the Chronicler, centuries ago. I had Homer try to propagate it, but it was beyond his skill." Clavius looked on proudly as Mortuus tasted his first cautious nibble. The fruit, a light, reddish-green skin, about the size of a large olive, changed to a purple color as Mortuus chewed away. Clavius studied his face, and the others grew quiet. The assistants of Clavius took copious notes. "The tree has only recently begun to fruit, but quite heavily," one of them said.

Mortuus became quite elated, curiously filling with joy inside as he ate. The fruit had a sweet enough flavor, though it was not remarkable, but it caused him to remember a similar feeling from an earlier time. The memory, however, did not connect him to anything more than the remembrance of a familiar feeling. Mortuus stomach had been very tight, yet he had not noticed it until now, as the fruit seemed to settle his insides and release a stress he had not noticed. He also became acutely aware of his extreme hunger. Curiously, his back started to itch, but he could not stop eating until the very last of the fruits was gone. After, he sat, satisfied, drinking from the vials again and scratching his back.

"I was very hungry, I did not know how so until I started eating." enthused Mortuus as the assistants added to their notes, scribbling excitedly. Just then he caught himself and, embarrassed, looked sheepishly at the group. "I… am sorry," he stuttered, "I did not mean to eat all the fruits…"

Clavius and Barak laughed out loud.

"Have no shame, my friend. The fruit was all for you. Socius is usually the only one who ever gets as hungry, because he is still a growing boy," smiled the short, stout man, "It was our pleasure, our pleasure!" Clavius assured him. "Now, I need you to remove your robes so I can inspect your back, Mortuus."

The assistants eagerly helped to remove the tattered cloth. It was very light for its thickness. They laid it across one of the tables, examining the fabric closely, looking through small round glasses that made the fibers much larger to the eye. Mortuus quietly noticed the assistants had a similarity to Clavius, but seemed younger, thinner and taller. He forgot his thoughts as Clavius and Barak moved behind him. Darius, who had been sitting quietly in the corner of the room the whole time, stared at Clavius, waiting for the next revelation.

Clavius scanned the back of Mortuus as Barak and Socius watched curiously. "Ahh – here. Do you all see this?" Clavius pointed to a small area just above the left scapula. "Watch as I press it. Barak, Socius - move back a few more steps."

"I see nothing Clavius." said Socius. "What are you looking pointing at?"

"His wings. They are hidden magically when not in use, but a slight pressure to the proper area and they should open reflexively. Unless an angel wants to use them, they stay concealed. Now watch." Clavius pushed his finger into a spot on Mortuus' back. Mortuus flinched in discomfort for a moment, but did not make any other movement. Suddenly a pair of thin ridges appeared in the skin along Mortuus' backbone, and then the ridges extended into an elongated row of bloody stumps down each side. The stumps then retracted into Mortuus's back quickly, leaving no trace or sign they existed at all.

"I suspected this." said Clavius grimly.

"What was that?" asked Darius.

"The Fallen must have been very upset with Mortuus for something. They sawed his wings off, and I would assume those of the others. This is very bad thing for an angel to do to another." Clavius shook his head gravely.

"That row of stumps was what was left of the wings of Mortuus," said Clavius. He was examining the face of Socius, who seemed, in particular, to have been jolted when the wing stubs were revealed.

"Socius, are you feeling alright? Looks like I shocked you a bit. Maybe this is too much for a young-"

"I...am fine," replied Socius weakly. "I've seen far worse in the battle games. It just seemed too horrific, even for Hell." Socius looked at Barak and Clavius, who were staring at him with concerned faces. "I am fine!" he insisted. Clavius and Barak knew better. They would take it up with Socius later. One of the assistants jerked around toward Socius, scribbling more notes.

"Socius, Barak – you must take Mortuus to the Chronicler immediately," Clavius advised urgently, and to Mortuus he was reassuring. The Chronicler will help you, Mortuus." He turned to his assistants. "Summon the runner; tell him to get to the society's meeting place near Basel and tell him to say 'there is a theory' as the password when he arrives. They will know what to do. And tell them I have positive confirmation this time."

The assistants left the room hurriedly. Socius handed Mortuus his robe, and they all turned to follow the path of the assistants.

"What did you mean 'this time' Clavius?" asked Socius as they walked out into the large cavern.

"The last time we thought that Hell was near to change," replied Barak.

"We all agreed then, Barak," said Clavius irritated. "Even you."

"I am not denying it." responded Barak.

"What is this theory you two speak of?" asked Socius.

"The theory?" stalled Barak, looking at Clavius with a small amount of caution.

"I believe it will be okay to explain the theory to our friends, Barak," said Clavius. "Would you like to, or should I?" Barak considered a moment.

"I will," said Barak. "This will be brief, however because we need to move again and soon." He stood, pacing as he spoke. "There is a group of people in Limbo that believes we will one day be freed from Hell. Clavius and I are members of that group." Mortuus and Darius stared, unbelieving at what they had just heard. Socius winced. Barak noted their reactions and continued. "The group believes that we will one day befriend a member, or members, of the Fallen, who - I do not need to remind you, but it is important to remember - are the most powerful beings in Hell. Because the Fallen have been exiled from somewhere and it is in their nature to return from whence they came, we feel that they will, in fact, one day do just that...return to wherever it is-"

'Heaven?" injected Darius, incredulous.

"Wherever it is, Darius," said Barak. "Or, the Fallen will find a way to escape from this place.

"Hell?" injected Darius again.

"Wherever this is," returned Barak.

"We know from the logs of Aristotle that Fallen always fly straight upward, passing through the mist, although we do not know what exists beyond. We do expect that there may be much more to Hell than we are aware of." Barak paused and searched the eyes of his ardent listeners.

"Is that it?" asked Mortuus, eager to hear more.

"No," said Barak. "There are many ideas, and many variations, but the generally agreed upon thought is that we will, we must, befriend the Fallen first before any change can occur. This revelation, Mortuus, has just happened, varying slightly - we had not considered that the Fallen would be warring within their own society." Clavius suddenly became animated.

"We can discuss more on this later, Barak, when we arrive at Basel," he urged, "We must leave now!"

"I would like to hear more about the theory while we walk, Clavius," said Darius. Socius and Mortuus nodded in agreement. They all began moving toward the hallway.

"Yes," said Socius, "As would I. I have spoken with you many times, Barak. Why did you not discuss this before?" Socius was slightly miffed.

"Take no offense, Socius," answered Barak. "This was very much a secret to be kept from the Elders. We suspected they were friendly with the demons for some time, and now this has been confirmed. We have merely been waiting for you to get to the proper age -"

"By the Astrochron I am well over six hundred years old, Barak," grumbled Socius, "How old must I be to get to the 'proper' age?"

"Yes, Socius, but you were born and raised here," said Barak, stopping a moment to address Socius directly, "and your life has been a learning experience for us all. According to the laws of Hell that we have observed, you should not have aged at all. Yet you grew older, and now appear as an adolescent. You eat, you sleep because you must. No others require food or drink here Socius. We only eat to feel alive, and sleep so we can dream about our lives and those pleasant memories we once experienced. You, youngling, are another one of Hell's mysteries. It does not matter that you are six hundred years old," Barak smiled as he paused, "you are still an adolescent."

"Everyone, we must go. Now," demanded Clavius. "Mortuus, you and Darius need to put on the new robes Socius brought you." Clavius gestured toward two folded piles of cloth on a nearby table. "These new robes should make it more difficult for anyone to tell you are from the outside. I only hope we have no problems from those who have seen you already."

Clavius, Socius and Barak exited the room as the pair of men dressed quickly and joined them outside the room. As they traveled back through the cavern, Mortuus saw a distant glow of many colors coming from a tunnel under the sloping path that led up to the hallway.

"Clavius," asked Mortuus, "What is that glowing I see?" He pointed to the tunnel.

"That tunnel leads to the tree of the Chronicler," answered Clavius, "And the glow is the tree itself. It is unlike any tree you have ever seen, or will see. I will take you to the tree another time Mortuus, right now we really have to move along."

Mortuus was compelled to stare into the tunnel. For a brief moment, a memory flashed, and then dissipated before Mortuus could grasp its meaning. He recognized the tree, but his memory faded, and was no more.

They continued to the hallway, and to the surface. Mortuus was feeling much better than anytime ever before, but back on the surface of Limbo, he could not help but feel the crushing weight of Hell, which lay just outside the walls.

Chapter 50
The Secret Society of Limbo

The group had been walking for a long time on their way to Basel. Basel was the meeting place of a secret group of the oldest citizenry of Limbo. Whenever irregular occurrences were reported in Hell, this group, who had no ties of friendship with the Elder's Council, would rendezvous. The last meeting had been prompted by the disappearance of the three Elders over a century earlier, and now they were meeting again to discuss the appearance of Mortuus, the only member of the Fallen ever to have befriended Limbo's citizenry. On the way, Barak told them about the history of the society. He had been a member for many centuries.

The Chronicler, the oldest member of Limbo and charismatic teacher of Barak and many other students of Hell, had founded the discrete group, though he rarely attended any of the meetings. Mortuus and Darius learned that the Chronicler was the keeper of the history of Limbo, recorded and copied by his followers, and placed in his own private library. His library was open only to those he personally picked. He would not allow the Elders to peruse his tomes and though the Council protested loudly and indignantly, it was to no avail. The Chronicler kept his volumes hidden well and according to legend, or perhaps rumor, there were other volumes in this private library, containing non-historic information. This fact was apparently of great interest to Clavius, who began chatting freely.

"I have not seen these volumes. They are said to contain the language and spells of the Angel-folk, the race of the Fallen. I am hoping that he will reveal his volumes as a natural consequence of our having brought you, Mortuus. He has denied me access since I first revealed my interest in angel lore and magic. The information I have heretofore spoken of has been gleaned from many places, and I had even considered traveling to the underground where you were kept comatose for Gods know how long. I wish Aristotle had returned with just one of the tomes in that underground library. Ahh but he was brave for finding you there. I have not been outside of Limbo since my descent into Hell at my death. Before reading that last travel log of Aristotle, I had not considered ever leaving Limbo. Can you imagine? I had only wished to access the collection of the Chronicler. No one knows where the Chronicler obtained these tomes either. Now he is another great mystery of Hell, that one."

"Aristotle has never brought back any books, but I believe he would have if he had the chance," said a gloomy Socius. "He stopped taking notes along the way a long time ago. It was too dangerous to stop and write so he would dictate his journey to me for scribing and placement into the Great Library when he returned. I thought they would have been of interest to the Chronicler, but the Chronicler has not been seen anywhere near the library."

"The Chronicler has read all of Aristotle's travel logs, Socius, and with great interest," contradicted Barak, "Do you think it a coincidence that I was nearby when Mortuus fought the demon Elder? Little goes on without the Chronicler's knowledge. I was at the library copying the last travel log of Aristotle when I heard from other members of the society that you and the warriors had left Limbo. I dispatched a runner to the Chronicler immediately while I waited for your return. We have known for a long time about the problems of the Elders, though not to the extent of there being a transformed demon among them."

"But Mortuus is one of the Fallen," said Socius. "He might be able to beat another."

"Yes. He might be able to overpower another," added Clavius, "And he might not. Mortuus has only recently awakened, and without memory of the incantations and spells used by Fallen, he would be defenseless against their conjuring. Remember, Mortuus and a great roomful of other Fallen were incapacitated by their fellows. These are a most powerful and cruel lot. Fortunately for everyone, the Fallen would not condescend to skulking about in disguise; they use demons and Elder's to do their base work for them."

Suddenly, a loud horn sounded in the distance. Everyone froze in anticipation.

"What was that?" Mortuus finally asked. Clavius had a worried expression on his face.

"We must hurry. The horn was the summoning for Fallen."

"Perhaps it was Minos reporting a fugitive?" said Socius. Barak, in his fear, was agitated with Socius' guess.

"Have you ever heard Minos blow the horn, Socius? No. Something far more serious has occurred. Make haste my friends!" said Barak, breaking into a semi-run. No one needed more prompting.

"We can hide Mortuus in the forest until we hear from the Chronicler. There is a place there made for just such a purpose," Barak spoke in a rush.

It would be some time before they reached the dense wooded area known as the Dark Forest. In the interim, the group, who had slowed their pace to a brisk walk, had passed through a large vineyard, or fields of what appeared to be grapes. The caretaker was a man called Homer, who Barak described as nearly as ancient as the Chronicler, though not as interesting. Homer was working in his fields when the group passed by. Barak waved and shouted a friendly greeting while still walking hurriedly.

Barak explained as they walked that there were many others who helped Homer, some harvesting, others transferring the grapes into a vast vat, and others who would stomp the fruits into juice. The barrels full of juice were stored in small underground caves until fermentation occurred. This spirit was not the only source of fermented beverage in Limbo, but it was known as the finest. According to Barak, Homer had grown interested in making this version of wine long after arriving; when the scientists first announced the developing of fruits in their laboratories. The fruits were not real grapes, but the nearest imitation in Limbo, and these fruits were far juicier and delicious. Homer had cultivated the variety he was using far beyond that of the scientists. When fully fermented, the wines were very powerfully intoxicating and highly desired, especially by the demon smithies and guardians of the Whirlpool Building. Homer was forced to hide most of his harvests after the beasts had depleted his first few crops.

"So, the demons enjoy a bit of the drink?" inquired Clavius. "I was not aware of this. It would have been a very useful bargaining chip while I was working in the mines, though I do not believe it ideal to be near a demon when it has a belly full of drink. I am certain they would act as the worst angry drunkards." Clavius became quiet, lost in his thoughts.

"They go absolutely mad for Homer's wine," said Barak, searching the face of the introspective Clavius. "My friend, I can almost hear gears grinding when I look at you. Does this mean something to you?"

"Perhaps. I keep notes on the beasts, and this is a very interesting addition. Has anyone seen the creatures in their intoxicated state? I am curious as to the effect upon them," said Clavius.

"No one has reported seeing them in a drunken state yet," said Barak. "As you said, no one would like to be in close range when the beasts become inebriated. Their temperament is volatile in their most sober state."

"Yes, Barak. I would agree." said Clavius. "I am curious though. Do you or Socius know why I went to work in the mines?"

"I recall there was a great deal of chatter about your move to mining. You went from a well known and respected scientist to a miner very quickly. No one understood why, and the only explanation seemed to be that you were just a sort of quirky fellow. That would be the unofficial explanation."

"That would be partly correct, Barak. There is more though. Did you not ever wonder how I know so much about the Angel folk and their spells and incantations?"

"Of course, it did cross my mind, but I am sorry to say, for one reason or another my time has been taken up to the point of distraction, and I was never able to satisfy my curiosity. But you have our attention now, Clavius. Would this not be an appropriate time to fill us in?"

"Very well. It will do me good to enjoy a little boasting," smiled Clavius, who needed no other encouragement. "I left the Hall of Science for a particular reason which I will not disclose lest it distract from my story. I had no idea of what I would do to pass my eternity, except that my desire to know about the Angel culture has always dominated my thoughts." The dwarfish man looked up at Mortuus. "You have no idea what impact your presence has on my heart and soul, my friend." Clavius looked ahead again. "I was passing the mines, and, like you, Exaro and Abreo were there, and called out to me. They asked me to sit and stay a while, and share any news I might have, as they offered theirs. I learned, during this conversation, that the demons who claimed a share of the ore from the mines would often converse with Eruos, the chief of the three miners, on a regular basis. I listened, interested to know what anyone had to say to demon workers. Eruos, it turned out, was one of those odd people who can talk to his own worst enemy safely. Something about him put the beasts at ease, and always they would tell of the news of their own world. Since the creatures were the closest to the Fallen, I determined that I might get more information about the angel folk from them. Soon after this encounter, I volunteered to work with the three miners."

"The information I gathered was either from eavesdropping on their conversations with Eruos, or asking them directly myself. Of the latter, I did very little, I might add. I am not the silver-tongued Eruos, and the demons' volatility spilled out on me a few times. I had been warned not to speak to them by Exaro and Abreo, but my desire got the best of me, and I was painfully reminded of my hubris on several occasions. To remedy my inability to query the beasts, I would speak with Eruos before they returned for ore, and he would ask the questions in his particularly pacifying mannerism. Thus, I became educated in much of the culture, lore and magic of the Angel folk."

"So did you not like the mines, Clavius? You went on to create quite an underground terrain of your own," said Socius.

"I created the underground within a few days, if you would believe it, my boy."

"I do not," returned a surprised Socius. "I do not believe it possible at all."

"I do not lie," chuckled Clavius. "I learned well from my work in the mines. By the time I left, I had Eruos convince the demons they would get far more ore by sharing their spells with him. They considered for a while, and after a few more visits to pick up ore, Eruos had been entrusted with a particular spell, useful for mining work. The only setback is that using it drains humans heavily. It is very productive otherwise."

"Amazing!" exclaimed Socius.

"Yes it is Socius. I may teach it to you one day. And there are other spells too, but I want first to see about our theory." They continued walking, and talking along this line of Clavius' Angel folk knowledge, and the time seemed to pass quickly.

Just before arriving in Luton, Darius began to feel unusually insecure. Though he had been washed of the mud and filth of the Vestibule, the odor seemed always present, though no one else seemed to notice. He would have been content to spend his eternity at the rocky oasis of the Vestibule, where he and his two companion fugitives traveled to after escaping the hell flies. Yet here he was, according to Socius, a full-fledged citizen of Limbo. Darius knew if his true identity was discovered, he would be expelled from Limbo as violently as his friends had been captured and mutilated by the demons, and his torment would surely become far more horrific than his sentence in the Vestibule. Now that his new friend had been discovered to be one of the Fallen, his thoughts became doubts, and an underlying anxiety began to eat at him.

He did not belong in this place, this utopian oasis tucked within the walls of Hell. His friends had been captured while he hid, cowering under a rock as they screamed in pain. He did not belong in the company of Angel-kind. This being, who had befriended him, was his better. All of them would see his inferiority eventually, and then he would be cast out, left behind. The reasoning of Darius, the lifelong slave, was lethal and a darkening depression began to overtake him, when just then, his thoughts were broken by Mortuus, who had been walking at his side most of the way.

"You are troubled still, Darius," said Mortuus, "…and it has to do with your feelings of unworthiness to be here?" Darius was astonished, and Clavius focused in on the conversation. Darius, caught, nodded nervously, guiltily. "I do not understand why, but I sense your pain. You are wrong to feel this way, Darius, and you are causing damage to yourself with this mindset. It is guilt, and a kind of faulty thinking that does not serve you. It is much to bear, your burden. But you overload yourself… unnecessarily." Clavius interjected, staring at Mortuus.

"Is this true, Darius? Is Mortuus accurate in his assessment of your dark mood?" asked Clavius. Barak and Socius turned to look at Mortuus and Clavius. The group had stopped.

"To my shame…it is," said Darius quietly. "My life has never been my own. I was a lifelong slave - always the bottom of society - and I cannot seem to feel any other way. I wait for you all to wise up and dismiss me, more so since discovering Mortuus' true identity. I just cannot shake this feeling of impending abandonment."

"You are highly empathic, Mortuus, an excellent ability but not one I had considered present in the Fallen. You can sense the feelings of others. That can be good as long as you are able to separate yourself and keep your boundaries; otherwise you could get swept into their feelings, experiencing emotion that does not belong to you. It is impressive," said Clavius, who turned to address Darius. "Darius, you are no doubt feeling guilty about your fellows, and maybe having guilt about being in Limbo while so many are tormented on the outside. That can only mean you are a truly good man, a man of virtue, and you absolutely belong here. There are many more that seem to have been misplaced by the mirror of Minos, people of considerably low character. *They* never question their placement. I have not determined the mechanism used to decide eternal placement by the mirror, but you have reached Limbo, Darius. And here you shall stay as long as you like."

Darius smiled at this, as did Socius, Barak and Mortuus, who felt the weight lift from Darius. Barak cautioned the group.

"We have to keep moving." Everyone quickly restarted, resuming a quick walking speed as Barak explained places and their route along the way.

"We have been staying near the outer wall for some time. Soon we will enter Luton, another village known for its specialization. It is there the wine is mixed with herbal concoctions. Our best herbal healers reside there, and we will pass through the village on our return trip. All of Limbo will be alerted and looking for anything out of the ordinary soon. We will circumvent Luton so as not to stir curiosities that might bite us later. Keep your eyes searching skyward. If you should notice any movement, dive to the ground and sit as if we have been talking for ages. Try to appear oblivious to the flying demons, as if we are another philosophizing or storytelling group, chatting and not noticing the world around us. You have noticed a few seated groups already during our travels, my friends?" Barak turned toward Mortuus and Darius, who nodded in acknowledgement. They had seen small clusters of people along the path who did not appear to respond to their presence.

"Barak. How far to the Dark Forest?" asked Socius. "I have not been back this way for ages; it seems the vineyards have grown in size."

"The people of Luton have enlarged the vineyards to increase the spirit production. Demand is very high these days," explained Barak.

"Will we get to sample some of the wines, Barak?" asked Darius. "I have not tasted a good wine for some time. In fact, the last time I recalled the scent of wine was on the breath of my master, who whipped me to death in his drunken state. I am sure it was accidental. Slaves were valuable pieces of property, and none were more faithful than I." Mortuus was walking alongside Darius, listening horrified at his tale. "I should be honest, my friends, I was angry at the master for raping a servant girl in front of all of us as a lesson, and as a display of his power; I provoked my beating by goading him, and insulting his honor. It was the only time I stood up for anyone since my early teenage years." Darius waited for judgment from the others, nervously watching as they reacted. Mortuus stared at him, appearing saddened and frustrated, then amazed at what Darius had gone through. He had no words to express his feelings.

"That is some bad exodus from living, Darius." said Socius. "Did you never fight back against this cruel master?"

"Only once. When I was a teenager, my anger was peaked many times, but mostly I did not act out. One day, after a particularly wicked son of the master spit upon me, I slapped him in the face as hard as I could. His shock at being able to be hurt by me was total, and caused him to run, unable to believe what had happened. For my transgression, I was almost beaten to death that day by the master. The house servants begged his mercy, and reminded him of the high cost of slave youths, and saved my life. From then on I promised my saviors, the servants of the house, to never touch the son or act out again, and that I would be obedient. And for reasons I never fathomed, the cruel boy kept his distance ever after."

"Why be born at all," asked Socius, "if such would be your fate?" Mortuus and Barak nodded, and in an attempt to pick up the spirits of the group, Barak answered Darius' original question.

"Of course, my friend, we will get to taste the wines." He winked at Darius, who smiled as he followed.

Luton appeared on the left of the travelers, through trees that grew sparsely in a field of high grass, roughly 100 meters away. They moved between the wall, which separated them from the river Acheron, and the trees. The path turned toward the outer wall halfway as they came upon the path into the Dark Forest.

There, in the Dark Forest, trees grew tall and stood tightly together. The wood smelled of musty, damp earth, and the trees seemed as serene gods in a state of deep sleep. The path was winding and narrow, and visibility was limited. The forest had meager lighting, only enough to portray a late twilight. It was a beautiful and ominous arrangement.

When they had gone a far distance past Luton, the trail suddenly opened out into a huge lake, circled tightly by trees. Few narrow openings between the trees could be seen, and where they stood looked to be the main entrance to the water's edge. The water was dark, reflecting the forest that surrounded it. Mortuus gazed intently; he could see a shimmering dance of colors across the surface that phased in and out of his vision.

"What are those waves of color across the surface?" he asked. The group looked at the body of water, then at Mortuus questioningly.

"Where do you mean, Mortuus?" asked Barak. "I do not see what you speak of." Mortuus looked at Barak.

"There. Toward the center," Mortuus pointed.

Socius winced as he looked at the water, not sure of what he saw. Darius looked and shook his head.

"I see nothing but the dark lake, Mortuus," answered Socius.

"As do I," said Barak. "Clavius?"

"Aye," replied Clavius. "Just water. Perhaps you are weary, Mortuus. We have traveled a great distance, almost a quarter circle since leaving my cottage in Porto."

But Mortuus looked again, sure of what he had seen. The colors were still present; fading a bit, then suddenly appearing brightly and plainly in his sight.

"I am tired, though I still see the colors. Can we stop here for a few minutes?" asked Mortuus. Barak, addressing Mortuus and Darius, spoke.

"Actually, that was our intention, Mortuus. My friends, I would ask that step into the lake. For you Mortuus, this water will begin to regenerate the magical power within, restoring that which was lost or stolen by the Fallen's spells and the foul liquid they fed you to keep you unaware and forgetting." Mortuus looked puzzled, but seemed to understand why he was seeing the colors on the lake, as they wavered in and out – it was the magic, the same magical power he had seen concealing the demon Elder. What did this lake conceal, he wondered, or was it only the signature of magic? Darius began to remove his robes.

"Will this water do anything for me?" asked Darius. Clavius smiled, as did Barak.

"You will no longer smell even the faintest scent of outer Hell." said Clavius. "And you will feel invigorated even more so than when you drank from the Second Waters." Mortuus was staring at the surface, looking down to see the bottom. He could see nothing but blackness.

"Mortuus. Please, enter the water. We need to hide in the trees again soon. They will be coming soon for you and I want your angel healing to begin promptly. You will be much more useful at your strongest, both magically and physically. When you two finish, we will move quickly to our rendezvous point. Luckily, we do not have to go all the way to Basel. In fact, we need to backtrack a bit."

"Where is this meeting, Barak? I understood it to be *in* Basel." said Socius.

"You'll see." said Barak. "Now jump in – I know it is cold Mortuus!" he yelled to the shivering angel. "Darius – there you go!" And both were in the water, underneath, then up, gasping for breath as the shock of the coldness of the water convulsed their bodies. "Feels good, does it not?" Mortuus looked at Barak as if he were crazy. "Very well. Now, both of you out. We need to go."

Soon, the group was walking along the path, back through the thick, dark forest. Just as Socius was about to ask Barak how much further, they came to a sharp turn, past a large boulder that was on their right when they came this way earlier. Barak stopped them all with a silent wave of his hand, then, looking at the large boulder, he spoke. The words were familiar to Mortuus, but he did not know why.

"*Gahdtwer!*" said Barak directly to the stone face. The boulder rolled slowly out onto the path as Barak moved back. A small passage hole in the forest was revealed behind where the boulder had been, a crawlspace carved through the thick tree bottoms. It was not high enough for anyone to stand upright, and so Barak motioned to the group to get on all fours and crawl. When they had passed him, he backed in on his hands and knees, then spoke again to the rock face. He scampered into the hole and caught up to the group. The blunt sound of the boulder rolling back into place followed his movements.

"Are you okay, Barak?" asked Clavius. "I could have cast the spell."

"I am fine, Clavius." replied Barak. "Just a bit weak. I have felt worse." Mortuus was puzzled by this exchange, as were Darius and Socius.

"Did something happen? Clavius, why did-" Mortuus was cut off by Clavius.

"It was the spell, Mortuus. Perhaps we should have let you practice your art. Magic use by humans causes severe energy drain. We do get better with practice. It takes so long to get our energy back after a heavy spell like moving that boulder. The long hallway under my hut incapacitated me for a week. The bigger the job, the bigger the energy drain."

"You learned the magic spell from the smithy demons?" asked Socius.

"That one I learned from the Chronicler," said Clavius. "All the members know of it. Tell no one of this, Socius, not even your dearest friends. One member of the society used the spell publicly and was reported to the Elder's Council by a so-called friend. He mysteriously disappeared soon after. Now that we know the Elder's are in league with the demons, I correctly assume my old friend is suffering in outer Hell."

"I must rest, friends." said a weakened Barak. "I will catch up with you."

"Enough about the magic." said Clavius. "We are almost there and my knees are getting raw; pretend as if you did not hear the spell word when we are in front of the others."

The group crawled for a short time, taking in the ornate carving along the way. The trees had been etched carefully all through the path. Then a circular, hollowed rock had been wedged into the hole, like an earring, to keep the trees from growing back together. Barak explained that the trees healed up quite fast; that was how so much wood could be found in Limbo. As long as the trees were not fully cut down they would regenerate, just like humans, and keep up the supply of wood for Limbo's usage. This stand of trees hid the group and any others who ventured through. No one else knew of the passage except for the society, who had used it for meetings for millennia. The only other way in or out was to fly, but the space was camouflaged very well by the canopy of the treetops. They crawled until they reached a small trickle of a stream that flowed toward the dark lake, where another path opened up. They stood up, relieved, as the roughness of the tree roots and gravel on their knee caps was gone. A thin path took them to a small, rocky mound. Barak caught up just as they arrived.

"*Gahtwer Viatra!*" whispered Clavius. A second later, the mound opened wide and revealed a rocky stairwell. The opening was large enough to easily walk in, single file. They stepped downward, and a set of torches flamed up as they walked near, surprising Mortuus and Darius. They were in a large room again, not unlike the cavern which led to Clavius' work area, though not as grand. The meeting was held in a corner of the cavern. There were eight people already seated around a long, flat table of stone, each of them studying Mortuus intently, staring as if none of the others of the group were present. Mortuus, uncomfortable at their scrutinizing, stared back at each of them.

"So much for tact and grace," said an irritated Clavius. "Please do not stare at Mortuus; he is *very* sensitive, and your staring is *very* rude." Clavius berated his fellow members for their lack of consideration. "Mortuus, Darius and Socius - please sit here." He pointed to the empty far end of the table. "You are our guests, and get the good seats. Do not mind their rudeness, Mortuus. They have never seen your kind before."

"When will the Chronicler arrive, Percival?" asked Barak of one of the members. He waited for an answer, and then studied the eyes of Percival, who was still gawking at Mortuus. "Well? No answer?" Barak was getting impatient.

"Barak, I think Percival has bad news," answered a frustrated Clavius. "Percival, speak already." Percival, looking quite stunned, began to speak, though he stammered at first. The other society members stopped staring at Mortuus, and turned toward Barak and Clavius while Percival answered, though occasionally shot glances randomly at the newly awakened member of the Fallen.

"There is a great disturbance, Barak. This angel…pardon me… Mortuus, is known to be missing from the custody of the Fallen. Their high demons have been to the Elders, and some have inquired as to the whereabouts of Morpheus." Mortuus began to tighten up, fear gripping him in a cold vise. Percival continued, "I do not know if you heard it, but-"

"Yes. We all heard the horn," interrupted Barak. His face was pasted with worry and irritation. "Back to my original question. What about the Chronicler, Percival? Is he coming or not?"

"The Chronicler has been made aware, Barak. You know how he is – no one can predict what he is up to, but I suspect he will not appear, as usual. The demons will visit him first when the Elders have no answers. There are guards who work for the Elders without questioning their commands, and I am certain they will be dispatched to find… answers." Percival looked at Mortuus and Darius with worry and unexpectedly cut to the chase. "The strangers will have to leave," he sputtered.

"Wait!" roared Clavius, 'What of the theory? This is not part of it, Percival, damn you!"

"The theory is vague, Clavius. What makes you think it would really manifest?" argued a predictably defensive Percival. "We have had this discussion many times-"

"That is your opinion only, Percival. We have a great chance if we can only grab it by the reins. Our fear is all that keeps us from realizing our dream." said a red faced Clavius.

"*Our* dream, Clavius?" asked another society member seated next to Percival.

"Is it not our reason for meeting all these millennia, Justinius?" asked Clavius. "Why do we gather at all? Do you not recall our original intention? Or are we some snobbish social club with a foolish wish list!" Clavius was yelling.

"We meet to keep abreast of news and the happenings in Limbo, Clavius." replied a worried Justinius. "This is to our mutual benefit. Were it not for the Elders, we would have great chaos in –"

"The Elders?" asked Socius. "The Elders? The Elders who allowed the demons into their ranks? The Elders? Are you beyond sense?!! Since when did we trust those pompous old fools?"

"I do not care for your tone, Socius." said Percival sharply. "The times are too dangerous for secret schemes and foolish uprisings. The angel and the fugitive have to leave before we are persecuted along with them!" Percival's desperation was growing more apparent. He turned toward Mortuus, whose face had softened into a deeply hurt sadness. Darius began to stare downward, sighing, and Mortuus closed his eyes.

"I am very sorry. I realize you have come through much pain and trouble. Of course it is for the safety of the whole -"

"Say no more Mortuus - you will stay, the sycophants can leave and hide their cowardly faces in their Elder friend's robes!" Socius was livid.

"Mortuus, Darius and Socius – please wait for us outside," interrupted Clavius loudly as he stared directly into the face of Percival. "We will not be long. Barak and I must confer with our *fellows*."

The three left the cavern while the society members began a shouting match. The three sat outside the rocky mound, each stunned or angry and contemplating their next steps. Mortuus thought about how he would miss Limbo. Nothing good existed in outer Hell; even the rocky oasis in the Vestibule could not touch the experience of Limbo. He thought about his healing and if that would continue in outer Hell, now that he would be without the waters and fruits. His thoughts went to the revelations that he was an angel and just what it would mean outside these walls. Could he fight throughout Hell? And what would happen if he was captured by the Fallen, who had cruelly cut his wings off? They would surely return him to that place he had awoken from, erasing his memories and removing the magical energies that were renewing within him. If he had just had more time…

Clavius and Barak emerged from the rocky underground. They looked disheveled and beaten, worn out from their arguing and frustration.

"The news is grim," reported a somber Barak. "I would speak to you when I have calmed down, my friends. For now we will turn back on our path and get away from these fools I had mistaken for friends."

Quietly, the group walked, and then crawled back the way they had come into the secret meeting area. Gloomily, they avoided Luton, on their right this time, and passed the vineyards of Homer much later. The demons would be searching in the inhabited places for the fugitives; Percival, Justinius and the other members of the society had informed Clavius and Barak that the guards were in fact looking for two persons who had entered Limbo, not just Mortuus, although he was the higher priority and thus in the greatest danger.

Clavius was shocked at the attitude of the society when he had ultimately proven the theory of change and how it would come to Limbo. The long talked about and speculated change was the object of conversation for many centuries of society meetings, and now that it was really here, the society was suddenly grim and fearful, obedient to the Elder's Council. All Clavius could think of was how badly he had misjudged his friends. The long walk was silent until Barak finally spoke.

"My friends, I am in grave pain over the society's decision to expel you. We are going to return to Bremen, despite the judgment of my fellow society members, and seek answers from the senior scientist Benjamin, who we met with earlier. Benjamin is about the wisest person I know besides the Chronicler, and who I trust the most. Militus will send runners past us if there is news we should be aware of. I look upon your faces, I see pain and fear. Know this; we have no intention of expelling either of you; do not fear. You are among friends."

Mortuus and Darius half smiled, happy for this support from Barak, but uncertain if they should hope. Both knew their presence was causing a great disturbance in Limbo, and though they were safe within the walls, always there was the knowledge of Hell outside that played in the background of their awareness.

"Why do you give them false hope, Barak, when we are being watched even now by the society members?" Clavius was suddenly cynical. Mortuus watched as the sad, dwarfish man spewed out his pain in the form of negativity. Barak angered and shouted back his reply.

"Clavius! Fool! I am not expelling anyone. This IS part of the theory. We cannot destroy our one alliance with a real member of the Fallen! They will find him and place him into the deep sleep again."

"We do not have a choice!" yelled Clavius. "I want the alliance too, Barak, but we have no say in the matter."

"No. We do not seem to." said Barak. "But until we find out, we should not expel them. Let the society complain. Will they report to the Elders? I do not think so."

"Barak," said Clavius. "Gather your wits. Justinius is in favor of the Elders. The society has already been compromised. Can you not see that? The society is infiltrated. How long do you think it will be before the demons disguise themselves as society members? Justinius was the strongest proponent of the theory, yet he has sided fully with the Elder's Council. And I had spoken with him not so long ago…" Clavius trailed off, disheartened, as Barak hung his head sadly.

"This is so wrong," whispered Barak gloomily. "So wrong…"

The group continued walking, saddened, angry, and confused. Mortuus, considering that this would be the last part of his visit to Limbo, studied his surroundings, taking in as many details as possible for his own memories, as if it were the last time he would ever see such sights again. Darius wept to himself quietly, briefly, a sudden knowing overtaking him.

"They will be waiting for us outside the gate," he said. "Just like Aristotle. They must have ambushed him as he left. That Elder, Alcander, knew it would happen. Now they will wait for us."

Concern spread on the faces of the group. Darius was correct. Socius recalled his last meeting with Aristotle, and the feeling of being watched from atop the inner wall. It made sense to him. Clavius growled angrily at the treachery of the Elders, and Barak suddenly became hopeful.

"We would not send you out until it was safe to do so, and I will do all in my power to insure we do not have to part," exclaimed Barak. "Socius, you could send a party of your warrior friends out to ascertain the path is safe, as you did when you found them."

"Against a force of demons, Barak? Aristotle was adept at protecting himself against the imps, and yet still almost lost a few times," cautioned Clavius. "I'm sure one demon is enough, though I would wager the Fallen will use more." Barak grimaced at his blundered thinking; he was trying too desperately to overcome this very unpleasant situation, and obviously losing his battle.

Socius nodded in agreement with Clavius a fraction of a moment before he hit upon a way that the wanted pair could leave safely. He considered this as they walked toward Bremen. If Mortuus and Darius had to return to outer Hell, they could elude the demons waiting outside the gate by taking another passage that Socius had learned of long ago. He had almost completely forgotten about this passage as there had simply been no reason to use it in hundreds of years. Smiling to himself, he walked and planned, but did not bring up his thoughts yet to either fugitive. He would see to it the pathway still existed. Denying the demon fugitive hunters their prey would be his greatest revenge for what they did to his teacher, his friend, and his father.

Chapter 51
The Final Judgment

It was my turn for judgment. I stood outside the doorway of the room, dreading what was to come next. Inside, the centaur and the great, large man were talking in their booming, powerful voices, almost arguing, though in my haze of fear I could not give their conversation my full attention. The last person in front of me had gone inside a few moments before, and I was standing by the entrance trying to seek some escape from my predicament.

The line behind me had stopped queuing not too far back, and the other passenger in the boat, the man who I hated for causing Charon to strike me had begun crying again. I was weakened, and I could not pull together enough energy to hate his weeping. At this point, hate was a waste of energy I could not afford; and I was crying too, the wetness running all over my face, lips and chin. I could not stop it no matter how I tried. It was uncontrollable, like when I first experienced death at my grandfather's viewing.

I was a young boy, age eleven. My mother, stepfather and brothers all went to the funeral home. I was not expecting to cry, and yet as soon as I saw my grandfather's body laid out in the coffin, I lost it. Completely. No one else was affected, it seemed, but me. It was uncontrollable, and for my young self, rather disconcerting. Now I was here, in Hell, and would never see anybody I loved again, and I would suffer permanently, and not know why. There was no way out, no legality, no one to feel pity, and pull me out, no nothing. Period.

Just then, the loudest, most deadly roar came to my ears, and I stopped.

"NEXT!" yelled the voice of the great man. My wits came back to me and I stood tall. I would go with dignity; somehow I would find the will to carry myself through. I had never had a feeling so strong, and I was not sure why the first time it would occur would be in Hell. I began to breathe in, the foul air passing through my nostrils and into my lungs, but I refused to gag. Instead, I ignored this 'flavor' of Hell and became calm. I closed my eyes and breathed deeply, and searched within myself for a space of peace. I would remember my life one last time, as positively as I could, and hold my memories as best I could. I entered the room of my final judgment, and I embraced my lifetime as I walked toward the mirror.

The centaur was much larger close up, as was the great man. They were conversing as if I was a passing leaf on the wind, and that was fine with me. I walked straight up to the mirror, a door-sized silver slab set in an ornately carved metal piece that looked like it was solid gold. But I was not interested in anything but my reflection, and as I strived for peace within, I watched as my entire life unfolded in the reflection.

Chapter 52

The Newcomer's Arrival

Mortuus saw a bright light ahead, just through the trees on the group's left. A line of light had appeared from out of nowhere, splitting reality from the misty ceiling to the ground just behind the trees for a single moment, yet no one else seemed to notice it; everyone continued the hurried pace, walking as if nothing had happened. Mortuus stopped and struggled to see through the trees, to view the ground where the light had touched. Something was there, but he could not quite get his eyes on it. It was hidden just out of sight. Darius had noticed Mortuus had stopped and saw his erratic head movements. He looked also in the direction of his friend, and saw what Mortuus could not. He turned back to Mortuus.

"What are you looking for?"

"There is something there, behind the trees, but I cannot see it. Can you see it?" asked Mortuus.

"Yes," replied Darius. "It is only a man; he appears to be a newcomer by his dress. I say this because everyone in Limbo wears fine robes, like ours."

"I must see. Come with me. I want to see this newcomer." Darius saw that the others had kept their pace and were disappearing as the path curved ahead. They had not noticed the trailing pair had stopped. "We'll catch up," continued Mortuus, "I am in no hurry to leave. Did you see the strangely beautiful light Darius?"

"No. I did not," said Darius, "but I thought I detected the scent of outer Hell for a split second. It passed so quickly, I am wondering if I really smelled it."

"Yes - I also caught that scent. I must see what caused it."

Darius was happy to follow Mortuus, like when they first met. This time they walked through the dense forest in the direction of where he had seen the newcomer. The newcomer had silently stepped behind a tree ahead, but was still partially visible. He appeared to be hiding, but from whom wondered Darius. Mortuus was ahead and now seeing a lot more than Darius. The strange newcomer was poorly hidden, looking around, with a puzzled expression on his face, but his body was surrounded by a sparkling field of energy that only Mortuus could see. The light was fading slowly from his vision as Mortuus cautiously approached. The newcomer, seeing the large presence of the angel, stared fearfully, not sure what to do or think. He searched the forest, checking for a quick escape route. Mortuus, sensing the fearful man's desire to flee, stopped and motioned to Darius to stop behind him.

"Wait, please friend, I would speak with you only a few moments, if you are willing." The newcomer stood silently for a second, then relieved, beckoned to Mortuus. Mortuus moved closer, watching as the last of the sparkling light faded. Darius followed on the heels of his Angel friend.

"I do not know where I am. Or who you are," said the stranger, scanning Mortuus and Darius.

"You have been sentenced to Limbo, my friend. Where were you last?" asked Mortuus.

"I stood in the room of the hall, where I was before a large mirror."

"And when did you arrive here?"

"Just now. I just arrived here. This is Limbo? Are you sure?" The man was searching the eyes of Mortuus, trying to discern that he was real and of a peaceful nature. He was strangely comfortable, as was Mortuus.

"Yes. You have been given the lightest sentence in Hell." The man heaved a sigh of relief as Mortuus said this. Swooning, he fell back into a nearby tree, knocking his head. He stood up, holding the back of his head, but still he smiled as he cursed under his breath. It was clear the man knew just how lucky he was. Mortuus now recognized the colorful light he had seen was the magic of the mirror teleporting the newcomer.

"I have been transported to Limbo then?" said the happy newcomer, his spirits rising. "Where do I go first?"

"You seem to need new robes, my friend," said Mortuus. The angel was feeling he and Darius needed to return to the path; their friends would be searching for them. Before Mortuus had seen the beautiful light, the group had passed Porto and were approximately half way between Porto and Terni, an easy walk for the newcomer. Mortuus offered his help to the stranger. "You may follow us back to the path, and we will point you toward Porto where the robe makers will dress you as finely as we are." Mortuus said this as he turned to display the fine craftsmanship of his robes; Darius also turned to offer a view of his. The newcomer looked at the pair's dress robes, a strange look on his face.

"So…they don't have jeans here then?"

Chapter 53

Demon Attack

Mortuus saw it first – a projectile moving so fast toward the group that it defied all that they knew. No bird had flown so fast nor creature moved so quickly that they could not follow, yet it was coming at them, a blur of movement. Clavius and Barak did not see it, nor did Darius. Mortuus yelled loudly to alert them, but only Socius acknowledged seeing the creature moving toward them. It was a huge man shape with giant-wide wings. When it neared them, it turned its body upward and stopped in the air, then dropped to the ground. Its wings vanished, and the creature stood before the stunned and terrified group. It was a demon, only it was more like a human than the Morpheus demon who Mortuus had beaten. It had the distorted features of a demon, but it looked like a cross between each. They were being attacked by a high demon.

"*B'rithjall – mahe!*" spoke the creature suddenly, in a hissing voice. Everyone, including Mortuus, could feel their joints stiffening up, the legs and arms frozen, all movement inhibited. They could not even speak. It had cast a spell that paralyzed them. Even Mortuus could not fight this beast.

The demon stared at Mortuus and approached, throwing him to the ground roughly. The beast turned Mortuus face down and tore his robes enough to bare his full back, speaking a strange spell as it did so. Mortuus felt a familiar twinge along his back that he first felt in the laboratory of Clavius – his wings had opened, or what were supposed to be his wings. The group saw for the second time the elongated rows of bloody stumps that had once been full wings. The demon angrily kicked Mortuus in his ribcage, sending the angel on his side in pain, and unable to move even to hold his pained ribs. The demon cursed him even as he rained down abuse, fueled by his rage.

"Worthless, filthy creature," spewed the violent demon. "Hiding among these simple children!" Several kicks struck the helpless angel-fugitive. He was on the ground cringing in pain as his ribs cracked, the paralysis disabling any protective movement. "You will wish you had remained asleep!" A kick to the face smashed his nose and it erupted with blood. "Superior, angel?"

Socius, watching his friend at the mercy of this giant beast, grew red in the face, and felt his body begin to loosen up – he was able to move again. He looked around at the others, still motionless. The demon landed another kick in the legs of Mortuus as Socius got up and approached from behind. "I think not!" The demon, sensing Socius, backhanded him with barely an effort, sending him flying into a tree ten meters away, and then resumed his violence on Mortuus. Socius lay still against the tree.

The demon, tiring of his abuse of Mortuus, reached into a sash around his waist, pulling out a long metallic horn tucked there. It walked over toward Socius nonchalantly, and readied to blow the horn as it kicked the youth against the tree. The hand that held the metal horn, which had been in the process of raising the horn to its mouth, was pinned into its throat as an arrow abruptly appeared to grow out of it. Its face was a question, not understanding what had happened. Another projectile followed, penetrating the right side of the demon. The creature fell to the ground, writhing in pain and anger as it had never before, the impertinence of violence against it seeming more to fuel its rage than even the pain of the shafts impaling it. As the group, who had been paralyzed in place, watched, a small company of fifteen heavily armed warriors suddenly surrounded the fallen demon, followed by a giant centaur, its crossbow firing into the demon as it scanned the furious, pained creature.

The soldiers, who had a range of weapons from spears to maces and long bows, and swords, jabbed at the demon, stabbing or smashing any body part exposed. The demon turned over, rolling to its left onto its belly, and the warriors who stood nearest it were suddenly flying away, as wide wings appeared from nowhere. The remaining warriors yelled to stay back, as the centaur shot bolt after bolt into the wings, pinning the beast to the ground like some macabre butterfly. The warriors stayed out of the way, striking, slicing and stabbing the demon at any sign of movement.

The soldiers kicked the horn out of the creature's pinned hand. The centaur walked up close, clearing the men from the area, before addressing the demon. It looked up at the centaur, with fear in its eyes for the first time in its existence. The centaur spoke in a soft and strange language, not the common tongue of Hell, and before everyone's eyes, the beast became smoke. The demon was destroyed.

Mortuus, still laying in pain, began to be able to move again, but he was in too much pain to get up. The warriors helped him up gingerly as he had some broken ribs. Socius was also brought to his feet by the warriors, who mostly turned out to be his friends; Socius also thought he knew who this great centaur was from Aristotle's descriptions. Barak and Clavius were in a state of joy, as was Darius. The spell soon wore off fully, and they met their saviors and this greatest of warriors, the Master Centaur, Chiron.

The friends of Socius, his warrior playmates with whom he had trained and combated with in the battle games, were happy to see and save their long time friend. And they were happy beyond belief to have fought a greater demon alongside the greatest of warriors, Chiron. The Master Centaur had been searching for Socius, and wanted to meet Mortuus. The warriors, who had proudly escorted Chiron, told him along the way of the arrival of Mortuus and the subsequent demon slaying.

Coming up from the back of the crowd of warriors was Militus, newly arrived on the scene. The warriors, who were buzzing in the joy and excitement of this great adventure, surrounded Militus, telling him of their hand in the destroying of the demon, their fighting alongside Chiron. Militus walked toward the wounded warriors who had been thrown aside by the mighty wing opening of the beast, seeing that they were tended to before moving toward Chiron, who was retrieving his arrows from the kill site. Mortuus was held up by Darius and Socius as he rubbed his ribs and gently touched his battered face; he was already regenerating, his ribs were very sore, but no longer broken from the violent kicks.

Militus, with serious face, gave Socius a note, passed on, he said, from Benjamin. Socius took it, reading it quietly, and his disdain apparent. The youth then handed it to Barak, who read and passed it to Clavius, who read it aloud – his tone was defeated.

> *My friends – danger is coming. You must leave by another way. I know the predicament the society has put you in. Get to the mine. Chiron will take you back to his circle until danger has passed.*
> *Benjamin*

Mortuus winced as he suddenly touched his sore nose too roughly, and Darius shoulders sunk as his head fell to his chest. Their fears were truly confirmed; they would be exiting Limbo, returning back to outer Hell. They had feared this all along, sensing it within, but allowed hope at the prior words of Barak. Clavius frowned. Now it was a certainty. The joy left the air around the odd fugitive pair. Socius wore his disappointment clearly; his countenance was sadness.

"Militus – what have you done with Alcander?" asked Socius. The Elder was not with the group, as Socius had suspected he would not be.

"He is being detained, silently, until the demons leave. They have gone to search from the other end of Limbo. The Chronicler will be getting a visit if he has not already met them." Militus looked very serious. "I would introduce you all formally. And I want you to know this is a very old friend of mine." Militus pointed in the direction of the Master Centaur. "My friends, this is Chiron." The centaur stared at each person, bowing respectfully and causing slight discomfort with the natural intensity of his stare. Mortuus seemed to understand the centaur protocol, and bowed back, as best as he could while rubbing his ribs again. Chiron stared for a full minute at Darius, who squirmed and did not follow Mortuus' lead. Finally Socius nudged him with his elbow, and whispered for him to bow his head politely. Socius knew the protocol well as he had copied it into the logs of Aristotle. Darius nervously bowed, and Chiron moved through the rest of the group. Darius sighed loudly in relief as Socius chuckled.

"My friend," said Militus to the towering centaur, "These are the two who have visited us recently." Militus gestured to Mortuus. "This is Mortuus, of whom Phlegyas spoke to you, recently awoken by Aristotle. He does not know of his origins, or history or even what his real name is. Aristotle provided him with the equipment and a name to pass through to Limbo, although it was still quite challenging-"

"I am aware of the challenges of traveling through Hell, Militus. My own wounds are not fully healed, even with your waters and elixirs." Chiron examined Mortuus, studying him as if no other thing in Hell existed. Suddenly, he stopped looking, though his eyes were open and staring widely into open space. Militus knew what was happening, though he had not seen it for so very long. Mortuus, confused, started to speak to Chiron as if trying to snap him out of his trance; Militus' hands flew up immediately, to silence Mortuus and all the others. Chiron was in one of his trances.

Chiron was back on the ice, the same ice as in his prior vision. Eight Fallen were before him, and their demons growled and snarled. He could see his centaur herds, and within their ranks were warrior humans, armed heavily. There was something in the freezing, windy air overhead, something that Chiron strained to see...

Then it was over. Chiron was back, confused momentarily, with the entire group watching, staring at him. Some of the warriors had joined the group and were looking at the dazed centaur. Militus watched and waited.

"Are you alright, my friend?" asked Militus.

"I am fine. Do you remember my inner visions?" asked Chiron. Militus nodded. "Well," said Chiron, "Even in Hell I have them. We had so much to talk of I did not get a chance to discuss them with you yet." Now Chiron looked at the group of four. "You are one of the Fallen, Mortuus. Why did you not fly at the creature when it attacked your group?"

"I was paralyzed by the beast's incantation, as were we all. But even if we were not so immobilized, I have no wings," replied Mortuus sadly.

"No wings?" Chiron was stunned. "What happened to your wings?"

"They were removed by those who imprisoned me in the sleep," said Mortuus.

"Removed?" Something was not right, but Chiron would not venture to guess. It was a time of urgency for them all.

"Sawed off," offered Clavius. Chiron considered, disbelief pasted on his face, and felt much sympathy for Mortuus. He was aware of the cruelty with which such an act must be perpetrated, and he sensed no disdain or the grand hatred that he usually felt in the presence of Fallen. In fact, he experienced Mortuus as quite the opposite, a gentle being, but with a strength perhaps even the angel himself was unaware of.

"This demon was far more dangerous than Morpheus. It was terrifying," said Mortuus.

"Until your strength rebuilds, I would recommend you avoiding any direct confrontations with demons. It was luck that the demon, disguised as the Elder, was weaker. That may be why he was assigned to infiltrate the Elders Council. You might be in very different circumstances had this been your first encountered demon." said Clavius. Mortuus nodded in agreement as Chiron studied the disabled fugitive Fallen. Chiron generally disliked angel folk – the Fallen had tasked him and his kind as workers in Hell for eternity. Yet somehow, he liked this angel Mortuus, and he would learn more before making any judgment. Militus waved to get Chiron's attention, calling him toward Socius.

"Master Chiron, here is the person you have sought since coming here. Socius, you have been told of Chiron by Aristotle?" asked Militus. Socius was wide-eyed, excitement brimming. He was finally meeting the head of the centaurs, the fabled Chiron himself, subject of many lessons from his various teachers. He smiled widely.

"Yes – I thought I would never get to meet you," said Socius. "Yet, I would prefer that circumstances were better for our meeting. You have heard of the misfortune of my teacher?"

"Yes." The centaur was abrupt. "That is my purpose for coming here." Socius, curiosity peaked, focused intently on Chiron. "Aristotle was spotted near my post, in a cave that is forbidden to all centaur folk by the Fallen. The cave has watchers standing outside, ready to sound off should anyone approach the entrance; I suspect there is a horn to summon the Fallen in their inventory. My commanders informed me that your teacher, Aristotle, has been taken inside the cave. It is most, most unfortunate. This cave is where the Fallen hide special prisoners, whom they personally torment, though on very rare occasions. We do not know why, nor do we know how or where they caught Aristotle. It is my belief that-"

"Alcander and the demon Elder betrayed Aristotle!" interrupted the bitterly angry Socius with a shout. Chiron was taken aback by the young man's rage and contempt; Socius put out a great deal of power in his outburst. "They work with the demons and Fallen, the Elders betray-"

"Whoa! Easy does it Socius," said Militus sternly. "You are among friends here." The whole group, with a few of the warriors who were now standing around, stared at the enraged young man. They watched and waited for Socius to calm down, and when he finally did, tears began to flow from his eyes.

"I am sorry, Master Chiron," said a wet-faced Socius. "I am not well myself; I get enraged and saddened easily, much more so since losing Aristotle. I did not mean to interrupt you, or to be disrespectful. Aristotle spoke very highly of you, and I would have you know I also regard you highly. Forgive my temperament - please continue."

"No forgiveness is necessary, young ward of Aristotle. I am not annoyed by your emotional outburst. Aristotle is missed by all, and I would hope the most by the one he considered as his own son, whom he expressed great pride in." Socius choked and sputtered a moment, as Militus and Clavius smiled. Darius wiped back a quick tear. Chiron paused and looked around at the group that was now standing around, staring, watching and waiting; most of the warriors were there, waiting on Chiron's words, their faces full of compassion for their saddened friend Socius. "I journeyed to Limbo to find out what was happening. This is a strange event for Hell. I learned that Aristotle had freed a member of the Fallen, related to me by Phlegyas, oarsman of the Styx, but I did not know that you had the angel in your midst until I arrived at the gate. The situation requires more serious action, and thus I have decided, not lightly, what must be done." Chiron paused for a few moments. "I am going to rescue Aristotle, Socius. Angel Mortuus, I would ask your help. No others have defeated a demon barehanded. We will not be alone in this risky undertaking. Your human friend from the First Circle will be of no use, however, in our extraction of Aristotle." Chiron looked at Darius, who shrank timidly under the powerful gaze. "But you will stay protected by a few of my fellow centaurs."

Socius could not believe his ears; the warriors were silent, some wishing for the adventure of real battle, but none actually willing to leave Limbo or combat the Fallen. Clavius and Barak stared in disbelief. Socius was ecstatic. Militus' thoughts were also racing, questioning, strategizing.

"How will you face the Fallen?" asked Militus. "That demon was only a fraction of what a Fallen will be. You will end up trapped and tormented alongside Aristotle."

"The Fallen do not frequent the cave," said Chiron, "And as far as they know, Aristotle has been captured and imprisoned there, left to the attentions of their demon workers. I will bide my time, and study their patterns of visitation. Before I made this journey, I could only dream of rescuing Aristotle. But there were signs laid out for me, signs I cannot ignore."

"I met and conversed with Asterion, known to many of you as the Minotaur." The warriors gasped in unison at this. "The Minotaur, Asterion, may be accompanying us if he can get down into my circle. Another sign occurred as Phlegyas spoke to me of you, Mortuus. But alone, even that would not be enough. The ferryman of Acheron, Charon, is missing. His craft was found empty on the landing of the Limbo side of Acheron. This I saw for myself." Mortuus and Darius looked at each other like guilty children as the leader of the centaur kind spoke of Charon.

"Master Chiron," interrupted Darius. "I can tell you what happened to the ferryman." Darius did, and the entire party watched as the usually serious and well composed Chiron displayed stunned disbelief. By the end, the centaur was smiling at Mortuus and Darius.

"So, there is more to you than meets the eye, Darius. By sacrificing yourself, you saved Mortuus and in turn have rid Hell of the menace of Charon. Another sign I cannot ignore." Chiron continued, "Upon entering Limbo, I was informed of the bare-handed destruction of the demon Elder. Luckily, this company of fine warriors and I entered the scene when this beast appeared. I am no friend to demons and I received great satisfaction felling this one like wild game. Wild game, however, gets my respect when I hunt for it." The warriors laughed at this, nodding their heads simultaneously.

"I could not destroy a demon by myself, for I did not know how without a large herd. I met Minos on my way from the Second Circle, and he bade me stay and visit. The King Judge showed me the spell. He demonstrated on an imp, which also, interestingly, became a cloud of smoke at its demise. I was not certain the spell would work on a demon, especially one so powerful, but once I saw the look of terror on its face, my doubts departed. Also, I am weary, as Minos said I would be from casting the spell. So you see there are far too many signs to ignore." Chiron looked at Militus.

"Militus, you were one of my finest students. I am proud to see you have won the admiration of these able warriors." Chiron surveyed the proud men, who were smiling and staring at this centaur anomaly. Chiron was spoken of many times by Militus as the inspiration for the strategies used in many of their mock battles.

Now they were really face to face with the centaur, and the stature and strength of the Halfling were far more awesome than any tale.

They all stayed in each other's company, not unwary of the danger around them, for hours, speaking to the centaur, asking questions about his life and adventures. Chiron regaled them with stories of his students, the harpies in the circle below, and his study of medicines and healing herbs. Aristotle, who had been a go-between of the humans and centaurs, had shared much of this information in his logs, but many of the warriors were not so inclined to read. In return for the stories of his adventures, the men shared the fruits of Limbo, which Chiron ate readily. He had earlier filled up at the pool of the First Waters, cleansing himself soon after. He would have stayed in the pool far longer were he less responsible; he had not bathed since his entry into Hell, and the waters rejuvenating effects were quite addictive.

Darius and Mortuus almost forgot that they were going to be leaving Limbo. It was Militus who finally snapped them back into the current reality.

"I am sorry my friends – you will have to go with Chiron." Militus looked slightly worried. "I did not want to send you out, but there are events and challenges ahead of us that we must prepare for. We have overcome two demons; we must not press our good fortune by remaining in place. Better to wander safely outside the walls than to be captured. Master Chiron, my old teacher, you must go soon."

The fugitive pair, Darius and Mortuus, returned to a gloomy state, but neither could help but feel better about the fact that they would be among the great centaur for their trek to the Seventh Circle.

The warriors departed sadly. Militus dispersed them back toward Bremen, where they were to join Benjamin at the Hall of Science. Chiron, just before the warriors began their return trip, thanked them for their hospitality and their courage, and declared all 'Centaur Friends and Allies', a gesture of honor on his part, as they cheered and thanked him repeatedly. In return, they vowed to respect the centaur race, and to honor them as friends and allies, and of course welcomed guests to Limbo should the opportunity arise. The warriors bowed as the Master centaur placed his hand on his chest and nodded, then turned to leave.

Militus walked with the group, unsure of what might come out of the sky. They were between Graz and Almere, and the original traveling party of Barak, Mortuus, Darius, Socius and Clavius had passed the mines many hours ago on the return toward Bremen in an effort to find Militus and Benjamin when the demon attacked them. Chiron kept his eyes upward, his crossbow ready to launch deadly projectiles instantly. His strength was slowly returning after eating the strange fruits; he hoped to be fully restored before exiting Limbo. Barak and Clavius were deep in thought, sad and happy at the same time. They had a revelation before that they wanted to speak of, especially to Militus and Socius, but they would not talk in front of Chiron, Darius or Mortuus, because, known only to them, the actions of the three had to be natural, not forced by any knowledge of prophecies.

Soon, they reached the path outside of the pit. Militus and Barak walked ahead until they could see the path was clear of demons. Barak ran ahead, down the circling path to the inside of the excavated hole, yelling for Eruo, Abreo or Exaro to come out of the mine. He wanted to be sure that none of the smithy demons were inside picking up processed ore. Militus waited on the upper ledge, the rest of the group hid themselves behind the rock piles in the front of the path.

Militus observed the pit center, and after a long while, Barak came out of the mine, three dust covered miners trailing behind him. Militus could not hear, but he was aware that Barak was speaking to the miners through his body language and gestures. Finally, Barak and the three miners looked at the upper ledge toward Militus, and Barak waved his arms to signal the party to come down to the mine entrance. Militus took a last look around, and then whistled in a high pitch. Chiron, Socius, Clavius, Mortuus and Darius walked out onto the ledge. Now the three soiled miners only stared in shocked surprise and awe. Abreo grinned a toothy grin, the whites of his teeth contrasting brightly with his dirty face. Exaro and another miner, Eruos, a taller thin framed man watched stood frozen in disbelief. What happened next they could not have prepared for.

A demon appeared, high up against the misty ceiling; it was flying from the same direction as the smithy demons, but it was not like the smithy demon they had seen enter the pit on their first visit. This one was much more similar to the demon they had recently destroyed, more human in countenance. The creature spotted them and descended quickly, almost dropping to the ground.

Chiron was the first on the offensive. Before the rest of the group knew it, the human-like beast had crashed to the ground at their feet, surprised and flailing in agony, outraged at the impudence of being attacked. Chiron had managed to put six arrows in key locations to disable the creature, and all before it hit the path in front of them, such was his skill. It had not expected rebuttal – no creature in Hell ever fought back, nor would it have mattered if they did. These were the strongest, free roaming denizens in Hell, second only to the Fallen. Now it was writhing on its back, inhuman screeches emanating so loud and piercing that Darius thought he would pass out from the pain in his ears. Between shrieks, Militus yelled out to Chiron.

"Now Chiron, before it casts any spells!" yelled Militus. Chiron spoke his spell, and the creature stopped and stared in horror as it began a slow dissolve into dark smoke, leaving only a final stabbing scream. Stunned at the quick destruction of the demon, Barak and company sat on the ground to recover from the encounter. It had exhausted him just by stress and fear. The three miners walked up toward the group, smiling and excited by what they had just witnessed. Barak was the first to comment.

"Well. That was easy enou-"

It was he who saw the next shadow and yelled, but too late. Another demon had appeared overhead when they were all looking downward at the smoke of the demised beast. Mortuus was hit first, clawed in his face and sent flying via kick into a wall of rock. The demon hit them each of the traveling party and the three miners, fast and hard, and sent each airborne over a ledge or into a wall of stone. It was enraged by their destruction of the other demon, and it slashed its claws at Chiron the most, ripping out pieces of his rear and side rib flank. The centaur was bleeding heavily, and a still reeling Militus jumped up and grabbed it from behind, pulling his arm around its neck. This was a futile move, he knew, but he would think of nothing else in the moment to relieve his old master, if for only temporarily. To his surprise and slight relief, Darius joined him, grabbing the left arm of the demon, as it suddenly opened its wings against both men violently. They were thrown easily, and the creature turned and targeted the pair of badly wounded men.

Walking toward Militus, it ripped a claw through the air so fast that Militus could hear his neck snap. He crumpled to the ground, as the demon turned toward Darius. Barak had gotten to his feet, and, picking up an arrow moved behind the demon, preparing to stab it in the back. The demon, effortlessly spread its left wing out without flinching the rest of its body, and Barak flew 20 meters into a wall. A spate of blood marked where he struck the wall. Darius lay on the path, wounded and terrified, awaiting the gory violence.

"*Bascaria – batah!*" A voice, but not Chiron's', came over the shoulder of the demon. Mortuus had cast the spell. The demon stopped, and knew fear, its face became gnarled and warped, and with a loud screech the beast darkened and floated off into the heights, dispersing with the movement of the air. The joy and relief of the group was more overwhelming, but they were all seriously injured. Chiron laid down on his side and was bleeding profusely, pulling his skin together where the demon had ripped it open. Mortuus was limping weakly as he tried to stand up, looking around at his fellow travelers. He managed to walk, but then hobbled over to where Militus lay, his head bent in an unnatural position because of his broken neck. Mortuus instinctively placed his hands on the base of Militus' skull, and muttered a few words. Militus' neck began to straighten, and his head turned back to its correct position. Militus, feeling suddenly well again, sat up. Mortuus had healed his wound by magical incantation; Militus, because of the extreme pain he was in, could not hear anything more than mumbling emanate from Mortuus. Mortuus, in a weakened state, lay flat on the ground to rest. Darius, severely bruised, went to help up the three miners, each of whom had been knocked into a wall. Socius, Barak and Clavius were down on the next level of the path - they had been thrown over the edge by the force of the blows.

"Son of a harpy!" said a sore and embittered Eruos.

"I will concur, Eruos. Socius! Are you well?" Abreo stood up on his own before Darius could reach him, looking over the edge at Barak, Clavius and Socius; they were getting up, helping each other to stand. "Darius, see to Exaro, he looks awful! Oh wait. That is how he always looks; never mind." The group laughed, even in their great pain. Exaro half-scowled, half-smiled.

"You are very humorous. For an idiot."

They were shaken up by the incident, and for many hours they stayed to regenerate, and each kept his eyes peeled toward the ceiling of mist over Limbo. Militus went to retrieve his soldiers, and returned much later with a dozen men, plus glass pitchers of the healing waters, fruits and herbs. They all drank deeply, the most damaged being urged on by the warriors who had brought the pitchers. Militus sent six men to watch for demons on both sides of the pit, and he presented Mortuus with a broadsword that befitted his large size. On the heels of this, another warrior gave a spare short sword to Darius. The pair of fugitives were gracious and thanked their benefactors. Finally, Chiron spoke.

"Angel…Mortuus – that is your real name?" asked Chiron. "It seems unusual. I know of the angelic realms and Mortuus does not seem to be a name from the angelic tongue."

"That name was provided by Aristotle upon his awakening, it means 'dead.' Do not worry; it is not his real name. That we do not know. " stated Socius.

"Interesting. I have many questions for you Angel Mortuus," said Chiron. "I generally distrust Fallen, but I sense you are… different."

Mortuus had felt some mistrust from Chiron since meeting him. It saddened him, but he understood, especially considering where they were.

"You do not trust me, Lord Chiron." The centaur gazed silently at Mortuus.

"I am unsure. The Fallen I have ever interacted with would hardly bother with me and my kind. But your own, the Fallen, have placed you and many others in a comatose state, a prison of eternal sleep. I do not know why, though I will assume you are their enemy. My fear is that you will suddenly recall who you are, unfriendly to centaur-folk." This struck a chord in Mortuus. His fear was to awaken his memories and consider his friends as enemies. It was a worry that he suppressed, but would not speak of. The idea was, at this point in his awakening, a monster he would not be able to overcome.

"Fair enough," replied Mortuus. "Truthfully, I have harbored this concern since discovering part of my identity. I would say I do not have any recollection of a past and I see no reason to have any problems with you or your fellow centaurs. Should my memories heal, I will honor–"

"Do not make promises you may not be able to keep. I hold you to nothing; I only wish to free a friend from the Fallen overlords. There are no oaths you need swear to."

"Very well," returned Mortuus. He felt no more need to speak to Chiron on this subject. Chiron seemed a creature that would not judge Mortuus by his words. There was a moment of uncomfortable silence before Militus queried Mortuus.

"Mortuus, how did you feel after casting that spell?" he asked. Mortuus' concerns were pushed aside. Militus was uncomfortable before, but could do nothing to alter the conversation between angel and centaur, nor did he feel it was his place to.

"I felt weakened, yet more powerful at the same time, as if I had stirred pleasant memories, if you can understand that. It is an awkward explanation, but I seemed to lose energy, causing me the weakness. At the same time, movement of the energy seems to have made me feel…better, as if flowing and more alive. Why do you ask, Militus?"

"I needed to see that your experience was different from others, like Clavius. Master Chiron, how did you feel?" asked the seasoned warrior to the centaur.

"I was quite weakened, almost sickened with fatigue." Militus nodded to himself, his theory confirmed.

"Ahh. You see, Mortuus. Being of the angel folk, it is important for you to flow magically, to use your magic, practice it, and explore it. When the energy is not used, it becomes as stagnant as still water. Clavius, you recall how you felt when you tried some of the angelic magic?"

"Yes – I could hardly move for some time if I tried any sort of spell – I listened to the demons cast the spells to excavate the mine in its earlier days, and when I experimented and tried the spells elsewhere in Limbo, it was as if I had performed all the work of the spell myself. I attempted to move a boulder, and when I cast the spell, I fell to the ground and could not stand up again for a long while. Illumination spells tired me much less."

"Interesting," added Socius. "I would like to try some of these spells sometime to see-"

"You must wait until we get Aristotle back here, Socius!" Militus was stern. Socius fumed for a moment, and then consigned this to the protectiveness of the teachers and warriors who raised him. Militus sighed deeply. "I only wish to protect you, Socius. I apologize for my rashness."

"It is time we depart Limbo for the seventh circle. Mortuus, Darius and I will leave all of you from here. Eruos, will you guide us now?" asked Chiron. Eruos spoke and the bitterness he had expressed earlier had disappeared.

"Follow me, my friends," He addressed the angel, centaur and Darius, "I do not know when we will meet again – if you return us our fellow Aristotle, we will be in your debt." Socius seconded the notion. Eruos arose, Mortuus bowed goodbye to all the warriors, to Socius, Militus, Clavius and Barak. Darius followed suit. Mortuus spoke one more time.

"I am in your debt my friends. If I never get back here I will at least have been here and always have these memories, if none other." He looked at Socius. "We will rescue our friend Aristotle from these beasts, Socius. You saved me, assisted me greatly by daring to venture outside the gate, when you could have remained safely behind and not placed yourself in opposition of the corrupt Elders. I will not forget your kindness."

"Neither will I," said Darius. Clenched up with the fear of leaving Limbo, he had to push himself to speak. The words choked out of his throat. Outer hell caused great pain just in its anticipation. But he had hope this time, something not available outside, because he could return. A light in the darkness that was outer Hell. Just then a distant, shrill whistle sounded. Militus motioned his men to watch the air above the pit. The warriors focused their gaze upward, an equal number of men watching from each direction.

"Good luck my friends – you must go now. The men have seen something, and I think you had better disappear into the mine. Hurry!" Militus shouted as he looked back and forth between the three and the soldiers above. Into the opening and down the darkened cave they ran, following Eruos. Exaro and Abreo trailed the three.

Once they were far enough into the cave, Eruos pulled a switch on the wall and the entrance they had entered closed up with a snap. It was as if the wall behind them never had an opening at all. The journey through the mine was a test of its own for both centaur and angel. Neither creature was well-disposed to the close overhangs and tight openings that composed the mine. The miners asked questions of both Mortuus and Chiron, and their queries were useful distractions from the almost overwhelming claustrophobia. Chiron had trouble fitting inside more than a few openings, though for the most part he could squeeze into the caverns and miniature passages. The three had no idea how long or far their journey would be to the exit. Mortuus was of an aviary race of beings, and began to slowly feel the walls and ceilings enclosing him; this was different than

Clavius' underground, particularly the lighting and dimensions of space. He recalled the fear and unknowing in the aftermath of his awakening, and how he had finally stumbled to the surface exit from the underground of the Seventh Circle. Though he was far different now, memories of that unpleasantness and panic were welling up inside him, as if he was in a dungeon.

Angels did not belong in the dungeons of Hell.

Chapter 54

Back to Circle Seven

It had been a long, hazardous journey to get back to Chiron's place and people. The three had left the secret exit from the mine into the putrid sleet fall of the Third Circle, completely bypassing the Second Circle. Eruos had not disclosed where he would lead them, though he had several exits on the Second Circle, and was even working on a passage to the Fourth currently. The trip through the mine was grueling for Mortuus, and humiliating for Chiron, who had to be pushed through many openings by his rear end because of his size. Darius had no qualms except for the dirtiness of their surroundings, having enjoyed being cleansed in Limbo after many centuries.

The three emerged with great sighs of relief, though short lived, as they faced outer Hell's sound and stink. Looking around as they walked onto the landscape, Chiron saw the three-headed giant dog Cerberus not far away, being harassed by a pack of eighteen imps. The beasts were throwing rocks at the giant dog as he backed away whimpering against the wall, a short distance from where they had just emerged.

"I had assumed this monstrous dog was far fiercer than these imps, Chiron," whispered Mortuus. "Why does it cringe away from them when it could easily rip them apart?"

"The dog is probably trained to obey Fallen and their workers," guessed Chiron, "Imagine the cruelty they must have inflicted upon it to gain its obeisance if they would cut off the wings of their own."

Motioning Mortuus and Darius to be silent, Chiron walked silently in the opposite direction, tiptoeing as well as a large half-human, half-horse could. They were nearly out of sight when Mortuus accidentally stepped onto the frozen face of a human buried in the slushy vomit.

"Damn animal! Watch where you step, filthy dog! Isn't it bad enough you chew our entrails…" the imprisoned man's face blinked his slushed-over eyes, looking at Mortuus more clearly, and then started yelling. "Fugitives! How dare you tread on me!" yelled the voice of the bloated face, as Mortuus jumped back in shock. "Fugitives! Fugitives!" repeated the man, yelling at the top of his lungs. Chiron looked back toward where the large dog had been cornered by the imps, trying to see, hoping they were out of earshot. The sight of the pack running and flying in their direction, confirmed they were not. Mortuus, now angry and irritated, kicked the shouting distended face, and the man quieted immediately as he spit blood and teeth.

Darius, who was in the rear of the three, pulled the short sword the warrior had given him earlier. It was heavy for its size, but Darius could see that it would easily cut whatever it touched, so finely honed was the sharpened blade. Mortuus pulled the sword given him by Militus, and he and Chiron walked alongside of Darius as the pack drew near. Darius, although emboldened to fight alongside his companions, had never yet fought one of the smallish vermin; his face was the picture of fear.

"Stand apart!" commanded Chiron, "They will divide and we will each have fewer to kill. Darius – this is your first time to defend against these creatures; do not underestimate them, but no matter your fear or pain, you must continue to fight."

Mortuus turned toward Darius.

"Be brave my friend. Let your rage power the fight." The imps were nearer, and Chiron dispatched several at a distance before they were on the group. Two flyers went down, and another six of the demon miniatures smoked instantly. This encouraged all three, but the pack was still large enough to be of concern.

Darius, shaken, barely managed his sword, and, ignoring the warnings of Barak earlier, spoke the spell he had heard both Mortuus and Chiron utter in Limbo at the pack, causing three of the creatures to morph into dark clouds. Casting the spell enraged the imps so much that they fought harder and with more daring and ferocity than Mortuus and Chiron had ever seen, and Darius was severely disabled for using it. He fell to the ground in a hunched-over clump, weakened so much that he was unable to move or lend assist any further.

Chiron, irritated, assessed the matter with incredible speed, and quickly hefted the immobilized Darius onto his back as he spun and loosed his bow into the swarm. Popping sounds emitted from the creatures, and sometimes twice at a time as the centaurs' great archery skills answered the growls of the imps.

Some of the creatures had gotten to the fighting pair. One imp, a flyer, landed on the back of Chiron, and had begun to rip at the slumped form of Darius, who could barely make a sound in his physically immobilized state. Another pair of imps had gotten a hold of Chiron's rear legs, biting into his powerful haunches, causing him great pain, and distraction. The centaur staggered for a moment before shaking them off and firing into them in a fury. They had done some damage, as he would not walk well until Darius had recovered a long time later.

Mortuus, however, had suffered the most bloodying from the attack. His back had been ripped open, and his clean, new robes shredded and bloodied. Mortuus sight was blocked by the smoke of the recently dispatched imps, allowing the remaining imps to slip through the smokescreen and get at Mortuus before he could see them coming. He was swinging wildly in his pain and panic, and accidentally sliced into his own leg trying to get free. When it was finally done, and all the imps had been destroyed, the three spent many hours regenerating, and Chiron retrieved his arrows. They had no alternative, even though the putrid vomit laden sleet was overwhelming their senses. Cerberus did not find them, and they thought he must be avoiding the pack, unaware they had been exterminated.

"I have not seen so many of these beasts in one place since my awakening. Do you suppose they-" said Mortuus. He was cut off by Chiron's reply.

"-were looking for you? Yes, I believe so." replied Chiron. "We must move before anymore arrive. The demons believe you to be hiding out in Limbo, and so they are focusing their energies there."

"Why did they attack the dog?" asked Mortuus.

"They are undisciplined – without their masters to order their actions, they slip away to mischief and cruelty, even when it is forbidden or illogical. In my circle, we dispatched many of these who wandered near enough before they were able to determine it was a danger zone for their kind."

"Foolish beasts, then," said Mortuus. "How is Darius doing?"

"He will have to be carried on my back for some time," said Chiron. "I would have you know that this is humiliating for my kind; to be a beast of burden is a high insult. *I* am not belittled by helping your friend, but my kind would find this disparaging, and some might challenge my leadership. When we approach my circle, I will instruct you on what to expect and how to act."

"Do you wish me to carry Darius, Lord Chiron? I would rather you had your hands free; you are the best fighter among us."
Chiron looked at Mortuus.

"I can carry him easily – I only wished to inform you of the nuances of my culture. Thank you for the offer."

Finally, after a long trek through the vomit precipitation, the three found the path that lead down to the Fourth Circle. They had a quick run in with Plutus. Chiron did not hesitate. He filled Plutus' hide with enough arrows to slow him down until they could get to the Fifth Circle. Mortuus and Chiron had anticipated Plutus. They had not, however, anticipated the two fugitive hunter demons that appeared in the distance. They were found.

Chiron had discussed a strategy for dealing with demons with Mortuus as they were climbing down through the mine. The spell was to be used when they encountered only one demon; two demons would have to be disabled, filled with Chiron's' arrows, then strangled by Mortuus and Chiron to conserve Mortuus' magical energy. It was during this exchange in the mine between the angel and the centaur that Darius got his notion to use the angel magic. He would not do so again this trip.

Chiron pulled his bow back as the pair approached. They were cursing the centaur in their half-growl, half-human tones, and it reminded him of his life among the humans that hunted and exterminated him and his kind.

One particular hunting party had attempted to corner Chiron against the side of a sheer mountain wall, cliffs high above; they were outcasts from their village, criminals, misfits, untouchables who earned their lowly status by their own actions. Chiron knew this because he had friends in the village with whom he would secretly meet. When the three village criminals were exiled, they grouped together and decided that bringing back the head of the Master Centaur, Chiron himself, would earn them the right to live among their fellow humans in the village. Chiron waited, knowing their plans to stalk him, and drew them into a large brushy area, a naturally formed maze. When they re-emerged later, far from where they entered, Chiron waited, and had his bow drawn. They were cursing him in the same low, guttural sounds as he now heard emanating from the demons.

When one of the men attempted to throw his spear at Chiron, Chiron dispatched him quickly, redrawing his bow before the others knew what had happened. When they became aware, they ran from the centaur in a panic, into the cave of a napping mother bear and her young cubs. Chiron sealed the cave until the screams had faded away.

The rage from that time in Chiron's life washed over him, and he used it to fuel a speedy delivery of high speed arrows into the two demons. They screamed and shrieked in pain and rage for a few seconds. The barrage of arrows stuck into their throats and silenced them. It was a relief to dispatch the disabled pair. Chiron kneeled onto the throat of one of the demons with his front leg (the demon was very strong Chiron thought, even full of arrows). After a few seconds, the demon transformed into smoke. Mortuus wrapped his arm around the throat of the other, and it, too, became a floating smoke shape.

In the Fifth circle, along the bank, Phlegyas had been standing by the shore next to his skiff. Chiron addressed his friend, and Phlegyas stared at him blankly. The centaur stopped his movement, and Darius and Mortuus followed, sensing the danger. Looking around quickly, Chiron and Mortuus could see no imminent danger. Chiron looked into the face of his friend. Phlegyas was different looking from their first meeting. Mortuus looked, closely, and then yelled his warning.

"DEMON!" His angel sight caught the creature in its disguised form. Reacting violently, the creature that was almost Phlegyas quickly morphed, grabbing onto Mortuus. This creature was so strong that Mortuus could hardly move within its grip. It spoke, a harsh, fast word, Mortuus remembered the word, then felt the strength draining as his limbs froze in place. Mortuus was paralyzed, just as he had been in Limbo.

Chiron saw Mortuus' situation. He approached the transforming demon, thrusting his small sword through its neck. Chiron repeated the paralysis spell - he had just heard it - and watched the beast freeze, then slide off of his sword onto the squishy ground with a splash. Chiron sank to the ground next to the beast; unable to move, so complete was his exhaustion. Darius, the only one of the three able to stand, though barely, placed his knee on the throat of the paralyzed demon, leaning into it and slicing it weakly across the chest and abdomen until the creature finally smoked. Chiron struggled to regain his footing and gave Darius a weak smile of approval, then collapsed again to the wet ground. They remained there for a short time.

Chiron arose first, shakily. Mortuus finally felt his strength return as his movement was no longer hindered. They removed much of the putrid slush that had been on them since the Third Circle by rolling around on the waterlogged ground. It was full of roots and small vegetation, which seemed to be what held it together. Thankfully, they did not have to enter the river to wash off.

They found Phlegyas in a weakened state on the flaming tower side of the Styx, at the landing where Mortuus and Chiron had first boarded. He had been stunned by the demon, which ravaged the oarsman grotesquely with his claws after disabling him, then used a spell to transform into the likeness of Phlegyas. Phlegyas, a bloody mess, required a long regeneration period. The group stayed with him, though they wished to hurry through the gates, into Dis and toward the relative safety of Chiron's circle. It was this charity that saved them from capture. After a long time, Phlegyas was able to speak to them, weakly at first.

"My friends, you must not enter the gates. The Fallen know of the angel's escape." Phlegyas motioned toward Mortuus. "You are able to defeat one or two at once? Behind the gates you will find more, many more, searching between the tombs; they remain near this very gate. You must not pass this way."

"We wish to get to my circle, Phlegyas. How will we pass through the tombs?" asked Chiron. "There is no other way to -"

"There is, Chiron. I will take you when I am regenerated." Phlegyas paused, "Why does the angel follow you, Chiron? Was not Limbo more ideal?" He laughed with this question – it was not really a question.

"The beasts have entered Limbo – in fact, they have been there all along, Phlegyas. One of them was disguised as an Elder! They have infiltrated even the 'virtuous' humans. We left in haste, as they were nearing us. Two we destroyed just prior to our exit." Phlegyas looked surprised, and contemplated this news.

"Hell is changing. And you, angel, what will you do? They will return you to the dark dungeon under the tombs. Many demons pursue you." Phlegyas was grim. He started to move around, then, picked himself up. They got into his boat and left the mucky landing, but instead of turning to the left toward the opposite signal tower, they went right, heading into the deep mist of the Styx. It was a long, slow trip, and on many occasions, the humans were looking out of the water, staring at the strange, immense frame of Chiron. Some were too near the boat, and Phlegyas cracked their skulls with a deftness of oar swinging skill. After Phlegyas swung, the river dwellers scattered, returning to their madness, gnashing, tearing and ripping their fellows long after the skiff was out of sight.

Phlegyas was taking the three to another entrance to Dis, and explained the alternate passageway that had been built into the far side of Dis' protective wall. The small doorway had been part of a much larger opening, long closed by the Fallen. Originally, Dis had two large gates. The second gate was rarely used, and so very few, besides wandering imps and demons, along with a handful of fugitives, had ever encountered the opening. Somehow, the landing in front of the gate had eroded over time and simply disappeared into the Styx. The Fallen sent their worker demons to seal the gate, along with the appropriate spells. The demons, ever mistrusting, left a small doorway that could only be opened with magic. They had used a combination spell that was difficult to cast.

Phlegyas had learned the combination spell from a demon. The demon had recited the spell right in front of Phlegyas. At the time, Phlegyas could not understand the spell, but he was able to figure out how to use it eventually. The only problem was that it was a one way spell; no one could return back through once they had entered into Dis.

This was not normally a consideration. No problem, unless you were the ferryman of the Styx and left your skiff behind the door. The three chuckled at the oarsman's wry humor. Phlegyas had to blow his horn to bring the Fallen once he discovered the unidirectional property of the doorway. It was easy to get out of, however; he informed them he had been jumped by some rogue demons, and had his skiff taken. The Fallen brought back his skiff angrily, but Phlegyas knew they had no choice but to believe him – the demons were often unstable and lied easily.

The skiff arrived at the small opening without incident; aside from the inhabitants of the swamp nearing the skiff to see Chiron and a few skull-cracking swats of the oar from Phlegyas, no other occurrences inhibited their boat ride. Phlegyas, having rarely had company, spoke of his own life and exploits, telling the tales that led up to his death at the hands of Apollo. Mortuus and Darius listened intently, enjoying the stories, except, of course, for the death of Phlegyas' famously beautiful daughter. The pain of this event showed even on the grim countenance of Chiron.

Phlegyas, in life, was King of the Lapiths. He had two children; one, a daughter, was named Coronis. The God Apollo had taken a deep liking to Coronis, and even had blessed Phlegyas with a prosperous kingdom. Phlegyas, knowing of his daughter's fickleness with male suitors, had warned Coronis not to partner with Apollo. Phlegyas paid his homage to Apollo regularly, and honorably, as did all the subjects of his nation, and even named Apollo the father of their country. But Coronis, unable to withstand the pressing of Apollo for her love, fell into a relationship, and each evening would meet with the god in the forest near the palace. On certain evenings, Apollo would not appear, busy with some of the many works of gods, unknown to Coronis. In his absence, and in her youthfulness, and insecurity, she was wooed away during one of these nights, by a handsome young man, Ischys, who had been watching her meetings with Apollo. After a few nights seeing Coronis alone and sad, Ischys approached.

Phlegyas knew of his daughter's interactions with Apollo, and had men follow and watch the princess during the day. He had charged them with keeping any and all would-be suitors away. On many occasions there had been royal suitors who visited and requested consideration for the hand of Coronis. Some, of great wealth and fame, could not understand the refusal of Phlegyas. They pursued the princess, and met with mysterious, accidental deaths.

Phlegyas could not stand to lose his daughter, and would have sacrificed a hundred suitors for her life if he had to. The men who watched Coronis were unaware of the forest visits by Apollo; when it was time for their meeting, the entire palace, everyone who worked inside and out, were ordered to their sleep chambers to provide Coronis an undisturbed walk to her rendezvous. This became automatic, occurring each night whether Apollo appeared or not.

Soon, Coronis became pregnant, and Apollo had a crow follow her to assure her safety during the pregnancy. It was on one of the nights that Coronis had met with her other lover, Ischys that the crow returned to Apollo with his report. The god, outraged, had his sister, the goddess Artemis, kill Coronis shortly after giving birth. The child was taken by Apollo. Phlegyas swiftly had Ischys murdered, and soon went to the temple of Apollo at Delphi, and burnt it to the ground. Apollo struck Phlegyas down in person, and he awoke before the Fallen. The Fallen charged the king with boating the Styx.

It was a long while before anyone spoke. Mortuus could see the pain of these times on the face of Phlegyas.

"Phlegyas, did you ever find out what happened to the child of Coronis and Apollo?" asked Chiron.

"No." answered Phlegyas. "I was dead soon after Apollo carried off the babe; I barely saw my grandson. I saw only the back of Artemis as she vanished from my daughter's bedside. Why do you ask?"

"I am sorry, Phlegyas. So much has happened since I left my circle; I neglected to consider you would not be aware." Phlegyas face showed a grave concern at hearing this news of Chiron. What was he sorry for? Had something happened to his grandson as well as his daughter? "Apollo gave the child to *me* to raise. Your grandson's name was Asclepius. I instructed him in medicines and hunting, and in his day, he was as famous for medicines as Hercules was for his feats of strength." Phlegyas eyes widened in surprise and delight. "Asclepius specialized in the medicines and incantations that have been used for love and sickness, and love sickness, of course. His skill was legendary." Phlegyas smiled broadly. He had heard of Chiron and the plight of the centaur race, and had wished to intervene on their behalf. His counselors and court nobles advised against it. To their dismay, Phlegyas proclaimed that no citizen of his Kingdom should ever harm the Master Centaur, and later expanded his edict to include all centaur kind. This turned out to be a difficult law to enforce, due to the mounting hatred and violent actions of a small minority of his subjects, and the drunken misbehavior of a small minority of centaurs. Chiron and the centaurs did not disappear until long after Phlegyas had been murdered by Apollo.

"Then I am grateful to you, and in your debt for all time my friend." Phlegyas was exuberant. "Tell me, I have only one fear, is my grandson in Limbo, or any other place of Hell?"

"Not as far as I have knowledge. Aristotle has not been able to penetrate to the farthest depths, but I have heard no news of Asclepius since my arrival." Chiron, normally grim in speaking manner, stared at Phlegyas, and for a moment, smiled. The Ferryman who was once King lost all control of his grin.

"Thank you, my friend. Thank you."

Chapter 55

Guests on the Blood River

Pholus could not believe his eyes. Sitting near the rocky slope of the Seventh Circle with several of the centaur commanders, he stared as Chiron emerged from the mist. Following behind the leader centaur were two humans, one large and one small and gaunt, and more astonishingly, one whom Pholus had chased away on many occasions, the Minotaur. The group of four was walking down the slope in single file fashion, and Pholus knew this was at the behest of his friend Chiron. Pholus and the commanders, Tacitus among them, stood frozen in place, mouths agape at this very odd entourage. Chiron, seeing Pholus and his commanders at the base of the slope, changed course and headed in the direction of the meeting of the centaur leadership.

Ironically, Pholus had called this meeting after Chiron had not returned for more than forty turns. The Second in Command of the centaur herds had Titan trot the entire circumference of the Seventh Circle and report each time he completed a lap. Pholus began to worry when Chiron did not reappear after the twenty-fifth round, but withheld taking action for another fifteen rounds, considering he really had no idea how long Chiron would be away. The herds had begun to whisper, rumors of their missing master circulated widely, and Pholus gathered his leaders to initiate counter-measures. The commanders, only a small sampling of the total number of herd leaders, were those whom Pholus trusted the most. They did not include Nessus in their number.

When Chiron and his strange herd approached, Pholus and the commanders followed the usual protocol, though none took their eyes off of the Minotaur. Even the thinner, frail human Darius seemed wary of the bull-like beast, looking behind him with each step. The Minotaur did not miss the fearful wariness of the human; every so often he would emit a low rumbling growl, stopping only when the group neared the meeting centaur commanders. Chiron returned their bows and introduced his queer company, though not without prefacing with an explanation of his arrival.

"Commanders, I am happy to see you all. I have returned from a lengthy and not uneventful journey, and I have much news to report. I know all here to be loyal and faithful to our centaur kind, and the wisest and most trusted leaders of the herds. I know this from my own observations, and those of Commander Pholus, who has summoned you in a most timely manner, unbeknownst even to himself. I have returned from a visit to the First Circle, the area known as Limbo, and with those I would have you accept on my word as friends to centaur kind." At this, the leaders scanned the guests of Chiron, feeling at ease to do so now that he had requested their acceptance, and they scrutinized even the Minotaur, who stared back at each commander in turn.

Chiron continued, "This is a most unusual request, Commanders. I understand, and I will assure you I have not lost my senses. I ask your discretion - do not speak with any outside of this group of what I tell you here and now. Do you agree to this?" The commanders bowed deeply, indicating their oath of silence as Chiron moved to the bull-man. "I give you Asterion, a Halfling, like ourselves, though he is a bull Halfling, and his halves are reversed from ours. He has been wandering the rocky slope, his assigned patrol by the Fallen masters. Like us, he was brutalized for his differences by the humans, and in turn defied them by being the monster they had labeled him."

Chiron moved to Darius. "This is Darius, former slave, sentenced to the Vestibule. Yes, he is a fugitive. He and two others escaped their aimless running. His fellows were captured by flying demons, and taken to the Eighth Circle early after their escape."

Chiron moved toward Mortuus. "And here, though you may find it hard to believe, is the strangest guest to our circle. You may have thought that would be Asterion, and you would be wrong. Tell me, Tacitus, what do you see here?" Chiron motioned toward Mortuus.

"I see a human, a large human, but only human."

"Pholus. Tell me what you see," requested Chiron. Pholus had a puzzled expression on his face.

"Human." The remaining commander's nodded agreement as Chiron polled the group one by one.

"As I thought," said Chiron. Mortuus prepared himself for their reactions, and that of Asterion, who also did not know.

"This is Mortuus. He is our friend. And he is of the Fallen."

Chapter 56
New Tricks for Old Centaurs

The commanders, including Pholus sat there stunned at the revelation Chiron had just given them. Friend? Fallen? This could not be - the Fallen were the jailers, the cruel prison wardens of Hell for thousands of years. The air was silent, but the expressions on the faces of the herd leaders spoke volumes. Chiron broke the silence after a long pause.
"You have said nothing, Commanders. Do you not have questions? I believe you see why there is a necessity for prudence." One of the commanders spoke.
"Master Chiron, truly, I wonder how this came to be, and I would ask that you share the story of your journey to the First Circle, that we may gather the pieces of this puzzle together and enjoy your travel tale. It has been too long since we have been imprisoned on this boiling river of Hell, and I would hear of the outside, even though it be Hell."
Chiron smiled, relieved, and the other commanders grunted and neighed their agreement, and joy to hear a new story, a fresh adventure. After thousands of years, it would be like a jug of cold water in a desert. Mortuus, also relieved, sat down on the gravelly ground, and Darius joined him. Mortuus had felt the regard of Chiron change as they fought their way to the Seventh Circle together, and the introduction to the Commander centaurs confirmed this. Only Asterion seemed to be upset, but no one noticed. A low rumble again emanated from deep within the Halfling, who was glaring at the angel and causing alarm with the Commanders and Chiron.
"Asterion, please. You must trust what I tell you. He is our friend," said Chiron. Asterion continued to glare, but ceased his growling.
"I will trust your judgment, friend Chiron. But I will watch the Fallen one carefully." With that, Asterion sat on the ground, looking

at Mortuus periodically, distrustfully, and causing the angel discomfort.

Chiron told his story, about his ascent up the rocky slope, and his meeting with Asterion. His encounter with Plutus, the once demigod transformed into wolf demon by the Fallen, his meeting with Minos (and Asterion, for the first time since his early youth, wept at this); finding Charon missing (and he would defer to Mortuus and Darius to fill in details of this later), plus the events of Limbo, including the demons who had been dissipated into smoke. The centaurs recalled the events of long ago when they had shot the demon left behind by the Fallen and thrown it into the river. Chiron finished with his entry through the back entrance of the Sixth Circle and meeting Asterion, who had been evading the demons as they searched for Mortuus near the front gate of Dis. The Master Centaur then asked Mortuus to explain his origin as he had on the trek through the mines of Limbo, from his trip to the Vestibule to his entry to Limbo. The commanders were in awe as Darius interrupted and told of Mortuus' defeat of the demon Elder barehanded. In all, this was the best round of storytelling the centaurs could remember, all the better for the destruction of their common enemy, the demons.

"Commanders," said Chiron, "I am happy to have shared these events with you, and I would speak with you of matter more pressing to myself and our human and angel friends. There is a human recently captured and removed to the forbidden area."

"Your friend. The teacher, Aristotle," said one of the commanders. Chiron looked at him squarely, confused as to how he knew of Aristotle. Chiron had considered his meetings with Aristotle to be discrete, kept from his fellows for his and their sakes. Humans were not liked by centaurs, and Aristotle would be safer if the herds did not know of him, in case of an uprising or challenge.

"Why…yes. How do you know of my meetings with Aristotle?"

"We have heard of it, mostly from Commander Nessus, Master Chiron, though we thought he told us only to sow discord in his usual manner, and so we kept it to ourselves and forbade him to speak of it with the herds lest we inform on him. Since then, he tells us nothing, though whispers come to us on occasion; Commander Nessus is unwelcome among most of the herds now." Chiron exchanged glances with Pholus, each understanding what the other was thinking. Nessus had always been distrusted, though they did not share their suspicions with the commanders. It was fortunate the herd leaders could discern the manipulations of Nessus and both Chiron and Pholus felt justified in their trust. Chiron was astonished at their independence of thought and decision making; he had not checked in with the herd leaders in millennia, and assumed they retained the intelligence he was accustomed to. They were growing.

"Thank you for that, Commander," said Pholus. "We will deal with Nessus later. For now, Master Chiron, please continue."

"Yes. Thank you," said Chiron. "As I stated, Aristotle has been imprisoned in the forbidden area cave; his actions have made him a key in the destruction of the demons, and I wish to free him." Chiron looked at the faces of the herd leaders. They were blank and unemotional, and he could not read them, making him uncertain.

"I will assist you Master Chiron," said one of the leaders. And like a wave, he was joined by the entire group. Chiron's story had somehow emboldened them to fight against the demons, and each of them desired the glory of defeating one of the beasts. Like the battle with the harpies, it proved to be a greatly bonding summons to service. His people loved the thrill and adventure of battle.

"You honor all our kind with your loyalty and dedication, my friends. All can assist in some manner, though some will be less directly involved in the success of the operation. I did request Mortuus to join in extracting Aristotle, as the great teacher was the one who found and woke him from the eternal sleep. There is also a danger the Fallen may arrive, and he alone would be nearest their equal. I -"

"I will assist," interrupted Asterion, curt and assured, leaving no question of his involvement. Chiron, surprised, looked at Darius for a moment, cutting him off as he started to speak.

"No, Darius," said Chiron calmly. "This is no fight for humans. You will wait for us to bring Aristotle in the Wood." Darius conceded his agreement, understanding he would be the least effective in such a venture. He would be more than honored to help the legendary Aristotle, the sole reason he dared to cross from the Vestibule and the temporary safety of the rocky oasis in the first place. It had seemed so long ago that he and Mortuus colluded on crossing over the river Acheron together.

"I am happy to assist and hasten the regeneration, Lord Chiron. I have brought many vials of Limbo's waters." said Darius. Chiron smiled and nodded thankfully.

"Very well, then," he said. "We shall now make our plans to enter the forbidden area cave and extract Aristotle." And so they strategized, human, Fallen, and Halflings, working together for the first time.

It was an odd day in Hell.

Chapter 57

Reunification

Chiron and the commanders had been sitting and strategizing for some time before a member of Tacitus' herd approached. The commander excused himself, and trotted away with his subordinate, returning a short time later. In the distance, a trio of centaurs stood and talked with each other as a smaller figure walked around nearby. Chiron stopped talking with his commanders as he saw the human form in the distance.

"Tacitus. Why is there a human standing among your herd?" he asked.

"That human is a fugitive, captured by the harpies as he came through the Wood," replied Tacitus. "He was saved from the bird beasts, at the same site where we did battle with the harpies, but he had been so mutilated we could not communicate with him. He is just now regenerated enough to speak and his guard had thought this might be a good time for you to question him."

"Why are we keeping a fugitive?" asked Chiron. "Do we not usually just return them to the plain?"

"Yes, normally, Master Chiron. This one is different. He had the smell of the First Circle on him," Pholus chimed in.

"I requested we hold onto the fugitive until you could question him."

"He smells of the Vestibule?" asked Chiron. "I would like to ask him now, if I may interrupt our planning for a few minutes, commanders." And to this they all nodded. Tacitus galloped to his guards assigned to the human, then returned as they followed in the distance. The human was slower than they, and no centaur would dare allow a human to ride upon his back. Darius and Mortuus, who had been sitting on the outskirts of the meeting, stood and watched as the centaurs and human approached. Darius gasped as they neared.

"Panos!" he yelled. "Panos!" The centaur commanders and Chiron stared at him as he took off running. Chiron, fearful Darius might be attacked by the centaurs, who did not know him, trotted ahead of him quickly, and waved his arms to the centaur guard, who were just pulling their bows back.

"Stand down brave fellows," called Chiron. "He is a visitor here - not to be harmed." The centaurs bowed, acknowledging Chiron's wishes. The human, who had ran behind the centaur guards as Chiron came running at them looked sheepishly at the Master Centaur.

"I would speak to you as to your origins, but I have just determined who you are…Panos." Panos, overwhelmed by this, spoke but could only choke the words out. His voice was barely healed. His fear turned to joy as he saw Darius run up behind Chiron.

"Panos!" yelled Darius, now out of breath, but overjoyed at the sight of his friend. "You escaped once again!" The centaur guards watched the pair hug curiously. Centaur protocol did not permit bodily contact; it would have been considered a sign of weakness. Chiron continued his questioning.

"So this is Panos, of whom you spoke in the mine Darius. It seems his luck is great if he has escaped the flyer demons."

"How did you escape Panos?" asked Darius, still smiling. Panos tried to speak but could not. His throat had been ripped apart by the harpies. He gurgled some sounds, shrugged at the futility of it, then smiled again at his friend. He then placed his hands up, one with the fingers moving to look like wings flapping, and the other attached to the bottom, trying his best to show how he had been dropped from the flyer. Chiron understood.

"They dropped you? But why did they not retrieve you after? You surely were unable to run from them?" At this, Panos made motions with his hands again, and sounds that were near enough to the whooshing of the fireballs of the burning plain for Chiron to comprehend.

"Ah. The fireballs. Of course. The demons dropped you upon the burning plain, and so would not pursue you. The fireballs that fall there are quite intimidating. Although you must have suffered greatly, you were saved from being deposited into the deeper circles." Panos nodded.

"Very good for you, Panos. You were not aware of the harpies, unfortunately, but we shall remedy their damage for you shortly. Darius, take him back to where you and Mortuus are sitting. I believe we have enough vials to share some of the healing waters." The centaur guards, relieved to not have to watch the human fugitive any longer, returned to the greater herd across Phlegethon. Chiron returned to his meeting, resuming his planning with the commanders, as Darius and Panos strolled along. They had a lot to catch up on, and of course it would be Darius who spoke first, just after introducing his friend to his new friend, the angel Mortuus and Asterion, also known as the Minotaur.

Panos would have been stunned to silence even if his voice worked.

Chapter 58
Secret Society No More

Benjamin walked the Hall of the Science in his search. In room after room, Benjamin walked in and out, asking those scientists attending the various botanical gardens, laboratories and meeting rooms, where he might find the scientist. Each person shrugged his shoulders or shook his head, then returned to the conversation or work in which he was previously engaged. On the fourth floor, Benjamin got his answer from an apprentice of the senior scientist. Another man looked at the apprentice with disapproval. Benjamin was considered a pariah by many of these scientists, and this one was a known supporter of the Elders and their policies.

"He was just here moments ago." said the apprentice. "I believe I heard the roof door slam just now. You may check up there."

Benjamin headed toward the end of the fourth floor hallway and climbed up the small stairway to the open roof of the building. He looked around the roof looking for the senior scientist and found no one. Walking toward the edge of the building, he looked down and saw the small band of warriors standing there waiting. He waved his arms to get their attention, side to side, shrugged exaggeratedly with his arms, signaling that he did not find who he was looking for. Benjamin turned, looking toward the small, square shaped protrusion that led back to the stairs and down into the Hall of Science and was suddenly grabbed from the back of the shoulders, by hands that were like steel claws. The fingers with their sharp as talon nails gripped his shoulders so hard that they pierced his skin, drawing blood from under his robes. The pain caused Benjamin to scream. Up he was lifted, high off the roof, and out over the center of the small village huts below. He could make out the formation on the ground, watching him as he flopped like a fish on a hook, desperate to escape the pain. He looked up, and saw the creature that carried him, a demon, but wearing the clothing of the senior scientist. It was as he suspected. He began to breathe deeply, trying to alleviate the pain as he began to speak the words of the spell that would destroy the beast.

"Mmph!" The creature had been aware Benjamin was readying the spell, and covered his mouth, leaving him to dangle from only one clawed hand, more painful with his weight distributed from only one side. The beast's fingers penetrated Benjamin's face; so tight was its grip. It flew more precariously with the imbalance of weight.

"Where is the angel?!" hissed the creature, growling loudly. The two were flying lower, and the formation had disappeared from underneath. Benjamin was alone; this beast would rend him to pieces whether he talked or not. He shuddered, then braced himself, letting go of hope. "Where is it?!" hissed the former senior scientist. Benjamin would not answer. The creature began beating his wings faster, and began to climb up toward the misty ceiling that overhung Limbo. "Very well, Benjamin. You will need to think about it. I will let you keep your secret while you linger at the bottom of Acheron with the other fools."

They turned in the air, and Benjamin saw the Hall of Science building fly underneath him in the opposite direction, and then the wood behind the Hall. He would be sacrificed for Mortuus. He lost hope, just as the projectile thudded into his lower back. The sharp pain of the arrow caused him to scream as never before. The demon, startled by the arrow impact on his prey, turned them around in the air, just in time for Benjamin to see the hall with the company of warriors on its roof. The demon screeched indignation and pain, its own hide covered with several arrows in the wink of an eye. Benjamin was dropped. Militus, on the roof, yelled to his men again, and now the arrows rained at the sky in a line toward the demon. It faltered and flew away from the building, then tumbled down into the wood. With a crash, it struck the trees, shrieking in pain. Benjamin had landed near the hall, a sickening thud denoting his arrival on ground. He was laid flat on his back, the wind knocked out of him, and most of his bones broken and protruding through his skin or into his internal organs. The arrow had pushed through on impact, and the point and shaft were protruding from his belly as the fletching was inside his body.

It was only a minute before Militus and his soldiers came to the aid of Benjamin. The men quickly produced several vials from the First Waters and poured it into and on the broken body of the scientist. One man pulled the arrow out as the broken scientist groaned loudly. Barely able to move, Benjamin motioned toward where the demon had fallen in the wood.

"Do not concern yourself, Benjamin. My men are hunters, and they revel in the hunt as much as the battle. They are on its trail. Quiet yourself for now, my friend. We will carry you to the healing waters soon enough," assured Militus. Benjamin smiled weakly. Soon, a soldier came up to Militus, spoke to him briefly, then left, joined by more of the soldiers who surrounded Benjamin. Benjamin did not know that the demon had somehow escaped the hunting party, wounded as he was. Militus looked worried as he turned back toward his friend, taking out another vial.

"Drink up. We will move soon. I'm sure the beast is making his way back to you. This one has lured away most of the men. Now drink." Each vial of cool water made Benjamin lose a bit of the pain, and so he forced himself to drink.

Moments later, there was a loud screech and the demon reappeared. It had made its way back around the wood, taking a long way in order to avoid the arrows of the soldiers. It came up, around the hall, surprising the soldiers who remained with Militus and Benjamin. They notched their arrows, pulled and loosed. But the creature was ready this time. It ducked behind a wide tree faster than they could see, then suddenly, it had climbed all the way up the tree, then flew and rammed into the soldiers. They were sent flying into a stand of smaller trees, two impaled coarsely on jagged branches sticking out. The other hit a tree with a thud, and was immobilized. The demon turned, and stared at Militus and Benjamin, pulling out the remaining arrows.

"Where is the angel!?!" it yelled at them in its low hissing voice. Militus walked toward the demon, and the demon stared at him as he approached. "This is not one of your foolish games, Militus," it hissed. The demon walked toward Militus, who was pulling out his sword. "You cannot destroy me." The demon watched as Militus flexed his wrist, swooshing with the sword as if warming up for a fight, much as an athlete would stretch before a tournament event. The demon, disdainfully curious, watched the flicks. "What are you doing, Militus?" asked the creature. "Am I to be frightened by your display?" The demon pulled out the last arrow, and Benjamin, despite his pain, sat up enough to look at Militus, puzzled. Militus smiled, and the demon seemed to portray a curious look on its deformed face.

"You are a slow thinker, imp." Militus was poking at the demon's ego, and the demon became visibly enraged. "I am only buying time," confessed Militus. And with that, the demon flinched and screeched in pain as it was struck with arrow after arrow from behind, it's back filled with feathery shafts. It fell to the ground screeching, and before it could get up, the soldiers who had been tracking it appeared out of the tree line. The beast stretched its wings, trying to push up from the ground. The soldiers pinned the wings with spears and swords, and sat on the beast to keep it still. They steered clear of the legs. Militus moved next to it, and sat down on the ground near its head. It gnashed and cursed him repeatedly. When the beast finally calmed and glared in exhaustion, Militus questioned it.

"How many of you reside within Limbo, demon, and where?" asked Militus. The beast cursed more, and when it grew tired of cursing Militus, it quieted, only to be aroused in pain by the soldiers standing on its shoulder and wings. It was a long interrogation, and when Militus determined he would get no more than the few answers from the beast, the demon was placed into a choke hold by the largest of his men. It took a long time, as it did for the Elder demon destroyed by Mortuus, before the beast smoked, a black cloud denoting its former state. The strangling warrior was cheered by his fellows. The men picked up their arrows and departed to recover at the First Waters, carrying along Benjamin and the others disabled in the encounter. Various scientists who were within the Hall watching the situation moved away from their windows, trying to be unseen by the soldiers and Militus.

Benjamin and Militus sat near a tree on the edge of the stream bank. Soon, they were joined by Barak, Socius, and Alcander, who was in chains, Alcander's two guards, and Clavius.

"The Society is no more," said Benjamin. "We just had a *talk* with our old friend, the senior scientist. You were correct Clavius, he was a demon." Socius winced, and Clavius shook his head. "The infiltration by these demons is deep. They are among the Society members."

"Why do they come here?" asked Socius. "What are they watching us for? Mortuus has not been that long escaped from the underground sleep. They have been here far longer."

"They watch us for their Fallen masters" answered Benjamin grimly. "Though you may not have gathered this, we are prisoners in a gilded cage, and we must be kept under control. At least as far as they are concerned. They know we helped the angel to escape, and it will not be long before they appear. I am afraid we may be sent to the outside." The idea of being placed outside of Limbo's pleasant environs weighed upon all of them.

"I am troubled by this possibility also," Militus stated frankly.

"Why do the Fallen not come and find Mortuus themselves," asked Socius.

"Fallen would not bother with our lot," said Clavius. "We are insects in their eyes, and they would rather train their demon dogs to keep us in line than dirty their hands. Since we threaten the established order, we may have severe consequences. There is only one who can help us at this point. We must go to the Chronicler."

Barak looked at the group. He was the most loyal and dedicated follower of the Chronicler, and even he would be allowed to see the secluded teacher only on the rarest of occasions. But they were in need, desperately, and the answers could only come from the Chronicler. Barak nodded his head.

"Very well. I will take you, and we can try for an audience. Drink up. It is a very long walk, and we shall need to watch much more carefully for the beasts. They will be hunting for us this time."

Barak started to fill vials from the stream, and secretly wished, for a split second, that Aristotle had never woken Mortuus.

Chapter 59
Nessus and the Centaur Rebellion

The band of centaurs, the angel Mortuus and the human Darius had gathered outside of the cave, as close as they dared prior to making known their intention. The planning for this event had been successful: many centaurs had volunteered, far more than could fit into the cave mouth, and so Chiron had proposed that the remaining herd could spread out, making a warning system to indicate the Fallen approaching from anywhere around the seventh circle. Across the river from the cave, the herds had also formed a line of a score of meters apart.

The imps of the forbidden area cave, seeing the crowding centaurs in the nearer distance, on both sides of the cave, watched and hissed and shrank back into the large dark opening. Chiron waited, watching as the numbers of centaurs increased by the minute. He was as a proud father, but wary that taking his herds into so much danger would hurt the race of centaurs and their morale forever after if their fight was unsuccessful. And, by all accounts of the powers of the Fallen and their demons, there was no reason to believe this fight could have a good ending for any of the rebels. Chiron was flanked by Asterion, who was shadowing the Master Centaur more as time passed.

Asterion was still, but his large bull eyes darted back and forth, nervously, feeling all but swallowed in the sea of centaurs. Asterion had only one friend during his harsh lifetime, a servant child who, in her naïveté, did not fear him; but she had been taken from him when their friendship was discovered and reported to the guards. Her removal from his life was a cruelty in itself, and the advisor to the King made certain to beat the child severely where her cries could be heard by Asterion. It had caused the tortured half-bull the most pain and rage, and his full hatred of humans came to a pinnacle at that point in his life. Now he had a friend again, but his joy was dampened with his insecurity in this large crowd. The best he could do was to stand still and wait for the battle to start, calming himself with deep breaths that made him appear angry. The centaurs staring so intensely did not help either. They had been briefed by their commanders about Asterion, and many were curious and wished to approach their newest fellow Halfling. His bull-countenance was far too foreboding, and they were preparing for the fight of their afterlives. Fellowship would have to wait.

Darius and Mortuus stood behind Chiron and Asterion, each in frightened anticipation for the battle to come. Panos was strutting about nervously, as several of the younger centaurs watched. One centaur mouthed the words "filthy human coward" to his fellows, wishing to grasp the fearful, pacing human and toss him into the boiling river. This circle's centaurs could tolerate humans, but had absolutely no threshold for fear. Panos, in his state of worry, was unaware of anyone's current views and judgments. He knew fear. It was all he could do not to turn and run away. Were it not for the presence of Darius, Panos would have scurried away hastily and been up the rocky slope heading toward the First Circle. The centaurs, disgusted, turned and talked among themselves, distracting themselves with the coming glory of battle which they heavily anticipated.

Pholus was behind, watching as the centaurs strutted toward Chiron. He would be the last to enter the cave mouth. As he watched the last of them arrive, Pholus noted another formation, coming up slowly, moving very uniformly. Thinking that they were a proud company, he smiled. But Chiron did not. His inner eye had begun another vision, and he appeared to stare into space blankly.

The centaurs were shooting at each other, and those wounded were attacked by the harpies, who shredded them easily in their wounded state; Chiron saw a leader, smiling as he pulled his bow and shot the arrows into his fellow centaurs, then hefted them into the red river, cursing them loudly. The leader was familiar, but Chiron could not make out his face. The Master Centaur stepped forward in his vision, just to the edge of sight and the vision faded.

Chiron returned to consciousness, and suddenly motioned Pholus and the company nearest him to assume an attack formation. The alarm in Chiron's voice caused the centaur companies to move quickly, quieting them immediately. The silence and formation occurred speedily, as Chiron looked to and fro for his foreseen nemesis. Mortuus, Darius and Asterion followed the movements of Chiron, but he waved them to stay put as he addressed the herds.

"My fellows," Chiron called, "We are betrayed by our own. Turn and look behind you. And prepare for battle." Chiron trotted toward what was now the front line of the centaurs, who, although puzzled, followed their chief commander to a fault. Seeing the large company of centaurs drawing near, they readied themselves. It was clear this regiment would easily have come up from behind had Chiron not had his vision. Pholus, the closest to the oncoming centaurs, began cursing loudly. Chiron's suspicions were confirmed.

Nessus was the leader of the opposing force in his vision.

Nessus shouted to the company to halt, and approached Chiron and Pholus, both of whom had moved between the companies. The two had only moved a short distance from their company, causing Nessus to move far from his standing company. Chiron stared at Pholus, and then winked. It was then Pholus knew that his old friend was up to something.

"Master. I have grave news." Nessus began, "The Fallen know of your plans to enter the forbidden area cave. They will arrive any moment. I fear you will be removed from your post, along with Master Pholus." Chiron and Pholus were in a state of false shock, playing to Nessus' lies and treachery, yet still somewhat astonished that this fool of a centaur had performed the ultimate act of treachery and sided with the Fallen.

"And how did they learn of our undertaking, Nessus?" Pholus stabbed his words at Nessus, because he knew the answer already.

"I told them," said Nessus, calm and cold. Pholus was enraged, his anger grown to violent proportion. Chiron, however, remained calm, and motioned Pholus to stand down. The company of centaurs behind Nessus were ready to battle, and the company brought up by Pholus began their stance. Chiron smiled and waved to all the centaurs, and they returned his greeting with bows. Suddenly, the Master Centaur began to shout, talking loudly for both opposing companies to hear him. The face of Nessus was a question.

"YOU WOULD CHALLENGE ME THEN NESSUS, FOR THE MANTLE OF LEADERSHIP? I ACCEPT!" The herds on both sides began their cheering, as they had so long ago when Chiron was challenged before. Brutus had fulfilled his penance after challenging and losing to his leader. Now the herds would witness Chiron against Nessus. No one would fight today except these two warriors. Chiron had sidestepped Nessus' attempted overthrow with a shout.

Nessus almost collapsed at his self-inflicted misfortune, reeling at his easy loss. He knew he was no match at all against the Master Centaur. Chiron had tricked him into moving out of hearing range of his company, and then issued the challenge. Centaurs could not call their kind to help in the challenge for leadership; it was against their code of honor. Even the traitorous centaurs would not abandon this code in the face of the larger herds. Nessus, his dreams of power destroyed, galloped and jumped into the boiling river rather than waiting to be thrown in. His screams faded as he moved away, swimming to complete his five rounds, the prescribed punishment for the loser of the challenge. Adding to his pride's injury, the humans who inhabited the river watched as Nessus swam among them.

The rebellion was over before its start. Chiron saw the harpies in the background, circling quietly in the air, and watching the centaur companies. The harpies rarely ever traveled to this side of Phlegethon, and their presence indicated that Nessus had made what had to be a pretty good deal with them. The company who came with Nessus dispersed, puzzled, and returned to their former posts, never knowing why Nessus had promised them glorious battle. Nessus had sought out the least intelligent and the most easily misguided members of the herds and recruited them over a long period of time, promising them commander status and glory if they would fight against the oppression that Chiron had put upon the herds; and mentioning many times Chiron's secret dealings with their greatest enemies, the humans. Their surprise at his sudden decision to challenge the Master Centaur was great, and their disappointment greater. Nessus had cowered in dishonor, and thus humiliated, could never again be recognized or respected as any sort of leader of the herds. To have placed their trust in such a leader would cause them misery for the rest of their stay in Hell, and none were too dimwitted or misguided to miss that single, cogent fact.

Chiron questioned the second in command of Nessus' company, who told him Nessus had setup a lone centaur to stand ready to blow the horn that would summon the Fallen. This centaur had luckily not blown the horn, because Nessus' command never came. Pholus retrieved the horn, placing it in the safekeeping of Commander Tacitus. Nessus' Second in Command insisted he knew no more and several of the trusted centaur commanders agreed he was probably telling the truth, verifying the centaurs' lack of intelligence in general. Chiron and Pholus speculated that Nessus would have informed the Fallen of Chiron's intent to enter the cave after the battle was complete, thus granting the traitor the role of leader of the centaurs. The scale of the treachery was unbelievably foolish, even for Nessus.

"Fool! Traitor! What will you do with him and his traitors?" asked Pholus.

"I do not know but I will have decided something by the time he is finished his rounds." returned Chiron.

"Now to our task."

Chapter 60
Inside the Cave

The battle was no more than a few minutes long. The centaurs, directed by Chiron to surround the cave entrance, watched for Fallen or their demon counterparts in the air above. Not a single creature was sighted beyond the few imps who were always present. Chiron, along with Mortuus, Asterion and Pholus went into the cave first. Darius and Panos were sent across the river to a hiding place within the Wood. The pair of humans were carried across the boiling river by Titan, the youthful centaur who was the least affronted by their riding upon his back.

Many centaurs, aroused for a grand battle, were disappointed at the prospect of being mere lookouts, but Pholus reminded them of the power of the Fallen, and the threat if they were to arrive suddenly. Still, they could not understand why the 'human' Mortuus was allowed to enter, along with the Minotaur. Chiron and the commanders decided to keep Mortuus' identity a secret for the time being; the Fallen were the unmistakable grand lords of Hell, undefeatable. This reputation would surely cause his kind to size up and attempt to challenge Mortuus' status as Fallen. Chiron's people were not shy to challenge power, and he did not feel they were ready to understand an alliance with one of their jailers.

The small imps loitering at the outside of the cave shrunk back inside at the sight of the approaching party, hissing and growling. The odd company of centaur, minotaur and angel approached the cave warily, ready for anything. A handful of imps, half the size of demons, had been waiting at the entrance, just back in the shadow. They jumped out suddenly and startled the company. Before Chiron and Pholus could turn them into screaming smoke, a score of arrows whooshed by their ears and into the beasts within seconds. Mortuus stood, in shocked awe as the two mighty centaurs looked around. The lookouts, eager for battle, had unleashed their projectiles from far away at the sight of the creatures. Chiron and Pholus glared at the lookout centaurs sternly.

"Do not draw your bows again. You are to keep watch only!" yelled Pholus. A distant commander replied.

"Apologies, Master Chiron and Master Pholus," he said, embarrassed.

The guard imps had no chance. Falling down in pain, they writhed for a moment with several arrows protruding from each of them. Asterion, newly equipped by the centaurs with a large spear, wasted no time and finished them off. The entrance became a smoking barrel, and Chiron and Pholus collected the arrows from the ground to leave as little trace of their visit as possible.

There was little light inside the carved hallway going into the first chamber of the cave. Chiron and Pholus struggled to see ahead in vain, but Mortuus saw the danger ahead easily.

"Chiron, Pholus – aim where I point. There, straight ahead!" said Mortuus. The two needed no prodding. Their arrows thudded into something, and the screeches which followed were deafening in the cave acoustics. Mortuus ran ahead, followed by Asterion. A loud pop followed as Mortuus and Asterion stabbed at the ground. Another imp dissipated. The company entered the inner chamber.

It was a large compartment, and the smell and look reminded Mortuus uncomfortably of his recent origin. Two sets of doorways, covered with heavy wrought iron bars were placed at the far sides of the room, both on the left and the right of a flat, back wall, made of solid black rock. Behind the bars were stairways, carved into the rock, leading upward and out of sight. This inner cavern was lit more brightly, like Clavius' hallway in Porto. Mortuus surmised the same magic was used to create the light. An ancient, ornately carved table next to the left wall held a large opened book. It was the only furniture they found in this strange cavity. Behind the table and against the wall, a fine, filthy old cloth veiled a large rectangular area. Chiron went to the cloth and pushed it aside cautiously. Behind the cloth was a dusty mirror, a duplicate of one in the Hall of Minos. He quickly released the cloth and it fluttered back to its former position covering the silvered glass. Chiron did not wish to trigger the mirror if it had the same magical teleportation function as Minos' mirror of judgment. Everyone watched as he moved back from the wall.

"Stay away from this - all of you. I will explain later..." No one in the room had ever seen the mirror of Minos; it was only used to judge humans. The two centaurs, Chiron and Pholus, searched the room and found near the barred doorways, levers jutting out from the walls.

"Try the lever on the right, Mortuus," said Chiron. "Though cautiously..." In a moment Mortuus had pulled the switch, and opened the right gateway. "This way friends." They followed Chiron, as the stairway was fit only for one centaur at a time. A short climb later, they were at the top of the steps, and Mortuus started to feel claustrophobic again. He recalled his hellish awakening, and his journey through the mines with Eruos. Angels must not be accustomed to caves, he thought. He swallowed hard, determined to get past his fear, and kept walking. The hallway at the top abruptly turned right, and the group followed Chiron further into the rocky structure.

Mortuus noticed something suddenly. As they walked, an entrance appeared on the left of the hall. It was closed but nevertheless there. He stopped, looking at the shape of this doorway. It reminded him of the first demon he had found in Limbo, hidden by magical means. It phased in and out of his vision, a surreal, gossamer veil appearing as rock, then door opening. He decided to check his theory.

"Chiron – stop for a moment. Asterion, Pholus – look at this wall. Do you see anything strange about it?" asked Mortuus.

"I see nothing but rock." returned Pholus. Chiron and Asterion nodded in agreement.

"Then only I am seeing this," said Mortuus. "Pholus, please help me to push, here." Mortuus showed Pholus where to put his hands, and struggled as they pushed into the wall. Chiron started to look around the wall, for any sort of device that would have helped open the doorway. Asterion had his own ideas. He began to brutally butt the wall with his head, hoping that his rage driven strength would open a passage. It did nothing. Then, Mortuus, looking directly across from the phasing doorway saw it. A small lever, a miniature version of those that opened the bars at the base of the steps, was hidden just like the doorway. Mortuus grabbed the lever cautiously.

"Watch my friends." Mortuus pulled the lever and the hallway wall opened. The four walked inside a low-ceilinged room, barely higher than the centaurs.

Chiron saw them first; on a single carved rock table, three large gems, looking polished and perfectly cut. They were each the size of a human heart, and two were clear, sparkling like diamonds. The other was a deep crystalline blue, giving off a slight glow that seemed to brighten as they neared it. Mortuus looked closely at the stones, stunned. His memory stirred in the darkness, but he was still disconnected from it. Instinctively, he knew he needed to take the blue glowing gem. Almost involuntarily, Mortuus reached for the stone and, holding it gently, caressed it as if it were a dear pet. For a moment he thought of Socius, and did not know why. The gem glowed more brightly and the glow fluttered, then subsided back to its original radiance. Mortuus placed the stone into his pack gingerly as Chiron and Pholus watched.

"What is this stone, Mortuus?" asked Chiron. "You seem as if you have found something dear. Precious gems mean nothing here. Do you have a recollection?"

"No," said Mortuus, "But I am compelled to take it. If I can trust my feelings to be correct, this is a living creature, though I know not what. My heart would suffer to leave it in the hands of these despicable Fallen, though I have no other explanation to offer."

"That explanation will do for now. And what of the other, clear gems?" asked Chiron.

"When I look at them, I feel great sadness. They are brilliant, but empty, unlike this one. My memory has been stirred, though not yet enough." Chiron nodded.

"I will take these two also." said Chiron, placing them into his pack. "We will get our answers later. If these are so guarded, the Fallen must place some value in them. I believe your memory will return, and when it does, we shall have many answers. For now, we shall have to be patient."

"Hurry friends. We delay too long and I have concern the Fallen will find us within," interrupted Pholus. Asterion grunted agreement as he rubbed his sore head. The intruders resumed their path up the hallway, which climbed to another set of stairs that wound left, then ended in a large, long room. Large stone slab tables lay in the middle of the room, and another table on the far wall was pressed into the corner. On the floor was a bloodied, ripped robe, a once fine garment crafted by the weavers of Porto. Chiron and Pholus recognized the colors and patterns immediately; this robe had been given to Aristotle many centuries ago.

Within seconds the group assessed the room. Two tables, those nearest the entryway, had multiple sharp spikes protruding from their surfaces. Over the tables, a flat stone was suspended by chains attached to the top of the room, with holes in the underside directly corresponding to the spikes coming out of the table beneath the hanging rock. The chains holding the stones up were attached to a single chain, in turn attached to a sophisticated gear system next to a lever. The levers of the first two tables were up, but the third table lever was down; the flat stone slab, with chains piled on it, gripped them all as, coming out from between the two stones, a slow trickle of blood made a tiny stream onto the filthy rock floor.

They had found Aristotle.

"Quickly!" motioned Chiron, "Pull that lever Pholus!" The group surrounded the table, and the stones began to slowly part, as Pholus struggled to push up the lever switch. Asterion, seeing the efforts of the centaur were not enough, placed his giant hand over that of Pholus', and the lever moved up almost effortlessly. They watched horrified, seeing the great teacher, the explorer, the awakener of angels, in this most hideous form, crushed, bleeding, mangled; unrecognizable. Chiron wept and Mortuus stood quietly as the leader of the centaurs covered his eyes.

"Ugh," came an unguarded sound from Pholus. He shook his large head at the mangled mass of flesh that was Aristotle. "Shall I use some of the remaining vials, Chiron?"

"If you have them use them," replied Chiron, "just do it quickly." Pholus opened up his pack, moving some small items out of the way. From its bottom, he pulled out the last three small vials of the waters packaged from Limbo.

"Mystical, I would say," said Pholus, "that the teacher was so generous with the healing waters that will begin his own restoration. I am beginning to feel hope for some reason." Asterion looked as Pholus spoke, and said nothing. He stared at Aristotle's mutilated form, and swore curses at the Fallen who would do such a thing to anyone.

"Pour the waters on his midsection, Pholus," directed Chiron, "The healing will be best begin there. I will administer one onto the head and neck. We will transport him as soon as we can. The longer we stay here the more peril we are in."

It was a relatively long time before they were able to move Aristotle's body. As soon as he was able to groan in an audible tone, the pair of centaurs picked him up and placed him into the arms of Mortuus. The blood and gore were almost too much for Mortuus to bear, but he put aside his revulsion as best as he could.

The human who had awakened him would not suffer long as far as Mortuus was concerned. Chiron led as the search party left the torture chamber behind. They went back to the large room at the opening, when Mortuus thought he had heard Aristotle speak.

"Wait, Chiron, Pholus. Aristotle has said something. I cannot discern it. Come closer, maybe one of you can make out his words." The bloody gore that was Aristotle moved something that had once been his jaw. The centaurs bent closer, but heard only a light muttering of pain. Asterion bent near, and the rescuers tensed up in concentration.

"Other," said Asterion. "Other. He has asked to get another." Chiron looked intensely around the room, searching for some clue as to what Aristotle was talking about. "Perhaps he is just in too much pain," said the half-bull.

"No. I have known this human for many centuries. I believe we may have to go into that other entrance. Mortuus - take Aristotle out of this place. Have one of the commanders escort you to where Darius remains hidden in the Wood, awaiting our return with Aristotle. They will lead you to the rill, under the tree covering. You and Aristotle are who the Fallen will be searching for, so remain hidden until I arrive. Farewell if I do not see you again. You have given me new respect, and hope, for angel kind." Mortuus was moved by Chiron's words, and turned to exit the cave.

Upon exiting the cave, Mortuus was met by a company of centaurs who had been waiting to take him and Aristotle to the Wood. But the centaurs were reluctant to carry Mortuus and the bloody pulp that was Aristotle across the river, so Mortuus began walking across at the rivers shallowest point. The centaurs stood in disbelief that Mortuus did not falter, and insisted that he wait and they would call for Titan to carry the pair across. Mortuus continued walking, grimacing with each step. The burning on his feet was worse than he had imagined, and he nearly dropped Aristotle. The river seemed wide here, but he could see that it was just his imagination. The pain intensified, and was unbearable, and Mortuus began running as he neared the bank on the other side, collapsing awkwardly into a small heap, still holding his damaged, dear awakener. Aristotle's moaning grew louder, prompting Mortuus to stand again on his burnt feet. The centaurs led the way. They reached the trees much later, and were soon met by Pholus, Asterion and Chiron, who were carrying another gory inhabitant from the cave whom they found in the other room Aristotle mentioned. This one had had no water sprinkled on his wounds, and was as quiet as death. He looked quite horrific and moldy, as if he had been there a very long time.

"We will need to conserve the waters for this one." said Chiron. "I want to know why he was being kept hidden by the Fallen. He has been there much longer than Aristotle. Do you see how his wounds have tried to heal in such a strange manner? His legs seem to have grown back together with holes in them."

"Aye - and his blood hardly flowed away from the table." added Pholus. "I do not think he will be able to speak for quite awhile."

"We will first heal Aristotle, and find out why he wanted to save this one," said Chiron. "I do not believe he is angel."

"Nor do I Chiron," said Mortuus apprehensively. "I see no magical energy flowing in him. He might just be a very troublesome fugitive to the Fallen. I wonder what kind of secrets he knows to get such special treatment?"

"He is no mere fugitive to receive this treatment, Mortuus," said Chiron, changing his mind. "Plutus was a troublesome wanderer, and he had no such punishment. This one has truly incurred their wrath and fear. I will get my waters and return shortly. Both will need to be regenerated promptly. Where is Darius? We can also use his water." Chiron left, and returned shortly with a few more vials of waters. Behind him were Darius and Panos. Darius gave up his water without hesitation, as did Mortuus, and between them the pair of crushed corpses that were Aristotle and the stranger regenerated greatly.

Despite their efforts, it still turned out to be a long wait.

Chapter 61

The Chronicler

The band arrived at the Chronicler's cottage in small fragments. They had decided to travel in packs of three, dividing themselves up to not arouse suspicion. They also had grown by two when they left the mine. Barak, Socius and Militus went in the first group and were followed by Benjamin, who was cloaked because of his high profile in the scientific community, along with the two miners Abreo and Exaro, who were insistent on traveling with the group. Eruo remained behind in order to handle the worker demons who might be coming for more ore, thereby deflecting any suspicion from the mine area.

Behind Benjamin and the miners were the warriors, who had been accompanying the group, split into many groups of three. Militus had seen to the hiding of Alcander deep within the mines, two of the warriors guarding him in a hidden wing. Clavius had volunteered his laboratory for holding the corrupt Elder, but Socius and Militus balked at this suggestion. Clavius stayed behind in Porto, arranging his cottage to appear more like his neighbors in the odd case that it was searched.

The walk was long. The Chronicler's cottage was near the far wall of Limbo, almost a complete circle from the entrance to Limbo. Many citizens of Limbo had requested the Elders to petition the Fallen for an entrance way across the path that ran through the Second Circle, and had been refused by the Elders, who stated the Fallen wanted only one entrance into and out of Limbo. The petitioners objected strenuously, but the Fallen were quite immovable.

When they had reached the cottage, they found several groups of students outside, sitting and apparently talking as they waited for the Chronicler. Barak knew many of the students, and walked over to ask his familiars as to the whereabouts of the Chronicler. Meanwhile, Socius and Militus sat down on the grass, waiting to see their trio of companions come along the path soon after. Socius began to have a conversation with Militus while they sat waiting. The grass was cool to sit upon, and the trees in the distance, known as the End Forest, were invitingly beautiful in their soft greenness, some with a silvery brilliance.

"Have you been here before Militus," asked Socius "I mean, to visit the Chronicler, or just to travel somewhere different?"

"I have," answered Militus, "though I have not been back here in ages. The Elysian fields are where I feel most at home, but this traveling we have done of late has stirred me to do more and see more. Do you see those trees in the distance?" Militus pointed toward the End Forest. "They were not here the last time I ventured out this far. It must be the Chronicler's doing. Behind the trees, hidden well, is the far wall to Limbo, across the path from the gateway. It's a wonder that no opening has been built there – we would surely see this part of Limbo more often."

"The work of the Elders, I'm sure," replied Socius, "Bureaucrats for the Fallen." Socius was bitter, angry at the injustice of those whom he understood to rule by fear, the ones who betrayed Aristotle. "Militus, are the Fallen so strong that we can never come up against them?"

"The Fallen are the most powerful beings in Hell. As far as we know, Hell was created for them to rule. They are cast out of their natural domain, but no one knows why, only that they were given rulership over Hell to mock them. But save your questions for the Chronicler; he will surely know more than I. Ahh – Barak is returning." Barak walked toward them, his face the picture of concern. Socius and Militus saw it immediately, and their hearts dropped as they anticipated grim news.

"We must go, there is danger here. I know most of these people, but they treat me as a stranger, as if I had *not* known them for centuries. We have to leave before our friends arrive. These impersonators claim not to have seen the Chronicler. I was going to press them with questions they should have been able to answer but thought better of it." Socius was looking beyond Barak at the small groups that were sitting on the ground, all eyes glaring at Militus, Barak and himself.

"Oh. Quickly then. Do not turn around Militus, just start walking back the way we came." As the youth looked, the grim gathering seemed to waver, as if a shimmering heat was rising off the ground and distorting them in the distance. The youth squinted, and then looked again. The watching mass was normal, so he decided his eyes were playing tricks on him in his alerted state. Then he saw it - they were walking toward the three. "Hold. They're moving toward us. Pretend we are not aware they are – different. Try to look normal." Militus put on a false smile, one he had used during his life dealing with politicians and his military superiors, and turned toward the cottage and the mob that formed. Barak pretended to talk to him, peripherally looking at the crowd, and when the pack moved nearer the three, they stood, as if to greet, and have Barak introduce them.

"We cannot destroy this many when we drop at the first casting of the spell," whispered Militus. "We will have to run."

"Play the fool my friends – they have no reason to suspect we know anything" replied Barak.

"What if they try to replace us with their fellow demons?" whispered Socius.

"We shall have to improvise as we go along," said Militus. The group surrounded them, appearing to be quite menacing. Barak addressed one of them, who looked in appearance like a very old friend of his, and started to introduce Militus and Socius, playing the friendly host as best he could to keep his countenance steady.

In the blink of an eye, Barak was flying backward, the victim of a sudden forcible backhand by his old 'friend.' Militus made to move into the man when he was suddenly picked up from behind and tossed into a stone pile not far from where they stood. His leg was broken and the wind knocked out of him, and he could not get to his feet. Socius fared the best, ducking reflexively as two of the men tried to grab his arms.

More of the masked demon assembly tried grabbing Socius, and he evaded very well, moving to keep out of their clawing grip, instinctively dodging their clawed hands as they tried to latch on to him. Pulling out his long knife, Socius waved it in front of several of them, trying to discourage them. Growling, they began reverting to their true forms; demons of many shapes and sizes, winged and not. In a moment he was underneath the swarm of these vile creatures, thrashing for his freedom, and damaging them as best he could. It was all he could do to utter the words of the spell. He would take out at least one of them before they ripped him apart. Before he could utter the spell, at the last moment, loud screams and screeching, intense heat, and the filthy stink of the beasts smoking were his universe, and then, he was no longer under a pile of demons.

Socius got to his feet, slowly, choking on the foul smoky air. He had been slashed and bitten on his legs, and his robes were ripped and shredded; his eyes were irritated by the stream of blood dripping from cuts and scratches on his forehead. He looked around and saw Barak, moaning as he slowly, painfully, got to his feet. He had stood up and limped slowly, leaving a bloody trail to mark his path. Militus was gone, as were the demons. All the demons. Socius, puzzled and afraid, ran to Barak to assist him. Socius could see out of the corner of his eyes, coming from the cottage, a man. He was moving in their direction. He waved his weapon at the figure and in a blink of the eye the man appeared next to Socius. The startled youth barely kept his wits, and though afraid, aimed his hostility at the man.

"Where is Militus?" yelled Socius. The large man, cloaked in a robe that looked as if it had been worn in outer hell many, many times, stared at Socius, examining him, seeming to scan his body, and then - smiling. Socius noted a gleam in the man's eyes of friendliness and warmth, behind a serious, mature, yet boyish face. The man, to Socius' surprise, began to help the stunned Barak to his feet.

"The demons have taken your commander Militus, Barak." said the cloaked man. "Come - I have healing potions that will have you and the boy as good as new." Barak smiled feebly at the man. "Let us walk to my cottage."

"Thank you master," said Barak. "I was afraid they had impersonated you as well." A new understanding swept over Socius. This was the Chronicler himself.

"Do not worry yourself, Barak," said the Chronicler, "And this, finally, is the one who you told me of, the babe delivered so long ago?"

"I would have to say yes by the way he dodged the demons." Barak smiled and motioned to Socius. "I am sorry to have waited so long to assist you, Socius. I only just arrived."

"Yes, it was he who came to Limbo as a child, and grew up among the warriors and teachers. Socius, I would like to introduce Master Avius, whom you know as the Chronicler." Socius smiled – here was the Chronicler himself, known to give an audience only once a century, standing with him and Barak.

"Brilliant," said Socius excitedly, "I am honored sir –" They were approaching the cottage entryway, where none entered, except the highest followers of the Chronicler, and very rarely. Barak had told Socius he could count the number of times he had entered the cottage on one hand, and each time the interior had been entirely different. "We are entering, Master Chronicler?" he asked respectfully. Aristotle had taught him good manners.

"Yes Socius – we are going inside. Welcome to my cottage. Please pardon my messiness - I have not cleaned in centuries." They walked inside, and found the interior was not much to look at, especially for someone so highly revered. Bare furniture, covered in dust, a table, a wooden floor, a large mirror, candles on the walls for light and some simple stones were all that Socius could see. It was a plainly normal interior. "Wait," said Avius and he turned to close the door behind them, then secure it with several large boards across the top, middle and bottom. He stepped over to a wall and tilted a candle holder that was tipped slightly sideways. Walking to the other side of the room, he did the same to another candle. In a moment, the mirror began to brighten, emitting a strong light around its edges, and the walls became stony, replacing the previous wood and thatch. The door behind them disappeared and was also replaced by a wall of stone. The room was, in a moment, far larger. Socius looked at Barak, who smiled through his bruises at Socius, who stood with his mouth agape. Avius returned to the side of Barak, and the three walked toward the mirror. It grew wide as they approached.

"Do not fear, Socius. Barak, you have told no one of this?" asked Avius.

"No one Master Avius," returned Barak. "Socius, you are the only other person in Limbo to enter this place."

And all at the same time, they walked, disappearing into the mirror of the Chronicler

Chapter 62

The Flight of Militus

Militus was screaming in pain. He was being carried, like prey caught and stretched between two large hawks. Strong claw-hands held him so tightly that they were causing him to bruise, and would have penetrated his skin were it not for his thick robes. They had picked him up from the rock pile and flown off, up into the air, transforming into demons in a split second, just as he had seen before with Alcander's Elder, the demon who was Morpheus.

He could see the ground falling away slowly as the creatures flew their hardest to lift his flailing weight. They did not see that they were flying over a group of three men, each with jaws agape in surprised horror. A great flash lit up the mist above Militus and the demons carrying him, as multiple shrieks assaulted their ears. the flash came from the field outside the house of the Chronicler. The demons screeched in angry surprise, and flew lower to inspect the scene they had just left.

Three of Militus' warriors, who had earlier grouped by threes to avoid suspicion as they traveled, had their bows pulled back, and aimed. They had seen the flash moments before and immediately readied for whatever was next. All at once, they loosed their arrows. The demons faltered, as two arrows pierced one of them. The last shaft missed its mark. The wounded demon, arrow shaft sticking from his gut and free shoulder, let loose Militus as the pain disabled and enraged him. Pulling the arrows out in irritation, the wounded demon screeched at the soldiers below while the other demon sank nearer the ground with the full weight of Militus. Not willing to endure more pain, the injured demon flew away, out of reach of the arrows. The demon still carrying Militus, soared upwards, joining his peer. Militus could hear them, speaking to each other in their coarse, barely understandable voices.

"I must regenerate. Take him to the pitch and throw him to the devils. Return here and we shall punish their impudence." The demon carrying Militus growled in agreement.

"Miserable, filthy humans."

"I will inform the masters of this. The humans had help. That was strong magic. Go now, and return when he is in the devil's care." And with that they split up, the demon carrying Militus rising high up, high enough to see the wall coming at them, and at the last moment, flying over the wall.

Militus decided to stop struggling and use his energy to assess an escape plan. The creature had in its belt a long knife and meat hook; Militus briefly remembered the description of how Darius' friends had been hauled off, and was thankful not to be dancing on the end of one of the hooks. He would wait for the right moment, and make his move. The pain of his broken leg was hardly bearable, but Militus had no choice but to hold onto his wits.

The demon and his cargo flew very close to the wall of Limbo and it seemed as if Militus would be smashed into it. At the last minute, the demon lifted higher. Militus watched the ground below. He could see they were just below the misty ceiling. His nose was suddenly assailed, as the smells of outer Hell reminded him of the terror he had experienced when he had first entered Hell, before being sent to Limbo by the mirror.

His memory flashback was interrupted, when below him, just appearing, were people who were floating, it appeared, or hovering, before suddenly being smashed into the wall that enclosed Limbo. The people would fall downward only to be picked up again and tossed around violently. The wind was the cruel torturer of these damned. Militus looked left and right, and everywhere below him were people being tossed against the wall.

The demon remained very high up, hugging the dark gray ceiling for a short while, and then, as the ground dipped, indicating the next circle, began to descend.

In the next circle, Militus could smell the putrid smell of rotten food, vomit, and long decayed flesh and blood. The flight continued down to the next circle, and now the ground was full of groups of people, frantically pushing large boulders at each other, the sound of the boulders hitting loudly, booming up enough for Militus to hear. Further down they flew, the demon and his prey, towards the bowels of Hell.

Another cliff indicated the next circle, and the ground became suddenly black, darkening, with large slime green spots, and a wide body of black water. It reeked of swamp decay, stinking of swamp gases mixed with human excrement, even at this high altitude, and somewhere in the distance to his left, far off, a light, a flame erupted. The demon leveled off, and Militus prepared for his final move. He knew they were nearing the walls of Dis. He saw the huge, rusty metallic form appear.

Once over the wall, Militus could feel the heat wafting up from below. He had listened to the stories of Aristotle many, many times over the centuries, and he remembered the gruesome description of this area and its inhabitants being slowly burned alive. There was no way to describe the stench of the burning flesh rising out of the glowing tombs and caskets which lay below. The red, glowing patches on the ground indicated where the tormented were cooked alive. It was horrific to behold, even for the seasoned battle veteran.

In the distance, Militus saw the next circle approaching fast. The demon began to descend again, and Militus, defying the pain of moving his body with the broken leg, not to mention the painful claw-fingers of the demon flyer, flexed his torso upward, enough to get his hand into his belt pack. The demon looked down, and squeezed his claws tighter, pulling each of Militus' shoulders apart so hard that Militus thought he would be ripped apart, so strong was the beast. Militus grimaced and yelled as he felt his collarbone break. The demon cursed, and Militus made his daring move. With a painful flick of his wrist, he turned the knife he had grabbed from his belt into the bicep of the flyer, turning it as much as possible to maximize the damage and disable the beast. Screeching in pain, the demon squeezed the broken collarbone of Militus, but released his grip on the other shoulder. It slashed into the side of Militus' face, deeply lacerating him, and causing blood to flow heavily. Using the pain that was filling him, Militus slashed the knife again, but with a greater arc behind the blow. This time the demon howled with rage as its blood poured onto Militus' face, temporarily blinding him. The struggle in the air did not miss the attention of those below. The two were struggling, each trying to do as much damage as possible to the other; the demon was unable to do much except take each blow from Militus; its left arm was hanging, disabled because of the sinews cut by the veteran. It descended quickly, preparing to drop Militus and smash his body on the ground, disabling him until it could regenerate and finish the flight to the Eighth Circle. Militus, deciding that he would not like to drop, grabbed onto the hanging forearm of the beast, and flailed around until it had to land. The landing turned out to be its fatal mistake.

Both flyer and prisoner impacted on the ground. Bones smashed and broken, Militus was unable to move, and gasped as the wind had been knocked out of him once again. The demon, enraged beyond comprehension, was heavily damaged, but able to get up and round upon Militus' disabled, gasping body. Militus readied himself, waiting to be ripped apart and stared defiantly at the beast as it limped toward him. It began to ravage Militus, clawing his abdomen, ripping at his belly until it was opened and then shredding it into bloody pulp; the weathered warrior gasped out screams and blood, choking and coughing in pain. The creature reveled in this power over his crippled prey, laughing in madness at the overpowering of the prisoner. It stood up tall, screeching in joy, ready for another round of bloodying, taunting Militus in his powerlessness.

"Foolish human. I will open up your – arghhhh!" The demon screeched, and many sickening thuds later, on the ground, flailing as it lay full of arrows. Militus could only turn his head now and watch. Over him, another creature was aiming its bow directly at his face. It was a centaur, but not Chiron. It pointed the arrow at the chest of Militus, and let it loose. Militus was blinded by the unbearable pain, unable to scream or breath. The next few moments were a fog for him, and he wished he could pass out from the pain, as he had from his last battle, when he was alive. Then a gruff voice sounded over all – he knew it was a centaur, because he had seen them, but it did not sound like Chiron's.

"Hold your arrows! Hold your arrows!" roared the voice. Moments later another centaur stood over Militus, and leaning over, pulled the arrow out of his chest. The centaur turned away, and began to yell at another. "We must inform Master Chiron. As for the filthy demon, keep filling its hide; do not let it escape. We will drag it to Master Chiron and the half-bull. Carry this one, who fights with demons."

"He is only a fugitive!" replied the other voice.

"Take him and do not question my authority or you will swim with Nessus!" roared the voice. Militus was quickly picked up, roughly, and thrown over the back of one of the centaurs, face down. This was a more proper way to transport a human and would not be considered a domestication of the centaur. The pain rolled through Militus in waves, and after a long, bumpy gallop, Militus noticed they were entering a grove of gnarled-looking trees as his head bumped up and down. He was still unable to move when they stopped, but he had regained his breath. Militus saw the demon writhing as it was dragged up behind them.

"Master Chiron – " said the centaur that was holding Militus. "This human was found on the bank. The demon and he were fighting in the air and fell to the bank. It had overtaken him before we arrived, but it was badly wounded by the human."

"I would see the human." said a familiar voice. A hand lifted Militus' head from the side of the centaur. It was Chiron.

"Militus!" exclaimed the Master centaur. "Gently take him off and place him onto the ground! He is to be treated with respect, a friend to our kind was he in life."

The centaur warriors lifted Militus, who expected their gentlest to still be quite rough, and was surprised at just how easily and painlessly he was placed on the ground. To his delight, Mortuus stood over him, smiling.

"Welcome Militus – it is good to see you again, though I am sorry to see you in the state you are in. The beast did quite a bit of damage," said Mortuus as Darius walked up alongside of him.

"You'd better pick weaker opponents to fight my friend," said the smiling Darius.

"Master Chiron," another voice, a centaur, that Militus did not know. "We thought him for a fugitive, and Theos sank an arrow into his chest before Master Pholus –"

"Leave me, now.' replied the unmistakable voice of Chiron. "You will spread the word to all your fellows. Do not attack any humans, even if you think them to be fugitives! Have Tacitus bring me the summoning horn."

"Yes, Master Chiron. I will tell all, especially Theos." And with that, Militus could hear the sound of the centaur galloping away. Mortuus and Darius were busy, ripping off pieces of their tattered robes and wiping the blood off of Militus.

Militus smiled weakly, for just a moment. Mortuus stepped away, and as Militus turned his head to the side, he beheld the ghastly sight of a pulverized human, barely breathing, crimson red in a bloody, pulpy mass. The head and side of the face were bleeding; it was covered in gore and what looked like brain matter coming out of some places. He turned away, the nightmare reminding him of some of the worst battles in his lifetime.

"Drink this Militus." Chiron poured a small vial of fluid into his mouth. It was bitter, and very bad tasting, but somehow Militus found it desirable. "This is one of the concoctions from Limbo, a fairly strong regenerative." Militus choked as he swallowed it down.

"Who is this lying next to me?" asked Militus.

"It is the teacher." replied Chiron.

"Oh no." said Militus, in surprise and anguish.

"Yes," said Chiron's voice, "That is Aristotle. We retrieved him, but he will need much time to regenerate. Now rest, Militus, and let your own regeneration occur." Militus was silent, and his friends sat near him as he closed his eyes and rested.

Chapter 63

The Fall of Limbo

In the time after the disappearance of Militus and the re-emergence of Socius and Barak from the cottage of the Chronicler, Limbo underwent a massive shift in theme. The great buildings were demolished. The Great Library, the Hall of Science, and the Amphitheatre were all destroyed in moments, as the Fallen made their appearance at the front of each building, uttered their incantations, and disappeared up into the misty ceiling as each structure fell into ruin. No warning was given to the occupants of the buildings or inhabitants of Limbo, and many people were trapped beneath the rubble and debris.

The Keep alone was spared, as was the Whirlpool Building. The individual cottages of the citizens of Limbo were searched and razed to the ground without exception. The warriors were attacked by hordes of demons, and their weaponry removed. Those who fought or spoke back were tied and tortured in plain sight of all outside the Keep as examples for the rest of the people. Many warriors fled toward the more deeply wooded sections of Limbo, hiding within the dense forests. Warriors who had any weapons hid them well. The other members of the citizenry were interrogated and ravaged by the demons randomly, ripped apart with the meat hooks and seized weaponry. In more extreme examples, the victims were taken to outer Hell and discarded.

The beginning of Limbo's fall saw the demons appearance within the populace. People who had known each other for centuries suddenly realized they had been infiltrated by the brutish, sadistic beasts. Terror filled them as friends and neighbors transformed into demons right before their eyes.

The paths around the Pool house were heavily guarded. None could pass unless accompanied by an Elder. Even then, the person might be interrogated and mutilated due to the normally violent nature of the demons. There was little comfort or reprieve for Limbo's people.

Clavius' laboratory was almost found after the demons had destroyed his cottage. They found the passage underneath and followed it to the end. Not seeing any visible exit other than the way they entered, they assumed it was not finished being dug. Clavius' neighbors were interrogated and tortured into giving away his identity. Clavius himself, aware that he was discovered, hid well, staying clear of demons and blending in to the crowds to avoid capture. The soldiers loyal to the disappeared Militus stayed nearby Clavius, flowing with the crowd whenever demons were sighted.

The mood of Limbo, once happier, with the smell of the grasses, woods and the general freedom of the people to move about and pursue their interests, became polluted with suspicion, brutality and fear as the Elders, reminding the populace that they had been warned for centuries about breaking the rules imposed upon them by the Fallen, walked about freely. They lorded their status, pointing out those who they did not like, for whatever reason, and that person was hauled off for torturing by the demons. They blamed Aristotle, and Socius and all others who had publicly discarded their 'wisdom' as the cause for the walking terror of the demon hordes.

The gates of Limbo were sealed shut, and according to the Elders, for good.

Chapter 64

Limbo for Beginners

I am convinced now, beyond a doubt that my life is a series of tests. I survived the mirror test of Hell, after waiting in a state of anxiety for what seemed too many days, though days and nights do not exist in Hell. The gray overcast remains very much static, and only the wind changed direction from time to time while I stood in the line.

I went before the mirror, in the same room with the centaur and Minos, both of whom are huge. The mirror sent me to Limbo, which left me in a state of relieved joy unlike any I had ever experienced in my lifetime. I ended up in a wooded area, a place between some small villages called Terni and Porto, respectively. The villages are located clockwise in Limbo, and the locals explained to me that the placement would be roughly one-hundred and eighty degrees from the path entrance into Limbo. The start of the path was where I had passed the door while in line, so I had apparently been sent very far away from the mirror. This was a good thing.

The trip was interesting, because I seemed to just be there, no sudden rush or stomach turning flight or bizarre science fiction spinning portal; time and space just bent around, and the walls of the hall became forest. There was a slight feeling that I had lost some time, like when you accidentally fall asleep; but I shrugged it off, since I had all the time I would ever need, and more. Minos was supposed to wrap his tail around me and toss me into some nasty pit of Hell, at least according to the story. But Minos did not have a tail; and I do not recall reading about centaurs being located so far up in Hell. Not to be too literal, I didn't expect this place to exist, but since it does, and I am sentenced to it, I would expect a bit of accuracy. Nevertheless, I felt I was the luckiest new dead guy in the universe after the mirror trick.

Things were going very well. Once I landed in the forest, a large man and his smaller companion approached me, and I considered that to be a lucky break as well. At first I was scared, not knowing what was coming at me, and I tried to hide behind a tree, worried that some monstrous Hell-hounds were going to chase and eat me for eternity. They were strangely dressed, as are most of the people here, but they took me to the path and pointed me in the direction of Porto, where I could find proper clothing. The death shroud cloth I came into Hell with was just too weird, even for a not-picky dresser like me. Polo shirts and jeans were my uniform of choice.

    I reached the village of Porto some time later, enjoying the scents and smells of the wooded forest. Outer Hell had savaged my nostrils with its violence, and inhaling felt great. I wasn't hungry or thirsty, but being somewhat shy, some concern rose up as I arrived in the miniature village which turned out to not be a problem as I was quickly surrounded by the locals. They pressed me, asking questions suspicious of my identity. In fact, they were alerted to the presence of fugitives just before I arrived. The fugitives had been reported to have entered Limbo illegally and were wanted by the leaders of Limbo, some older folks known as the Elders Council. Apparently, I happened into Limbo when all the interesting business of fugitives began.

    Once the local villagers were convinced that I was absolutely not a fugitive - my newer untarnished cloth assisting them in their decision - I was surrounded by men with makeshift tape measures, not manufactured types, but pretty good handmade versions that were actually more fancy looking. I was asked what styles of clothing I preferred, and said the same as I told the large man and his companion in the woods. Jeans.

    Of course, the tailors had no idea what I was talking about. I was the first newcomer they had seen in many hundreds of years, which told me I was far luckier than I knew. But that meant they had never seen a pair of jeans in their lives, and that they had some method of telling time. In regards to my pants, I was able to pick out a material, and diagram a rough draft of a plain pair of jeans. They created several pairs, and I took one and put them on. The fit was good, and the material was very soft, weightless like spider web, but very strong for its lightness. They created a shirt and I happily removed most of the cloth I had come to Hell in. My new shirt was also light.

    Finally, I finished talking and telling stories with these men; they were very generous, and the tailor who made the clothing I wore beamed as if he was the proud winner of the 'dress me' contest, smiling and lording his skills playfully at his tailor friends. I was pointed in the direction of Terni as the men thanked me for the visit. They wanted to share some wine to celebrate my coming into Limbo. As opposed to having been sentenced to anywhere in outer Hell, being sent to Limbo is a very big deal. I declined though because I was excited to see more of Limbo. The people had a great amount of time on their hands and they seemed to use their time very well. There was a library and an amphitheatre, and a building known as the Hall of Science which they recommended I see. They boasted of its giant height with its incredible four stories, the tallest building outside of the Keep, which was a castle that the Elders Council held meetings in. Honestly, I was happy just to have trees. I imagined Dante had either lied or exaggerated, or there had been a great deal of tree planting and construction in the last 700 years. The walls alone were quite an accomplishment, and I was glad to not have to breathe the air or see the outside of Limbo. As I left, the main tailor, the leader of the group, informed me that I might pass near a building that was situated on a large lake. He identified it as the Whirlpool building, and told me only to steer clear of it. 'Hug the inner wall' he said.

I passed through Terni later, and the people, like those who had surrounded me in Porto, looked at me, but did not attempt to interact. I expect my clothing had a great deal to do with this, but I was feeling good, and did not try to stop and chat. The woods were always my comfort, even in my life, and I continued on, sighing every so often at the good fortune to have landed in Limbo. The Whirlpool building came up some time after Terni, and I veered to the left path nearest the inner wall. I stepped up my pace, and passed through quickly. As I watched the building, I saw in the distance something big fly up and out from the other side, nearer the outer wall that bordered the river Acheron. It was human shaped, and fast, and disappeared over the trees that were in front of me. The flapping was hard, like meat being hit with a wide hammer. It was a signature wing beat that I would recognize many more times. In fact, another of the creatures flew over and past me not so long after in the same general direction. I continued walking, hoping I would not see the beasts again while alone. I was quite shaken, and had not realized it.

Much, much later, the forest thinned out, to my dismay. It reminded me of my trek with my family. We took a road trip once and were enjoying the rocky wilderness of Colorado for some time in our drive. Later, the trees thinned, then disappeared and we were in the northern hills and desert, with only minor brush filling for trees. This was how I felt as I approached the mines. The locals of Porto had told me as much, but I was daydreaming as I walked through the forest, and enjoying the long, peaceful surrounding of wilderness. The landscape became sparsely treed, then flat and rocky.

It was empty, except for the tall walls on either side of me. In the distance, large piles of rocks blocked my view. As I got nearer to the piles, another of the flying creatures passed over, flying directly over the rock piles. It looked as though it dropped down behind the heap. I stood still, feeling some amount of dread. I got a better view of the creature, and I did not like what I saw; it was an odd, purplish color, its face like some gnarled tree knot, twisted in anger. The beast was well muscled, appearing powerful in build. I looked at it without expression, but inside, I was actually trembling. I stood still for a long time, trying to gather any semblance of courage I might need. Finally I began my walking, deciding I would just have to work around an encounter with it as best I could, Surely the people here had to deal with the beasts once in a while. And I was very curious at the same time, so I wanted to have a closer look.

A path was made through the piles, easy to see, and I followed it. It was a strange path, but I followed as it opened into a wide pit, with concentric circles that wrapped around and down to a central area with an entrance to a mine. Across from me, a bunch of people were sitting or laying on the ground, and I noticed the two guys, one very big and his friend who had directed me to Porto. Interestingly, there was the centaur again, but he appeared to be bleeding, and in fact, all of the people here looked a little beaten, even from as far away as I was. Honestly, I turned around and walked back behind the rocks; I was too new here to be scrapping already, especially since I did not know who the good guys were. And just what was this centaur doing here? *Dante must have had his head in his goddamned ass*, I thought angrily. I was scared, and when scared, I complain.

I had no idea what to do, so I stayed put until sometime later, when a small band of men came around the corner of the rock pile.

They were armed with bows and arrows, spears, and actual real long swords!

"Halloo stranger." said one of them. The others looked at me, waiting for my reply.

"Hi." I said this shyly, still stunned at the weaponry.

"You would be wise to remain here for the moment, stranger. There may be trouble coming. Did you witness the earlier attack?" I shook my head; I knew something had happened here.

"No, though I saw injured people, and the centaur around the pit."

"Yes. Even Master Chiron was not spared this round."

"Chiron?" I said. The centaur was Chiron? "Chiron? Really?"

"Yes. Master Chiron hails from the Seventh Circle, on business of his own." replied the man. "He and the others were on their way out of Limbo when the demon attacked." And now I was quite enthralled.

"That purplish flying thing was a *demon*?" I said.

"Yes. Frightening, are they not?" I was once again stunned. Weren't demons red with horns? Jeesh this is a weird place.

"Very," I answered. I was relieved he seemed as fearful as I did. "What happened to it? I didn't see it in the pit, only those wounded."

"It has been destroyed." said the man.

"Destroyed? How do you destroy a demon, if I may ask? I thought they would be eternal here ...being it's Hell and all."

"Suffocation, or if you impale them rapidly enough. They are very very strong, so no human can best them. Only recently have we seen one perish at the hands of Mortuus. There is one other way-" He was cut off by another.

"Appis. Use your discretion."

"Yes. Of course." he said. "I will not burden you with too much information in case you are questioned. Where do you normally dwell, stranger?" He had changed the subject.

"I am a new arrival and just finding my way around. I was on my way to the Library."

"Ahh, then welcome to Limbo stranger. What is your name?"

"I am John Moore. Is there some other way around this pit I am unaware of Appis?"

"No, John Moore, there is only the way through the pit. In a few minutes you may go. Have you washed in the waters yet?"

"I passed but I did not wash. Why do you ask?"

"The waters are quite healing to drink, and will wash the stench of outer Hell if you bathe. "

"Interesting. I will see to it when I pass again. I hope I do not offend."

"You do not, I only wished to share the knowledge of the waters. You will pass another before you reach the Hall of Science. It is advisable that you bathe on the part of the water that opens to the path first. The rapids of the far end are too perilous, and may cause you injury."

"Thank you for that. I will bathe then before I reach the Library."

"You are welcome." I noticed the others of Appis' party were looking up into the air, like they expected more of the demons to fly in.

"Appis, why is it the demons are coming? Has something happened?"

"It is a long story," he replied, "and should not concern you. The beasts will not find what they seek, and all will return to normal soon."

"What do they seek?" But Appis only smiled and looked up into the air like his friends. I looked up, then parted from the men. I crossed the pit around its edge to the far side, where a similar path exited and continued my walk.

This was a strange land of mysteries. Luckily, I had plenty of time on my hands.

Chapter 65
Emergence

"Socius – where would you like to be returned to?" asked Avius. The Chronicler was browsing in one of his large spell books, perusing the incantations he could use to return Barak and Socius back to Hell.

"I took it for granted we would return to your cottage Master Avius?" Socius had a puzzled look on his face. Avius, not looking up from his opened tome, paused for a moment. Barak looked at Avius curious. The three had walked into the mirror within the cottage of Avius and arrived in a large room with many books; it was the library of the Chronicler, a very rare visit by an outsider, as Barak had told Socius on many occasions. Barak had been to the vast book collection of the Chronicler before, but his visit was short. On top of that, the Chronicler had blindfolded him. He had waited many centuries for this visit, and he did not wish to leave. The tomes, giant bound volumes in aged fabric, were full of information about Hell, angel magic, and so many other topics that Barak could spend years savoring the data within. The only problem was the language. Each tome of the angel magic and lore was written in the language of the Angelics, which no one, except the Chronicler himself understood. Socius was indifferent to the texts and their value, despite the multiple repeated attempts by Barak to explain it to him. Finally, in frustration, Barak gave up his efforts. The Chronicler taught him some spells, simple angel magic that would be of more use when he returned to Limbo.

Upon their entry, Socius had asked where the three were. Avius told him.

"You are in the library. More precisely, a deep sub-basement of the Great Library." Socius was dumbfounded.

"How can this be? We were fully on the far side of Limbo."

"The portal can be set to transport us to many places Socius."

"I see no doorways to the upper floors. How do you get to the exit?"

"There are no passages out of here except for the mirror itself, Socius. It is unfortunate for Barak since he has to get me many books from the Great Library. It would be far quicker to install a stairway. But it would also provide access to my own library, which I cannot allow."

"How did you build this room? How deep under the library are we?"

"It is almost as deep as the library is high, Socius. I did not trust my skills at using the mining spells to create this large room, so I started deep. Happily, the upper library was not harmed during my dig."

"Very impressive. A very good hiding place right under the noses of the Elders. No wonder no one can find you." Socius was in awe. They had stayed underground for a lengthy period, however, and he was about ready to leave. "Can we return to the field by your cottage?"

"Limbo has undergone some unfortunate changes since we left, my friends. I did not wish to tell you, but it was probably caused by my 'interaction' with the demons that were attacking you. The spell I cast to remove them was a bit noticeable, apparently."

"Remove them? But they were shrieking very loudly, as if they were in pain. I thought you had destroyed them. Where did you send them?" asked Barak.

"Back to their creators, of course." Socius stood agape, then Barak chimed in.

"Their creators? The Fallen?"

"Yes. They are not appreciated by their Fallen masters either, especially in their private area. They will cause much havoc, and eventually be removed or destroyed."

"Could you not just destroy them?" asked Socius.

"Yes. However, I prefer not to. My solution is far better. Wish I could have been there to enjoy it." Avius smiled as Socius and Barak stood in shock, then laughed heartily.

"You have an unusual sense of humor, Avius." chuckled Socius.

"Indeed." added Barak.

"Where do the Fallen reside?" asked Socius.

"Winged creatures live in aeries, of course," stated Avius, matter-of-factly. Socius wore a look of puzzlement.

"Where?" asked Socius. "I am very curious."

"That will be revealed to you soon enough, youngling. Now, returning to my question – where would you like to be returned to?"

"I have my reasons, Barak. Socius will need your assistance when you leave here. And for where you are going, you will need his protection. I'll ask you two again. Where would you like to return to? Limbo is not the same place you left, and the demons may be expecting you to return in close proximity to my cottage." Socius pondered this for a few moments.

" Do you mean outer Hell? I am not certain where we should go, Avius. I have barely been outside of Limbo myself, and I really did not like the experience. Do you have some recommendation? I will tell you, I am a bit fearful of the outside, yet I have always wanted to go to see it." Socius reminisced. "I had expected to go with Aristotle, but…then he never returned."

"Very well. I will send you to Phlegyas; he can guide you to the centaurs where you will be safe. You will have to protect Barak, Socius. He is a clever student, but as a warrior, I think he comes up a bit short. Phlegyas liked Aristotle, so be certain to mention his name when you two meet. He will surely help on your journey. You do remember Phlegyas, from Aristotle's stories?"

"Yes of course. The oarsman of Styx, the swamp surrounding Dis." answered Socius. Barak nodded. He had read many of Aristotle's accounts of his travels, and he was familiar with the various workers of outer Hell.

"Good. Now," Avius placed his hands together, interlocking his fingers, "Prepare for the portal opening. Socius, you have packed the regeneration potions for Mortuus?" Socius nodded and held his pack up. "Good. I will see you again, Barak. You have been a faithful student, keeping my secret for many centuries. Both of you will need to find Mortuus; remember, he is in need of one of the large vials. These remedies are only for the worst needs of regeneration. When Mortuus begins the change, stay with him. It is very painful." Avius was stern on this point, his face revealing the seriousness. He bent over his tome, reading again, then, looked at the pair.

"Do not move until I signal you. Once you arrive at the edge of the swamp, look for the signal tower and do not enter the swamp. Prepare yourselves." He read aloud. "*Basqi ites mufeza'viaeta…como unlni rasz!*" The mirror on the far wall began to glow, a luminescent bluish light pouring out for a moment, then smoothing out into a lighter blue, an aqua glass. "Walk through together. Good luck my friends!" he shouted.

Socius and Barak turned and stepped into the widened mirror as the odor of fetid, stinking swamp filled their nostrils.

Chapter 66
The Encounter

Phlegyas was a large, sinewy tangle of angry muscle, not an ounce of body fat to smooth the knotted strings. Socius, still reeling from the revelations of the Chronicler, studied the oarsman, comparing this real Phlegyas to his own previously imagined version. This Phlegyas was more intimidating, and his booming voice alone had frightened Barak when they first met. Phlegyas had been less than friendly, but warmed considerably when Socius identified himself. Barak was shaken up and shied away from the brusque oarsman; outer Hell was always only a theory; the true experience was very much overwhelming for the student of Avius. He imagined it must have been quite a rude awakening for Mortuus.

Phlegyas pushed the skiff along slowly, wanting to maximize his time with the friendly company; they were going to the rear entrance of Dis that earlier Mortuus, Chiron and Darius had been transported to. Of late, the transport's passengers were all demons and imps, and their ill tempers had caused them to rake Phlegyas on more than one occasion. The imps were particularly troublesome, not willing to sit still, and almost discovered Phlegyas' private stash. One imp had been pulled overboard by a small contingent of angry swamp-dwelling humans, making its demon master so angry, it ripped at Phlegyas' back and chest several times.

"Phlegyas – I have noticed your wounds. Have you been attacked recently?" asked Barak, trying to overcome his fear. Phlegyas had caught Barak's aversion to him, and decided to taunt him in jest.

"Yes. What of it, peon!" yelled the oarsman. Phlegyas stared at Barak in mock anger for a minute as Barak slowly backed away as far as possible within the skiff before Phlegyas finally burst out into hearty laughter. "Do not fear me boy, truly, I am on your side. The demons have been at me for some time, and I am transporting many demons since the awakening of Mortuus. Far removed from their Fallen lords, their temperament is more horrid than Hell itself. I cannot get them across this swamp fast enough."

Barak, relieved, looked at Socius who was smiling at Phlegyas' joke.

"I believe we have enough water to spare some for our humorous guide, Socius. What do you say?" asked Barak.

"Absolutely. I have heard you assisted Mortuus as well, Phlegyas? We are in your debt. Limbo is astir now; Mortuus has been long waited for by many, though I have only found this out recently." Barak passed two large vials to Socius, who extended them to Phlegyas. Phlegyas smiled as he took the waters.

"Many thanks, friends. What of Limbo, Socius? The Fallen are angered at Mortuus escape? Chiron said the demons had infiltrated the place, and that some demons have been there all along."

"Limbo is filthy with the beasts, Phlegyas. They replaced an Elder, and many of my own friends, students of the Chronicler. Who knows where else the beasts are lurking. Our secret society, unknown even to me until recently, seems to have also been infiltrated." Phlegyas pondered this.

"If they have gained so many places in Limbo, then they must have taken those they replaced to lower Hell. It is the most difficult to escape; it is patrolled by dark devils, more dangerous and twisted than the demons and imps, who will not go there unless directed by Fallen."

"How do you come by this information Phlegyas?" asked Barak.

"I am here many, many centuries my friends. Until I met Aristotle, I had no one to speak to except fugitives and demons. As for the fugitives I am required to alert the Fallen masters; but surprisingly, I rarely ever do. As for the demons, they talk amongst themselves or not at all. The flyers carry their captives to the lower pits and according to what I have heard, they throw their prisoners on top of the unsuspecting devils as their own sort of entertainment."

"Do you know anything of the pits, Phlegyas?" inquired Socius.

"I have heard stories from the fugitives. One told me there are many pits, some of fire, boiling pitch, rivers of stinking shit, flesh eating monsters, though differing from the imps, and all serviced by the dark devils. This particular escapee hailed from a pit where he wallowed in human excrement and he said that pit was the easiest to escape. The beasts rarely go near it because of the smell, and he was ripe with it. When he escaped, the devils in the next pit spotted him. He had to stand under a waterfall of hot red water to hide; like the demons, each had a lengthened meat hook. Although burned badly, he was grateful for the cleaning, though he stilled stunk. I would have thrown him into the Styx if I had not been longing for some human company. It's just as well I let him go. He was eventually caught - I saw them flying over and I knew from the stench it was he," Barak shuddered.

"As if the normal smell of outer Hell was not enough. The red waterfall?" asked Barak. "I recall it from Aristotle's travel logs. It falls from the blood rill. But how did the fugitive get past the flying monster?"

"The monster is Geryon." said Phlegyas. "The guardian of the Eighth Circle – it patrols the outer rim. It is some sort of bastardized creature, and is quite vicious. The tail is that of a scorpion, and if it stings you, the poison lasts for some time. The poison inhibits regeneration, and burns as it courses through your body. The demons are terrified of the beast, and apparently it is not fond of them either." Phlegyas paused. "I received a sting from this beast. It took almost a century for the burning to completely cease."

"How did you get stung by the monster? The Eighth Circle is far from here," asked Socius.

"I attempted to escape." replied Phlegyas. Socius and Barak looked at the oarsman in shock. "The beast caught me climbing down the wall near the rill. It stung me and threw me out onto the burning plain. I lay on the burning sand until I could crawl back to the rill, then worked my way back here."

"*You* attempted escape?" asked the astonished Barak. "But you are a worker. Why woul-"

"I am a prisoner, just as you," said the oarsman. "Only now it will become obvious to you that you are as much a prisoner as any other in this place. Now that your pleasant stay in Limbo has been compromised, you will see the extent of your punishment. Did you not ever wonder, in all your centuries, that there might be something more?"

"But what did you hope for, Phlegyas?" asked Barak. "You might have become one of the tortured…"

"Indeed. But Hell was young, and the torments were not all in place yet. The Fallen had not finished building their 'kingdom'. I had hoped for an exit below. I had already tried to leave by the entrance in the Vestibule to no avail. Geryon was a surprise."

"Darius and his two fellow fugitives tried that escape too. We understand," said Socius.

The skiff neared the greenish red rusty metal walls of Dis. Socius and Barak had read of Aristotle's description of the entombed, eternally roasted and the moans came from this circle. They heard the moaning and smelled the scent of burning flesh from across the swamp; now the pained sounds were louder, and the odor more offensive.

"My friends" said Phlegyas. "We have reached the back entrance to Dis. Prepare for the gruesome experience of the burning city of tombs. It is quite a horrific experience from what you are used to, and I am afraid you may swoon, overwhelmed. Aristotle had a great deal of trouble his first time through, and I expect you will also." Socius and Barak saw only weathered, rusty metal and rivets as they docked against the wall; it appeared to be the same as any other panels. As Phlegyas spoke the combination spell, an outline formed in the metal, shaping into a small doorway.

"Pass through the doorway together. Once through, you must head as straight away from the wall as the tomb configuration will allow. There is no returning through this way – only the front gate, located clear on the other side of the circle, is usable for that. Pull your packs tight and wield your weapons. Whatever may be on the other side, you will have no choice but to fight it. You have no time to get used to the heat from the tombs or the stench of burning flesh that fills the air in Dis. Farewell, my friends. Until we meet again. Go, now!"

The two pushed through the doorway, falling to the ground on the other side. The heat came in waves, but the odor turned out to be far more brutal. They had tried to emotionally prepare for the sounds of suffering and pain, but the actual sight was frightening beyond their expectation. Barak froze up, starting to go into a paralyzed shock, and Socius, not faring well himself, focused on getting his friend through the nightmarish landscape; it was his willpower that pushed them through the tombs unceasingly. Once they faltered, slipping against a glowing casket, and burned themselves badly. The pain seemed to pull Barak from his stunned state, and the two walked faster, not stopping until they had reached the rocky slope that led down into the circle of the centaurs.

The coppery smell of the boiling river was the newest odor to assault their noses as they walked down the slope; that, mixed with the smell of the burning flesh became a disturbing new stench. It was repulsive, and the newcomers to outer Hell now fully understood the bravery which Aristotle had to have in order to leave Limbo.

A large centaur patrol saw the pair walking down the slope. A company of twenty-five centaurs trotted uphill to intercept the pair, as one centaur raced toward the area where Chiron and Pholus stayed with the recently rescued humans. Barak was surprised by the speed of the centaurs. Fortunately for Socius and Barak, Chiron had ordered his centaurs not to harm any humans. The commander of the company watched as Socius bowed to him, keeping his head down until the centaur returned the gesture. This caused a curiosity among the herd, and they began to question Socius.

"Who are you and why are you here?" asked the commander.

"I am Socius, and this is Barak," said Socius. 'We are come to meet with Master Chiron. We have come from the circle of Limbo. We are friends."

"How do you know of our customs, young human?" asked the centaur.

"I learned your custom from my mentor," answered Socius. Aristotle had taught him to bow, letting the centaurs know he meant only respect. The leader signaled to the other centaurs, and they stood in formation.

"We shall take you to Master Chiron, humans. Follow us."

And off they went to meet Chiron.

Chapter 67
Changing Priorities

Only Pholus, the human Panos, and four centaurs remained in the hiding place in the Wood, standing over the regenerating fleshy pulp of the unknown human, the one who had not been given the healing waters. Chiron, Darius, the mostly regenerated Aristotle, Militus and Mortuus went off to the rill. Chiron took them to explore the Seventh Circle, crossing the burning-sand of the fiery plain, all the way to the cliff edge where the rill dropped its boiling liquid down to the Eighth Circle. Pholus, like most of the centaurs, would not venture too near to the fire of the plain. Panos, having suffered on the plain for a length of time before escaping to the Wood, chose to stay with Pholus and the herd. Asterion had befriended a small company of centaurs, and he decided to walk along with them, talking as they patrolled the Wooded side of the Seventh Circle.

Pholus went out to meet the newest strangers from Limbo before allowing them to see the hiding space within the trees. The strangers smiled as they were gently lowered to the ground by the centaur that had carried them across Phlegethon's shallows.

"I am Pholus, second to Master Chiron. Identify yourselves, and tell us why you come this way." Pholus was very stern and commanded respect with his direct approach and generally strong poise. He was as large as Chiron, though slightly rougher in appearance facially. He appeared somewhat more sensitive and intelligent than the centaurs who had met the pair on the slope.

"I am Socius, and this is Barak. We are friends of Aristotle, acquaintances to Master Chiron," said Socius, quite formally. "We seek Master Chiron." Socius smiled as he said this, knowing he was dealing with another of Aristotle's contacts in this circle. Pholus was well known from the travel logs.

"I have heard of you, Socius, through my encounters with Aristotle. Chiron has recently mentioned your name, Barak, in his travel to Limbo. You are both most welcome to our circle. We are hosting quite a few outsiders these days." The second centaur and the visitors from Limbo finished their introductions, gradually warming as they shared their individual stories. The conversation continued uniformly, until the mass of bloody, raw flesh on the ground behind Pholus shuddered, and in an instant the mixed party of Halflings, Limbo's refugees and the fugitive Panos was thrown into tree branches, trunks, and each other, smashed so hard that some of their bones were sticking out through their skin.

A quiet explosion had occurred in their midst, and they were all in shock from the noiseless concussion. Barak was sent high into a tree, caught in its branches as overhead a flock of harpies, previously unseen, but apparently there the whole time, took to flight, screeching in fear and panic. A lone centaur trotted into the place where Panos, who had been standing over the mutilated human, stood seconds before. The unknown, looking painfully up at the centaur, began to moan in a deathly fear. The human could still barely speak or move since the rescue from the forbidden area cave. The centaur looked at the raw flesh, and pulling out a large meat hook, slung it into the bloody mass, then turned and walked away, dragging the faintly crying form out toward the river. The stunned centaurs, battered and bleeding, could only watch in pain, groaning as they tried to regain their mobility. They were deafened by the trees which were now screeching from being struck by the party.

Socius, the least damaged of the entire group, dropped down from a tree, landing on his feet, though still dazed. A tree branch stuck through into his lower leg, and he swore as he slowly pulled it out. Getting up as quickly as he could, he followed the rogue centaur and the mystery human being towed behind the centaur.

"Centaur!" yelled Socius. The centaur did not turn or flinch in response. Socius looked harder at the centaur; it seemed to be unraveling before his eyes. "Centaur!!" Socius yelled louder then got an idea. "Filthy half-breed! I challenge you! Walk away then – run!" As Socius said this, Pholus limped up behind him, battered and bloody.

"Centaur!! Stop now! I command you!" Pholus yelled. The centaur did not flinch, or make any acknowledgement of Pholus as it kept dragging its bloody cargo, leaving a trail on the ground. It was nearing the river, and soon would be dragging the body across. A company of centaurs approaching in the distance were staring, not aware of what had just happened. Pholus motioned them to come hastily The centaur that was dragging the human away stopped. It considered the approaching herd, then turned in the direction of Pholus and Socius.

"Demon. I see you. You are not worthy to wear that form." said Socius, turning to Pholus. "That is no centaur, Pholus."

"Though my eyes deceived me, my nose did not." The demon centaur raised its hands, waving them as it reverted into its true form. It spread its wings in a sudden display, enlarging itself, trying to scare off the approaching centaurs.

"It is going to fly off!" yelled Socius as he boldly ran at the demon. The herd was galloping quickly toward the demon, readying their bows along the way. Pholus could barely walk.

"Socius, stand back. The herd will take care of the demon!" Socius stopped and the demon placed its hook back into the immobilized human form. It spread its wings wide and began to beat them rapidly. In an instant, its wings filled with arrows, some penetrating fully and others remaining stuck in the wing and the back of the demon. It shrieked and turned toward the galloping herd. An arrow appeared within its throat and no more sounds emitted from it. Choking and bloody, it fell to the ground, writhing in pain. Socius walked up to it and repeatedly stabbed it with his long knife until it stopped moving. Moments later it was a cloud of smoke, and dissipated rapidly, carried away by the heat of the river Phlegethon.

Pholus, in utter, joyous, disbelief, walked into the circle. A smallish centaur traveling with the herd was summoned by Pholus.

"Titan," asked Pholus of the youthful Halfling, "do you fear the flames of the plain?" Titan thought about the question for a moment, and replied hesitantly.

"I do, Master Pholus, why-"

"I need a brave youngling to seek out Master Chiron and his acquaintances; they are traveling on the rill, though they may be near to getting back. Will you perform the task? Titan did not hesitate in his reply.

"Yes, Master Pholus. But the Wood may be-" Pholus cut him off.

"I would not send you into danger, Titan. I want you to tell Tacitus to accompany you to the edge of the Wood, where the rill meets the flaming desert. They are to stay there until you return. Is that acceptable?" asked Pholus.

"Very much so, Master Pholus."

"Good. Make haste, courageous Titan. Tell Master Chiron this is an urgent matter." Titan did not wait to be told twice, he began a gallop toward the rill, where he knew to find Commander Tacitus and his company. Pholus turned toward the company of centaurs standing around Socius.

"Go, and assist our brothers in the Wood – they were hurt badly by the demon's spell." They left as Pholus looked at the mass of human that had been the cause of the magical attack. "You are apparently a very important prisoner of the Fallen, human. We will need to hide you much better. We have underestimated your importance." Pholus, examining the important prisoner, took hold of the meat hook, and carefully, gently, removed it. Socius walked over to the shredded mass.

"I have something to help regenerate this one more quickly if you like, Master Pholus. The Chronicler gave me some of his herbal medicines and instructions for their use. We can speed up his healing greatly, which I would recommend – he looks very, very bad; it is painful to look at his condition."

"Excellent Socius. Please do whatever you can; we need to find out why this one is of such value to the Fallen." Socius opened his pack and began treating the important prisoner of the Fallen. He had expected the healing and regeneration to take several hours. Within minutes of application, the wounded prisoner was able to speak, and another few minutes saw the previously mutilated man become whole right before their eyes. Pholus and Socius could only stare in disbelief as the wounds closed and bones restructured themselves before their eyes. It was a miraculous event to behold, and Pholus wished Chiron had been here to witness it. The Master Centaur was also a master medicine maker, and this would interest him to no end.

Chiron, Mortuus, Darius, Aristotle, and Militus returned at once; Aristotle, seeing Socius once again, was overcome, and their reunion was as a father and son event, each weeping joyously, as if Aristotle had returned from the dead, which he had. Shortly after, Asterion returned, having heard of the attack from centaurs they passed while on patrol. He was running, angry for leaving his friend behind, more relieved when he saw that Chiron was unharmed. The group was huddled around another human, whom Asterion could not see until he got closer. When he was near enough, he could see he did not recognize the human.

"It is good to see you again, my friend," said Chiron to Asterion. Asterion nodded happily, but the half-bull was staring around at the new faces of Socius and Barak, and particularly at the man in the middle of the gathering.

"Who are these new faces? Who is this one?" grunted the Minotaur. Pholus, Chiron, Militus and Socius looked at each other momentarily, then back at Asterion and the stranger. Barak and Panos, still injured, and sitting on the ground, studied the stranger curiously.

Chiron spoke, "First, Asterion, I would introduce you to Socius and Barak, who have arrived here just now from Limbo." Socius and Barak smiled at Asterion, but the half-bull stared at them grimly. He was quite fierce in appearance, whether that was his preferred countenance or not. Chiron continued, "I will start the questioning of our unknown guest now."

The mystery man, short, uni-browed, and very thin, like a half-starved wretch, sat in the midst of the assemblage, looking around fearfully, shy and insecure of this strange band of his rescuers. He was breathing nervously, and his eyes, which were darting from face to face, settled on Mortuus. He was drawn inexorably to this large stranger's strong yet gentle appearance without question because it was easier on the eyes and disposition than the intense stares of the centaurs or the half-bull. The Minotaur was staring a hole through him.

Chiron prodded, "Who are you human? What is your name?" The thin man looked down, unsure of his own ability to use his voice. He was not quite clear-headed or free from perhaps centuries of disorientation. Finally, with great effort, swinging his head around to meet all their eyes, he croaked out his reply.

"I am Dante…Dante Alighieri."

To be continued in

AngelFall
Book IV

Available July 2012

Printed in France by Amazon
Brétigny-sur-Orge, FR